# ROBOT TITANS OF GOTHAM

A MASTER
OF MEN
THRILLER
BY

# NORVELL PAGE

## THE SPIDER: ROBOT TITANS OF GOTHAM

This is a work of fiction. All the characters and events portrayed in this book are fictional, and any resemblance to real people or incidents is purely coincidental.

A Baen Book

Baen Publishing Enterprises
P.O. Box 1403
Riverdale, NY 10471
www.baen.com

ISBN 10: 1-4165-2127-5
ISBN 13: 978-1-4165-2127-3

Cover, logo, interior art and design by Jim Steranko

Special thanks to consulting art director
J. David Spurlock and Vanguard Productions

First Baen printing, June 2007

Distributed by Simon & Schuster
1230 Avenue of the Americas
New York, NY 10020

Library of Congress Cataloging-in-Publication Data

Page, Norvell W.
   The spider : robot titans of Gotham / by Norvell W. Page.
      p. cm.
   ISBN 1-4165-2127-5 (trade pb)
   1. Spider (Fictitious character)--Fiction. I. Title.

   PS3531.A2355S65 2007
   813'.6--dc22

2007010025

Printed in the United States of America

10  9  8  7  6  5  4  3  2  1

# CONTENTS

# A C K N O W L E D G E M E N T S

# FOREWORD

# GOTHAM HOUND

## BY JOEL FRIEMAN

**D**ARK, OVERCAST SKIES OUTSIDE, and diffuse lighting inside, contributed to the gray feeling that made Norvell W. Page withdraw into himself, that day in January 1941. He was lost in thought as he proceeded through the main reading hall at The New York Public Library on Fifth and 42nd.

While exiting the card file room through the large doorway leading out into the hallway, he was so preoccupied that he was absentmindedly brushing past those entering.

Having finished his research on the new mini-submarines that were constructed for the Japanese Navy, he was reminded of some of the past subjects that he had spent time researching for The Spider.

The Spider demanded cutting edge action, and Page had to do the research. The Spider was his bread and butter.

Page recalled the work he did in developing the giant robots that attacked New York City. He had spent hours in the engineering stacks just to perfect the concept, right down to how the control panel operated.

Page enjoyed sharing his ideas. He even borrowed an idea from "The Green Madness" story that his editor, Loring Dowst, had written and had suggested that Page use for *Slaves of the Laughing Death*, which, in turn, Page's close friend, Theodore Tinsley, had borrowed for The Shadow entry, *The Green Terror*.

1

However, now, there was a new element that was unsettling to Page. It was barely perceptible when he had sensed it back in 1939, but, by 1940, it became a major problem that could not be mistaken for anything else.

Page retrieved his things from the library coat room mechanically and, as he walked out of the 42nd Street exit, the chilled fresh air snapped him back into awareness, and he hurried down the steps to the sidewalk.

Page walked briskly across Fifth Avenue, keeping to the south side of 42nd Street, with the wind whipping at him and the cold stinging his eyes.

Walking eastward on 42nd, Page clutched a large manila envelope to the breast of his dark blue overcoat with his left hand and held his black fedora firmly on his head with his right. Nearing the Lincoln Building, he caught sight of a man with a saturnine expression striding towards him. His former literary agent.

"Norvell!" Lurton Blassingame called out as he approached. "What a coincidence, someone was just asking for you."

"Hi, Lurton," Page said dourly. "Let's talk inside. It's rather windy out here."

Page hoped that this was not a ploy to get him back to the agency. He liked Lurton, but his output did not require an agent.

Inside, near the miniature of the famed Lincoln Memorial statue that is set on a pedestal centered in the Lincoln Building lobby, they spoke.

"Norvell, someone—probably an 'acquaintance' from your days as a newspaper reporter—came by this morning and wanted to get in touch with you. I told him you were no longer represented by my agency, but could be reached at the offices of Popular Publications. He had a raspy voice."

"I think I know who it is."

When the elevator stopped at the 25th floor, Page got off and entered the maze of corridors, which the Lincoln Building sported, and trusted to memory and instinct locating the offices of Swiger, King and Chambers.

Upon setting foot in the reception area, a secretary looked up from her typing and greeted him.

"Good afternoon, Mr. Page. Mr. Harragan is expecting you and will be with you shortly. I'll take you to the conference room, where he will meet with you."

"Thanks, Georgine."

Inside the conference room, which also served as a law library, Page made himself comfortable. He put his hat and overcoat on a chair in a corner. Then, he placed the manila envelope underneath the overcoat.

Page inspected his surroundings and was fascinated with the framed prints of old maps that were hung on the walls.

While he was closely examining the "Ukrainia" map, a man dressed in a dark suit, and looking like a benign Jack Dempsey, entered.

"Hello, Norvell," Edwin J. Harragan said warmly with a slight drawl, as he reached out to shake hands. "Glad you could make it."

"This is one meeting I wouldn't miss for the world."

"Norvell, thanks to your diligent efforts," Ed Harragan began saying as they sat down, "a settlement has finally been reached. However, there is one key provision: silence."

Smiling, Page looked at Ed Harragan and asked wryly, "They don't want Superman to be known as 'The Man of Steal'?"

"Under the circumstances, since a settlement was reached, think in terms that it was 'borrowed'."

"I could, if they had acknowledged that the storyline of 'Bandit Robots of Metropolis' was based on The Spider novel that I wrote!"

"I happen to agree with you—it's all highly irregular and not the way that I would have addressed the matter—but it was completely done verbally by Harold Goldsmith of Popular Publications, with Jack Liebowitz of Detective Comics, and not me. They had known each other since 1932, when they met at the creditors meeting for the Eastern News bankruptcy." Reaching over to a bookshelf close by, Harragan extracted a plain business-size envelope that was secreted between two legal volumes and handed it to Page.

"This is for you."

"What's this?" Page asked incredulously, taking the envelope, then lifted up its unsealed flap to peer inside.

"Your share of the settlement. Two hundred dollars for each installment of the Superman Sunday comic strip published, plus two hundred dollars additional to cover whatever expenses you had incurred."

Page counted eighteen hundred-dollar bills. Then he whistled when it struck him that he had originally received only $550 for the novel that was "borrowed" for Superman.

Norvell Page enjoyed his visits to his editor's office, located high above East 42nd Street. Popular Publications was now the undisputed leader, and he was among the cherished writers who had helped to make it a formidable pulp magazine empire. Here, he was treated with deference. Even though it was bustling with activity, Page could amble through the corridors of the suite unescorted, saying hello to old friends, viewing recent cover paintings displayed on the walls like at an art gallery, and quietly approach his editor's inner sanctum unobserved.

Halting right before the threshold, Page looked in to find his editor, Loring Dowst, meticulously at work, in his shirtsleeves, editing a manuscript with blue pencil in hand and a green visor shading his eyes.

When Loring placed the pencil down on the desk and began to neatly arrange the edited portion of the manuscript before him, Page took the large manila envelope from under his arm by one of its corners, and tossed it on to the top of the desk, ruffling loose sheets of paper and causing the blue pencil to roll off the desk and on to the floor.

"Thanks, Norvell!" Loring grunted, bending over to retrieve his pencil while still seated in the chair. "I knew you wouldn't let me down."

"Anything for a pal," Page said. "Once it hit me that The Spider should have a submachine gun in each hand—and both blazing away at the same time—everything fell into place. It was finished in no time!"

"You really know your stuff," Loring said, as he was eagerly opening the manila envelope. "But then, you are The Spider!"

"By the way, has a check been cut for my novel for the April issue?"

Hearing the very words that he was dreading to hear, Loring began to blush.

"Yes, Norvell. But, it's difficult to tell you this," Loring said sheepishly. "Due to prevailing economics, the check is only for $450—your new rate for The Spider."

"Comics?"

"Yes, comics," Loring said, adding, "Eva Walker is holding the check for you, since Harry Steeger wants to see you."

"Mr. Steeger is at a meeting in the art director's office," Eva Walker said in her high-strung nervous way, "but he instructed me to take you directly to his office."

Page was alone, knowing that Eva Walker had a million other things to do, and Lucy, Harry's secretary, was on vacation.

Listening keenly, and hearing no sound in the immediate vicinity, he finally had the opportunity to discover the secret inside the mysterious four drawer legal-size green metal filing cabinet near Harry's desk.

He opened the top drawer, looked in, and closed it promptly.

Then, he opened the next drawer, looked in, and closed it promptly.

Then, again, he opened the next drawer, looked in, and closed that promptly.

Finally, crouching down, he got to the bottom drawer. He took a deep breath, opened the drawer wide, and looked in expectantly.

"Comics!"

He was about to close the drawer, when he noticed something and picked it up to examine.

It was the original .45 automatic replica used for The Spider covers. The current cover artist for The Spider wanted a .45 automatic that was larger than actual size, and had turned in the old one.

Page relished holding the faux pistol. It was a connection to his past, when his rate was $700 per novel, when there were no comics around.

He looked around the office and noticed a small bronze statue of a bull on the top shelf of a bookcase. "Perfect target!" he thought.

He placed the pistol model in the waistband on the left side of his pants, its butt facing forward under his suit jacket, hands at his sides. He looked squarely at the small bronze bull statue.

"It's a present from my mother," Page heard the voice of the head of Popular Publications say from behind him, and sheepishly turned around to face a man who looked like a young Lew Ayres. "She thought that spot needed something."

With an embarrassed grin, Page extended his right hand forward and said, "Hello, Harry!"

"Good to see you, too, Norvell! How's the project coming?"

"How about a sneak attack on New York Harbor?"

Using the 43rd Street exit, Norvell turned left and headed for Grand Central Station in the early evening darkness, putting his black fedora on his head and pulling his overcoat closed.

Just a few paces westward, someone emerged from a darkened spot on the side of a building and stood in his path, with his hands in the pockets of his overcoat.

Immediately noticing that the bulge from one of the pockets was the outline of a gun, Page drew out the mock pistol and aimed it squarely at the target in front of him.

The man with the gun in his pocket squinted at the pistol.

Just as he finished saying, "Are you kidding?" a bullet hole appeared in the center of his forehead. The man lurched back slightly, then pitched forward, crashing face down on the sidewalk, hands still in his pockets.

Three men came out of the darkness from in back of Page. One of them was holding a smoking gun, from which a silencer was being detached with a gloved hand.

Norvell looked at one of the three and smiled, "Hello, Frank."

The leader of the three was Frank Costello, his "off the record" contact during his newspaper reporting days, who said, in a raspy voice, "Page, just what the hell do you think you're doing with that?"

"Research!"

# SATAN'S

## MURDER MACHINES

# CHAPTER ONE
# THE MASKED MAN

THE MAN WAS A WATCHMAN, wearing the uniform of a private police agency, and he walked with his head bowed into the bitter winter wind that whimpered through Sutton Place. He moved swiftly, yet it was not the cold that he fled. Ever and again, he looked back the dark way he had come.

He was looking the wrong way, for, half a block ahead of him, the shadows of a doorway concealed a curious figure. There was nothing furtive about the broad shoulders, superbly set off by the tailoring of a Chesterfield coat that covered evening dress; nor about the arrogant carriage of the head beneath the gleaming silk hat. He seemed a gentleman of leisure about to take a bed-time stroll, except for two things. The upper half of his face was hidden by a silk mask; and in his white-gloved hand there lay an automatic pistol, its snub nose brutal as a rattlesnake's head!

The eyes of the masked man were riveted on the approaching watchman, whom he intended to kidnap, but all his senses were preternaturally alert, as became a man who must fight both the police and the Underworld through every waking and sleeping hour . . . as became Richard Wentworth, who, in another life, was that lone wolf of justice known as the *Spider!*

None but Wentworth's ears would have caught the distant, slowly authoritative tread of feet coming from the opposite direction. Nor did he need to look that way to know that a policeman—a municipal cop—too, had entered Sutton Place! Beneath the black mask, Wentworth's lips drew bitterly thin. The officer's presence would make the *Spider's* task more difficult, but it could not swerve him from his purpose. More than personal safety was at stake. Four men had died this night, butchered with a brutality that had shocked to fury even the death-hardened Homicide Squad. And this watchman, whom the police had exonerated, held the key!

The watchman did not see Wentworth, did not hear him until he had passed the shadowed doorway that hid terror—then a thin voice reached out and froze him in his tracks!

"Hands down!" it whispered harshly. "Turn the corner left, and keep your head front, mug—*or you won't have no head!*"

On the lips of the masked man there was a slight smile. His friends along Fifth Avenue, in the exclusive clubs to which his name and wealth gained him easy access, would have been shocked to hear such accents from Richard Wentworth! The tones were crude, but the watchman recognized something else in that voice—and he obeyed! It was not an empty title that had been given the *Spider,* that of Master of Men!

The watchman moved stiffly toward the corner and, when he could no longer see the shadowed doorway even out of the tail of his eye, Wentworth stepped casually to the pavement. His movements were easy, his pace a careless stroll, although he covered ground with deceptive speed. The gun was ready in his fist. His eyes probed ahead to the approaching policeman!

At a distance of two blocks, the cop could see no details of the two men on Sutton Place. His back was to the wind and it pressed his heavy coat against his calves, sliced coldly about his wool-clad ankles. His eyes ached with the cold. . . . That watchman was hurrying to his warm bed, off-duty, the lucky stiff! And a gentleman out for a bed-time stroll. Imagine a guy that didn't have to, going out in the cold on a night like this! The cop frowned a little then. Funny, both those guys turning toward the river where the wind was coldest; funny, both of them turning into a dead-end street! The cop shook his head, cursing the cold, and his eyes lingered on the dark entrance to the dead-end street. His pace quickened a little. . . .

✿ ✿ ✿

Just turning that corner, Wentworth detected the quickened stride and swore softly under his breath. He needed no more than that quickened step to tell him the policeman was an old-timer, and already suspicious. That would make his deception more difficult—but he was still determined to take the watchman a prisoner. It did not matter whether the man would talk or not; it would become known that he was a prisoner. Wentworth intended to let the man's criminal pals know who was responsible so that they would come for him—and walk into the *Spider's* trap!

A long stride brought him close to the watchman, and he jammed the muzzle of the automatic against the man's ear.

"Don't try no funny business!" Wentworth said hoarsely. "This is a stick-up!"

His left hand ran deftly over the pockets of his prisoner, filched gun and a few crumpled dollar bills. In that swift moment, his plan was fully formed. He would rob the man, knock him out—and then play good Samaritan for the benefit of the policeman, and the watchman! It should not be too difficult to start for a hospital, and finish up somewhere else where the watchman could be held prisoner! But he wished the wind were not so loud in the narrow canyon of the street. It rattled the skeletal boughs of stunted trees . . . and drowned out the footfalls of the cop!

"Listen, guy," Wentworth's prisoner whined. "Listen, you don't want to do this to me! It ain't healthy!"

Wentworth's eyes narrowed. It had been no part of his plan to question this man now, but if he would talk . . . and the policeman did not arrive too soon!

"Why not?" Wentworth demanded, and put a quaver in his voice. "I need the money more'n you! You gotta job!"

"I got friends!" the watchman said arrogantly. "You give me that money back, and—"

"What friends?" Wentworth snapped, hopefully.

The watchman made a sudden sideways lurch, started to whirl and grapple with Wentworth. It was the one thing that Wentworth could not permit. If the man glimpsed him, there would be no chance to kidnap him under the policeman's nose. Instead, Wentworth's arrest was certain . . . arrest and disgrace! Wentworth's blow was off-balance, but fiercely positive. It slammed under the man's ear and checked his turn. Before the man could recover, Wentworth struck again—and caught the watchman before he could slump to the pavement.

For an instant, Wentworth stood rigid, listening. He caught the tread of the policeman faintly. The cop was running toward the dead-end street! Wentworth swore raggedly, and his eyes flicked over the narrow *cul de sac* in which he stood. There was no place of concealment, no place to which he could flee, for the end, too, was sealed by a high wall. His eyes flicked toward the man whose unconscious body he held in his arms and Wentworth's eyes widened in amazement.

He had not known when he trailed this watchman just which private agency the man served, but the name was plain on the badge which gleamed on his chest: *The Drexler Protective Agency.* Wentworth shook his head incredulously. He knew the chief of the agency, Frank Drexler; knew him well. He was an honest and courageous ex-cop. It was incredible that Frank Drexler could be involved in such horror as had taken place this night, and . . . Wentworth jerked the thought from his brain. That would have to wait. Unless he could escape from this trap, which a running policeman was rapidly closing, the investigation of this horror would be impossible for Richard Wentworth. He would be locked up in a cell!

A grim smile touched Wentworth's lips. There was just a chance. . . . Without further delay, he heaved the unconscious watchman of the Drexler agency to his shoulder and broke into a staggering run—straight toward the policeman who at this instant rounded the corner from Sutton Place!

"Help!" Wentworth shouted as he ran. "Help! Police!" And he remembered then to slip the black mask from his eyes. . . .

The policeman jerked to a halt beneath the corner street light, and a finger of illumination glanced from a revolver in his right hand. It showed the bitter thrust of his cold-reddened jaw, the aggressive forward roll of his shoulders.

"Thank God!" Wentworth gasped, and staggered against the wall with his burden. "Get that man, officer! I think he killed this watchman!"

Wentworth sagged to his knees with the unconscious man, let

him slump to the pavement. With his left hand, he ripped aside the watchman's loosened coat, gripped his shirt and tore it so that his fingers rested against the man's flesh. His voice sounded exhausted, and he felt the officer standing tautly over him. But Wentworth did not check his purpose. His left hand slid to a vest pocket and slipped out a cigarette lighter, thumbed open the base.

Wentworth twisted his face up toward the policeman, meeting the narrow suspicious glare of the eyes beneath the visor. "A man was lying in wait for this watchman!" Wentworth gasped. "A man in a long black cape, with a black hat low over his eyes. He looked like he was hunch-backed or something. . . ."

"What?" the cop gasped. "Say that again. . . . A hunch-back in a cape! Good God, man, do you mean . . . the *Spider!*" Wentworth said, blankly, "*Spider?*" He staggered to his feet. In the street-light glare, his face seemed pale. Certainly, his eyes were stretched very wide. "God," he whispered. "Do you mean I was fighting . . . the *Spider?* I saw this man in the cape knock this watchman down, and stoop over him. He ripped open the man's shirt, and seemed to search him . . ." Wentworth turned then, and stared down at his victim. The cop gasped hoarsely.

Suddenly, the beam of his flashlight reached out and laid its dazzling circle upon the watchman's exposed chest. That chest was curiously marked. On it had been tattooed a strange and awful design. It seemed to represent a gruesome face sketched upon a modern steel helmet . . . but it was not that which the policeman indicated with a shaking finger. He pointed to a figure etched in blood-red vermillion, a thing that seemed a living creature of hairy legs and poison fangs!

"Jeez, oh jeez!" he gasped. "You was right! See . . . *the seal of the Spider!*"

Wentworth's lips moved in a secret smile and his fingers touched absently the slim cigarette lighter in his pocket with which he had imprinted that seal. He had taken the only way to convince the policeman that there had been another man in the dead-end street . . . for the street ended in high walls. The cop would never have believed a third man could vanish from that trap; any man except the *Spider!* But that other design on the victim's chest proved that a Drexler man was involved.

"Listen," Wentworth said in nervous tones. "I want to get away from here. My car will be here in a moment. . . . There it is now! Suppose I take this man to the hospital and call for help for you. You can stay here and stand guard!"

The cop was staring back up the length of the short dead-end street, toward the big limousine to which Wentworth had pointed. It rolled almost silently to a halt beside the curb. Its powerful motor made only a faint whispering beneath the long sleek hood. Wentworth gestured with a hidden hand to the man behind the wheel, indicating the unconscious body on the pavement. He needed to do no more than that, for the man behind the wheel was Jackson, his faithful comrade-at-arms who had fought through a hundred battles beside him. But even as Jackson stepped out of the car, the cop whipped about—and his revolver was pointed straight at Wentworth!

"Just a minute!" The cop's face was drawn and white. "Just a minute, now. I don't like this. I don't like it at all. That car comes up too pat, and how do I know. . . ." The cop swallowed noisily. "How do I know . . . *you ain't the Spider!*"

Nothing of the tension that jerked all his nerves taut showed on Wentworth's face. But the cop could have no genuine suspicion, of course, and there was no proof unless . . . unless the cop searched him! He would find no proof that Wentworth was the *Spider* even then, but he would find the gun taken from the watchman, and he would find a silken mask! Easy enough, of course, to knock out the cop despite the leveled gun, but the policeman's trained memory would not be so easily overcome. The cop had seen his face!

Wentworth put exasperation into his voice. "Really! Of all the stupidity!" he said shortly. "No wonder there is need for such a man as the *Spider*! I've been warned that the police were even harder on witnesses than on criminals, and I was only trying to help a fellow human being!"

The cop had his shoulders against the wall and did not waver. He was close to the watchman, who was lying strangely quiet. Wentworth had used his fists too often not to know the efficacy of each blow he struck, and he knew that the watchman should be conscious now; should have been several minutes ago. He glanced covertly at the man's face and hid a smile as he saw that the eyes were too tightly closed. The man was shamming!

"You can say what you like, mister," the cop said doggedly, "but you ain't going nowhere until I can get the chief here!"

Wentworth shrugged slightly. "This is very easily settled," he said easily. "I saw this man here meet the *Spider,* and he's got the *Spider's* seal on his chest. They met on a dead-end street. It looks to me like this watchman is one of the *Spider's* assistants and they met by appointment, and had a disagreement over something. I'm entirely willing to go with you to headquarters. We will give that story out to the newspapers, and see what happens."

Wentworth's eyes were closely on the watchman's face while he spoke, and he saw the eyes open a fraction, saw fright begin to draw taut the lines about the man's mouth. . . . If he could frighten the crook into striking the cop, and fleeing, it would be easy enough for Jackson to follow and take him prisoner. And the officer then would have no evidence and no complainant. . . .

"If he's the *Spider's* man," Wentworth continued softly, "the *Spider* will come to free him. If he isn't the *Spider's* man, then he's a crook, for otherwise the *Spider* would not have attacked him. The newspaper story will make his crook pals think he's been two-timing them with the *Spider . . .* and they'll come after him, a different way! How does the plan strike you, officer?"

The cop shook his head, "Listen, I don't get what you're driving at, but if it's some plan to trap the *Spider . . .*"

Wentworth saw determination clench the watchman's jaw, and behind him, Wentworth motioned Jackson not to interfere. Then the watchman flung himself into action! His foot struck upward hard against the cop's gun wrist. The revolver sailed high through the air and, the next instant, the watchman was on his feet and racing for the mouth of the dead-end street and Sutton Place!

The cop clutched his wrist in an agony of pain. "Catch him!" he gasped. "Catch that dirty louse and I'll crucify him!"

Wentworth turned casually to Jackson, "You might see what you can do," he murmured, and he winked deliberately!

Jackson needed no more than that for instructions. He snapped his hand up in salute, like the soldier he had been, and still was . . . though it was in the service of the *Spider* that he had enlisted now! As

Jackson sprinted up the short street in pursuit of the fleeing watchman, Wentworth moved toward his car. The policeman was reaching for his revolver with his left hand, but Wentworth had no fears that he would be able to drop the fugitive. Jackson would overtake and capture him. This skirmish was won . . . and the story the policeman would give headquarters would help to notify the criminals behind these ghastly murders concerning the whereabouts of their vanished watchman! Meantime, Wentworth thought a call on Frank Drexler was indicated!

Wentworth reached in through the window of his car and flicked on the radio—and in the same instant, he heard a man scream!

Wentworth twisted about beside the car and stared toward the mouth of the street. The watchman had vanished around the corner into Sutton Place; he it must have been, who uttered that tearing scream.

As Wentworth stared, Jackson flung himself at the corner and then—Jackson seemed to go mad!

The whole scene was painfully clear in the bright pool of illumination beneath that corner street light. One instant, Jackson was hurling himself confidently forward in pursuit—the next, he was striving frantically to check his forward dash! He managed to grab the iron standard of the traffic light with his right hand, jerk to a standstill.

For that first, terrible instant, Wentworth thought that a bullet had found its billet in his comrade's body. Then he saw Jackson's head lift stiffly and stare down Sutton Place! His head was just beneath the green eye of the traffic light, and its ghastly glare fell across his drawn cheeks. Jackson's strong jaw was knotted, but there was no mistaking the rigidity that gripped his body. Jackson, who had dared death gladly a thousand times to serve his master; who had fought through a great war . . . *Jackson was afraid!*

Through the long instant, the tableau held, while the light still sprayed green across Jackson's face, while the scream of terror and despair sounded through the night. Then that scream broke, and Jackson wrenched himself free from the iron post. He began to claw for his gun. Jackson, whose draw was the swift strike of a snake, fumbled with a shaking hand for his gun! The traffic light changed to red, and the gun came free, began to spit its harsh thunder down the street. Beside Wentworth, the cop swore curiously and with his retrieved gun in his left hand, ran awkwardly along the dead-end. He had taken only three paces when a man whipped around the corner and charged into the street. The man ran wildly, with both arms flung high above his head, and the screams still came from his lips. It was the Drexler watchman.

"The Iron Man!" he shrieked. "God save me! *The Iron Man!*"

And abruptly, Jackson had abandoned his position beside the traffic light. He turned and ran swiftly toward Wentworth, and he was reloading his automatic. Twice he twisted his head about to stare back across his shoulder.

"What is it, Jackson?" Wentworth snapped.

He had his own gun in his hand and was striding to meet his comrade. The policeman already had passed him, was scrambling toward the corner. Wentworth knew the cold tightening of horror in his own heart, for he was remembering those looted homes and the distorted bodies of the four murdered men. They had been literally torn apart. And now Jackson fled, and a man screamed . . . "*The Iron Man!*"

Jackson whirled, and at the street's mouth, the policeman shouted hoarsely and unintelligibly . . . and then Wentworth saw— and he knew why the watchman had screamed, and why Jackson had been stiff with fright; and how four living men had been torn apart!

The thing stood there for an instant beneath the swaying street light, a monster of steel, an iron man! Its head towered almost to that light, and the red glare from the traffic signal spilled like lucent blood across a gigantic torso. Arms swung from ponderous shoulders and the head—the head was a replica of the helmet tattooed upon the Drexler watchman's chest! Two blank eyes that were plates of glass glared emptily; the mouth had teeth like a steam-shovel—and the empty glare of those awful eyes was fixed upon Wentworth!

Even as the *Spider* ripped himself free from the paralysis which that sudden apparition had placed even upon the Master of Men, the giant in steel lifted a ponderous foot and set it upon the sidewalk. And under that colossal trend, the concrete crackled and broke like ice! A hand moved carelessly, and wrapped about the iron traffic signal standard . . . and that post snapped off with a sputter of electric sparks!

Once, twice, the robot whipped that heavy post about its head and then hurled it like a war-club at Wentworth's head!

# CHAPTER TWO
# WHEN BULLETS FAIL

D EATH WAS VERY CLOSE TO RICHARD WENTWORTH in that moment. There seemed a weight in limbs and brain, stupefaction over this thing his eyes saw, but his mind could not quite believe. It is certain that any other man would have been caught by that steel club and died miserably in his tracks. Wentworth managed somehow to wrench his frozen muscles into action. He shrank aside by a hair's breadth and the wind of the missile's passage whipped his silk hat from his head, fluttered the tails of his Chesterfield.

The policeman stood motionless, a paralyzed pigmy in the path of the steel monster. His gun was in his fist, his head wrenched back crazily to peer up at that travesty of a face. The watchman ducked behind Wentworth and crouched like a cowed dog and Jackson had his back flattened against the wall; automatic ready in his fist again.

"This way, officer!" Wentworth's voice cracked like a whip and, even in that paralysis of fear which gripped the man, the cop heard the accent of command and discipline stirred within him. He jerked up his revolver and fired at the monster.

"Retreat, man!" Wentworth shouted. "Come to me!"

Wentworth whipped up his own automatic and took careful aim. He knew without further trial that the steel body would be impervious to bullets. Jackson's shrewd lead already had searched that out. One shot, Wentworth squeezed off. He knew that his lead flew true, caught the monster in one of its glass eyes—and nothing happened! The monster stood within a few yards of the policeman and slowly bent his head to stare down at the puny thing at its feet. A steel hand lifted casually. . . .

With an oath, Wentworth leaped toward the Daimler. The policeman was fleeing in crazy, scrambling terror, and the monster was walking . . . slowly, ponderously. The tremor of that tread came through the pavement, seemed to vibrate in Wentworth's very bones.

"Keep away from it!" Wentworth shouted. "It can't move fast! Keep out of its way! Dodge!"

He flung himself behind the wheel of the Daimler, and wrenched it into gear, whipped it in a U-turn. The car was too long for that narrow street and he had to wrench it backward again while aching moments passed; while death moved with ponderous ease and on feet of steel. He glimpsed the giant, saw it lift a hand and point a finger like an accusation at the crouching watchman. The man's scream rose terribly, and then—fire spurted from that pointing finger! The scream cut off. The watchman was a twitching, dying huddle upon the ground!

Wentworth fought to hammer sane thoughts through his own brain. This thing of steel could be no living monster, of course. It must be a robot, though marvelously under control. A robot that could point a finger made into a gun barrel and kill with perfect aim! Wentworth jerked his head, struggling against the daze of incredulity that still gripped him. A robot was only a machine, an intricate and necessarily delicate machine. A profound blow, such an impact as would knock the thing to the ground, undoubtedly would disarrange its mechanism. It was simple, really. Whoever was master of this monster of steel had calculated on the terror its mere appearance would generate to prevent rational attack. He had not counted on meeting the *Spider* face-to-face!

Wentworth had whipped the heavy limousine about now, so that its nose was toward the robot. He swiftly flung it backward until its rear bumper nudged the wall at the street's end. He would need all the momentum he could generate in this short dead-end street to upset that creature! He jerked loose the half-cushion beside him, and wedged it between his chest and the steering wheel, jerked the gear into second. . . .

❂ ❂ ❂

Even as his foot hovered over the accelerator, the radio emitted a faint click . . . and suddenly a voice sounded in the car. That voice was disguised, but Wentworth recognized it at once. He would always know that voice, in whatever circumstances he heard it, for it was that of Nita van Sloan, the woman he loved! He had been at an after-theatre party with Nita when word had come of the tragedy which had called the *Spider* to action—and he had sent Nita to keep watch on police headquarters while he flung himself into battle! That was terribly necessary now since, on every hand, the police hounded the *Spider*. Her speech now could mean only one thing: the police were on his trail again!

Nita spoke softly, as if she would whisper those words into his ear, and her words would make no sense to others.

"The big blue cat," said Nita, "is going to the mouse's home to retrieve some stolen cheese!"

The words ran like an electric shock along Wentworth's nerves. *The big blue cat. . . .* That meant Stanley Kirkpatrick, commissioner of police, who was at once Wentworth's friend and the *Spider's* enemy. And the mouse was Wentworth himself. *Stolen cheese. . . .* Even as Wentworth jammed down the accelerator and drove the heavy Daimler toward the steel monster, the truth of that broadcast struck him, and shook him. It could mean only one thing: Kirkpatrick was going to Wentworth's home on a tip-off that he would find some stolen goods there!

Nor did Wentworth even need to speculate on the nature of that loot, or whether he would find it! The loot would be there, and it would be loot from those three homes that had been rifled this night! By God, the enemy moved swiftly! Already, they had spotted Wentworth's interest in the case and moved to checkmate him—by planting in his home the evidence that he had been responsible for those lootings and awful murders! Strangely, Wentworth smiled. At least it proved human agency behind this robot!

Wentworth wrenched his mind to the battle at hand, but the delay had proved costly! The robot had closed up some of the previous distance Wentworth had gained, thus lessening the momentum which the car could build up. As Wentworth stared, and started the car leaping forward, the robot bent forward and plucked up the policeman from the earth! He grasped the screaming man by one ankle and, casually as a child might whirl a stick about its head, the robot spun the policeman! Two, three times he circled the helpless, doomed man . . . then flung the dangling thing that remained headlong toward the charging car!

A sickened horror surged through Wentworth. He tried to wrench the big car aside, but was too late. Headlong, against the bullet-proof glass of the windshield, the policeman hurtled, then slithered off to one side!

Wentworth's lips drew thin and bitter across his face and pallor crept into his cheeks. He leaned forward and flicked on the windshield wiper . . . shuddering involuntarily.

He needed to see very clearly to drive straight at this monster in steel who could perpetrate such horror. His anger seemed to lift the heavy car and hurl it forward, wringing the last ounce of power from the engine. His knuckles shone white as he gripped the wheel.

He saw the robot take a stride forward, and swing a foot like a football player about to kick off! And that foot was aimed at the radiator of the Daimler! In that horror-sodden instant, Wentworth knew that even this mighty attack would fail against the robot! On the moment, he batted open the door beside him and, as the Daimler surged toward the steel monster, he hurled himself toward the pavement!

Wentworth struck the pavement rolling in the same instant the robot crashed its foot against the radiator of the Daimler! He saw what happened then in flashing glimpses as he spun dizzily toward the curb and reeled to his feet. The thing was timed as beautifully as a dropkick. The smashing impact of the robot's foot, whose tread could crack the concrete of the walks, caught the Daimler just at the front axle!

Fenders and headlights leaped from the limousine, and glass flew like a shattering grenade! The front of the car lifted, while the powerful drive to those rear wheels urged it on—and the whole machine spun dizzily aside, turned over and slammed against the wall of the house to the right! For an instant, the robot tottered. An outflung arm reached to the wall of the house, and the bricks crashed inward. A rubble of broken masonry clattered to the earth and plaster dust lifted around the monster of steel like battle-smoke. But it was only an instant, and then the robot's head revolved slowly and the blankly awful eyes picked out Wentworth where he reeled, dazed from his heavy fall, against the opposite building wall. Jackson was beside him. His gun was spitting lead hysterically, but he might as well have been throwing pebbles at a seventy-ton tank.

Slowly, the right arm of the monster lifted . . . and Wentworth remembered that its forefinger could spurt lead and death! He flung himself sideways toward Jackson, carried the hysterically cursing man to the pavement . . . but there was no crash of a shot from the robot. Evidently the impact had partly disabled the monster! The thing was no longer braced against the wall but as it stepped toward where Wentworth fought to get Jackson to his feet, to retreat, he saw the left leg drag curiously. The *Spider's* charge had achieved something then! The monster was not working perfectly!

Wentworth reeled to his feet. There was no gun in his hand, for a gun would be useless. He stood slowly erect and watched the monster take another dragging step toward him . . . then the robot stopped. The great head bent slowly and the blank emptiness of those eyes of glass peered down where the *Spider* stood, a pigmy in the path of Juggernaut. A moment passed, a long dragging moment while the two confronted each other, monster of steel, and he who was known as the Master of Men. And in that moment a queer doubt shook Wentworth. He had termed the thing a robot, as surely it must be, but there was a human mind here . . . a human mind whose evil reached out to touch him through those blank staring eyes! Wentworth felt the impact, as genuine as a bullet blow, and more dreadful; and he knew what horror it promised for himself, for the humanity which, as the *Spider,* he selflessly served!

Wentworth felt the coldness of his anger mount within him, and while his eyes still gazed at the soulless blank depths of that steel helmet, he spoke in tones of quiet command to Jackson.

"Quickly, Jackson," he snapped. "The First Avenue garage is only a block away. Hurry there and get the heaviest car you can find. This thing is damaged and can't get away very fast! *Hurry, Jackson!*"

Jackson scrambled to his feet, the gun in a shaking hand, but Wentworth knew now that it was anger at his own helplessness that made brave Jackson's hand tremble like that.

"You go, Major," Jackson said hoarsely. "Let me keep watch over this damned thing! You're hurt, and—"

"It is a command, Jackson," Wentworth said quietly.

Jackson flinched as if from a blow, stiffened to attention. "Yes, Major!" he acknowledged. He saluted and whirled to sprint along the street.

Still, Wentworth stared into the blank eyes of the creature of steel. He found an instant then to wonder that there had been no alarm, but he realized the cause instantly. Actually, only a few seconds had elapsed. He was in a neighborhood of wealthy homes whose owners had deserted them for warmer climates at this period of the year. There would be no one here to give an alarm, save guards—and this dead Drexler watchman who lay a score of feet away belonged to the Iron Man!

Curiously, Wentworth became aware of Nita's whisper in that silence. Somehow, the Daimler's radio had escaped being wrecked in the crash, and the voice of the woman he loved came to him softly.

"The big blue cat travels fast!" she said, "and takes many kittens with him!"

Wentworth's grey-blue eyes tightened to hardness. The police were already on the way to his home, and they would be swift and thorough. Commissioner Kirkpatrick was his friend, but for that very reason would be the more stern in his execution of justice. Kirkpatrick was a man who served the law with all his strength and keenness—and with all the integrity of his upright soul. If there was stolen loot in his home—and Wentworth had no doubt that it was there—Kirkpatrick would have but one course. Useless to plead that it was a frame-up by criminal foes.

Wentworth shook his head sharply. Damn it, he could not afford to be imprisoned now! Though eventually he might clear himself, those lost hours would mean that he would be out of the war against this monster and his criminal servants—and yet he would not abandon this fight now when he felt it was so nearly won! Let him but charge a car once more against this monster's legs. . . . It was typical of the *Spider* that he did not even hesitate in his choice. Personal safety, as always, must make way for the demands of the selfless service to which he was pledged!

Abruptly, the robot was in motion. Wentworth stood alertly, waiting for an attack, but the monster ignored him now. Resolutely, the robot turned . . . toward the wall at the end of the dead-end street! It moved a little awkwardly, and the left leg squeaked a little at every movement. Light slid in glittering contours across the smooth metal back, and it came to Wentworth suddenly that the creature was retreating! But where did it seek to go, when walls lifted on every side?

Wentworth swore and his eyes quested sharply about. Was there nothing he could do to stay the thing's flight? He whipped out his automatic and aimed at the creaking knee joint, pumped out a swift and careful drum-roll of bullets. He could trace the silvery streaks where the bullets struck. They whined off into the night . . . and the robot did not even turn its head! Fiercely, Wentworth ran toward the shattered traffic standard which had been hurled at him. With a heave of his powerful shoulders he lifted it, and balanced it across straining biceps.

The *Spider's* face was grimly twisted, for he knew what risk he ran. He had not the strength to hurl this weapon. His only chance was to run with it, like a battering ram. If he missed, if the robot turned at the last moment . . . Wentworth brushed those considerations from his mind, and began to run, straight toward the monster! At first, his pace was no more than a lumbering trot, but as he gained momentum, his stride lengthened. Finally, he was sprinting at fierce speed with his awkward weapon laid in rest like a spear!

When he was still a dozen feet away, the robot reached the wall at the end of the street. A hand rested against that wall, and there was a muffled concussion! Under the touch of that steel palm, the bricks and mortar fell apart . . . and the robot stepped through! An instant later, Wentworth crashed his battering ram against the robot's knee, saw a steel hand swoop toward him! Somehow, Wentworth flung himself backward from the path of that careless blow. The robot's hand caught the iron standard, and plucked it from his grip, sent it tumbling like a stick of kindling across the street . . . and then the robot walked on into darkness!

At the gap in the wall, Wentworth leaned while the breath whistled through his distended nostrils. He was gazing down upon the black, rippling waters of the East River, gazing at the retreating back of the robot. Even as he watched, the monster of steel stepped into the margin of the water . . . and an instant later, the black flood swallowed it entirely! There was left only a widening ripple in the waters breaking the streaks of reflected light from the stars, from the calm cold moon!

Not suicide, no. The robot had been merely beating a strategic retreat. Wentworth choked down a wild impulse to laughter. Suicide, for a monster of steel? But there was a human brain within it, an inhuman brain . . . and Kirkpatrick was hurrying toward Wentworth's home to gather up evidence which other servitors of the Iron Man had planted there. By the heavens, this Iron Man moved swiftly and terribly! And it had a sure and safe retreat beneath the waters of New York harbor!

Wentworth took long steps, that at first were uncertain, along that shattered dead-end street. A moment he stared, and then keenness came into his eyes. If Jackson returned, if he moved swiftly, there might still be a way to defeat the Iron Man's trap and disarm Kirkpatrick's suspicions. Then he could assume the offensive once more, track down these killers. . . .

Grimly, Wentworth bent over the body of the slain watchman. His lips twisted with distaste, but there was no help for the thing he must do. He leaned the man's body against the side of his overturned car, backed away across the street—and fired a single shot! The corpse jerked to the impact of lead, and there was no longer a *Spider* seal upon his chest! Instead, another wound gaped there beside the one that already had drained his life. An instant later, an auto swerved into the street and Jackson leaped to the pavement.

His voice rang out to Wentworth hoarsely, "Where is it, sir?" he asked.

Wentworth shook his head. "No time for that!" he snapped. "Help me with this body!"

Jackson ran the car to Wentworth's side and, within moments, the body had been placed in the tonneau of the small sedan Jackson had rented. At a word from Wentworth, the car leaped forward, speeding toward his home. This would have to be terribly fast; Kirkpatrick already had been on the way for a couple of minutes and only the fact that Wentworth was nearer his own home than Kirkpatrick gave him any chance at all.

"What's up, sir?" Jackson asked quietly, but there was still strain in his voice, and the muscles made white ridges along his jaw. "God, I hope I never see another thing like that!"

Wentworth's lips parted in a harsh smile. "We're apt to see many more—and battle many more—before this criminal uprising is crushed!" he said swiftly. "I don't know the motive behind this business yet, but it's plain enough that that robot or another like it committed the crimes on Sutton Place! If you could have seen those murdered men . . ."

"Another like it!" Jackson echoed. "Good God, *more of them!*"

Wentworth made no answer, but his thoughts raced ahead. The dilemma at his home now was a matter of speed. His plans were partly laid, but he had left trouble behind him in the side-street off Sutton Place. The Daimler was wrecked past any removal, and he would have to explain plenty to Kirkpatrick. God in heaven, how could a man explain that monster of steel! But there was a dead policeman back there in the street, and Wentworth's wrecked car . . .

Jackson said grimly, "I'll double back and . . . remove that dead cop. Mr. Kirkpatrick won't believe what happened."

Wentworth glanced at Jackson with a smile. As always, Jackson's thoughts were first of the man he served, never of himself. Of what might happen to him if he were caught in his self-assigned task of removing the body of a murdered policeman he made no mention. Wentworth felt a warmth creep through the coldness that had been his heart. By the heavens, with men like this to serve him, he was an ingrate to despair! He would down these robots. . . .

Jackson cried out softly as the car whipped into the side street that flanked Wentworth's Fifth Avenue apartment house, and Wentworth saw the reason why. A long black limousine was just sliding past the street's end, slowing to a halt before the main door—and that limousine had blood-red headlights! It was the car of Stanley Kirkpatrick!

"The private elevator!" Wentworth snapped, and as he spoke, he was stripping off his overcoat, wadding it around his silk hat. "Take this body to the apartment—"

"But the police will come there, sir!"

"Orders, Jackson!" Wentworth snapped. "Listen to me! Take this body to the apartment. In one of the rooms, probably the music room, you will find some objects of art that don't belong there. You will put the fingerprints of this body on several of them, then lay it face down beside the doors of the terrace, or window, with a gun in its hand. Here's his own gun. Fire that gun a couple of times, and let the bullet marks show on the wall, but muffle the shots with a wet cloth. Watch fingerprints! Now, hurry! I'll delay Kirkpatrick!"

As he spoke, he was out of the car, sprinting toward the side entrance of the apartment building. He raced down the hallway to the main lobby which led past the public elevators to the front of the building. Through the main doors, closed against the biting cold of the night, he saw the lean, dapper figure of Kirkpatrick. He was gesturing men into positions about the building! Heaven grant that Jackson already had the body inside the elevator! Kirkpatrick wheeled then and strode toward the main doors, and Wentworth ran. He staggered a little, slipping on the smooth tiled floor, and leaned hard across the information desk. He shouted toward the man at the telephone switchboard.

"Why in the devil didn't you answer my signal!" he cried. "Get an ambulance! Get a policeman! Don't sit there staring at me, *call a policeman!*"

Wentworth heard the swinging of the outer doors, felt the gust of cold air that came in with the opening. He pushed himself back from the counter, whipped out a handkerchief and mopped his forehead.

"Will you hurry?" he demanded of the still-gaping operator. "I must have a policeman right away!"

Beside him, Kirkpatrick spoke and there was a harder ring than usual to his metallic voice. "Won't I do, Dick?"

Wentworth started violently, then whirled toward his friend and put a smile on his lips. "This is lucky, Kirk," he said energetically. "I—wait a minute. Never mind that call to the police, operator."

The operator shrugged slowly, "What about the ambulance, Mr. Wentworth?" he asked.

Wentworth stared at him as if he did not understand the man. As he figured it, Jackson could not possibly be more than half way to his penthouse by now. And he had to make the full arrangements before

Kirkpatrick reached his apartment. He *had* to! Anything he could do to delay their arrival. . . . "What ambulance?" he asked the operator blankly.

The operator stared in bewilderment and started to explain, but Kirkpatrick cut in sharply. "Dick, I'm waiting for an explanation!"

Wentworth wheeled to face his friend. There was a frown on Kirkpatrick's saturnine countenance, and the mouth beneath the spiked mustache was a harsh line. Wentworth knew he must be careful not to overdo the delay. Kirkpatrick had seen him in too many emergencies for him to believe in any extreme befuddlement.

Wentworth said quietly, "Certainly, Kirk. I'm afraid I'll have to submit to arrest. Technical of course. I just killed a man in my apartment, but—" He massaged his temples. "God, I never saw such a night! First, one of your policemen is killed—"

Kirkpatrick seized him by the arm, "Snap out of it, Dick!" he said fiercely. "What in the devil are you talking about? You've killed a man . . . Surely, not a policeman!"

Wentworth said, "No, no, I only thought that at first. The man has on a private police agency's uniform. But there is one of your men killed."

Kirkpatrick said violently, "Will you talk sense, Dick? I demand that you give me the whole truth at once! It isn't just luck that I'm here, you know!"

Wentworth said slowly, "Do you want to have someone take down this statement?"

Kirkpatrick started to gesture toward a plainclothesman who had followed him through the doors, then he stared at Wentworth with suddenly narrowed eyes. "We'll take the statement in your apartment," he said sharply. "Come along!"

Wentworth looked at him while his mind raced desperately. Kirkpatrick had seen through his stall, or at least had become suspicious of delay . . . and Jackson had not yet had time to arrange matters as he had ordered. He shrugged heavily.

"Oh, all right," he said and started toward the elevator, then turned toward the telephone operator. "By the way, if Miss van Sloan should call—"

"Disregard that!" Kirkpatrick snapped at the operator. "By God, Dick, if you're trying any hocus-pocus on me! Why should you come down here to call a policeman? You have two private lines into your home in addition to the one through the switchboard!"

Wentworth faced Kirkpatrick, and there was no smile on his face. "The way you have been behaving lately Kirk," he said shortly, "with your suspicions and persecution of me, I find it expedient to have witnesses for every movement of mine."

Kirkpatrick did not quail under the direct gaze of Wentworth's grey-blue eyes, but a small frown knifed between his brows. "I warn you, Dick," he said quietly, "that every second of delay increases my suspicions of you! I told you it was not luck that I had come here! I have a tip that—"

"That what?" Wentworth demanded as Kirkpatrick broke off.

"That will come later," Kirkpatrick said shortly. "Into the elevator at once, or I'll go up without you!"

Wentworth nodded and stepped into the cage. The uniformed man and Kirkpatrick's secretary followed and the elevator sped upward. Wentworth said, wearily, "I suppose I'll have to put up with these suspicions of yours, Kirk, but I warn you they're wearing hard on my liking for you. After all, friendship is based on mutual respect, and really—"

"I'll ask you to account for your movements, Dick," Kirkpatrick interrupted sharply, "from seven o'clock tonight onward!"

"Under the circumstances, perhaps I'd better call my lawyer first," Wentworth snapped, "though I fail to see why I should fall under suspicion for having killed a burglar in my own home! A burglar I tried to capture, and who fired on me twice before I returned a shot!"

"So that's what happened, is it?" Kirkpatrick asked. His voice was utterly without expression.

"Would it be asking too much?" Wentworth went on bitterly, "to demand the reason for your presence, since you would hardly bring your secretary and other officers on a friendly call?"

The elevator sighed to a halt, and Kirkpatrick strode out of the cage without reply, jabbed hard at the bell beside Wentworth's door. Wentworth stood idly aside. He had done what he could to delay the police. If Jackson were not ready now, he would have to make a break for it! He peered covertly toward the two men who accompanied Kirkpatrick. Sergeant Reams, the officer in uniform, was not a man who needed orders, otherwise he would not have been Kirkpatrick's bodyguard. He stood by the elevator with a revolver ready in his fist!

The door of Wentworth's penthouse opened on the safety chain, and through the opening Wentworth saw the dark bearded face and turbaned head of his other confidential servitor, Ram Singh.

"Open the door," Kirkpatrick ordered brusquely.

Ram Singh's dark eyes regarded Kirkpatrick impassively. "Pardon, Kirkpatrick *sahib*," he said in the deep rumble of his voice, "but do you come in friendship or as the police? If you come as the police . . ."

Kirkpatrick's anger flushed into his cheekbones, but he checked the angry retort that sprang to his lips. "Confound it, Dick!" he snapped, "there is a reason for these delays!"

"Quite," Wentworth murmured, and his smooth black eyebrows arched in mockery. "The reason lies in your own anger and impatience, for as the Hindus say . . ." he lapsed into the Hindustani which Ram Singh understood. "*If all is well, open the door, my comrade. Otherwise, have trouble with the lock.* Which means, Kirk, that the angry man maketh his own impediments."

"Will you order this stubborn Sikh—" Kirkpatrick began, but cut off as the door swung smoothly open.

Ram Singh bowed low, and hid the mockery in his dark gaze. "A thousand pardons, Kirkpatrick *sahib*," he rumbled. "My turban is in the dust! I did not know that my master accompanied his friend!"

Kirkpatrick strode past him with an oath, and from inside the apartment, Jackson's voice called out calmly, "You came quickly, sir! The body is in here!"

Wentworth followed the angry strides of Kirkpatrick across the drawing room toward the arch that gave into the music chamber beyond, and his quick eyes flashed over the chaste simplicity of the furnishings. He smothered an oath. The body was stretched out as he had ordered upon the floor, and there were bullet scars obviously from the gun in the man's hand . . . but Wentworth's eyes were fixed on a number of objects placed about the room. They were cleverly disposed, so that they seemed a part of the furnishings, yet Wentworth knew that they were stolen property!

On the grand piano, there was an exquisitely carved Ming vase of moonlight jade, and on the mantel a small antique clock of French fame caught glittering lights with the swing of a pendulum encrusted with precious stones! Surely, the Iron Man, or whoever directed the robot's movements, did not stint for money when he planned a frame-up! Those articles had a value in hundreds of thousands, and their possession might well tempt even a Richard Wentworth to robbery!

Kirkpatrick was standing over the body of the dead man. He reached down to lift the head by the hair, swore softly as he let it fall.

"Your burglar," he said acidly, "is a trusted agent of a private protection agency famed for its integrity. The Drexler agency! But I don't need to tell you that. You know Frank Drexler! Nor do I see that he has stolen anything!"

Wentworth said slowly, "You are quite right, Kirk. It is apparent that this is a most peculiar burglar. He came bearing gifts!" He strolled across the room toward the Ming vase, made a slow business of reaching out for it. "This vase, as I happen to know, being something of a connoisseur in such matters, belongs to one Aaron Smedley, whose house was robbed tonight, and—"

"*Don't touch that vase!*" Kirkpatrick snapped.

Wentworth let his hand freeze in mid-air, while he turned with lifted brows toward Kirkpatrick. "What have I done now?" he demanded.

Kirkpatrick was standing on braced legs, and his hands were clasped hard behind him. "I do not want your fingerprints on that vase, Dick," he said quietly. "*Unless they are already there!*"

Wentworth shrugged irritably, "Really, Kirk, you're going too far!" He turned angrily across the room. "I insist on an immediate fingerprint test. I have materials here. . . . And would it be asking too much if you also fingerprint the corpse? Or is it a criminal offense for me to make the suggestion?" He continued to fume while he jerked open the drawer of the desk, caught out envelopes of powder, a sufflator, ink pad and papers. "Apparently, you suspect me of robbery! Well, I've confessed homicide. That should satisfy you."

He flung the articles on the desk and Kirkpatrick took them quickly, but Wentworth stood staring down into the drawer. It was only an instant's pause that did not catch the commissioner's attention, but the discovery he made set Wentworth's heart to racing painfully. He had, perhaps, escaped one trap that had been set for him by the fiendish ingenuity of these criminals. It was unlikely Kirkpatrick could contradict the testimony of those fingerprints on the loot. He had hoped to get rid of Kirk now, race on with his investigation—and he had only discovered a second trap! The Iron Man had not been content with planting loot here and tipping the police. The same man who had placed the evidence here had, at the same time, set another snare!

In that drawer, Wentworth habitually kept an automatic registered in his name, and licensed to him. And that gun was gone!

Wentworth had no doubt as to the whereabouts of that gun, or what had been the purpose of the theft. As surely as death itself, that gun was planted now in one of the looted houses; and equally certain, too, was the fact that a bullet would have been fired from it into the mutilated corpse of one of the guards!

A slow and bitter smile disturbed Wentworth's lips. Truly, the Iron Man planned well! Somehow now, he must elude the police, and get to the murder scene before that incriminating gun was found!

Kirkpatrick's voice came to his ears with an accent of relief, but with a reserve that puzzled Wentworth.

"The fingerprints on the vase and clock are undoubtedly those of the dead man," Kirkpatrick said quietly. "Now, Dick, I must ask you to accompany me."

Wentworth turned slowly, and his face was expressionless, but he felt that he knew the answer to this invitation even while he phrased the query, "That's always a pleasure, Kirk," he said, "though I'm a bit weary just now. Would it be impertinent to ask where it is you wish to go?"

Kirkpatrick was unsmiling, too. "I want you to go with me," he said quietly, "to the home of Aaron Smedley."

Wentworth felt the shock of those words and knew that his suspicions were correct. Not only had the gun been planted as he feared—*but Kirkpatrick had been tipped off about that, too!*

Now there was no chance at all of evading Kirkpatrick, of getting there first. He must be with the commissioner when the police found the gun which would pin upon him one of the most atrocious murders the city had known! Against that evidence, the trickery played here would not stand up an instant! Kirkpatrick's keen mind would tell him how he had been tricked. But, damn it, the *Spider* could not allow himself to be imprisoned! The lives of many of the city's people would be crushed like ants beneath the iron tread of those grim robots, unless the *Spider* remained at liberty!

Something close to panic goaded Wentworth then, not a fear for himself, but the certainty of the fate that threatened the people he loved and served. Panic. . . .

Wentworth shrugged and, by a violent effort, made his voice easy. "Certainly, Kirk," he agreed. "I will go wearily with you to the home of Aaron Smedley. After that, I hope you will allow me an opportunity to sleep!"

Kirkpatrick's frown refused to lift. "Yes, Dick," he said. "I only hope that you will be allowed to sleep comfortably in your own bed, and not—"

"Not in one of your private guest chambers," Wentworth interrupted with enforced gaiety. "The ones with bars and tool-steel doors!"

# CHAPTER THREE
# THE TRAP IS SPRUNG

THROUGH A LONG MOMENT, the two friends stood face-to-face in the middle of that death-marked music room. The half-angry smile lingered on Wentworth's lips, but Kirkpatrick was completely grave. Wentworth knew that each move the commissioner made against him stabbed Kirkpatrick to the heart; he knew that Kirk would be the more grimly determined to press the evidence against him for that very reason. Wentworth's mind was racing ahead, canvassing every possibility. Somehow, he had to evade making the trip with Kirkpatrick, arrive before him at the looted home of Aaron Smedley. Not until then could he strike back at these murderous criminals who were, so early in the war, trying to destroy the man they must recognize as their most dangerous enemy! Yes, he must elude Kirkpatrick—but it must be done in such a way that no suspicion attached to him! Wentworth wheeled abruptly away. "I'll be with you, Kirk, as soon as I change to more appropriate clothing."

Kirkpatrick said, "Certainly. . . . Sergeant Reams, stay in sight of him the entire time."

Wentworth bowed swiftly, but made no demur and accomplished his rapid change under the watchful eyes of Kirkpatrick's body-guard—and Sergeant Reams kept his revolver in his fist!

Wentworth's stride was crisp with anger as he returned to the music room, clad now in the dark tweeds he preferred, and it put an edge on his voice when he spoke to Kirkpatrick. "As you know," he said, "Nita is always in danger whenever I have been attacked, and I can give no other interpretation to what happened here tonight. You won't mind if I phone her to be careful?"

"No objection," Kirkpatrick told him tonelessly. "You won't mind making the call from this room?"

Wentworth smiled thinly as he swung toward a wall cabinet and removed a portable telephone. He plugged it into a jack in the wall, and went through the routine of dialing a number. He had only one chance of evading Kirkpatrick, and that would draw Nita into danger as well as himself. There was no other way . . . and he had plugged the telephone into a radio circuit instead of the regular phone line. That very action would start the transmitter on the roof into operation. He could only hope that Nita would be listening.. . . .

"Nita, dear?" he threw his voice into the air. "I'm glad I caught you at home. Yes, I'm at home, too. I wish you were here!" He emphasized that phrase very slightly. If Nita heard, she would know what he meant, and she would get here as quickly as possible. "No, unfortunately, I have to go out again. Kirkpatrick has invited me most urgently. . . ."

Kirkpatrick said shortly, "Cut that short, Dick! You wanted to warn her!"

Wentworth's shoulders tautened at the peremptory tone. Kirkpatrick must indeed be on edge. He made no response, continued to speak into the blankness of the air. If only he could be sure Nita was listening!

"Dear, I want you to take particularly good care of yourself. Keep your gun always handy. Yes, I've been attacked once tonight by this new criminal gang, and that means danger . . . to you, dear. Yes, of course, I'll be careful. I'm always ready for any unexpected events that may develop. As you say it is the unexpected thing that is demoralizing. You know the Hindustani proverb?"

Kirkpatrick's heel thudded on the floor. "You will confine yourself to English, Dick!" he snapped.

Wentworth turned deliberately to face him, and it was in English that he spoke into the transmitter. He already had conveyed most of his message to Nita. She must come to him at once. He had mentioned his gun, and said he had been attacked; that he would be ready for "unexpected events."

"As the Hindus say," he went on, "'In peace, the thunder of chariots goes unheard; in war, the rattle of a small sword startles an army.' Yes, of course dear, I'll see you soon. The first moment I am free. I have to leave now with Kirk. Good night!"

Wentworth hung up slowly, jerked out the plug lest Kirkpatrick understand how he had sent out that message. If Nita had heard him, he had no doubt that she would understand his double speech. If she would only 'rattle a small sword' he would have a chance to escape from Kirkpatrick!

Wentworth accepted his coat and hat from Ram Singh, laid his gaze upon the Sikh and Jackson. "You two will remain here pending further orders," he said curtly. "Do you mind, Kirk, if I tell them to send my lawyers over to headquarters if I have not returned in a few hours?"

Kirkpatrick said grimly, "Not at all, Dick. If you have not returned in a few hours, your lawyers will be needed!"

The eyes of the two men met in challenge and it was only Wentworth who smiled, albeit grimly. He buttoned his coat and deliberately pulled the soft brim of his felt over his brows. He had done what he could to meet this crisis. If Nita had not heard him, there would have to be another attempt, regardless of whether it aroused Kirkpatrick's suspicions still more. He must recover that gun before it fell into the hands of the police!

"I'm ready, Kirk," he said quietly.

Kirkpatrick nodded, motioned to Sergeant Reams and they filed out together. Wentworth was conscious of Jackson's eyes on him appealingly, of the smoldering anger that Ram Singh barely suppressed. His two men were ready to hurl themselves upon the police at any cost. They did not know what threatened, but that he was in danger was abundantly clear—and yet he had ordered them to remain behind! But it was necessary. If Nita obeyed his suggestion, there must be no added danger to her sweet life!

As they crossed the first floor lobby, Wentworth glanced covertly at his watch and saw that almost five minutes had elapsed since he had first spoken to Nita. It was time enough for her to reach here . . . if she had heard! At the entrance, Wentworth tucked a cigarette between his lips and, just outside, he paused to flick flame to his lighter. He had a little trouble so that Kirkpatrick and Sergeant Reams passed him, turned stiffly to keep him under constant surveillance. Wentworth got the cigarette lighted, slowly pocketed the lighter . . . and still nothing happened. Had Nita then failed to get his message?

"Come on, Dick," Kirkpatrick urged impatiently. "I've never seen you so dilatory as tonight." He jerked open the door of the big limousine, motioned Wentworth inside. Sergeant Reams flanked the door on the other side, gun in his fist. Wentworth caught the sigh that pushed to his teeth. He would have no choice then but to make a break for it, to try and conciliate Kirkpatrick afterward. He settled the brim of his hat more firmly about his brows—and heard the squeal of skidding auto tires!

Wentworth stiffened at the sound. Out of his eye corners he saw a battered coupe sweep around the corner from beside the apartment house. The window nearest him was down and, even as he peered that way, he caught the silhouette of a slouch hat pulled low over the driver's brows. And then gun-flame blossomed from that dark interior! Lead screamed over his head and smashed through the glass in the door behind him!

A shout sprang to Wentworth's lips, a shout of exultation! Nita had heard him and understood! Wentworth changed the cry to surprise, to fright. He went down on one knee, and two more of Nita's bullets slammed overhead! Then he had his own automatic out and was sprinting toward the coupe! It had straightened out of the skidding turn and was darting across Fifth Avenue. Out of his eye corners, Wentworth caught sight of Sergeant Reams. He had dropped to his knee behind a fire hydrant and the light gleamed coldly on his revolver. Kirkpatrick wheeled stiffly beside the limousine and the long-barreled .38 with which he was so expert was ready in his hand. Good God! If those two marksmen opened up on Nita. . . .

Wentworth shouted fiercely. "Come on, Kirk! They're the crooks who tried to frame me! In that coupe!" He hurled himself forward in a violent sprint—straight into the line of fire of the two officers!

Wentworth heard Kirkpatrick cry out harshly, felt the breeze of lead streaking past his head . . . and knew that he had disconcerted the aim of the police! Wentworth's own gun was kicking in his hand, but he was throwing his lead deliberately high. Half-way across Fifth Avenue, he shouted his challenge back to Kirkpatrick.

"Come on! I got a tire on that coupe! We'll run it down!"

He put everything he had into a hard sprint, heard Kirkpatrick's feet thud against the pavement behind him, heard his order to Sergeant Reams to "follow with the car!" As if to put a period to his sentence, one final shot blasted from the coupe before it whipped out of sight—and there was a hissing explosion followed by the sharp curse of Sergeant Reams. Nita, bless her cool courage and intelligence, had fully grasped the situation. She had shot a tire of Kirkpatrick's car!

Kirkpatrick was fifteen yards behind when Wentworth rounded the corner into the side street. By the end of the next block, where the coupe, wobbling as if from a punctured tire, had turned, Wentworth had increased that lead to fifty yards. He heard Kirkpatrick call out breathlessly but answered only with a shout.

"Come on!" he cried. "We're gaining!"

Around that corner, the coupe was motionless at the curb, the door flung wide! With a long bound, Wentworth was on the running board and instantly the coupe lurched forward. Nita's quick, excited laughter was warm.

"How do you like me as a torpedo, Dick?" she cried, still laughing gaily.

The coupe whipped around the next corner and streaked on into the night. Briefly, street lights shone upon the smooth oval of Nita's face, glistened on her shining eyes. The tendrils of her chestnut curls twisted out from beneath the confines of the man's hat she had tugged low over her brows. She looked like a child at an amusing prank, but Wentworth knew what fears throbbed in her breast for him. It was part of the compact between them, the oath they had sworn when Wentworth had lost his fight against their love and told her the truth of his harried existence, and the fact that they could never marry while work remained for the *Spider*! She would never show her fears. . . .

Wentworth mastered his pumping lungs, and his hand was gentle upon her shoulders. "Eastward, dear, and fast," he said. "Stop near the first taxi you see. . . . Sweet, you took too much chance back there, more than was necessary."

Nita shook her head, and there was deviltry about the tender curve of her lips. "It had to be realistic, Dick. Is anything less than that worthy of . . . the *Spider's* true love?"

Wentworth laughed softly. "I think you'll have to stop the car," he said.

Nita's face was immediately sober. She glanced to the rear and asked sharply, "Are we followed?"

Wentworth shook his head, "No, but I doubt if even the *Spider's* true love can drive efficiently while being kissed!"

It was only an instant's pause on a dark side-street, half-way between danger and despair; then the coupe once more was boring through the night while Wentworth hurriedly explained the things that had happened this night; the things that still threatened to happen.

"Without a doubt, dear," Wentworth rushed on, "Kirkpatrick must have thrown a strong guard about those houses on Sutton Place the instant he received the tip about the murder gun being there. But he will want to make the search in person. As soon as I leave you—there's a taxi parked ahead, I'll take that—phone Jackson to get out of the building without being seen. He is to proceed at once to Sutton Place, put on the robes of the *Spider* and, when he sees me talking to the police guards, he will show himself long enough to draw those guards away!"

Nita drew in a slow breath. "The peril must be very great, Dick, for you to assign risky jobs to anyone except yourself!"

Wentworth's arm closed hard about Nita's shoulders as she eased the coupe to a halt. "Greater than anyone could realize who has not seen those robots, if that's what the thing was," he said grimly. "Heaven grant, dear, that you never come in contact with them. If you do. . . . If you do run as fast as you can! Nothing can stop them!"

The coupe halted, and Wentworth swept Nita once more into his arms. She was so small, so soft, in his powerful embrace; so vulnerable. Those monsters in steel. . . . His arms tightened. "When you've transmitted those orders, go to my home," he said. "You should be safe with Ram Singh to guard you. And—be careful, dear!"

Nita's lips trembled under his caress, but her voice came out clearly, even with a hint of laughter. "Certainly," she said. "It is a lesson we have learned from you! Always to be careful of ourselves!"

There was time for no more of these sweets stolen from a life of perpetual peril, of feverish battles. Wentworth flung around the corner, and sprang into the taxi, tossed a Sutton Place address at the driver. When he peered back, he saw Nita's brave figure turning into the corner drug store. Within a few minutes, Jackson would be receiving his orders. . . .

There was a grim tautness in the thrust of Wentworth's jaw as he tore his thoughts away from Nita and her peril. His ruse had succeeded against Kirkpatrick. Within a few minutes now, he would recover that stolen automatic and then he could turn his attentions to the criminals who struck such shrewd and wanton blows against him. This was a battle that must be joined and settled quickly. He could not permit such creatures as these robots to range at the will of criminals. The potentialities for awful slaughter were too great. And already, he had had proof enough that the will for slaughter existed! Those four poor devils in the homes on Sutton Place. . . .

A block from the looted homes, Wentworth paid off the cab and sauntered into an all-night drug store where he put through a call for his own apartment house, had the operator page Kirkpatrick. Within moments, the stormy voice of the commissioner blasted over the wire!

"Where are you, Dick?" he demanded. "By God, you ran out on me, and—"

"I trailed the coupe in a cab," Wentworth said crisply, "but the beggar got away from me finally on the upper East Side. I'm at Sutton Place now, where I expected you'd already be. Shall I wait for you here?"

Wentworth heard Kirkpatrick's smothered oath over the wire. "You will go at once and place yourself in the custody of the first policeman you see," Kirkpatrick ordered. "There are twenty stationed around the looted houses on Sutton Place. At once, you understand, Dick? It is now three-fourteen. You will make that surrender by three-sixteen."

Wentworth's voice rasped angrily into the transmitter. "This one time I'm taking orders, Kirk," he snapped. "Hereafter, you will come to see me on official business only!"

He slammed the receiver into its hook and swung out of the phone booth. His eyes were narrowed and hard. He could not blame Kirkpatrick for doing his full duty, but it seemed to him that the commissioner was too quick at accepting anonymous information against a friend. The tips could have been only anonymous. Wentworth shook his head, bowed into the bitter wind that moaned along Sutton Place.

The sky was overcast now, and only the transient beams from the street lights relieved the shadows. He saw the policemen ringed about the three buildings where the murders had occurred, and moved steadily toward them. A dozen blocks farther along was the dead-end street where he had battled the robot. But these police must have been thrown about the houses since that time. Had the murder of the policeman been reported?

At the memory, Wentworth stopped sharply in his tracks. Jackson had said he would remove that body and Wentworth had given no counter-manding of the determination. Jackson might well have concluded that his instructions to remain at home had been given for Kirkpatrick's ears alone. In that case, there would be no diversion created here to permit his entrance. But he could not turn back now. Kirkpatrick had given him only two minutes, and the police guard had already seen him approaching.

Wentworth sent his sharp gaze stabbing ahead, picked out the facade of Aaron Smedley's home. That was the most logical place for the planting of his gun, since the loot left in his apartment had come from that home. He must surrender to the police, yet elude them to recover that gun—and do it in a space of minutes. Kirkpatrick would be in furious haste to arrive now that he knew Wentworth was already here.

Wentworth walked straight up to the nearest policeman, nodded to him pleasantly. "I'm meeting Kirkpatrick here," he said quietly. "I believe he'll be here in a few minutes."

The policeman lifted his nightstick in salute. "Yes, sir," he agreed. "A bitter night to be on duty."

Wentworth nodded absently, and leaned his hips against the iron fence which surrounded the basement well of the Smedley house. Minutes, and then Kirkpatrick would be here. His own course was clear. He would have to absent himself, take a chance on allaying Kirkpatrick's suspicions. . . .

"Too cold," he agreed. "When the commissioner arrives, tell him I'm waiting in the bar room over there on the corner."

Wentworth nodded, started across the street and then an oath sprang to his lips. He muffled it, kept deliberately on his way. It was not for him to call attention to that grim silhouette on the roof of the buildings across the street, a figure of hunched shoulders, draped in a long cape—a silhouette which any of the police, and half the populace of the city would recognize instantly, and. . . .

Wentworth whipped about as a policeman lifted a hoarse shout: "Look! Hey, get him! *Look,* on the roof there—*the Spider!*"

There was that moment's pause while the man's frightened shout ran down the street, and then there was a concerted crash of gunfire! Even then the figure on the roof did not immediately dodge back out of sight. It stood peering down into the dark canyon of the street, the black cape sweeping out on the breath of the wind. Wentworth's teeth set fiercely. Why didn't Jackson get back out of range? He had exposed himself long enough now. He—instead of retreating, the caped figure suddenly whipped out a gun and emptied it in a swift drumroll which shattered windows in the Smedley house behind Wentworth! Then it turned and ran lightly along the front ridge of the roofs across the street!

The police went past Wentworth in a blue flood, their voices as fierce as the bay of hounds that rush in to the kill. Wentworth hesitated, while his eyes followed that flitting figure with the cape kiting at its shoulders. This was not like Jackson, to expose himself needlessly to gun fire. What was necessary he would do, but beyond that he was too wise a man, too experienced with guns and the carnage they wrought to take useless chances. Wentworth shook his head at the sudden, frightened thought that crossed his mind. He could hear, through the hammer of furiously released police guns, the thin distant wailing of a siren. It meant that Kirkpatrick was on the way; that Wentworth had only a few moments left to seize the chance which the *Spider* masquerade afforded him. But fear was still there in his heart as he darted, unobserved by the preoccupied police, through the smashed windows of the Smedley house! The figure of the *Spider* had seemed so *small*! But this was madness. It could not be . . . Nita!

Wentworth told himself that, as he quested swiftly through the lower floor of the Smedley house, but his mind was distracted. If Jackson had left on his self-appointed errand, this was exactly what Nita would do; come herself in the masquerade of the *Spider*! God, he had to make this fast! It would be just like Nita to continue the diversion until she saw Wentworth emerge safely from the beleaguered house! Wentworth's pocket flash eagerly probed the room, glittered on the smashed shards of art treasures which the killers had left. Wanton vandalism. Staring at the wreckage, Wentworth could see the work of the steel flails which were the arms of robots. Anger shook him. He sent the flashlight toward the window portieres . . . and it glinted on his gun! With a glad cry, he sprang toward it.

Outside, the hammer of guns went on, and the shriek of the siren was louder. When he reappeared, the false *Spider* could flee. Wentworth stooped swiftly toward the gun . . . and it was only belatedly that his caution returned to him. He remembered then that his light had passed this spot once before, and that on the previous occasion the gun had not been here!

Even as the significance of that fact flashed across his mind, he hurled himself toward the portieres while his left hand clawed for the heavy automatic that nested beneath his arm. He was too late. Before his hand could close on the gun, before he could touch the portieres, he saw a hand snake out from behind the curtain and a blackjack swung viciously toward his skull!

Brilliant lights exploded within Wentworth's skull, and he pitched to the floor. There was agony in his brain, but all his senses were terribly acute. He tried to drive strength into his limbs, and he could not move at all. But he could hear with a clarity that seemed to give him a new vision. Feet moved softly toward him. There was a thin snickering laughter just above his head, and then the chill touch of steel in the palm of his right hand. After that, only the clatter of guns and the mounting shriek of the siren.

Wentworth knew what had happened all right. That was the damnable part of the thing. His brain was startlingly clear, though he could move not even a finger. The crook, perhaps the leader himself of this dread combination of horror and robbery, had hidden here to make sure that the incriminating gun was not removed before the police were at hand. Wentworth, his mind concentrated on his fears for Nita, had walked into the trap. He would lie here unconscious now, and the gun beneath his hand was a murder weapon!

"Now," he heard that hateful voice just above him whisper. "Now, the *Spider* will walk no more!"

# CHAPTER FOUR
# ON THE SPOT

A LESSER MAN THAN THE *SPIDER* would have fought through brief seconds against the benumbing effects of that blow and, failing, would have been doomed. Wentworth's body was defeated, but his mind fought on; his will was a flame of naked steel. That siren dinned dimly in his ears, and the *Spider* commanded his body to rise.

Perspiration broke out on his forehead under the assault of his will. The muscles of his legs and arms twitched, and there was no strength in them. But it was the will of the Master of Men that commanded. There was that moment of pause and then, slowly, as if each individual limb weighed a ton, Wentworth's arm drew beneath him. His legs tensed—and the *Spider* staggered to his feet!

There was no feeling in his legs, and his head sagged like a broken thing. He moved and his feet scuffed the floor in the dragging step of a paralytic. He stood there in that dark room and forced his head up. His hands still gripped the gun, his soft hat was on his head. The siren shrieked furiously in the street, and the gunshots were dying. There was so little time; so little.

The window would not serve now. He could not trust his crippled body through it. The door. . . . It swung open under the grip of Wentworth's gloved hand. He stumbled out into the shadows of the portico, somehow reached the sidewalk. Kirkpatrick's car blazed past toward where the police where grouped excitedly in the street. Their

46

eyes were turned upward, but the silhouette of the *Spider* no longer showed there on the skyline. Fear like physical pain thrust through Wentworth's heart. What had happened then? Had Nita. . . .

He smothered the thought. Every shred of his concentrated will was necessary even to achieve movement. Close in the shadow of the building, he turned away from the police and presently angled toward the other side; toward the bar room where he had told the policeman he would wait. Thoughts drove through his brain like individual spikes. His will was the sledge. Kirkpatrick must not see him come from the direction of the Smedley home. Beyond that, he could not plan now.

He reached the center of the street, sought for no more. He turned then and moved toward Kirkpatrick's car. The cold stab of the wind was grateful in his lungs. He felt that presently the curtain of numbness that had dropped over his brain would lift, but not yet. Not yet. He forced his head erect, tried to put briskness in his stride, but twice he stumbled where there was no obstacle at all. His pain-squeezed eyes reached ahead to where Kirkpatrick's lean, military figure stood beside the big red-eyed limousine and shouted orders. Evidently, he asked some question about Wentworth, for one of the policeman lifted a pointing arm and Kirkpatrick pivoted sharply about to stare where Wentworth walked.

Steady, Wentworth cautioned himself: *Put your feet down briskly and keep your bearing jaunty. . . .* If Kirkpatrick discovered he had been slugged, it was tantamount to admitting that he had entered the guarded building. The gun . . . good God! He still had the gun in his pocket! Too late now to do anything about it.

Kirkpatrick's voice came crisply: "Where have you been?" he demanded. "I told you to surrender yourself to the nearest policeman!"

Wentworth tried to answer and his tongue moved thickly in his mouth.

"Well?" Kirkpatrick snapped.

Wentworth managed to shrug. His words lacked their usual precise delivery. "I . . . waited," he mumbled. He nodded toward the officer with whom he had spoken previously. "Officer will tell you."

Kirkpatrick frowned, and the policeman grinned slightly as he peered toward Wentworth. "Right, sir. He was with me when the *Spider* was sighted. . . ."

"With you?" Kirkpatrick demanded.

"Right with me," the policeman nodded. "The gentleman said he would wait for you in the bar around the corner. I . . . think he did!" The cop hid another grin, and Kirkpatrick glared sharply at Wentworth.

It was the cue which Wentworth had awaited. He laughed loudly. "Right," he said. "Did wait in the bar. Good lord, that last drink packed an awful wallop. Went right to my head!"

Kirkpatrick did not smile. He looked at Wentworth, but his words were addressed to the policeman beside him. "You were standing right in front of the Smedley house when the *Spider* was sighted, I take it," he said.

"Yes, Commissioner."

"You left this gentleman with free access to the Smedley house, officer?"

The red crept up the policeman's cheeks. "Why, yes, sir. The gentleman was waiting for you, and the *Spider*—"

Kirkpatrick's laughter was sharp, triumphant. "Exactly! Officer O'Holian, *search this man!*"

The command fell like a shock across Wentworth's mind, and the veil of pain finally lifted, though his head still reeled from a blow which would have rendered a lesser man unconscious for an hour. He stiffened at Kirkpatrick's words, and he took a step backward. He seemed merely indignant, but he was frantic. With that murder gun in his pocket, he dared not submit to search! There was no longer any doubt that Kirkpatrick had been told in detail what evidence he would find in the Smedley home.

"This has gone far enough, Kirkpatrick!" Wentworth said harshly. "You presume upon friendship!"

Kirkpatrick motioned the policeman forward. "You are wrong, Dick," he said. "No malefactor is my friend! If you have nothing incriminating on you, you cannot object to search! Now then, permit the officer to do his duty!"

Wentworth faced the policeman squarely. "I have not been arrested," he warned the man. "You have no right to search me, and I will not submit." His words were quiet, but the cold force of the voice of the Master of Men struck through his tone. The policeman checked, but Wentworth recognized that this was only momentary respite. Kirkpatrick would insist. He had to find a way out. Had to! If the murder gun were found, he would no longer be able to fight against the Iron Man and his criminal cohorts . . . Wentworth reckoned grimly that the Iron Man would have a terrific score to settle when this was finished!

"You have illusions of grandeur," Wentworth snapped at Kirkpatrick, and his voice rose. He was stalling desperately for time. He had only one slim chance . . . if Jackson or Nita were within sound of his voice. If he could make them understand what he wanted, he might still evade Kirkpatrick. Yes, a slim chance.

"This is America, and there is a constitution to protect my rights!" He declared. "God in heaven, haven't I been through enough tonight? An attempt to frame me in my home. *I have been been shot at in the streets!*

"Do you think criminals want me dead because I have *helped* them? *At any minute, there may be another attack on my life!*"

Kirkpatrick said drily, "I hardly think it possible with all these police around you. Enough of this—"

Wentworth laughed harshly. "There were police around me last time I was shot at! A bullet can come from any shadow. . . . But that is beside the point, merely a proof of my innocence." His words rang clearly. "*I would rather be shot than submit to the indignity of such a search!*"

Had his words been heard, Wentworth wondered desperately? He dared not make his meaning clearer—and there was always the possibility that Jackson, or brave Nita if it had been she in the disguise of the *Spider,* had been wounded. Kirkpatrick gestured impatiently.

"You will either submit to search here and now," he said shortly, "or you will be taken to police headquarters on charges of suspicion of murder! Take your choice!"

Wentworth said, stiffly, "The choice is easy!" He could not stall much longer. It was clear none of his comrades was within the sound of his voice. Better to make a run for it, and. . . .

The sound of the shot that was fired from an opposite roof was loud in the waiting silence of the street. The tongue of flame reached downward fiercely.

Wentworth blew out his breath in a thin whisper of sound and pitched limply forward to the street. For an instant, there was only shocked silence in the street, and then bedlam broke loose. A half dozen police guns blasted toward the roof ambuscade, but Kirkpatrick cried out and dropped on his knees beside Wentworth. He bent close over him . . . and it gave Wentworth the chance he sought. The incriminating gun already was in his hand. As Kirkpatrick bent toward him, his back was toward Wentworth's right hand . . . and Wentworth whipped the gun toward a street sewer opening a dozen feet away!

Through the racket of the street, he heard the gun rasp on metal, and knew that it had struck the grating accurately. It was a sound that would go unnoticed in the general clamor.

"Play it up," he whispered to Kirkpatrick. "If the killer thinks he got me, he'll stop shooting!"

Kirkpatrick swore and ripped to his feet. "Faking!" The commissioner glared down at Wentworth irresolutely through a long moment, then turned to peer up toward the roof from which the shot had come. Wentworth seized that opportunity to glance toward the sewer opening, and an oath sprang to his lips. The gun had struck the grating all right. But it still hung there, balanced on the edge of the grating, and to Wentworth it seemed that all light in the street concentrated on the exposed butt!

He sprang to his feet, and Kirkpatrick whipped toward him. His call brought O'Holian back to his side. "Once before, Dick," he said quietly, "you escaped my custody during gunplay. I am making no accusation—"

"I should be thankful, I suppose!" Wentworth mocked.

"—but my ultimatum holds good!" Kirkpatrick pressed on. "Submit to search, or you go to jail!"

Wentworth met Kirkpatrick's frosty glare through a long moment, then slowly he lifted his hands. "Very well," he said grimly, "but I think you'll regret this, Kirkpatrick!"

Kirkpatrick's face was rigid as frozen earth. There was both determination and a wincing dread in his expression. "It is possible," he said heavily. "O'Holian, get on with the search!"

While the policeman made his rapidly thorough search, Wentworth allowed his eyes to stray covertly toward the sewer opening. A uniformed man was sauntering that way. If he should catch sight of that gun-butt ... Wentworth shifted impatiently.

"It might help O'Holian, Kirk," he said shortly, "if you would tell him what he's looking for."

"A thirty-eight calibre automatic," Kirkpatrick said grimly. "A colt, with a test barrel."

"It ain't on him, sir," O'Holian reported steadily. "His gun is a forty-five, and he's got a license for it here."

Kirkpatrick's whole body seemed to relax, though his voice remained toneless. "Very well, O'Holian," he said. "That will do."

Wentworth saw that the policeman had reached the sewer. He was kicking the metal grating absently with his toe. How could he help seeing that gun butt?

"If you're through with your insults," he said stiffly. "I'm going home." His mind was very active.

Kirkpatrick nodded gravely. His frosty blue eyes were puzzled, but there was suffering in their depths. Actually, he detested these moments when he had to accuse his friend. Things would be a little smoother, now, with the searching over and done—if only . . . Wentworth turned aside and glanced once more toward the policeman. He was standing on the grating now, staring up at the front of the Smedley house. His toes were almost touching the dangling gun!

A grim smile touched Wentworth's lips. It was a time for hair-line measures! He turned excitedly toward Kirkpatrick, pointed toward the policeman.

"What is that man's name?" he demanded.

Kirkpatrick frowned. "Patrolman Kelly," he growled, "but what—"

"*Kelly!*" Wentworth called sharply. "Here at once!"

As he had calculated, the man started at the sudden summons. He executed a neat about face ... and his toe brushed the gun, sent it spinning down into the sewer! Wentworth blew out a relieved sigh, but masked it. He peered hard into the face of the policeman. He shook his head, puzzled.

"I could have sworn, from the set of this man's shoulders," he said slowly, "that he was the driver of that coupe that got away from me tonight, but I got a glimpse of the man's face, and it wasn't Kelly. I'm sorry."

Kirkpatrick said sharply, "Do you think the police harbor assassins?"

Wentworth looked him directly in the eye. "It is peculiar," he said slowly, "that both times I've been fired on tonight, it has been after police brought me out into the open!"

Kirkpatrick started an angry answer, but cut off the words before he began them. "You are at liberty to go, Dick," he said slowly. "I . . . I bear you no ill feeling, man, but you must realize I can show no favoritism in the execution of my duty!"

Wentworth was torn. He wanted nothing more than to grip firmly the hand that Kirkpatrick half extended, but friendship with the commissioner was becoming too hampering. There was a titan's battle ahead, and he must throw off all handicaps.

Instead of taking the half-proferred hand then, Wentworth bowed stiffly, swung on his heel and strode away. There was no time for personal grief. He must hurl himself at once into the fray, where he had been forced to leave off to avoid the traps of the Iron Man's hirelings. As he stalked toward the corner bar, his eyes quested once more, and vainly, over the building from which the shots had come. There, a few minutes ago, the *Spider* had flaunted his robes at the police. Heaven grant that his substitute had not been trapped!

Wentworth cut into the bar room, angled at once toward a corner phone booth. There was only one party in the narrow dining room behind the bar, two men and women noisily jubilant over their drinks. Wentworth ignored them to shoot through a call to his home. Now, in a few minutes, he would learn the truth. If Jackson had left earlier, then it had been Nita who had worn the *Spider's* garb!

His call went through swiftly, and in a few moments, Ram Singh's harsh voice rasped over the line.

"Orders, Ram Singh," he snapped. "In my stores is a rubber diving suit with a helmet and oxygen tank. Get a fresh tank of oxygen and rush the equipment to Sutton Place. Understood?"

"*Han, sahib!*" Ram Singh echoed deeply. "Fortunate it is that thy servant obeyed his orders. That foolish braggart, Jackson, left almost as soon as thyself, and . . ."

✪ ✪ ✪

Wentworth's face hardened at this confirmation of his guess. Jackson had gone to remove the body of the policeman from the dead-end street, and Nita . . . Nita had worn the *Spider's* robes!

"He went to risk his life for our honor, Ram Singh," Wentworth said gently. "Hurry, thou mighty warrior!"

Twice, he groped for the hook while his unseeing eyes stared straight before him. Once more, he was seeing that bravely daring figure flaunt defiance at the police, so small in the black and ominous robes of the *Spider*. God, if anything had happened to her. . . . Wentworth thrust at the door of the booth, and the fatigue of his strenuous night hit him all at once. The throbbing of his head seemed to swell. He stumbled as he moved toward the bar, and ordered a brandy. He could not search for her, not now, lest the police follow him. . . .

At his elbow, a voice spoke, "How about buying us a drink, big boy?"

Wentworth stared and whirled. "*Nita!*" he cried.

Nita was leaning her elbows on the bar beside him, and there was mockery in the gay smile that curved her lips. "So this is how you spend your spare time," she chided him. "I'm afraid, Dick, that you will be far from a model husband!"

Wentworth's hands gripped hers hard, and his eyes drank in the laughter in the violet depths of her gaze. "You come out of here, young lady," he ordered. "You and I are going to have a talk!"

Nita laughed, tucked her hand under his arm, and they were almost at the door when the barkeep returned with Wentworth's drink. The man swore, then shrugged and tossed the drink off himself.

"Quickest pickup I ever saw," he nodded confidently to himself in the mirror.

But Wentworth was not even aware he had spoken. He had no need of brandy, with Nita at his side, and he turned under her direction toward the coupe which she had parked two blocks away.

"You're taking too many chances, dear," he told Nita sternly. "Though in this instance I'll admit it was fortunate for me that you did. Nevertheless, you go home now as fast as I can ship you there!"

Nita shook her head in mock bitterness, though there was worry in her violet eyes. "That's the thanks I get for coming to you," she said. "I'm just beginning to enjoy myself!"

Wentworth smiled down on her. "You're fired," he told her grimly. His heart swelled at recognition of her bravery, for he knew that she was torn with terror for him; for the battle that lay ahead. As always, she thought not of herself, but of cheering him. Her hand clung to his now.

"Dick, surely now you can rest," she said. "Just for tonight—"

Wentworth jerked his head in negation. He said, "In this battle, every passing hour means more deaths! I'll take you to a taxi, and then—"

"And then?" Nita's question was no more than a breath.

"Why then," Wentworth said softly, "I shall hunt for robots! I have a theory about those monsters, and if I'm right it will be possible to stop them. I hope so, and—"

He broke off then as they stopped beside the coupe, for a man had suddenly darted around the nearby corner. Wentworth's hand flicked toward his automatic, but the man did not come toward them, did not even seem to see them. His breath rasped in his throat and he ran heavily, as a man would run at the extreme end of exhaustion. His shoulder struck a light post, and he reeled aside, but did not check his pace at all. He rounded another corner and was gone.

Nita said, "He looked . . . frightened!"

Wentworth whipped open the door of the coupe and thrust Nita inside and there was grim tension on his face. As he ducked in behind the wheel, he heard a woman's cry soar up desolately into the night. It was a hoarse cry, more animal than human in its intensity. Nita shuddered.

"In heaven's name, Dick," she whispered. "What can be happening?"

Wentworth said, "I hope I'm wrong. I hope to heaven I'm wrong!"

He sent the car surging forward, careened around the corner from which the man had spurted. Immediately ahead, the street was empty, but even as they sped forward, some people burst into sight from a side way. They were running desperately. The night swallowed them. The sound of their pounding feet was drowned out in a rumbling crash that spread its thunder like a tangible weight upon the air. The windshield of the coupe jarred with concussion, and afterward there were mounting, ghastly screams! The roar of mingled voices became a vast murmur of fear and horror.

Wentworth said, with difficulty, "I was right. The robots are marching!"

As if his words had brought forth the sound, a new rhythm in the paean of terror began to make itself felt, more than heard. It was even, deep as primitive drums, as if giant clubs were used to turn the earth itself into a drum. It was slow, with a heavy insistent rhythm; slow as a funeral dirge, but more ominous. It continued as Wentworth drove the coupe around another corner, and the scene burst upon his eyes.

At first, there was only the wildly terrified flight of people. They were in all stages of undress. Children screamed their fright as they ran barefooted across the freezing pavements; women raced with backward twisted faces and streaming hair, some falling, to rise and run again. A running man collided with another and lashed out at the other frenziedly. His blow fell viciously low in the body. The man he had struck did not check. He ran on, bent agonizingly forward, holding his body and still running. He did not even look at the man who had hit him.

In an instant, the street was blocked with the fleeing scores of people, and once more the *Spider* and Nita van Sloan heard the thunderous reverberation.

"Dick!" Nita gasped, and her voice was strained. "Dick, do you realize what they're doing! They're—they're pushing over buildings! Buildings in which people live! That must have been a huge tenement . . ."

The screams of the new victims were tossed up like sparks in the hot breath of a holocaust. Beside the car, a woman with a child in her arms tripped over the curb and fell! In an instant, she was buried under the rush of other people. Her cries rose weakly, but she was given no chance to regain her feet! The child wailed. . . . With an oath, Wentworth flung himself from the stalled coupe. Men collided with him as insensately as if he was a post. He had to fight furiously to divide the stampede so that he could reach the woman. She crouched miserably upon the pavement, elbows and knees on the concrete while she sheltered the child beneath her. In those few brief moments, her clothing had been torn almost from her; her left hand had been ground to a pulp.

Wentworth slammed his fists about him, knocked men aside and stooped to help the woman to her feet. His hands were gentle despite the stampede which in an instant had swept them past the coupe and into the eddy behind it. He placed the child in her arms.

The woman did not speak. Her drawn face peered once back the way she had come and then she was plunging on with the crowd, the child clasped in her arms. It was a fight to regain the side of the coupe. Wentworth flung himself to its top, stared down the dark way the people had come and, as he stared, he felt the strained pallor creep into his cheeks. The funereal rhythm was all about him, was palpable in the air. Heavy and slow and awful in its suggestion of power. For that single moment, Wentworth could see nothing . . . and then the drumbeat of fury was louder, was in the street itself. He was gazing at the glimmering steel helmets of an entire squad of robots. It was the ground-trembling impact of their steel-shod feet that he had heard!

# CHAPTER FIVE
## "LOCK ON THE HELMET"

EVEN AS HE STARED, two of the robots detached themselves from the squad and pivoted to the left. Their hands reached out—and the entire front wall of a small tenement gave way before their pressure! Falling brick rained down upon their steel-clad heads; collapsing walls lapped like furious waters about their inhuman legs. When the job was done, they turned and walked out of the debris as a man would wade a brook, and behind them people screamed in discovery of fresh horror. Wentworth saw a child dangling from the broken edge of a high floor; saw that hold slip. . . .

Eight steel monsters there were, swinging in a formal squad in the midst of destruction. Those who lingered in their path, died. The careless clash of steel feet, the swing of beam-like arms brushed human beings from their paths like flies, and always there was that awful, overbearing rhythm, the dirge-like crunch of those awful feet!

Wentworth found that his automatic was in his fist and he swore at the futility of the gesture. Somehow, these things must be stopped, but more important than that right now was the safety of these scores, these hundreds who fled through the bitter night from the path of death. It was more fearsome than any slaughter these poor victims could recognize, more awful than screaming gun shells or aerial bombs. Those at least were the fiendishness of men, but for this thing they saw no explanation at all.

The robots, if such they were, moved with the cold and silent efficiency of machines. They marched on and, now and again, two of their number would wheel from ranks to push down the front wall of a building. They were as systematic as a highly trained drill team. They towered enormous and the death they dealt was contemptuous. The overcast skies were releasing their pent clouds in torrential rain. The wet steel glistened as the massive arms swung, and still they marched on, and another tenement crashed; other scores fled screaming from their path—or screamed, trapped beneath the falling debris!

Nita called up to Wentworth urgently, "The police are on the way, Dick! I heard Kirkpatrick's voice. They're sending an emergency wagon, and reserves!"

Wentworth swore deeply. He jumped to the ground and snatched up the microphone that connected with the two-way radio of the car, swiftly sent out a call for Kirkpatrick.

"Wentworth calling Kirkpatrick," he snapped. "Wentworth calling Kirkpatrick . . ." He got his answer and rushed on. "Eight steel robots are wrecking tenements, killing people, Kirk," he said. "They are bullet-proof and even a car cannot knock them over. *Do not send your men against them. They will only be slaughtered!* Send for fire equipment! Send for Fifth Avenue buses. A charge by big trucks may knock them down! Nothing less will serve."

Even as he spoke, he heard the wail of sirens and Kirkpatrick's voice burst out from the receiver with a volume that meant the commissioner was very close. He was ordering his blue cohorts into battle!

Wentworth swore at Kirkpatrick's stubbornness, but there was a pallor in his cheeks at realization of what this meant. Kirkpatrick no longer even trusted him as an ally!

"But they'll be killed!" Nita cried. "Why is Stanley doing a thing like that?"

Wentworth shook his head. "That does not matter," he said quietly. "Take this car away from here, when I call to you. You may meet me later down Sutton Place."

"But, Dick, surely if the police . . ."

Wentworth had swung to the pavement. From the rear compartment, he removed the robes of the *Spider* and the steel mask which Nita had worn in lieu of makeup, which was a replica of the *Spider's* countenance.

"Go now," he said, "and there must be no disobedience!"

Nita nodded, white-faced, and fought the car into a U-turn. Men clambered on the running board, scrambled upon its top to escape from the on-pressing terror from behind, and the coupe limped out of sight with a dozen fugitives clinging to it. A long spring hurled Wentworth into a dark doorway and, instants later, a sombre and sinister figure crept out again into the shadows, a figure with hunched shoulders from which a long cape flowed; whose beetling brows were hidden beneath the low broad brim of a black hat. Any man who saw him now would recognize the *Spider,* but so great was the fear of these panic-driven people that they failed to see even the Master of Men!

Wentworth's eyes searched the facades of the tenements ahead of the robots. The people there already were aroused by the march of the steel monsters; the inhabitants already were fleeing. So much had been accomplished by the screams of the victims. The very air shivered now to the rhythms of the march of the steel men. Wentworth turned his back upon them and peered toward the shriek of the sirens. An instant later, the red-eyed limousine of the commissioner of police whipped into the street. On the instant, Wentworth was in action!

With the *Spider's* robes whipping out behind him, he hurled himself straight toward Kirkpatrick's car! Twin guns were in his fists and, as he raced forward, he began to shoot!

Two shots exploded the front tires of the police limousine. It yawed wildly, slewed to a halt, and the doors were batted open. A squad car whined around the corner in its wake, screamed to a halt, and police erupted from it also. Wentworth stood squarely in the middle of the street and the guns flamed in his hands—but the lead screamed high above the heads of the police!

For a long minute he stood there, a plain target for a score of guns, while he shouted defiance at the police. It was just the instant before police guns began to hammer at him that he leaped aside and fled toward the tenements that lined the way! It was a daring move, daringly executed, but the *Spider* was willing to risk his life endlessly to save these policemen. Lead made the air about him alive. He felt bullets tug at his whipping cape. His hat jarred upon his head, and then he dived into the shelter of a doorway. There was a smile on his lips. The police would follow him, and he would lead them a close chase, showing himself every now and then. By the time he had eluded them, the danger from the robots should be over. . . .

Even as the thought crossed his mind, he heard Kirkpatrick's voice rasp out on the loudspeaker attached to his car for direction of his men in battle.

"Come back!" Kirkpatrick shouted. "Return to positions! The *Spider* is only a decoy for these men in steel. Their ally! Return to your posts!"

Something like a sob drove out between Wentworth's clenched teeth. Even his risking death had not served to save the police from the doom that would overtake them if they attacked the robots! He whirled about to face the police, but they had already obeyed Kirkpatrick's orders. They were returning to their posts—and to certain death!

Wentworth darted back toward the street, heard the volley fire of the police. They had swung the squad car broadside across the street in the path of the marching robots. Machine guns hammered from behind that barrier. A gas gun boomed deeply and the shell burst against the armor of the leading robot. The giant of steel did not even falter in its even, implacable stride!

Glaring toward those impregnable titans, Wentworth saw them perform the maneuver they had executed before. Two of them swung ponderously from line and marched to the front of a tenement building. They placed their hands against the front wall, and there was a dull rumbling explosion. As they pivoted back then toward the ranks, the tenement wall crumpled in upon itself. It was a feast of destruction and the robots paid no more attention to the onslaught of the police than if the bullets had been a buzzing swarm of mosquitoes!

Wentworth saw Kirkpatrick knuckle his mustache, then turn

sharply toward Sergeant Reams at his side, as always. Reams ran toward the squad wagon and, a moment later, returned with a loose canvas bag that Wentworth knew contained hand grenades. With a final word to the police about him, ordering them to hold their positions, Kirkpatrick marched forward to meet the robots!

The sheer courage of that maneuver stopped Wentworth's breath in his lungs . . . but he did not wait to see the inevitable end of that reckless attack. Instead, he whirled and raced back through the hallways of the tenement, out into the street beyond. First Avenue was only a block away and there was a ceaseless parade of heavy trucks there. It was the only hope against these monsters. If he could seize a truck of sufficient mass . . .

Traffic stalled with screaming brakes when the awful figure of the *Spider* dashed out into the street, but Wentworth wove a rapid way through them toward the truck he had selected. It was a gigantic cement mixer, weighing more than ten tons. As he raced toward it, the driver slammed on his power brakes and leaped to the earth. He fled, screaming, toward the sidewalk. An instant later, Wentworth had hurled himself behind the wheel and had ground the accelerator to the floor. The great truck gathered speed slowly, then faster. Behind the wheel, Wentworth's face was set grimly. There was small protection for him here, but if he could save Kirkpatrick. . . .

Wentworth manipulated the truck into the street where the robots marched. As the heavy machine straightened out, he heard the burst of a grenade and saw the white fury of its flame as it shattered between two of the robots. One of the steel giants staggered sideways a half-stride. Afterward, it stood motionless and slowly lifted a long, steel arm! Wentworth knew what that portended! The thing was getting ready to shoot Kirkpatrick!

Before flame spurted from the leveled forefinger of the monster, another grenade burst nearby. This time, the giant did not stagger, but apparently Kirkpatrick was unharmed, for two more grenades burst among the huddle of steel men! Then a great voice boomed out in the narrow street, a voice that had the rumbling accents of thunder! It was the first time Wentworth had heard one of the robots speak, and, strangely, the *Spider* smiled! For the voice that issued from one of those tanks-on-foot was human!

Wentworth had not realized until that moment how powerfully these impregnable giants had worked upon his imagination. Despite their horror, and their incredible strength; despite the futility of the attack he was about to launch, it was a relief to know that they were human beings under their shells!

But the robots were mustering in close ranks now that filled the street from side to side, and even as Wentworth approached them from behind . . . the robots began once more to march forward! The grenades that burst among them seemed no more than the echo of their steely tread. They did not even bother to shoot! What need, when the ponderous weight of their march, the swing of their derrick arms could crush out anyone who dared to impede their progress?

Wentworth's lips drew bitterly thin. He slipped the steel mask over his face, and wrung the last ounce of speed from the truck . . . and headed straight for the close-marching ranks of the robots!

Yet, even in his extremity, Wentworth did not drive blindly. He knew by now that the robots were almost impervious to blows. The impact of the truck would be less than the force of an exploding grenade. But he had a plan. The robots marched in two ranks of four men each. It was Wentworth's plan to part those ranks, to smash into the steel giants squarely between two of the men in the rear rank. If he had enough strength, he thought that he would drive those two men aside against their companions. He might even reach the front rank. After that. . . .

Wentworth slammed the truck into second gear an instant before he reached the robots. One of the steel monsters turned its head, started a beam-like arm toward him . . . and was too late. With a crash like the collapse of a skyscraper. Wentworth drove the mighty truck squarely between the two middle robots! A grenade burst overhead at the same instant, and metal fragments punched down through the cab where Wentworth crouched. The impact of the collision hurled him violently against the wheel, but he kept his foot upon the accelerator, kept the truck grinding in second gear.

For an instant, Wentworth thought that even this attack had failed. Then the robot on his right was swung half-about and driven to its knees. Its upflung arms clashed against the giant on its right, and the steel fist rang like an anvil. The second robot reeled sideways, crashed against a tenement wall. The brick balustrade at the top of the wall tipped forward and rained down into the street. The fragments rang on the steel armor, but did not dent it. Two robots had partly fallen, and a third took long reeling strides forward, off-balance from the powerful impact of the ten-ton truck. But there were still five other robots which had not been disturbed by the charge. They were turning to confront Wentworth, with that ponderous slowness that was in itself fearfully ominous, bespeaking the power of those steel-thewed monsters. Wentworth thrust himself backward from the wheel, where the blow had thrown him. His breath had been driven from his body, and he was dizzy with shock. He saw one of the robots lift a slow, deadly finger to shoot him!

Wentworth slammed the gear into reverse and whipped out one of his heavy automatics. It was a futile thing in his hand, a popgun against artillery, but Wentworth flung up its muzzle with swift sureness. This was the gun that had saved his life in a thousand battles with the lords of the Underworld, and he was past master of its use. What he attempted would have balked many famous experts with firearms . . . but it was the *Spider* who held this gun!

One shot he fired, then the truck leaped backward under the surge of power he pumped into the engine. And the robot's hand suddenly spurted out a burst of flame! The right forefinger had exploded, for Wentworth had deftly plugged its muzzle with lead from his own swift gun!

The next moment, the truck had backed out of danger, and Wentworth had a moment's respite in which to plan his next move. He knew now that it was useless to charge the robots even with this mighty juggernaut. And next time, they would be ready; would meet him with a rain of bullets. He strained his eyes to see beyond the crowded ranks of the robots. Were the police retreating yet? Or was Kirkpatrick foolishly leading them to a new attack? He could not see—but he knew Kirkpatrick!

Even while he cursed the stubbornness of Kirkpatrick that would fling him again and again into this vain battle, Wentworth knew a grim admiration for the man. It was this very quality of perseverance that made him the most effective police commissioner the city had ever known! But he was beaten in advance this time. He and his brave men would only walk to their deaths!

With the thought, Wentworth knew what he must do, and he was already in action as the idea flashed across his mind. He backed the truck into the cross street, sent it lurching forward. A few minutes of maneuvering and then, gathering momentum, he headed straight for the tottering wall of a half-collapsed tenement that towered above the close-packed robots!

He knew that the wall would not destroy, or even stop the robots, but it would slow them for a few moments. It would give the *Spider* time enough to complete his work!

Grimly, Wentworth clung to the truck to the last possible moment, then he leaped from the running board, sprawled into the street. He bounded to his feet, and sprinted back the way he had come, but he had not taken a dozen strides when the truck slammed its tons of weight against the rocking tenement wall. There was an instant when a few bricks rained down on the battered steel truck, then a groaning crack opened up the face of the wall. It leaned gently forward. It bowed gracefully above the truck—then it lost its balance! Faster and faster, the solid wall of the tenement pitched forward. As it fell, many jagged cracks ran across its face. A window frame was popped out and sailed like a box kite ahead of the fall. That window frame smashed down over the head of a robot, and then the wave of bricks broke over the upright monsters of steel. Fragments flew upward as from an explosion, and the dust roiled high against the sleet-spitting sky. The concussion of the fall rolled thunder through the deserted streets.

But Wentworth took no notice of the collapse. Already he was circling toward where Kirkpatrick and his cohorts laid siege to the steel killers. They were rolled back by that wave of masonry. Kirkpatrick and Reams, their grenades exhausted, had quickly retreated before that impact. Wentworth saw this as he popped out of the doorway of a tenement which he had reached through the back court. He was within a dozen yards of Kirkpatrick's limousine, and like a black shadow, he slipped soundlessly across the street. There were a score of police within gunshot of him, but all stared where the dust of the building collapse still lifted a monstrous dark silhouette against the sky. Already, within that moiling cloud, there was movement.

Wentworth saw a single robot lift an arm, then a leg . . . and thrust out of the edge of the wreckage!

A shivered, concerted moan went up from the men in police blue. They were brave, these men, but they could not fight immortals! Wentworth was squarely beside Kirkpatrick's car now. He straightened, and the driver twisted about, his face bewildered. Wentworth's hand darted like a snake's head, and his stiffened fingers drove to nerve centers in the man's throat, spilled him unconscious across the seat. It was the work of a moment to dump the man into the back, to pull on his uniform cap. Wentworth's lips were grim as he reached for the microphone of the loudspeaker unit, but when he spoke it was crisply, in the metallic tones which Kirkpatrick used!

"Retreat, men," he said, imitating Kirkpatrick. "We have done all we can. Return to quarters and await further orders. And make it fast! These monsters in steel are after us again!"

Wentworth saw Kirkpatrick leap from the shadows where he had crouched to ambush the stirring giants, but the men behind the squad wagon did not suspect. They had heard Kirkpatrick's voice, they thought, and it was an order they welcomed. Within brief seconds, while Kirkpatrick raced toward his parked car, the squad car got under way. Then Kirkpatrick reached the running board, whipped open the door on the far side from Wentworth.

"Who the devil gave that order?" he demanded harshly. "Damn it, Cassidy . . ."

He did not notice until then that the man in the uniform cap wore a long black cape on his shoulders, or that the face that peered toward him through the gloom was the face of the *Spider*! When he did notice, Wentworth's fingers were already striking for his throat! Instantly the *Spider* hauled Kirkpatrick into the car. When Sergeant Reams bolted alongside the limousine, he looked into the muzzle of Wentworth's automatic!

"Get behind the wheel, Sergeant Reams," Wentworth ordered coldly, "and drive this car away from here. Never mind the blown-out tires. The robots can't move rapidly enough to catch you!"

Reams' jaw set stubbornly, but the grey-blue eyes that glared at him through the steel mask were relentless; behind them blazed the will of the *Spider*. Reams muttered an oath, and took the wheel. As the car wheeled away, with Wentworth on the running board, he cast a single backward glance—and relief flooded through him!

The robots had had enough of that battle, and they were moving off toward the river as they hauled themselves out of the debris which Wentworth had dumped upon them. Wentworth's teeth were clenched together, and there was a coldness in his soul that was fury. God alone knew how many poor mortals had died this night under the march of the robots. But, God being willing, he would track the monsters to their lair beneath the waters of the East River!

"Straight on!" he ordered Reams harshly. "And if you love Kirkpatrick, don't revive him until it's too late to fight those robots! They're in full retreat . . . and it would only mean his death!"

As he finished, Wentworth dropped from the running board of the limousine and ducked into the shadows of a dark doorway. For a moment, he stood there watching the limousine jounce on its flat tires down the street. His lips were a little twisted. Kirkpatrick could be so true a friend—and so harsh an enemy! Too bad that they could not work side by side against crime, but Kirkpatrick was first of all a defender of the law. And it was because the law so often failed that the *Spider* had been born!

With a jerk of his head, Wentworth bounded from the doorway and raced through the shadows. A half dozen blocks away, he ducked into the dead-end street where he had told Ram Singh to meet him; where Nita would be waiting. They called to him softly from a gap in the wall that surrounded the ruins of what had been once his fortress home—and which criminals had destroyed in one awful hour. Wentworth swerved toward the gateway, already stripping off the black cape about his shoulders.

"Quickly," he ordered, "get the diving suit ready!"

He saw Nita then, huddled against the broken wall for protection from the bite of the sleet. The Long Island shore was obscured and the black waters made a mournful obligato to the wind. A tug howled from the obscurity. Nita came toward him.

"Must you go . . . tonight, Dick?" she asked softly. "It will be terribly cold under the river."

Wentworth laughed harshly. "The robots are marching toward

the river now," he said. "When they enter, I must follow!" He could see how white and drawn her face was, could see how she tried to smile as he stepped into the tight fitting rubber suit, and Ram Singh hurriedly made the fastenings secure.

"But, Dick . . . you'll be helpless under water! Those great murderous things will know you're following them."

Wentworth shook his head. "Perhaps," he said softly, "but under water, I will have a weapon against them! There are men inside those suits, Nita, and I will carry a knife!"

Nita stared at him incredulously. "A knife against bullet-proof armor!"

Wentworth laughed grimly. "It is the one weapon that can win! Hurry, Ram Singh, hurry. They will be here soon!"

Ram Singh prepared to hoist the heavy copper diving helmet high, and Wentworth rapidly adjusted the oxygen valves. But Nita was standing very close, and he saw her shoulders shiver a little. Brave Nita . . . afraid. Wentworth laid his hand upon her arm, and then his head lifted. Stiffness ran through all his body, a stiffness that was the eagerness for battle.

The air was vibrating dully to that funereal rhythm he knew. He felt the earth quiver under the remorseless tread of the steel robots, and for an instant he looked dubiously at the long blade of the knife which would be his only weapon beneath the black waters of the East River. Then he laughed, harshly.

"Lock on the helmet, Ram Singh!" he ordered. "The hour of battle is here!"

# CHAPTER SIX
# UNDER THE RIVER

THE BLACK WATERS OF THE EAST RIVER heaved sullenly, dimpled by the slash of sleet. The thunderous tread of the robots was very close and, in the ruins of what had been his home, Wentworth crouched against the wall and drew Nita close to protect her. Ram Singh growled in his throat, his big hand close to his dagger.

Past the concealing shadows went the robots, whose marching feet had become an intolerable weight upon the brain, upon the heart. Only when they were past did Wentworth release Nita.

"Keep watch, if you like," Wentworth told her gently. "I'll be back within the hour. I won't follow too closely, but if I can track those robots to their hideout, I'll contrive a way to smash this whole damnable murder conspiracy!"

He pivoted then and moved heavily in the wake of the robots. They were already entering the water, one by one. The black waters lapped against their steel flanks, then closed quietly above those rounded helmets. Wentworth moved as heavily as a robot. There were leaden weights fastened to the belt that held the knife, and in his hands he had other leaden weights which could be fastened to his feet. He would need them beneath the surface of the river, but on land they made walking too difficult. When the last robot had disappeared, Wentworth broke into a lumbering run. At the water's edge, he paused to tighten the window in the front of his helmet, to slip his feet into the straps of the shoe weights. He touched the hilt of the knife at his belt, and his lips locked grimly. He floundered into the water.

The shore was slippery with mud and the river closed about his ankles. The water deepened instantly and within four strides, he was up to his neck. The weights were less hampering now. He was beginning to feel the buoyancy of his suit—and the cold of the water struck through the rubberized material. There had been no time to don heavy garments beneath it. No matter. . . . He would not be below the surface long. Within a few minutes, he should know the lair of these monsters of steel, or be defeated. His grey-blue eyes narrowed, he rapidly checked the valves of his helmet—and took a final step.

The water lapped against the window in the helmet. For a moment the slap of the waves against the metal casque was thunderous . . . and then it stopped and he knew he was wholly beneath the water. The blackness was impenetrable. He groped across the chest of the suit, touched a hard spot in the rubber, and a powerful beam reached out from a glass port. Its range was only a few feet, but it lighted the ground at his feet. He was already ankle-deep in the sludge of the bottom. Perhaps he carried too much weight. He could tell better when he was deeper in the river. But now his eyes focused on the mud, and a thin smile twisted his lips. As he had expected, the huge steel feet of the robots had left their trail! It looked as if a herd of elephants had waded through soft mud. But those footmarks were even larger!

Wentworth bent against the thrust of the tide and dragged his weighted feet steadily forward. He had forgotten the bitter cold that was seeping into his tight suit; forgotten everything save the chase. It was the first moment in all this mad night of battle that he had been able to put his mind entirely upon the problem of the robots. Mechanized monsters they undoubtedly were, but he was equally certain that they carried men inside them—and men as ruthless as if they were soulless robots! In heaven's name, who could be the leader, the director of this mad jehad of slaughter? But he had a clue to that, even though it was a lead he could not understand.

Three rich houses had been looted, smashed by the robots—and a fourth house just beside them, richer than the others, had not been looted. That fourth home had been guarded by a man of the Drexler agency, and on his chest was tattooed the sign of the murder monsters! Wentworth had always had the highest regard for Frank Drexler, and he was loath even now to believe the man capable of such infamies. And yet . . . there was the evidence of the Drexler guard, and the trail of the robots led upstream toward Drexler's riverside home!

Now that he was farther from the shore, the force of the current was extremely powerful. It was labor to set each foot before the other; labor too to drag his weighted legs free of the sucking mud upon the river bottom. Swirls of it lifted like torpid dust to cloud against the shortened ray of his lamp. There was a numbness in his limbs that was the creeping paralysis of cold. Wentworth was like that, canted forward at a forty-five-degree angle against the current, fighting for each step, when the light reached out and wrapped itself about him.

For an instant, Wentworth thought that it was the blinding reflection of his own lamp, hurled back by the higher swirl of the mud. Then he realized that the light was far more powerful than his own. A muffled oath burst from his lips and crashed deafeningly within the helmet. He twisted his head about, peered out of the small sideport in the helmet—and then his hand flicked to the knife at his waist! Peering at him from the black wall of the water were two great balls of light and he realized as he stared at them, that the light poured from the eyes of one of the robots! God, he had been a fool! He should have guessed that they would post a rear guard!

Wentworth ripped the knife from its sheath, but he had no intention of battling the robot in these depths if he could avoid it. His purpose was to find their lair, and then to arrange for its destruction. He wrenched his feet free of the mud, tried to thrust himself swiftly upstream. He moved with incredible speed for a diver, but it was slow, terribly slow. The robot moved with the same implacable pace that it used upon land, neither faster nor slower. It was too powerful to heed either mud or water pressure. The glare of the lights glittered from the steel. The knees lifted steadily, the feet swung forward six feet at a stride!

After that single instant of struggle, Wentworth realized that flight was useless. If he was to go on with his pursuit—and it was characteristic of the *Spider's* indomitable purpose that he did not even consider abandoning his task!—there was only one possible course. He must destroy this robot!

On the face of it, the thought was madness. Bullets and the headlong charge of trucks had not stopped these monsters, nor had the impact of a wall of brick done more than delay them for a space of moments! Yet, with only that slim-bladed knife which he gripped in a cold-numbed hand, Wentworth turned to face the enemy! His mouth was a lipless gash across his face, and his eyes were narrowed and intent. He shifted his feet in the silt of the bottom, kicked free of their weights. His left hand moved rapidly upon the weights that were attached to his belt. There were five of them, weighing ten pounds each.

The robot was only two strides away now and Wentworth swiftly unfastened three of the five weights from his belt. The buoyancy of his suit immediately made itself felt. His feet felt light. Wentworth poised the knife before him like a sword and, with a tensing of his leg muscles, he dived straight at the robot! The current plucked him up and hurled him forward. The light from the robot's eyes was suddenly dazzling, but in its reflection Wentworth could make out the great steel body. He saw then that the two massive beams of the arms were swinging forward, and that the steel talons were clenched to seize him! Once let those points rake his rubber suit, and they would tear it to shreds!

But Wentworth had no intention of being caught. With less weight he had gained considerable swiftness of movement. As the right arm of the steel monster swung toward him, Wentworth jackknifed and swept in under it. It was the moment for which he had waited. His knife point rasped across the steel armor until it found the armpit. As he had discovered when he hurled bullets at the monster, the joints of the armor were covered by overhangs of steel . . . but there were joints, and in order to keep out the water, *they must be covered by rubber!*

It was this deduction on which Wentworth had gambled his life. Now, probing deeply into the socket of the armor, he felt the knife catch on some soft, half-yielding substance and exultation coursed hotly through his veins. It did not matter whether this was a mechanical monster, or whether a human being was within it, if water trickled inside, it spelled the robot's doom!

Wentworth seized the shoulder of the robot with his left hand, and thrust more deeply with his probing steel. He knew that the robot was in violent motion, for the water swirled fiercely about him, but he clung tightly, fought to widen the slit he had made in the rubber. He thought that, already, the motions of the robot had become slower. A few more moments of clinging to this creature's back, where it could not reach him, and he would have the robot disabled. Afterward, he could press on with his pursuit, and then. . . .

A cry surged to Wentworth's lips. He had thought the robot could not reach him, but he had been wrong! Even in his moment of triumph, he felt a steel hand close like a vise about his ankle! It pulled at him resistlessly, and Wentworth's hold was instantly torn loose. He had just time to wrench his knife free when he was whirled in a frenzied circle through the waters! His arms flung wide, and centrifugal force drove the blood to his brain so that his senses faded. Presently, he realized that the motion had ceased; that he was being held aloft before the dazzling lights that were the eyes of the robot. But it was only for an instant, and then there was a tremendous pressure upon his helmet; blood started from his nostrils. He heard the thin creaking of strained metal and horror shot through him like the punch of a bullet. God in heaven, the robot *was crushing Wentworth's helmet!*

Even as the thought slashed through Wentworth's brain, the first jet of water struck Wentworth's cheek with the shock of a blow. It was fiercely cold, and the weight of the river drove it inward with terrific force. Then another jet. . . . The robot was deliberately delaying the moment when he would drown Wentworth, torturing him! Fury swirled through Wentworth's brain: Once more he struck out with the knife, and this time it found a joint near the throat of the steel monster. Savagely, Wentworth thrust the knife home, dragged its keen edge through the rubber inner shield.

There was a single convulsive drag at Wentworth's leg, and then his helmet was ripped from his head. The river crowded into his nostrils, beat in upon his eardrums, hammered its intolerable pressure upon every exposed inch of his body. His lungs were bursting; he was being squeezed to death, and still the steel talons of the robot gripped his ankle.

Then suddenly, Wentworth was in darkness. For a dizzy moment, he thought that his senses were blotted out and then, dimly, exultation crept through him. He knew then that the robot's lights were out, and he knew the reason . . . water had reached the mechanism of the robot! Dear God, suppose he had jammed the mechanism so that his foot could not be released? He—there was a swirl of water about him, and Wentworth felt himself dragged more deeply toward the river's bottom. The robot had fallen!

How many seconds had passed? How many more moments of consciousness remained? Wentworth could not estimate. He only knew that death was close. The coldness was already having its paralyzing way with him. He thought of his knife, and an idea drove itself into his fading mind. He began to hack at the rubber suit, to slit the leg of the diving outfit which was gripped in the robot's hand.

How he accomplished that thing, Wentworth could not guess. He only knew that he was shooting upward toward the surface, toward open air. His lungs were aching, and there was a heavy pounding in his temples, in his ears. He must breathe *now*. He must! His head broke the surface of the river!

Somehow, Wentworth managed to keep himself afloat, but when a hand clamped upon his arm, there was in him no will to fight. The cold had eaten into his bones. Presently, he knew that it was his powerful Sikh bodyguard, Ram Singh, who had plunged into the flood to save him. . . . There were moments when the whole universe whirled dizzily about his head, yet an urgency goaded him. There was a task he must perform, a task . . . if he could remember. . . .

At last he knew that Nita and Ram Singh were beside him, that they were hurrying him toward the car. The warmth of the heated interior swirled against his skin, yet did not seem to penetrate. He began to shiver, and he found that he could think . . . and remember.

"Northward," he ordered Ram Singh sharply. "Go to the Drexler home."

"No, Dick!" Nita cried. "Even you can't stand exposure like that!"

Wentworth shook his head and crouched toward the heater. There was a gauntness about his drawn face, and fierce fires in his eyes. "There is no time," he said hoarsely. "The robots are marching upriver. If I am right, and they are going to the Drexler home, my only chance is to be there when they arrive. No, Nita, I can't stop to get on dry clothing."

Nita said no more, but her lips tightened. She handed him a flash of brandy, and Wentworth tipped it to his lips. Its warmth was grateful, but it did not send the familiar tingle through his veins. Exposure, after the exhaustion of the night, had been severe. Nita was right of course. . . . He shook his head. There was no time. His eyes stared piercingly ahead through the half-moons the windshield wipers cut in the sleet. It was in the cellar of the Drexler home that he must look for the entrance of the robots. . . .

"As soon as I leave you," Wentworth said slowly, "you will find a taxi and go home, Nita. I must wear the robes of the *Spider*. Ram Singh will wait and rush me home afterward. And I'll get on something dry then."

Nita leaned close to him, "Dick, you mean that you will not be through then? There is still more to be done?"

Wentworth's blue lips smiled. Was it any new thing that the *Spider's* work was never done?

"There is one more job tonight," he said slowly, "if I fail at Drexler's. . . . I killed a robot on the bottom of the river. I must get another diving suit and arrange to recover that robot. Once we have learned the secret of the Iron Man, we can beat him!"

Nita caught hold of Wentworth's shoulder, forced him to look at her. "Dick, you can't do it," she said. "Let Ram Singh dive for you."

Wentworth laughed, but it was tenderly . . . and a sharp, painful cough broke his laughter. His jaw set stubbornly. "When I have finished, I will rest," he said. "Ram Singh, turn right at the next corner. Pull into a doorway of that warehouse and stop! Nita, there is a taxi stand around the corner."

Without a word, Nita climbed from the car. She reached up to clasp his face between her hands and kiss him, and then she half-ran, half-stumbled toward the corner. Her head was down . . . Wentworth watched her for a moment, and shivered. There was a weakness in his chest and the cold refused to leave his limbs. He swore at his own softness, donned the robes of the *Spider*.

Beside him, Ram Singh said eagerly, "Orders, *sahib?*"

Wentworth shook his head. "Stay in the car, Ram Singh," he said, "and watch. If I signal you. . . ."

Disappointment clouded the Sikh's eyes, but he salaamed his acknowledgment. Wentworth slipped away into the shadows. The wind prodded beneath the cape, but Wentworth forgot the cold as he peered toward the Drexler house. It was a survival of Manhattan's early days. Once a farmhouse on a point that jutted out into the river, it was walled in now by factories and warehouses, dwarfed by a modern apartment building. But, due to its location, it still maintained isolation. And it was very close to the river banks! That fact was important!

Only dim lights were burning behind the small old-fashioned windows of the house. Wentworth was a shadow that drifted across the street, sliding over the wall. A window on the second floor was open and, in brief moments, Wentworth had climbed to it.

Presently the *Spider* mingled with the darkness in the room. There was a bed against the wall in which a man slept. Doubtfully, Wentworth drifted toward it. If Drexler were at home, in bed. . . . A faint radiance was all that showed when Wentworth squeezed a masked flashlight. Its pallid light crept across the bed, fell on a frail, wrinkled hand that was almost transparent with age; stole up until it illumined the head upon the pillow. Straggling white hair, a ruff of whiskers, a lined and sunken face. This must be old Angus Drexler, Wentworth decided. He would have to be careful. The aged slept so lightly. . . .

Rapidly then, Wentworth canvassed the upper floor of the house, found the servant's room where a maid slept, but no trace of Frank Drexler! Wentworth's lips clamped together thinly then as he stole down the narrow, winding steps. It might mean nothing at all that Drexler was out on this bitter night when the robots marched. Still, Drexler's home was an ideal base for the robots. There were two possibilities of a hideout: One beneath the garage, the other under the house itself. An underwater entrance, perhaps. . . .

The warmth of the basement flooded up to meet Wentworth. He heard the whirring of an oil burner and his light reached out to quest over the stone walls, centered abruptly on a steel door that opened on the side toward the river! In a half dozen quick strides, Wentworth was before the door.

The lock yielded under Wentworth's skillful fingers and he listened a moment before he eased it open. Darkness beyond, and the musty rich odors of . . . wine! Once more, Wentworth's flashlight licked out. Stairs led downward into a wine cellar. Its stone walls were lined with bottle bins and hogsheads. Across the ceiling ran asbestos-wrapped steam pipes, and Wentworth's eyes followed them intently. They turned into an alcove on the left-hand wall!

Wentworth flicked on the lights and with long bounds crossed the cellar. The pipes burrowed through the stone wall into the solid earth beyond! Narrow-eyed, he studied those pipes. They ran in the direction of the garage. Was that their sole purpose?

Instantly, Wentworth was at work on the stone wall, seeking some hidden doorway. He frowned as he tried to make swift calculations of time. Could the robots yet have reached a secret hiding place here? Impossible to estimate the time spent beneath the surface of the river, but it could not have been very long. Probably the robots would be just arriving, if this were their destination. Wentworth swore softly. He could detect no signs of an opening in the walls, no trace of footsteps upon the earthen floor. The hogsheads . . . Wentworth approached them. They were backed against the stone wall through which the pipes pierced. In an instant, he was at the spigots. If any of these proved . . . *empty!*

But wine flowed briefly from each spigot. Aroma was sharp in his nostrils. Nothing here. Nothing that he could detect. There remained the garage, but he must be swift, swift. At any moment, Drexler might appear—or the robots.

"Up with your hands, *Spider!*" a voice commanded harshly. "What the hell are you doing here?"

Wentworth swore softly. He recognized the voice at once—Frank Drexler! Even in the face of that discovery, had he been sure of the man's guilt, he could have drawn his gun and fired, with a fair chance of escaping. But the *Spider* did not war against innocent men, not even suspected men. He had to be very sure! So the *Spider's* hands went up slowly, and he turned to peer up into the face of Frank Drexler!

The detective was fully twenty feet away, crouched at the head of the wooden steps that descended into the wine cellar. Pale fire glowed suddenly in the *Spider's* grey-blue eyes. *For Drexler's clothing was dripping wet!*

"Speak up!" Drexler ordered sharply. "What are you doing here?"

The *Spider's* disguised face moved in a smile that was full of mocking menace. "I had heard," he said softly, "that you possessed a very fine cellar. But I had expected to find your wines in steel casks."

Anger flushed Drexler's cheek, and Wentworth was aware of movement behind the man; saw the old, peering face of Drexler's father.

"The *Spider,* hey?" old Drexler's voice was thin, rasping. "What are you waiting for, son? Burn the man down!"

Drexler jerked his head. "Go call the police, father," he said. "He won't get away from me."

The wrinkled face blinked down at Wentworth. Aged hands trembled on the head of the cane on which he leaned. Old Drexler's eyes were as excited as a boy's.

"Are you sure," Wentworth asked softly, "that you want the police here, Drexler? You will gain considerable publicity by capturing the *Spider,* but you're already a rather prosperous man, Drexler. You are rapidly becoming more so, aren't you?"

Drexler said savagely, "I want an answer to my question, and a direct one. What the hell are you doing here?"

"I was beginning to tell you, Drexler," Wentworth said sharply. "Keep your mouth shut, and listen!"

The old man lifted the knotted cane and shook it. "Don't you talk to Frank like that!" he cried. "Burn him down, Frank!"

Neither of the two men paid any heed to him. Wentworth was close to the wine bins. It would take only a flick of the wrist to seize a bottle and smack out the single overhead light . . . but Drexler's gun rested on him unwaveringly. Yet Wentworth thought that he saw a way. The father seemed senile, and child-like in his adoration of Frank Drexler. If he could infuriate the old man to the point where he attempted to interfere. . . .

Wentworth said, "Three houses were robbed on Sutton Place tonight, just beside one guarded by your agency. *But the house your man watched was untouched!* That man had on his chest the symbol of a criminal who has killed dozens of human beings this night!"

The old man said, quaveringly, "He's calling you a crook, Frank!"

Wentworth nodded. "That's right! I'm calling you a thief who betrays his own clients, Drexler! I'm calling you a murderer!"

Drexler was unmoved, but the old man lifted the gnarled stick in his hand and shook it violently. "Why, damn you!" he cried shrilly. "You can't talk to Frank like that! Give me that gun, Frank! Give me—"

Drexler's face twitched with concern. "Be quiet, father!" he said sharply. "Remember your heart! Look out—"

As Drexler spoke, the old man pushed past him indignantly. Drexler's head whipped toward him . . . and Wentworth struck! He seized a wine bottle, flung it, and there was the sharp explosion as the light went out. Drexler's gun thundered, but the Spider already was in motion!

He vaulted atop the hogsheads and he ran lightly across them while Drexler's gun thundered again. Through the explosions, Wentworth caught another menacing sound. Somewhere above, a bell was pealing violently—a burglar alarm! Then there was the tramp of rushing feet! It was either the police, or more men of the Drexler agency, and either way it meant deadly peril to the *Spider!*

The thought lent fury to Wentworth's speed. Two more leaps put him beside the open-work of the stairs. He could hear Drexler's hoarse whisper as he urged his father to retreat. Wentworth waited for no more. His hand flashed out and closed on Drexler's ankle! A wrench sent the man stumbling wildly down the steps, and the *Spider* was racing across the windowless basement toward its only exit. The tramp of feet overhead was thunderous now. Long bounds took Wentworth up the steps . . . too late. As he reached them, the door at their head was wrenched open. An instant later, brilliant lights poured downward . . . and found only empty cellar, the steel door across its width swinging open, and an old man there who waved a knotted cane violently!

Sergeant Reams clattered fiercely down the steps, followed an instant later by Kirkpatrick. The commissioner's voice rang out crisply, "Kelly, take the head of the steps. Let no one out!"

Then Kirkpatrick, followed by two more uniformed men, was striding across the basement. Drexler's flushed angry face showed in the entrance of the wine room.

"There was shooting here!" Kirkpatrick snapped. "What was it?"

Drexler was tight-lipped. "Maybe I was having some target-practice," he snapped. "Who gave you permission to enter here?"

"Gun-fire gives any police officer the right to enter," Kirkpatrick said grimly. "Otherwise, we would have waited for you to answer the door. And you haven't answered my question yet, Drexler. I have a number to ask you about tonight's happenings!"

The two men glared at each other, and suddenly a voice rang through the basement. It seemed to be the voice of Kirkpatrick, and it was imperative.

"Kelly!" it ordered, "Down here! Quick!"

The guard at the head of the steps came down instantly. Kirkpatrick swore and whirled toward him.

Drexler's voice lifted, clearly. "It's the *Spider*! I thought he'd got clear!"

In that moment of confusion, a black figure darted from beneath the stairs. Before Kelly sensed a mistake, strong arms clasped him from behind. He was lifted off his feet, dragged backwards up the stairs. Sergeant Reams' gun was in his fist. Kirkpatrick whipped out his long-barreled revolver and raced across the cellar so that he could command a side shot at the steps . . . and they were all too late. Despite the struggles of the surprised Kelly, Wentworth had reached the head of the stairs!

For an instant, he paused there. Then Kelly reeled down the steps, the door clapped shut, and from behind it the mocking laughter of the *Spider* sounded. It died in a burst of savage gunfire as the police sent their lead screaming toward that flimsy door.

But Wentworth already had reached a side window of the house. He peered out long enough to spot the guards at the gate and, once more, he called out in the urgent tones of Kirkpatrick.

"In here, fast!" he called. "We've got the *Spider* trapped!"

There were sharp shouts and the men dashed for the front door of the house. In an instant, Wentworth was out the window and racing toward the wall. He staggered as he dropped to the street beyond, raced for the side street in which he had left the car. Even as he ran, he heard the shouts of his pursuers burst out more loudly, and knew that his subterfuge had been discovered. He reeled a little as he ran, and there was a sharp pain in his side. God, he could not afford illness now! He could not even afford rest. . . .

The robots must have landed, already; or the gunfire had kept them in hiding—or they had never headed for the Drexler place at all! The *Spider* must return to the river with a fresh diving suit and reclaim that fallen robot.

A shudder raced through him at the thought of those frigid depths. He staggered more violently, and then the coupe spurted from the mouth of the dark street, skidded to a momentary halt beside him and raced on as he sprang to the running board. He opened the door, dropped inside. Ram Singh was bent grimly over the wheel, and Nita was smiling up at him. She was holding a steaming thermos of coffee in her hand. "It's been laced with brandy, Dick," she said quietly. "Drink it!"

Wentworth looked backward. Already, Kirkpatrick's limousine was lunging forward. Its siren began to wail. Wentworth's lips drew thinly.

"You've put yourself in deadly danger, Nita," he said quietly, "just to make me drink a little coffee!"

Nita smiled faintly. "It's my right, isn't it, Dick?" she asked quietly. "I have so few. . . . Drink up, Dick!"

Wentworth's lips clamped grimly together, but he made no other answer as he reached for the coffee. Nita needed no other. She closed her eyes as Wentworth lifted the thermos bottle to his lips. Her hands clenched whitely in her lap. Wentworth shuddered and gasped at the drink.

"I know," Nita said hurriedly. "It's awful stuff, but the best I could find in the neighborhood. You should choose your parking places more carefully, Dick!"

Wentworth tilted the bottle again. There was a pain in his chest. It wouldn't help the battle any if he came down with pleurisy! Nonsense. Another hour now, and he could rest. A brief expedition beneath the river to fasten cables to that robot, and then. . . . He lifted a hand uncertainly to his forehead.

"This heat is making me a little sleepy," he said slowly.

Nita whispered, "If you would only rest a little while, Dick! Ram Singh and I can handle this robot."

Wentworth shook his head. "Has there been any word of Jackson?" he asked heavily.

Nita said, "None!"

Ram Singh looked toward her swiftly, but she shook her head and he did not speak. She was watching Wentworth closely. His whole body was relaxing. Her hand trembled as she slid her arm about his shoulders.

Wentworth shook himself, "Nita!" he said clearly. "Nita, you've drugged me!"

Nita's lips twisted with her smile. "Yes, lover," she whispered. "I promise your work will go on, but you must sleep! You must, Dick! I only hope it isn't too late to save you from pneumonia!"

Wentworth tried to fight off the heaviness that was in his brain and he could not. His head sank toward Nita's shoulder. Behind them, the sirens yelped with the vicious insistence of the chase. The powerful motor under the coupe's battered hood made the whole car tremble. But Nita heeded none of these things. Her face was very grave as she stared straight before her. She had taken a fearful responsibility upon herself; none knew that better than she. They were still in genuine danger from the police, and Dick was unconscious from the drugs. She depended on Ram Singh to take them to safety, but that was only the beginning. There was a task for the *Spider* still to be performed.

Swiftly, Nita began to remove the garb of the *Spider* in which Wentworth still was wrapped. With tender hands, she stripped off the disguise which turned his rugged, kindly face into the ominous mask of the *Spider*.

"This had to be done, Ram Singh," she said heavily, and she knew that she spoke more to reassure herself than to explain to the Sikh. "Otherwise, there wasn't a chance that he would escape pneumonia. And it would not help for him to know now about Jackson. It should be simple enough to clear Jackson now that everyone knows about the robots. It was a brave thing he did in trying to get rid of that policeman's body, even though it did end in arrest and a charge of murder!"

Ram Singh murmured, "*Han, missie sahib!*" His tone held no conviction.

Nita's jaw set solidly. There were doubts in Ram Singh's mind, too, but she would prove she was right!

"Shake off these police!" she ordered, and a sharpness of command crept into her voice that made it strangely resemble Wentworth's. "And hurry! We have so little time until dawn!"

Ram Singh said nothing, but his head lifted more alertly. He had never taken orders from any other woman. It would have been beneath his dignity as a lion, a Singh among Sikhs. But when that tone crept into the voice of the *missie sahib,* he knew that it was the mate of the *sahib* who spoke! *Wah,* no evil could come to the master through her! Was not her *karma* one with his?

Nita, watching him, nodded her head slowly as she saw the change. "There will be fighting ahead, warrior of the Sikhs!" she said softly, in the Punjabi Wentworth had taught her. "There will be a vengeance for thy knife!"

Ram Singh's laughter rumbled. "*Wah,* thy warrior is ready, *missie sahib!*" he cried. "Already, the jackals of the police lose our trail!"

Ram Singh was right. Fifteen minutes later the coupe slid to a halt on the street beside Wentworth's apartment house. Ram Singh carried Wentworth's body, tenderly as a child's, in his arms and they sped upward in the private elevator. Swiftly then, Nita aroused the aged butler, old Jenkyns who had served Wentworth's father before him. Into his hands, gentle as a woman, she gave the man she loved . . . and then swung to face Ram Singh.

"Another diving suit, Ram Singh," she said quietly. "We will need the *sahib's* diesel-powered cruiser."

The Sikh bowed in a low salaam. *Wah,* here was a woman a brave man could follow! She would do the master's work while he slept; Ram Singh hummed through his nose, a war song of his native hills, as he hurried about the tasks Nita had set him. Nita smiled faintly at the change in the Sikh, and then she bent gently over the sleeping Wentworth.

"Have the doctor in at once, Jenkyns," she said. "Tell him, I gave Master Richie codeine. When he wakes, I should be here. If I am not. . . ." Nita straightened and her eyes lifted to the wrinkled, kindly eyes of Jenkyns. Her voice grew crisper. "If I am not, you will tell him that I went after the robot at the bottom of the river."

Jenkyns' eyes were worried. "You shouldn't, Miss Nita," he said gently. "The master will worry—"

Nita smiled, "Please, Jenkyns. Give him my message."

She strode from the room and Ram Singh hurried down the hall with the equipment she had ordered. It was a heavy burden even for his stalwart shoulders, and Nita's own back straightened in anticipation of the load she must carry, both physical and mental. Her head was up as she followed Ram Singh down the corridor and into the elevator. At least Dick was taken care of. . . .

Nita sat quietly in the cabin of the Diesel cruiser as Ram Singh drove it slowly up the East River. The tide was slack at extreme ebb, and that would help a little. But she would have to do her work before it turned. She looked down at herself, encased in the thick rubber diving suit with the leaden weights at her slim waist. The helmet rested beside her on the seat. She was ready. Her lips moved in a slight smile. Ram Singh would be her only help. He had been ferociously eager to make the descent, but she could not allow it. She had taken the responsibility for placing Dick out of the battle. She could not permit anyone else to carry on in his stead.

Overhead, the storm whined and blustered. The cold was intense, but at least the overcast sky would delay the light of dawn. She would need the time. . . . Ram Singh's heel thudded twice on the deck. It was the signal!

Nita pushed herself to her feet, picked up the helmet and bore it before her in both arms. The weights were on deck. Ram Singh would attach them at the last moment before lowering her over the side. Nita thrust out into the night, heard the motors check and the rush of the anchor rope. Then she was clear of the cabin's protection and the storm was upon her. The sleet laid jewels upon her clustering curls, and Ram Singh moved with swift efficiency. He lifted the helmet over her head, spun the anchoring bolts fast.

"Any orders, *missie sahib?*" Ram Singh asked.

Nita shook her head. "Haul up if I yank the line three times," she said quietly. "Use the winch if I pull twice. That's all!"

Nita's hand rested on the knife hilt at her waist, but she knew it would be feeble in her hands. She had a gun beneath the rubber suit, and she did not even tell herself why she carried it there. She smiled into Ram Singh's anxious eyes.

"Don't worry, Ram Singh," she said quietly. "You know I've made these dives before. Help me over the side!"

The black waters seemed eager for her. She made an adjustment of the oxygen inlet, of the exhaust valve, took a few steps down the ladder. Then she swung off into the water.

Nita felt the vibration of the rope, slipping out slowly through Ram Singh's hands, felt the pull of the current. No light at all reached her here, but she needed none as yet. Ram Singh knew the spot at which he had rescued Dick, and the robot could not be far from there. If there were other robots here, she would not see them until they had come too close for her to escape!

Nita closed her eyes and tried to hold the smile on her lips. Dick, at least, was safe. She clung to that thought, alone beneath the black waters.

# CHAPTER SEVEN
# DISASTER!

WHEN WENTWORTH AWOKE from the deep drugged sleep into which Nita had plunged him for his own protection, he found his physician taking his pulse. Dr. Riggs nodded briskly as he rose to his feet.

"You'll be all right now, Dick," he said quietly. "Just rest up for a week, and you'll be fit as a fiddle. You escaped pneumonia by a hair."

Wentworth gazed blankly at the doctor for a long minute, and then the whole circumstance of the situation rushed over him. He raised up from the bed.

"What time is it?" he demanded.

The doctor consulted his watch. "Seven o'clock. Evening. You've had a good fifteen-hour sleep."

"Fifteen hours!" Wentworth echoed. He flung the covers aside, bounded to his feet. His jab at the bell-push brought Jenkyns at a run. His face wrinkled in a delighted smile at sight of Wentworth.

"Where is Miss Nita?" Wentworth asked quickly.

The smile left Jenkyns' face at once. He shook his white head. "She left here about three o'clock in the morning, sir, with Ram Singh. I have heard nothing from either of them."

"Jackson?"

"Not since last night, sir," Jenkyns said heavily.

Wentworth pressed down an oath of dismay. What was it Nita

had said just before he fell under the influence of the drugs in the car?

*"I promise you your work shall go on!"*

With feverish hands, Wentworth began to dress. He was not even aware that the doctor had left.

"Do you know where Miss Nita went?" he demanded of Jenkyns, with harshness creeping into his voice.

"I only know, sir," Jenkyns said miserably, "that Ram Singh spent some time in the supply room and left with a very heavy load on his back."

Wentworth was rapidly knotting his tie. He snatched double shoulder holsters from his closet and weighed two heavy automatics in his fists, checked their loading before he dropped them into their clips. He had small doubts as to what Ram Singh and Nita had intended. But had they run into an ambush, as he had, beneath the waters of the East River? And Jackson . . . Jenkyns came hurriedly in at the doorway.

"Mr. Kirkpatrick to see you, sir," he announced.

Wentworth whipped toward the door. This was all he needed now, to have Kirkpatrick spring some new trap upon him, inspired by the machinations of the Iron Man!

"How many men did he bring this time?" Wentworth demanded harshly.

Kirkpatrick spoke from the hallway behind Jenkyns. "I am quite alone, Dick," he said. "I bring you news that may have meaning to you. I'll confess we can make very little of it. Your cruiser was picked up by the river police today. It was anchored close to the channel off the site of your destroyed home. There was a diving ladder overside. Nita's slippers, at least I assume they are hers, were aboard, but nothing else."

Wentworth stared at Kirkpatrick fixedly, but made no response to the information. It was just as he had feared. Ram Singh and Nita. . . .

"A man answering Ram Singh's description," Kirkpatrick went on, "was picked up by a tug. He has a broken shoulder, and a slight skull fracture, and is unconscious in Bellevue hospital."

Wentworth made a small gesture with his right hand. "Phone the hospital, Jenkyns," he instructed. "You know what to do. All possible attention. Send Dr. Riggs there at once."

Jenkyns bowed and departed and Wentworth faced Kirkpatrick. His face was drawn and cold. "And Jackson?" he asked quietly. "I suppose he has been arrested?"

Kirkpatrick faced him with a still face. "It was about Jackson I came to see you, primarily," he said. "He was taken prisoner last night with the body of a murdered policeman in his arms. Apparently, it was his intention to throw the body into the river!"

Wentworth nodded heavily, "I was afraid of that," he said slowly. "I assume full responsibility. The policeman was killed by a robot I encountered off Sutton Place last night. In your present suspicious frame of mind, I was dubious that you would believe that such things as robots existed. Jackson volunteered to remove the body from the vicinity of my wrecked car, and I did not countermand him as I should have. That is the truth of it, Kirk. I give you my word."

Kirkpatrick's own voice was heavy. "I was sure there was an explanation," he said slowly. "If you will make that statement to my secretary and sign it, I think we'll get Jackson off in a few days."

Wentworth looked sharply at Kirkpatrick and saw that his friend was trying to make amends for the suspicions of the night before. There was a pleading that Kirk would never voice deep in his frosty blue eyes. Abruptly, Wentworth thrust out his hand.

"Thanks, Kirk," he said. "I know you could make it pretty tough for Jackson. And I think we'd better join forces. These robots are too much for either of us, single-handed. Shall we go to headquarters while I tell you what I know?"

The night was crystal clear, and bitterly cold. Wentworth muffled himself to the ears in a great coat before climbing into Kirkpatrick's car. He was desperately anxious to start out upon Nita's trail, but he had no starting point. If Nita had disappeared, there was no hope that the robot would still lie disabled on the river bottom.

"I had intended to check up on Drexler last night," Wentworth told Kirkpatrick quietly. "The same thought must have occurred to you."

Kirkpatrick looked at him sharply. "Are you sure you didn't pay Drexler a visit?"

"I gather that the *Spider* did," Wentworth said drily. "And yet I'm inclined to believe in Drexler."

Kirkpatrick nodded reluctantly. "There's a report about the city that people will be safe if they employ Drexler guards," he said. "A number of prominent men have called me about that report. Of the three who were robbed last night, Aaron Smedley at least had been warned to hire Drexler guards!

"Drexler swears he knows nothing of the matter. There is nothing to show that these racketeer threats were made by anyone connected with him . . . and Drexler voluntarily submitted his books for examination. He admitted that his business had been growing lately by leaps and bounds, that he had been compelled to employ many new men."

"Yet you believe in Drexler, too?" Wentworth asked softly.

Kirkpatrick's jaw set in a stubborn line. "I believe in Drexler," he said. "It's possible someone is using him as a scapegoat. That has happened before this."

Wentworth agreed, and told of his discoveries concerning the robots and of disabling one beneath the river; and of what he feared had happened to Nita.

"You should have notified us, Dick!" Kirkpatrick snapped.

Wentworth smiled slightly, but made no other answer. Kirkpatrick had scarcely been in a tractable mood yesterday.

"So I'd like your men to make all possible efforts to find some trace of Nita," he went on steadily. "And post a guard over Ram Singh to notify us the moment he regains consciousness. It's just possible he may know something. My guess is that Nita insisted on making the dive herself, that she was attacked by robots and Ram Singh dove to her rescue! He was probably disabled by a single blow that broke his shoulder and cracked his skull, and was lucky enough to be picked up."

Kirkpatrick said heavily, "It sums up to this: several hundred thousand dollars' worth of damage has been done, a score of people have been brutally murdered—and if the robots decided to march on police headquarters and wipe it out, we could not stop them! Something must be done!"

Wentworth whispered, "Something!"

His voice died in the whine of the radio in the car. "Sergeant Reams, call headquarters," came the announcer's voice. "Sergeant Reams, call headquarters."

Kirkpatrick stiffened in his seat. It was the code by which head-quarters indicated an urgent need to get in touch with him. The driv-er swung the heavy car to the curb beside a call box and Kirkpatrick leaped to the pavement. Wentworth leaned forward and deliberately tuned the radio to a news broadcast which he knew would be going on at this moment.

"The New York police have a new mystery," said the announcer, "which may or may not be connected with the great steel giants which are destroying property and killing civilians. A rowboat drift-ing down the East River was picked up today and in it was found a woman's clothing, complete to the last item except for the shoes. Police said that the clothing contained a secret message which would, and I quote, 'enable them to crack the case in twenty-four hours!'"

Wentworth's eyes narrowed as the full impact of the words struck him, and he turned to see Kirkpatrick leaping toward the car. "Get to headquarters fast!" he snapped, grimly. "Those damned fools!"

Wentworth said savagely, "That was madness, Kirk! They gave out on the radio the fact that they had a secret message. Before we can reach there, they may move her!"

Kirkpatrick stared at Wentworth without comprehension. "What in hell are you talking about?"

Wentworth explained rapidly. "Plainly, those must be Nita's clothes! It's a taunt at me, and she was clever enough to plant some message in them. Get me there fast, Kirk. I've got to see for myself what this message is!"

The car was already roaring through the streets, parting traffic with the shriek of its siren. Kirkpatrick massaged his brows with bony fingers. "I see," he said slowly. "I didn't know about that. The news I received was that the Iron Man telephoned a few moments ago to speak to me, and those damned fools let him get away! He's calling again! Dick, this may be the break I've been praying for!"

Wentworth's words were urgent. "It's more apt to be a threat, or extortion. Good luck to you, Kirk, I'll follow Nita's message!"

The heavy car slewed to the curb before police headquarters and Kirkpatrick strode swiftly up the steps. His forehead was knotted into a frown. He needed Dick's help in this struggle that lay ahead, but he knew it would be futile to attempt to interrupt him now. As for Wentworth, a great load had lifted from his heart. He knew at least that Nita was alive, otherwise they would not have submitted her to that indignity to taunt him!

"Where are those clothes?" he demanded sharply.

Kirkpatrick threw an order back at Sergeant Reams and the officer led Wentworth rapidly along the wide lower hall to an office on the first floor.

"Wants to identify them clothes picked out of the river," Reams said curtly. "Commissioner's orders, give him all help."

Wentworth thanked Reams, and the dumpy man with the eyeshade rose laboriously from his seat and began to poke over shelves with grimed fingers. He found a package in fresh brown paper.

Wentworth caught it from his hands and ripped it open. It took only a glance to assure him that the clothing was Nita's. The scent of her perfume lifted to his nostrils and pain clutched at his heart. Nita in the hands of those devils! Forced to this indignity!

"You identify them, hey?" the custodian asked shrilly.

Wentworth jerked his head in affirmative. "The radio mentioned a secret message," he said thickly. "What was it?"

The man cackled. "Funny business, that was. Funniest thing I ever did see. Inside her slip, we found this, and we can't make heads or tails of it, for a fact!"

The man poked among the clothing and brought out an envelope. In an instant, Wentworth had ripped it open . . . and there tumbled into his hand a fragment of white porcelain and gold, a removable bridge containing an artificial tooth! Wentworth gazed down at the bauble, and his throat closed. He remembered when a gangster, striking at him, had caught Nita in the jaw and knocked out that tooth. Strange, how the memory could close his throat. It was hard to force out words.

"Fastened inside the slip?" he asked, and his voice was a whisper.

"Yes, sir, that's right," the man cackled again, "and if you can make heads or tails out of it, you're a better man than anybody around here!"

Wentworth let the bit of bridgework slide back into the envelope. The muscles stood out in knots on his jaws. No question that Nita meant to convey to him her place of imprisonment, but that fool radio broadcast might already have alarmed the crooks. If they moved her . . . God, he had no time to lose!

Wentworth swung out of the room, into the hall and Sergeant Reams called his name from the head of the steps. Wentworth ignored it, went into the street and hailed a taxi. He had long ago learned the advantage of having a hideout near police headquarters and he directed the driver to that vicinity now. He flung a ten dollar bill to the front seat.

"I want speed," he said flatly.

He got speed, but once he had to stop the taxi to make a phone call. He put through a call to a friend on a morning newspaper.

"I want to know the whereabouts of an abandoned ferry slip, probably on the Hudson River, and near a bridge," he said rapidly. "My guess would be somewhere near the George Washington Bridge—some ferry put out of business by its opening. Can you get that information for me?"

"As it happens," the newspaper man drawled. "You have come to precisely the right man. I looked up that same information for a lad named Frank Drexler about a month ago."

Wentworth struggled to keep his voice calm. "I don't know the gentleman, but where is that slip?" He knew now that he was on the right track. Nita's message had seemed so painfully clear to him, a bridge fastened to a slip . . . and she had disappeared in the river. The Hudson River had been a guess, of course, but Nita had fastened the bridgework to the *wrong* side of the slip. It might mean that he had been interested in the wrong river. It might. . . .

"It's not much of a ferry," the newspaper man was drawling. "Last summer is the first it hasn't operated. Used to run across to Interstate Park, and it's just about a mile above George Washington Bridge. As a matter of fact, it may run again. I seem to remember hearing it had been bought."

"Get the name and have it for me," Wentworth told him. "This is worth money to me, and I'll mail you a check."

The newspaper man sighed, "Insulted again, but I love it!"

Wentworth did not hear him. He was leaping toward the taxi. That inquiry by Drexler was the confirmation he needed. He knew now that he was on the right trail . . . but thanks to the bungling of the police, it might already be cold! Wentworth forced himself to relax. It was madness that he planned, an open attack on a headquarters of robots, even though he would dare greater than that for Nita's sake.

Presently, at a dark corner in a district of slums and gaunt warehouses, Wentworth paid off the taxi driver. He waited impatiently until the machine had whirled a corner, and then he sprinted into the dark mouth of an alley. Half way along its length, there was an incongruous small brick garage, whose door mechanism was operated by a masked beam of black light which Wentworth interrupted at irregularly timed intervals. The doors slid open and Wentworth stepped inside.

Parked there was a replica of the battered coupe which he had used the night before. Wentworth's swift glance assured him that everything was in order and then his eyes quested hurriedly over the garage. They lighted on two old ginger ale bottles on a shelf and, as Wentworth stared at them, a grim light crept into his eyes. Not a weapon he liked to use, but against such monstrous murderers as these men of steel. . . .

He filled those bottles with gasoline. He twisted a bit of rag about each one then and, tightly corked, laid them beside him as he got behind the wheel. He fought the cold motor to life, emerged into the alley, and drove rapidly across town. The motor moaned with power, and Wentworth crouched fiercely over the wheel. Once his eyes strayed to those two innocuous seeming bottles upon the seat, and when they did, cold fires flamed in their depths. God grant that he would be in time!

The ferry house was a squat monster beside the dark Hudson. The slip was its yawning jaws. Above it, to southward, the inverted arch of the bridge laid a clear curve of beauty against the stars.

The roadway to the ferry house led under a stone arch that bore railway tracks. Beyond this, a battered coupe huddled like an old woman in the shadows. The black shape that detached from it, and drifted beneath the arch, was equally anonymous, but from under the black hat brim cold eyes surveyed the building. Its spire, that once had held a clock, pointed upward like a warning finger.

Through the archway, the wind moaned on the deep note of a

dying man. It caught the tail of a long black cape, flapped it once. When he was nearer, the dilapidated aspect of the building showed more clearly. The doors were locked. In Wentworth's nimble fingers a lockpick made little of that. The door did not creak as he eased it open, but afterward he stood very still inside, and a cold smile moved the lipless gash of the *Spider's* mouth.

This old building, abandoned for months, held a trace of heat! It was not that the gaunt waiting room was warm, but there was the smell of heat. Wentworth bent quickly, and his fingers hovered above the cracks in the floor. He nodded alertly. The warmth came from below! So quickly, so easily, he had located the hiding place to which Nita's shrewd message had guided him!

Briskly, his eyes quested over the interior. There was an elevator shaft which led to the upper deck of the ferry house; probably downward also. It would not do for the *Spider,* and there were no stairs in evidence. He whipped out a shielded flashlight and its radiance flickered and vanished, glowed again. He traveled silently along the walls, then swerved toward the deserted change booths. The opening he sought would be masked, and . . . in the second change booth, Wentworth stopped. His light burned steadily for a half minute. He had found the trapdoor he sought.

Nita lay huddled against the wall of the ferry house, arms and legs bound tightly. She was not given to despair, but her lot seemed almost hopeless. How many hours had passed since the robots had ambushed her on the river bottom? They seemed endless, horrible. Those men within the steel monsters . . . they had forced to her to strip off her clothing as a taunt to Dick. . . . It still brought a burning flush to her cheeks. Her present garments were inadequate, but she had small thought for bodily discomfort. If only she could hope!

There had been hope for hours after she had smuggled that vague message into her clothing. She had been left here alone with only a single guard, one of the Drexler men in uniform, and it seemed to her that her very thoughts must be summoning Dick. Now—she prayed that he would not come!

A half hour ago, three robots had entered the building. One of them had vanished into the elevator shaft, but the other two stood

near the trapdoor that opened into this basement room from above.
And Nita knew with a terrible certainty why they waited! They were
expecting Dick. . . .

At the thought, Nita saw one of the men in steel turn its head
slowly and the blank panes of glass stared at her. It was their utter
soullessness that was terrifying. A steel hand motioned to the uniformed guard and he pushed himself warily to his feet, grinned down
at Nita.

"Come on, toots," he said. "Me and you is going places!"

"Where?" Nita demanded.

The guard just grinned, caught her by the arm. "A safe place," he
said. "I think somebody is paying us a visit, and the Iron Man don't
want you hurt none. Not yet, anyway. Come on!"

With the man's hand gripping her arm, Nita surged to her feet. "I
can't walk like this," she said. "Untie my ankles."

The man hesitated, then shrugged and stooped to do as she bid.
Nita's eyes flashed to the ceiling, and she saw . . . the trapdoor begin
to lift! The robots saw it, too. Their heads were tilted back, their great
steel hands poised just beside the opening.

Nita cried, "*Back, Dick!* Two robots . . . waiting!"

The guard struck Nita across the mouth with the flat of his hand.
In the same instant, a gun blasted from the ceiling! Nita saw the
tongue of flame leap out of the darkness overhead, heard the surprised gasp of the man in front of her! His body jerked and pitched
heavily against her, bore Nita to the floor. But Nita did not tear her
eyes away from the opening in the ceiling. She cried her warning, but
there was no answer. She saw a small flicker of fire up there. Then
one of the robots took a single stride forward, and reached up into
the darkness with great taloned hands of steel!

With a sob, Nita tried to wrestle free of the slain guard's body. She
found that her ankle ropes were loose, and she braced her legs, began
to wriggle clear. A curious object sailed downward. For a hysterical
moment, she thought that she was mistaken. It seemed to her that
the thing that plummeted down toward the upturned head of the
robot was an ordinary bottle with flaming rags knotted about its
base!

There was only that glimpse, then the bottle struck the face of the
robot, and burst. That was all for a moment, and then, suddenly, the

robot was a tower of flames! Liquid fire dripped down its sides and burned fiercely on the steel legs. The head, shoulders and chest of the robot were blotted out in leaping flames!

For a moment the robot stood there, motionless, hands reaching through that trapdoor, and then the thing staggered backward. She had heard them speak before, through the diaphragm magnifier that was hidden somewhere about the great body, but she had never heard such a sound as this. It was a scream of absolute terror, its volume stunning, in this enclosed space. It was as if a ship's siren could take on the qualities of a human voice!

A sob pushed up into Nita's throat as she finally fought her way clear of the guard's body and staggered to her feet. She had been mad to doubt Dick. He had found a way to defeat the robots! The second monster was not waiting to battle against the flame bomb. Instead, it wheeled so quickly that it reeled off-balance against the wall. The battering ram of its shoulder cracked a gaping hole in the concrete, but it staggered on. It came straight toward her!

In terror, Nita turned to flee, and in that moment she saw a figure drop swiftly through the trapdoor, and hang there by one hand—a figure in a kiting black cape. Flat and mocking laughter poured from its lips, and in its right hand another of those absurd glass bottles was clenched. The rags at its base were flaming. Behind him, the other robot beat at its flaming armor, the blows dinning drum beats in rhythm to those awful screams. They were suddenly muffled, almost child-like, and Nita knew that the heat had disabled the amplifier. It was a human voice she heard now.

But the robot that remained on its feet was almost upon her. Nita gasped and turned to run. If it caught her . . . Dick would be beaten! He could not use the flame bomb! Even as the thought struck her, Nita stumbled, pitched helplessly to the floor. The next instant, the monster was upon her. She felt the steel talons close about her, wrench her aloft.

Her senses reeled dizzily, but she fought for sanity. Somehow, she must contrive to break free, to give Dick his chance! Her eyes quested frantically toward the trapdoor! Dick had not yet dropped to the floor. Instead, he swung in mid-air, now dangling from a length of web. He was driving, feet-foremost straight at the robot who held her prisoner—and then Nita remembered! She remembered that a third robot was hidden in the elevator shaft!

Even as the thought flashed across her mind, she saw the monster heave itself into sight, saw the great taloned hands reach for Wentworth where he swung.

"Behind you, Dick!" Nita cried. "Oh, look behind you!"

Wentworth twisted in mid-air. With a final swing upon the web, he hurled himself into space and landed lightly against the wall. And in the same instant, he hurled his bomb—straight into the face of the second robot!

As if that were the moment her own captor had awaited, Nita felt herself falling! The *Spider* had no more bombs, and the robot wanted both hands to close the battle. While Nita was still falling, the robot turned and plunged straight toward Wentworth! And now he had only powerless guns—and his wits.

Two of the robots were out of the fight. They battled with fires that were spreading. Over the head of the first monster, Nita saw that the tinder-dry flooring of the ferry-house had caught! In a space of minutes, this whole building would be a raging inferno! But Wentworth paid all these things no heed. He was crouched against the concrete wall, his hands empty at his side, waiting for the charge of the robot!

Nita had been badly shaken by her fall, but she struggled to her feet. She threw a frightened glance toward the two flame-wrapped robots, toward the spreading fire that was rapidly eating into the ancient timbers.

"Run, Dick!" she cried. "There is a door at the back. At water level. We can get away!"

Wentworth's voice, reaching out to her, was cold and crisp. "Go there," he ordered quietly. "I'll join you shortly!"

As he finished speaking, the robot struck at him with a taloned hand. Wentworth . . . was not there. He darted sideways and around the robot, and then Nita saw for the first time that a length of his silken web dangled from his hand! She knew the power of that cord which, scarcely larger than a pencil, would lift a thousand pounds with ease. But it would be no more than cotton string to this monster of steel. Surely, Dick did not expect to bind the robot!

Once more, the robot struck down at Wentworth, and stepped into the noose. The *Spider* snapped it tight about the jointed ankles. Now, he raced in narrowing circles about the robot, throwing loop after loop of the powerful silken rope about the monster's legs!

"Get to the door!" Wentworth ordered again.

"The right hand, Dick!" Nita cried. "It's getting ready to shoot with those fingers!"

Wentworth's head snapped toward the monster, and he flung himself aside just in time. He whipped out a gun, and tried to duplicate his previous feat of putting a bullet down the barrel of the robot's ingenious gun, but the thing's hand moved too swiftly. Frantically, Wentworth threw a knot into the silken line, then he whirled toward Nita.

"Out the door!" he cried. "Quickly! This building will collapse any minute!"

Nita moved toward the door, trying to open it with her bound hands, but her eyes riveted with an awful fascination on the robot. It swung a great arm about to bring the gun to bear again. It took a stride, and the silken line drew taut about its ankles. Nita saw the silk draw thin, saw a strand snap! But the other wrappings held, and the stride was only half-completed.

At the same instant, behind the monster, Wentworth thrust up both his automatics and emptied them in a swift drum-roll against the back of the creature's head. The lead would not penetrate, but each one struck with the force of a half-ton. Combined with the hobbling silk about its ankles, the blow was enough. The robot tottered, tried to keep its balance, and pitched violently forward to the concrete floor!

It was an incredible spectacle, the fall of that giant, like the death of some great redwood, pierced by the lumberman's saw. Under the impact, the concrete floor cracked like ice, and fragments of grey stone spun into the air. The jar loosened the timbers overhead and a great flaming beam wrenched free and speared down into the basement!

Nita had the door open now, and she called out to Wentworth, but he stood by the fallen monster. He was bending over the helmet which his bullets had battered.

"Hurry, Dick!" Nita called. "He may be stunned by the fall, but it's no more than that. Come on, before he revives!"

Instead of answering, Wentworth flung himself suddenly astride the fallen giant, and his hands tore at the base of the helmet.

"Get outside!" Wentworth called once more. "I'll be with you in a moment!"

As he spoke, the helmet came loose in his hands and Nita saw the lolling head of a man. He wore a curious sort of crash helmet, but blood seeped from his nostrils and he was completely unconscious. She stared incredulously at this human being who, encased in steel, was so ponderous, so terrible. He seemed as defenseless as an oyster stripped of its shell. As she watched, Wentworth whipped up an automatic and struck once, with carefully calculated force, at the base of the man's skull. Then he raced toward her.

In an instant, he slashed the bonds from her wrists. His arm flung about her, he sprang from the doorway to a narrow wooden walkway that skirted the black, oily waters of the slip. A hundred yards offshore, a barge piled high with gravel floated high in the water, and Wentworth's eyes raked it as he reached for a wooden ladder that led to the shore.

"That barge!" he cried. "It floats too high in the water to be loaded like that with gravel! That's how these monsters travel! An airlock under the water would do it. No wonder I lost them in the East River!"

Nita was sobbing, "Dick, oh Dick! I bungled things terribly, didn't I? But I was so worried about you!"

Wentworth laughed sharply. "On the contrary, my dear," he cried. "You have solved the case!"

He leaped over the verge of the shore, reached down to drag Nita upward, and she looked beyond him. Her breath broke with a gasp.

"Oh, Dick!" she cried. "Look, the police! Kirkpatrick!"

Wentworth swore as he set her feet on dry land, threw an arm about her waist. "I should have known better than to ask that newspaper man a question without satisfying his curiosity," he said. "That's what did it! Listen, dear, go to Kirkpatrick at once, but don't mention that barge out there! Tell him everything else. Understand?"

Nita's white face was turned toward him. "Yes, Dick, but what are you going to do?"

Wentworth set her from him, and his laughter rang out clearly, briefly. "I'm going to smash this case wide open!" he cried softly.

Police were running toward them now. Kirkpatrick's challenge rang out harshly. "Surrender, *Spider!* You're covered by a dozen guns!"

Wentworth laughed once more. He whirled . . . and ran back toward the blazing ferry house! Nita gasped, and her hands reached out to him, and then she did a daring thing! She stepped squarely between Wentworth and Kirkpatrick, between him and the line of policemen with lifted guns. And she turned her face toward Dick!

The ferry house was a soaring spire of flame. The angry crackling of the fire was like thunder and, even in the bitter cold, the heat struck like a mallet. Nita wavered on her feet, and suddenly Kirkpatrick was beside her. He flung a strong arm about her waist, leveled his revolver . . . and Dick was out of sight!

"After him!" Kirkpatrick snapped out his orders. "Block that slip in case he tries to leave by water. If he wants to commit suicide in that fire . . ." His voice trailed off.

Nita stood rigidly within the curve of Kirkpatrick's arm. She was trembling, but it was not from the cold. She had heard no splash of water after Dick had ducked over the edge of the slip. In heaven's name, had he gone back into that inferno? Nita lifted her hands to her lips.

"I hope he escapes," she whispered. "He is a very gallant man."

Kirkpatrick made no answer, but there was worry about the stern corners of his lips. "Surely, no man could live in that building," he muttered. "It will collapse in a moment! Back there! *Get back!*" As he spoke, a section of the roof crashed inward, and a flying brand flew out to hiss into the black waters. The policemen lining the banks of the slip drew back, vanquished by the heat.

"He went inside, Commissioner!" one of them called. "He's done for!"

Nita bit down a sob. It wasn't possible. Not Dick, who had been so strong and confident beside her a moment before! And yet . . . there had been no splash! A choked cry lifted into Nita's throat, and Kirkpatrick swore at her side. With a final, thunderous roar, the entire ferry house caved in upon itself! Afterward, there were only the twisting, lifting spirals of dark smoke and eager, exultant flames. Of the *Spider,* there was no sign at all.

# CHAPTER EIGHT
# LAST WARNING!

NITA SCARCELY HEARD Kirkpatrick's orders as he sent men along the shore line to keep watch on the black waters. She was only vaguely aware that a cloak had been thrown about her shoulders. This disaster, after her rescue had raised her hopes so high, sapped the last of her vitality. It was only much later, when the ferry house had at last caved in upon itself, that she remembered Dick Wentworth had warned her not to mention the connection of the barge off-shore with the ferry house.

At the memory, she glanced toward the barge—and it was gone! Frantic thoughts darted through her mind, but she dared not ask a question lest it draw attention to the fact that the barge had been there. If Dick had mentioned the barge, then he had had some plan! Slight as were her reasons for hope, Nita clung to them. She could even smile a little when Kirkpatrick came striding toward her, crisp and grave as always.

"Two of those robots in the ruins," he said curtly. "Can't find anything else."

"Two robots," Nita repeated after him, "but—" She bit her words off. There had been three. Perhaps that, too, she was not to tell Kirkpatrick.

"But what?" Kirkpatrick demanded harshly.

Nita shook her head. "I didn't know that they had been killed," she said slowly. "The *Spider* attacked them with some bottles, filled with gasoline I think, and wrapped in flaming cloths. But I didn't know they were enough to kill the robots!"

Kirkpatrick uttered a sharp exclamation. "By the heavens, I believe the *Spider* has shown us the way!" he cried. "They used bombs like that in the Spanish Civil War . . . against tanks, you know. They might work! Heaven knows, we'll have to find something and find it fast!"

A despair in Kirkpatrick's voice pulled Nita's attention wholly to him, and she placed a hand upon his arm. "Is it . . . very bad, Stanley?" she asked.

Kirkpatrick's lips stretched into a thin straight line. "That hardly describes it," he said slowly. "Before we got this tip-off from a newspaper man, I had a call from the Iron Man. He said he would 'give us a lesson tonight.' Tomorrow, if the police did not voluntarily surrender their jobs to the Drexler agency, headquarters and all major officials would be destroyed!"

"Then you've arrested Drexler at last!" Nita cried.

Kirkpatrick shook his head heavily. He was leading her now toward the stone archway and his parked car. "There is no evidence against him," he said curtly. "My men have been following him day and night; his books and office have been thrown open to us. There is no proof!"

Nita's laughter was sharp and taunting. "And you say there is no place for such men as the *Spider*!" she said ironically. "You know the man is guilty, and you cannot arrest him even to prevent wholesale murder!"

Kirkpatrick shook his head and stubbornness squared his jaw. "In the end, the law always wins," he said curtly. "It may muddle along, but the law always wins."

"Thanks to the *Spider*," Nita said quietly. "Where is Dick, do you know?"

Kirkpatrick glanced at her as he handed her into the rear of his police limousine. The police driver saluted respectfully, and Nita repeated her question.

"He'll be worried about me," she insisted. "I want to communicate with him at the first possible moment."

✪ ✪ ✪

Kirkpatrick's voice was impatient. "Dick left me at headquarters," he said shortly. "I don't know his whereabouts any more than I know those of the *Spider*. I'll drop you at your home, Nita. Meanwhile, will you kindly tell me just what happened? I might learn something that will help to trap the Iron Man and these steel monsters of his!"

"What, without legal evidence, Kirk?" Nita asked, her voice low with mockery, while her mind raced over the events of her captivity. Dick had told her to relate everything except his suspicions regarding the barge. She began to talk rapidly, but her thoughts were not on what she said. She had not lied when she said she wished to get in touch with Wentworth at once. He must be told that the Iron Man planned to inflict a "lesson" upon the city tonight. At the thought of that, Nita felt tension crawl through her body. There was so little she, or anyone else, could do—except the *Spider*!

Nita knew a new humbleness of spirit at thought of the man she loved. At such moments, he seemed more than human. His keen brain flashed always ahead to the true hidden meaning of criminal problems, and found the way to defeat them. He had needed only to glance at the high-riding barge to guess the secret of its use. Her despair of a short while before seemed a disloyalty now. Dick would not have dashed back into the building had he not a plan . . . and not a mere plan for escape. Wentworth had gone once more to battle giants!

Nita fell silent, dropped her head gravely. Her hands were clasped hard in her lap, as if in prayer.

"What you say doesn't help much, Nita," Kirkpatrick said. His voice sounded angry and puzzled. "If only I knew how they move under the water. Always, they seem to return to the water on the East River, yet their headquarters apparently was here! Well, we have to thank the *Spider* for destroying this stronghold!"

"Instead of thanking him," Nita said, scornfully, "you will chalk up two more murders to his name. Torch murders, would you call them? And the destruction of the ferry house! Tell me, Stanley, will your legal conscience permit you to use the gasoline bombs? Or must more people die under their attacks?"

"They are outside the law," Kirkpatrick said sternly.

Nita sighed and turned her gaze to the road ahead. The car had left the West Side highway and was tooling along Riverside Drive.

The high viaduct that spanned the valley at 125th Street was just ahead. She would be home soon, but how could she communicate with Dick?

"Has it occurred to you," she asked Kirkpatrick slowly, "that perhaps this 'lesson' may be an attack on yourself? The promise of an attack later, might merely have been meant to disarm you for the present."

Kirkpatrick nodded stiffly. "I am taking all possible precautions now," he said. "As soon as I can reach headquarters, I'll have some of those gasoline bombs prepared. . . . You must be careful, Nita. It's quite obvious that the Iron Man is intent on destroying you and . . . Dick."

Nita smiled, and there was tenderness in the curve of her lips, and pride, too. So many monsters had tried to destroy Dick. One and all, they had been vanquished, though she admitted with a thrill of fear, that he had never fought such impregnable creatures as these men of steel. Her eyes quested longingly ahead as the limousine swung out on the viaduct. If only she could be sure that Dick was safe now. . . . Suddenly her hand gripped Kirkpatrick's arm.

"In heaven's name, Stanley," she gasped. "Look! *Look at that Fifth Avenue bus!*"

A startled oath sprang to Kirkpatrick's lips, and he leaned forward to snap an order at the driver, but it was already too late! Nita saw the things that happened as a wildly fantastic dream. The huge double-decked bus was careening wildly across the viaduct, and stretched out upon its upper deck, crushing the steel framework beneath their colossal weight, were two of the robots! Nita saw that the powerful arm of one of the monsters was stretched down into the cabin, and that a steel forefinger was pointed at the head of the frantic driver. There was no other living being aboard the bus!

As Kirkpatrick shouted to the driver to whirl the limousine about and retreat, the bus shrieked in a furious turn and came to a halt just in front of the police car! The robots stepped to the pavement and heaved the bus over so that it blocked the viaduct. Then they turned and came toward the police commissioner's car!

The driver barely succeeded in stopping the car before it collided with the wreckage of the bus. He was fighting now to back out of range of those two oncoming terrors. Kirkpatrick had his revolver in his fist. He opened a compartment and seized a hand grenade, but Nita knew grenades were futile.

"Get out and run," Kirkpatrick said sharply. "I'm the one they want, Nita. I can hold them for a while!"

"Come with me," Nita cried. "They can't move very fast, and if we can dodge their bullets, we can still get away!"

She batted open the door on her side, but in the same instant the robot reached the car. Its steel hand smashed against the door, wedged it fast. The other robot reached through the front window as Kirkpatrick's gun blasted furiously. His futile bullets screamed off the metal of the steel talons. The driver screamed terribly through a single tearing instant. The hand clamped on his shoulder—and pulled!

The driver's scream soared to an incredible thinness. His head had caught against the top of the door as the hand dragged him through the open window, but the hand was inexorable. The scream broke off and there was a dull snapping sound. Afterward, Nita saw a blue clad body hurtle through the air toward the railing of the viaduct and disappear into the darkness beyond.

"Down on the floor," Kirkpatrick snapped.

She saw his hands wrench the pin from the grenade, toss it outside. The explosion made the heavy limousine jump. It seemed to drive in her ear-drums, and immediately thereafter she heard a scream such as had pierced her brain once before—when Wentworth had smashed his flame-bomb against one of the robots.

Cautiously, Nita lifted her head, and she saw an incredible thing! One of the robots had turned on the other, had moved up behind the steel monster while he was torturing the driver! Nita's gasp brought Kirkpatrick up from the floor. He was clutching another grenade, but his grip remained frozen. He, too, stared at the bizarre spectacle. The robot who had killed the driver was pitching forward on its face, still screaming. The second robot had stepped up behind it and seized its ankles in mighty fists . . . and lifted it clear off the pavement!

Even as Nita watched, the viaduct quivered under the impact of the thing's fall. She saw the flooring of the viaduct crack and give way. Paving blocks disappeared through a gaping hole in the pavement . . . and the scream stopped! But the second robot was not through. It stooped above its fallen comrade, and got a new grip. She heard a slow creaking sound, as when terrific strain is put upon a hoist, and then . . . and then the robot lifted the fallen monster high over its head. A stride, another . . . and the robot went sailing through the air toward the railing! In exactly the arc that the already dead police driver had described, the steel monster hurtled through space. The crash of its fall was like the explosion of a great bomb. And the second robot turned back toward the police car.

"I could not destroy him sooner," it said in a booming voice. "There was no time for a battle and I had to take him unawares. I am sorry for the driver's death!"

Kirkpatrick pushed to his feet, flung wide the door of the car and stepped courageously to the pavement. His fist was wrapped about the grenade, clenched to throw. Nita gasped, and flung herself forward to seize that wrist!

"Don't throw!" she cried. "Don't you recognize that voice? It's . . . it's the *Spider*!"

Kirkpatrick's wrist stiffened in her grasp, and the two stood staring up into the blankly unfeeling face of the steel monster. The yelp of sirens was thin in the air behind them and Nita's head whipped that way. Two Fifth Avenue buses were roaring toward them, while motorcycle police cleared a path with their sirens. A machine gun stammered from its motorcycle mount, but the bullets screamed overhead.

"Back in the car, Commissioner!" a voice trumpeted from the police. "Give us a clear target!"

The robot did not glance toward the attack. Incongruous in a great steel fist, Nita saw a slim platinum cigarette lighter which she recognized with a throb. Even as she gasped, the robot bent and pressed the base of that lighter to the break in the pavement of the viaduct, and when he had straightened, the gleaming red seal of the *Spider* shone there! But the robot was talking. . . . "The 'lesson' which the Iron Man intends to inflict tonight," the *Spider's* amplified voice boomed, "will be inflicted on the subway at Forty-second and Fifth Avenue. I will do what I can to prevent it, Kirkpatrick. Have your men armed with flame bombs, but if you value the salvation of your city, do not let them throw at me until after the battle! I will mark myself!"

As he spoke, the steel hand lifted again and, on the forehead of the helmet, he imprinted the seal of the *Spider*!

"Hurry, Kirkpatrick," he said once more. "I do not know how much time is left to us!"

With the words, the robot turned away toward the railing of the viaduct. There was a shout, and a roar of motors behind and the Fifth Avenue buses, police at their wheels, charged toward the retreating form of steel. Nita cried out, and flung herself at Kirkpatrick.

"Stop them!" she cried. "Don't you realize he is your only hope!"

Kirkpatrick wrenched himself free, sprang toward the car, but Nita flung herself straight forward—into the path of the onrushing buses! It was only when she heard Kirkpatrick's voice boom out over the loudspeaker of his car that she realized he had taken the more effective way to stop that charge.

"Stop!" he bellowed above the roar of the charging motors. "Stop those buses! Kirkpatrick's orders!"

Nevertheless, Nita stood firm, straight and slender in the path of those juggernauts. Through long seconds, it did not seem possible that they could stop in time, but finally they grumbled to a halt within feet of where she stood. Angry police poured from them. Men sprang from the motorcycles and charged toward her, shouting, but Nita looked toward the railing of the viaduct.

There was a great gaping tear in the steel balustrade, but of the robot, there was no sign at all. One of the men darted to the verge, and began blasting bullets down into the darkness.

"It's climbing down the pillar!" he shouted. "Circle around! We can still catch it on the streets below!"

Inside the steel shell he had captured in the burning wreckage of the ferry house, Wentworth made no effort to avoid the bullets rained upon him from above. Their hammering was like a trip-hammer in the curved top of the helmet, but all his attention was concentrated on the stupendous task of managing the robot in a climb down the steel pillar of the viaduct. He was crouched in the body of the monster, on an upholstered saddle to which he was strapped like an airplane pilot. His feet rode in stirrups which controlled the movements of the legs, and there were two hand grips before him by which he could direct the arms. Other specialized movements were controlled by a series of push-buttons set like a miniature typewriter keyboard before him.

Below and around him, there was the whirr of machinery which he had not stopped to examine and the oily stench of it was strong in his nostrils. The noise was terrific, deafening. And he needed the crash helmet which he had stripped from the man slain inside the ferry house. The lurching of the robot was impossible to control, and his head banged again and again on the steel sides of the monster.

His plans were carefully made. He would find a truck here in the heavy traffic that filed toward the ferry and, in it, would make his dash to Fifth and Forty-second.

How many robots would be sent to destroy the subway he could not guess. He only knew that, by means of the small radio receiver within the robot, he had received orders with another of the monsters to destroy Kirkpatrick and, afterward, to go to the appointed place of the subway attack. If there were many others there, and this double duty seemed to indicate that the whole force was involved—it was a question how much he could accomplish against them, even in this powerful robot!

Wentworth heard the thin wailing of sirens as he reached the earth beneath the viaduct and looked slowly about him through the great blank eyes of the robot. Men were running from him in screaming terror, abandoning their automobiles in panic. He saw a driver leap from an oil truck and, in the sheer blindness of his terror, dart almost straight toward him!

As gently as possible, Wentworth picked up the man, and spoke to him through the microphone which dangled before his lips. "I won't hurt you," he said, and tried to make his voice soft. "I need transportation. We are going back to your truck. I will sit astride it, and you will drive me to Fifth Avenue and Forty-second Street. Understand?"

He was holding the man high before the blank eyes of the robot, and he could see the writhing terror of the man's face, but the driver managed some sort of affirmative. Wentworth had never ceased to advance, and now he eased the man into the cab of his truck, swung astride of it.

Wentworth's gaze ranged ahead down Fifth Avenue, seeking some trace of the steel monsters he must destroy. His earphones were silent save for the ceaseless rasping of police orders. Twice, he heard Kirkpatrick's clear voice and heard the command to manufacture flame bombs!

Abruptly, he snapped to attention. Far down the length of Fifth Avenue, he caught the glint of street lights on steel. At first it was no more than that, and then his straining eyes made out the regular ranks of the robots, marching up Fifth Avenue. There were only six of them now, behind the taller figure of the Iron Man, but they were enough!

"Faster!" he shouted at the driver. "Faster, man!"

The bellow of his voice beat back into his ears, and he saw windows shiver and crash inward at the concussion of the sound! And then, dead ahead of him, two trucks swung out of a side street! For an instant, they clashed together and then they straightened out, completely closing Fifth Avenue. Wentworth surged forward as the power brakes of the oil truck took hold. Then, with a titanic collision, the three trucks slammed together and Wentworth felt himself falling!

Twice, he had seen robots fall from slighter distance than this and each time the men inside them had been knocked out! Even as the thought flashed across his mind, he saw oil gush from the torn side of the truck, saw flame flick upward. The robot, carrying Wentworth with it, plunged toward a lake of flaming oil!

# CHAPTER NINE
# BATTLE OF THE GIANTS

FALLING TOWARD THAT LAKE OF BURNING OIL, Wentworth did the only thing he could. He braced himself rigidly against the strap that bound him and thrust the arms and legs of the robot rigidly forward. If he plunged into the flames, he was done for. There was small chance that he would be able to extract himself from the suit before the terrific heat overpowered him, even if the police would allow him opportunity.

An eternity passed while he plunged toward the street, but the weight of the outthrust arms and legs decided the issue. They pointed downward and it was in that position, he fell to the street. The flames splashed toward him, coated his limbs almost to the joints. For an instant longer, Wentworth held motionless until sure that the robot was balanced, and then he straightened and plunged toward the sidewalk!

He held the hands of the monster straight out to the sides, and the flames flapped back from them, away from his body. On the legs, the polished surface of the steel shed the oil downward. So the *Spider*, flaming, hurled himself toward the scene of battle.

Wentworth turned the robot's head and peered at the traffic, spotted a bus from which the passengers fled in terror, and suddenly he saw how he could attack the robots! Wentworth lunged toward the bus, pointing a gun finger at the driver.

"Drive down Fifth!" he shouted, "or you die!"

Left-handed, Wentworth reached out to one of the light standards that rose on each side of the avenue. A single wrenching heave, and the iron post snapped off in his hand. The next instant, he had thrown himself prone atop the bus. He dangled a hand to point into the cab, and the truck lurched forward beneath him. Grimly, then, Wentworth straightened atop the bus, while it roared down the avenue.

He could see the robots more clearly now. They were passing Forty-first Street. It would be a close thing whether the robots or Wentworth reached Forty-Second Street first.

"Faster!" Wentworth shouted. "Faster! Pass the robots on the left! And do not be afraid. *I am the Spider!*"

His voice boomed hollowly down the street, and it seemed to him that after that the bus was driven more positively, more steadily.

At the last moment, two of the robots understood and tried to dodge aside, but Wentworth was ready! The iron post whirled like a polo mallet and crashed against the helmet of the foremost giant. There was a hollow clang, and the shock of the impact ran along the iron club . . . and the helmet was driven in as if it were no more than papier-mache! A shout of triumph burst from Wentworth's lips again, and he swung the war club a second time before the bus rushed past in that fierce charge.

"Turn!" Wentworth shouted. "Turn the bus and charge again!"

He twisted about to peer backward. Three of the robots were down after his headlong charge, but it was apparent one of them had only been overturned. Already, with stiff movements, it was climbing to its feet again. Wentworth was almost unseated as the bus whipped around a corner and headed for Madison Avenue. He set the robot legs more tightly about the truck body and braced himself for the next curve.

When the bus rounded back into Fifth Avenue, Wentworth saw that a line of blue clad police was advancing cautiously toward the robots. Guns were blasting futilely in their fists, and Wentworth could not determine whether they also carried flame bombs. It was a vain gesture they were trying if they carried any lesser arms, but Wentworth thrilled to the courage of the men advancing in the face of certain death. He saw the Iron Man wade toward them, deliberately crush one of the helpless police underfoot! A scooping hand picked up another and dangled him, screaming in mid-air!

"Faster!" Wentworth shouted. "Straight for that big one!"

The engine of the bus strained mightily—and then Wentworth saw what defense the robots would use against him! Two of them had caught up the steel giants he had slain, and held them poised above their heads! Too late, Wentworth recognized the peril and tried to shout a warning to the driver. He whirled the massive club about his head and let it fly straight at the nearest of the enemy! It struck solidly, and he saw the armor plate of the robot buckle inward at the moment it launched its awful missile! That robot, hurtling through the air, did not fly true. It struck in the path of the bus and Wentworth gripped hard with both hands to withstand the shock. An instant later, the bus struck. Its rear wheels lifted high into the air and, at the same instant, the second hurled robot crashed against it!

The double impact jarred Wentworth savagely against the sides of his steel prison. His head, inside the crash helmet, swam dizzily, but his hand-hold was not jarred loose. He sat through a long moment atop the wreckage of the bus and saw three of the remaining robots stride toward him. With a gasp of thankfulness, he saw that his club had penetrated the chest of the third victim. It lay flat upon its back, with the steel post jutting from it like a spear. But the Iron Man himself still dangled the policeman from his hand. As Wentworth shook himself free of the lethargy of shock, he saw the Iron Man clamp another hand on the helpless policeman's head and . . . and *pull*!

His senses still reeling, he hoisted the robot to its feet just as the robots charged upon him! Somehow, Wentworth floundered aside from that first attack. Three strides took him to another light standard and he wrenched it loose and whirled it fiercely about his head!

As he slashed down once more, a police car screamed around the corner behind the robots. Wentworth saw something that glittered sail through the air, something that flapped a thin trailer of flame behind it—and then the object struck the rearmost robot and flames splashed over the steel armor!

Laughter pumped from Wentworth's lips, the thin and mocking laughter of the *Spider*. Two other robots remained. One of them turned upon the police car, and it lashed out with a kick of its tremendous foot. There were screams from the car, and then the machine was overturned. An instant later, the wreckage burst into flames.

But Wentworth was once more in motion. The iron club slashed through the air and caught the robot across the back of the helmet. The casque split like a ripe melon and the robot pitched to the street. The remaining robot wheeled and began to retreat! For an instant, Wentworth hesitated, then he sprang toward the wreckage of the police car. With a swift surge of power, he set the machine right side up again, saw two men wrench themselves free and rush to safety.

The two robots that remained stood side by side before the entrance of the library. As Wentworth marched toward them, hands aswing at his side, he saw the Iron Man stoop toward one of the great stone lions before the library! Before Wentworth guessed his purpose, the lion was hurled at him!

It was the handicap of the robot monsters that they could not move swiftly. Wentworth pivoted, took a long step to the side, and the granite lion struck the pavement and shattered like a bomb. A huge fragment smashed against the left knee of Wentworth's robot and knocked the leg out from under him. Outflung hands caught Wentworth as he went down, and he was upon his feet before the two robots could destroy him. But when he moved forward the left leg dragged. Yet, as the smaller robot tried to wrench the other lion loose, Wentworth was upon it!

Wentworth's mechanical hands seized upon one arm of the robot, and he began to twist! For an instant, the other strained fiercely, then it lifted the finger gun and blasted at the glass eyes of Wentworth's robot! The bullet did not penetrate, but the glass frosted over. Wentworth did not change his stance, but kept up the inexorable twisting. He heard a shriek of sirens and guessed that a new squad of bomb-throwers had come. A blow on the side of the helmet jarred him to his spine, and he twisted the robot head to see the Iron Man himself.

It was a smashing downblow of the fist that had struck on the helmet. The seams of it had started to separate under that impact, and Wentworth knew that another would drive the metal into his skull! A shout of defiance lifted to Wentworth's lips. He flung all the power of his robot into a final wrench on the metal arm of the other, and swung toward the Iron Man!

The Iron Man staggered backward and the second blow miscarried. There was a shriek of tortured metal, and Wentworth found that he had torn loose the steel arm of the robot! It was the monster's fall that had driven the Iron Man backward!

Once more, the laughter of the *Spider* rang through the street! He lifted the steel arm like a club and struck downward. In the wreckage of the robot at his feet, nothing stirred and he lifted his head then toward the Iron Man himself! The Iron Man was fleeing!

Grimly, Wentworth pursued. He fought the crippled mechanism of his robot, saw a flaming bottle-bomb sail past just in front of him! What the devil—couldn't the police see he was fighting their battle for them?

"Fools!" he cried, "I am your friend!" His voice beat back on his own ears, but did not sound outside the steel casque. During the fight, the speech mechanism had been smashed! And the Iron Man already was turning the corner a half block away!

Wentworth drove the robot into a run—a killing task. Each stride drove the steel feet crackling into the pavement; each shortened stride of the left leg almost threw him, but he persisted. He felt warmth upon his back and knew that a flame-bomb must have burst there. His clenching teeth bit out curses, but he drove on violently, rounded the corner.

He stopped short then, staring in frustrated anger. The shell of the Iron Man lay prostrate upon the pavement—but the master criminal had fled!

Dimly, behind him, Wentworth heard the triumphant shout of the police and he felt the minor shock of another flame-bomb bursting against his back!

Blindly, Wentworth swung about. Without hesitation, he strode toward the high door of an office building on his right, and crashed through the metal framework with a single stride.

Swiftly, Wentworth's eyes swept over the interior. Double bronze doors opened into a bank entrance. He reached the doors, tore them open, and stumbled in and shut them. He eased the robot to a squatting position against the doors. He could count on its enormous weight to hold them shut for a few moments. He reached out then for the fastenings of the helmet.

They were hot to the touch, scorched his fingers, but finally drove the helmet free. In the same instant, he freed himself from the straps that held him and hurled himself head-foremost from the imprisoning oven of the armor! He struck the floor on his shoulders, came tumbling to his feet. Somewhere near him, glass crashed and he heard the heavy hammer of police guns, closer.

The *Spider* darted along the wall, raced for the rear door that he knew must open into a hall. He made it just ahead of the police who were racing to shut that exit. He plunged down cellar steps. The black cape kited out from his shoulders.

It was a work of minutes to find a way out of the cellar, to dart into a side street. Even so, he was only moments ahead of the police as he commandeered a taxi whose driver gaped in awe, ten yards away. Wentworth ground the accelerator to the floor and whipped about in a violent U-turn. He was flashing past the corner before the police could organize, and he had gained three blocks before he heard the first yelp of the sirens!

Wentworth knew where he was going, but there was a desperate need for haste. His only chance of proving what he knew to be a fact was to catch the Iron Man before he had the opportunity to remove the traces of his activity. And the police would give him so little time; this taxi was so damnably slow.

When presently he whirled toward the East River, sharp laughter burst from his lips. There was the wall about the Drexler home and there, just turning in through the gate, was a fast-driven sedan! It was too dark for Wentworth to see the man who drove it, but he fought another fraction of speed from the taxi and headed for the fast-closing gates. He caught them an instant before they locked, ripped one entirely free from its hinges. Ahead of him, the sedan was sliding into the garage. Those doors were swifter. They had slid into place before Wentworth could reach them, but he did not hesitate.

In an instant, he had leaped from the driver's seat and was racing, not toward the garage, but toward the house itself! His shoulder drove inward an ancient door, and he reeled across the room, to the stairs that led to the basement!

He cleared the basement stairs in two long leaps, cut toward the steel door that closed off the wine cellar. He checked there for an instant to manipulate the lock, and then he swung it wide. He flicked on the light in the wine cellar—and out of the darkness, a robot reached for him!

Blinded though Wentworth was by the instantaneous flash of the lights, he caught a glimpse of that steel-taloned hand as it streaked toward his feet! Wentworth sprang convulsively into the air, felt the jerk as the talons bit into the tail of his cape, and then he was hurtling through the air, toward the robot.

Wentworth had no hope of knocking the robot off of his feet, but for the *Spider,* police hard on his heels, there could be no retreat. There was only one way, and that was forward! His left arm circled the neck of the robot, he flung his legs high and went over the shoulder of the steel monster to land lightly on his feet in the middle of the wine cellar!

In the same instant, Wentworth wrenched out his automatics, but he did not turn them upon the robot, which was turning to attack him. He knew too well the uselessness of that process. Instead, he pivoted slowly on his heel and his bullets sped true. Each one knocked out the spigot of a wine barrel! In an instant, the ground was drinking in wines.

It took only an instant, and then Wentworth was forced to leap from the path of the robot. A huge foot had lifted to crush him, and a steel fist swung viciously at his head. The fist missed and swept on to bash in the front of a hogshead. There was an instant, eager gush of red wine and Wentworth leaped warily to crouch close against a stone wall in the protection of another wine tun.

Overhead, Wentworth caught the heavy pound of feet and knew that the police already were charging into the house. God, he had so little time! Even now, he was certain to be trapped when the police rushed to the wine cellar. He shifted again and the groping robot crushed another wine tun, released a fresh flood of liquor over the floor.

With a taunting laugh, Wentworth leaped into clear view of the robot. His guns were sheathed now, and the robot turned heavily to face him. It took a long stride toward Wentworth and, in the same instant, the *Spider* sprang into the air. His upreaching hands grasped the asbestos-covered steam pipe well up toward the ceiling, and as he swung there, the robot uttered a muffled shout and reached for him with fiercely powerful hands! At the same instant, Wentworth heard the door at the head of the wine cellar steps wrenched open, and the quick shouts of the police!

There was no time, no time at all. Wentworth ripped an automatic from beneath his arm and blasted lead upward at the ceiling. The light went out in the same instant. There were crazy shouts behind him, then the brilliant beams of flashlights cut the darkness.

To the men grouped on the stairs; to Nita, who stood in helpless terror there beside Kirkpatrick, they showed a curious sight! Wentworth was dangling by one hand from the steam pipes and, as the robot reached for him, he grabbed into the darkness over his head and then stabbed that hand toward the robot! Only Nita saw what he was doing, and a gasp tore at her throat. She saw the black electric wire in his hand, and guessed that the single bullet he had fired had cut that wire in half!

So much she saw, and then there was a blinding flash of blue-white light as the naked tip of the electric wire ground against the steel armor of the robot. Its feet were knee-deep in wine, a perfect ground. There was that moment of intense illumination, and when it was blotted out, the glare of the flashlights were dark by comparison. The robot seemed to leap clear of the earth, and then crash backward into the flood of wine. For a moment longer, the *Spider* clung to his high perch and then he, too, dropped into the knee-deep wine, harmless now that the broken wire no longer touched the steel robot.

Kirkpatrick was half-way down the stairs. "All right, *Spider*," he said quietly, "get your hands up!"

Before Kirkpatrick could protest, Wentworth had stooped. With a few deft movements, he loosened the helmet of the robot, and dragged the dead operator into sight. His face was distorted, but Nita looked at it in amazement, even while she was tortured with the certainty of Dick's capture. She had never seen the man.

"A stranger to most of you, eh, gentlemen?" the *Spider* murmured. "But you know him, Kirkpatrick, and you, Drexler. How about Drexler, senior, there, do you know him?"

Nita was aware then that the two men had moved up behind her, were crowding past her to the stairs, but it was Kirkpatrick who answered.

"Louis Montose," he said in amazement. "But he can't be the Iron Man!"

"You're right," Wentworth said quietly. "He was just a minor crook, who worked for the real villain of the piece, who stands just beside you on the steps!"

Kirkpatrick glanced to his right, and uttered a disgusted exclamation. "Drexler cannot be guilty!" he said sharply. "I have checked him on every point, and he is in the clear!"

Wentworth smiled, "It is queer what things a man can achieve when he has been a weakling all his life," he said softly, but still in the mocking intonation of the *Spider*. "It is queer what dreams that sort of life can breed, dreams of *power*! Look to your left, Kirkpatrick, and tell me . . . what are those red objects in the ears of Drexler's father?"

Kirkpatrick said, emptily, "Drexler's father? Now, *I* know you are mad, *Spider*! A weak old man. . . ."

"A weakling all his life," Wentworth said softly, "but within a robot, his strength becomes that of a giant. A touch of a lever and he can smash in a building. *What is that in his ears?*"

Kirkpatrick said, in bewilderment, "Why he has some of those rubber stopples used to keep water out of the ears in swimming!"

"Or to reduce the incredible racket those robots make, when you're inside one!" Wentworth threw in. "Also, if you will take off the hat of Drexler senior, you will see there the marks made by the straps of a crash helmet such as this dead man wears!"

Old Drexler's face was suddenly fiery red. He twisted toward his son. "You turned me in, you mealy-mouthed coward!" he said shrilly. "I was doing all this for you, to make you the greatest man in the world, something I never had the strength to do! You—"

Old Drexler whipped up his cane and made a violent swing with it. It just missed his son's head and the old man lost his footing and pitched headlong down the steps! His foot caught in the open work of the stairs and he lay there, head down, hands upthrown and dangling, just touching the wine that was red as spilled blood.

"No, don't touch him!" Wentworth said softly. "He's already dead, as you can see from the blueness of his face. Heart failure, I should judge." As he spoke, he bent forward and pressed the base of his cigarette lighter against the chilling flesh of the dead man's forehead, and when he straightened there glowed there the crimson seal of the *Spider*!

Inarticulate rage burst in a roar from Drexler's throat. "You killed him, you trickster!" he shouted, and leaped down the steps!

Kirkpatrick shouted, tried to stop Drexler, but it was too late. Kirkpatrick fired a single shot that went wide of its mark, and then the *Spider* was fleeing across the cellar with Drexler raging behind him. They reached an alcove in the left-hand wall, and Kirkpatrick shouted fiercely.

"Down here, men!" he cried. "And careful! We've trapped the *Spider* too often to have him get away now! I want every man down here, gun in hand!"

Kirkpatrick himself stood on the steps, with his gun poised while the men in police blue filed past him. Nita twisted her hands. There was no sound in the cellar save for the splashing of the policemen as they moved to close the mouth of that alcove. Nita looked desperately about. She could pull her gun and, perhaps, hold them all captive while Dick made his get-away. She caught the small automatic from her bodice . . . and a hand clamped rigidly down on her wrist.

"Not this time, Nita," said Kirkpatrick, sternly. "I know he saved your life, but he is a criminal!"

After he had spoken, there was deep silence in the cellar. There was a slow dripping of wine somewhere in the darkness, and that was all. Kirkpatrick lifted his voice.

"All right, *Spider*," he added quietly. "This time you're trapped. Come out!"

Silence through a long moment, and then the softly mocking laughter of the *Spider*! "*Come and get me, Kirkpatrick!*"

Kirkpatrick's flashlight, like every other one in that tight cellar, was focused on the entrance to the alcove, and now Kirkpatrick moved steadily sideways. His light moved with him, and he shifted his revolver to be ready.

Nita lifted her face, her eyes closed, and her lips moved silently. It was when she opened her eyes that she started violently. Afterward, she looked down at the wine that lapped around her knees. She began to plead brokenly with Kirkpatrick.

"He's such a brave man, Stanley," she said. "You would never have caught the Iron Man without him. You know that! Let me go! You can't do this to the *Spider!*"

She threshed her legs in the wine, and the policeman grunted and tightened his hold. Kirkpatrick did not answer. He suddenly made a wide leap sideways, and his light stabbed into the alcove, his gun raked out. . . . She peered into the recess in the wall. There was a man there in a black cape and hat. His hands were stretched high above his head, as if in abject surrender. But Nita's eyes saw that a light length of line held them upward, was looped over the steam pipe.

"So you surrender, *Spider!*" Kirkpatrick's voice was full of relief. "That was wise of you!"

He moved toward the motionless figure in the recess, and suddenly the light, mocking laughter of the *Spider* filled all the basement! It seemed to come from everywhere at once, but Nita's keen eyes placed it at once. She saw Wentworth slip from the overhead steam pipe along which he had crawled while the flashlights focused beams beneath him, saw him stand upright on the steps a moment before he laughed.

"Why no, Kirkpatrick," the *Spider* called gently. "I never surrender. And don't hurt poor Frank Drexler, who was forced to don my robes for a moment. He is quite innocent!"

Finally, Kirkpatrick spotted the source of that voice. He whirled, with his gun raking out, but the light laughter sounded again. There was a flicker of movement at the head of the steps, and then the steel door clanged shut, and a lock snapped into place. Kirkpatrick fired a single shot, and it rang like a gong against the closed door. And laughter still sounded in the cellar from which the Master of Men had escaped.

But it was Nita laughing. "Isn't that too bad, Stanley," she said softly. "I do believe the *Spider* has 'disappeared' once more!"

# DEATH REIGN OF THE

# VAMPIRE KING

# CHAPTER ONE
# THE BAT MAN

T WENTY MEN WITH SHOTGUNS patrolled the wide lawns of Robert Latham's mansion, crouching in the black shadows of night. Their hands were tightly clamped on their weapons and they cringed close against the walls of the house. They watched the moon-drenched sky fearfully.

From the dense shadow of a shrub a score of yards away, another man spied upon them. He was a hunched, grotesque figure and his long black cape made his body blend with the darkness. He held no weapon, but beside him was a large bird cage. On his lips was a thin, tight smile. . . .

Those guards feared different terror, but if they could have seen this lurking man, they would have fled screaming in panic behind the protecting walls of the house. Not even their ready shotguns would have reassured them. For they were men of the Underworld and he who watched preyed upon their kind. He slew and left a mocking vermilion seal upon their foreheads to show that full vengeance had been exacted by the champion of oppressed humanity—nemesis of all criminals—the *Spider*!

The smile lingered on the *Spider's* lips as he surveyed the mansion, blazing with a hundred lights, and watched the men move about furtively with their deadly guns. He was determined to enter that house, though he knew that discovery within those walls would mean certain death at the hands of these men whose fear of him was matched only by their hatred and their desire to kill him. Yes, his entrance must be secret . . . for a while.

The *Spider* rose slowly to his full, bowed height, lifted the cage at arm's length and removed its bottom. For perhaps thirty seconds, nothing happened at all; then a black form dropped from the cage, spread leathery wings and flitted off erratically into the night. Then another and another, until six bats had taken wing. The *Spider* laid the cage gently on the earth, crouched again into the shadows to wait. The lights of the mansion would attract insects and those bats fed on small, flying vermin of the night. When the bats flitted between those men and the sky, the panic of terror would reign. . . .

The *Spider* nodded. They had reason for fright, these men. Within two weeks, a dozen race-horses and four men who frequented the tracks had been killed by the bite of vampire bats!

Useless to say that vampire bats never had been known outside of the tropics; useless to state that they never killed. There could be no mistaking the type of wound, the tiny area of skin peeled away by the keen, painless teeth of the bat. But the bodies of the victims had not been drained of blood. They died instead . . . of *poison!*

The *Spider* smiled coldly in the darkness. His bats were not poisonous—not even vampires—but the men who watched the home of Robert Latham would not know that. . . .

Abruptly, one of the armed guards cried out shrilly. There was more than warning in the shout. There was panic, fear and dread. His shotgun belched flame and lead upward into the darkness; then another man also screamed and fired. A ground-floor door flung open in the mansion and the men streaked toward it, shotguns bellowing.

This was the moment for which the *Spider* had played. He wrapped his cape tightly about his body lest its flapping betray him and ran fleetly forward. When he burst into the moonlit ring about the house, he was shouting more loudly than any of the other panic-stricken men. He went in through the door with the rest, mistaken momentarily for one of their number.

Swiftly, he backed across the room in which the terrified guards were huddling. A man turned toward him:

"Geez!" he gulped, "the boss was right. Them bats—"

So much he said before he realized that this sinister, caped man with the hunched shoulders—with cold eyes gleaming beneath the wide brim of a black slouch hat—was no comrade of his. His mouth opened to cry out. His eyes stretched and terror glanced across his countenance. The *Spider* was recognized!

If this man shouted aloud the *Spider's* name, a dozen shotguns would blaze at once. These men feared him, but like cornered rats, they would shoot him down. . . .

The *Spider's* action was as swift as his thought. His left hand shot forward, the first two fingers rigidly pointed. They struck basic nerve centers in the throat. With the cry unuttered on his lips, the man collapsed. In two leaping strides, the *Spider* crossed the room, plunged through a door. The other men, staring fearfully out into the darkness, while the last of the guards still raced for cover from the threat of those harmless bats the *Spider* had loosed, saw nothing, knew nothing of the more frightful menace among them—until they turned and saw their companion on the floor. Even then they did not understand, but cried that bats—the vampire bats—had slain again!

Within the house, crouching now in the shadow of a stairway, the *Spider* heard that cry with tightened lips that knew no mirth. If the gods were good, he would find here tonight an answer to this mystery of vampire bats whose bite was fatal. Newspapers, even reputable scientists, talked of a new species of bat carrying the poisoned fangs of snakes. . . .

The *Spider,* waiting there in the darkness for the excitement to die, shook his head slowly. There had been other such foolish theories as this whenever the criminal great turned their hands to slaughter. In his many battles to protect mankind against them, the *Spider* had unearthed drugs that drove men mad, and others that made them docile as dogs; explosives which performed the impossible by absolutely disintegrating whatever they blasted; there had been a gas that destroyed steel as termites do wooden beams. . . . And now there were vampire bats which killed like snakes! No, he did not believe in such vermin. There was something far more menacing behind this nascent terror than a new species of bat.

The *Spider* was ever alert for new outbreaks of crime. It was only by constant vigilance that he had averted, a dozen times over, the desire of the Underworld to rule over the nation; the slaughter of untold thousands. . . . It had seemed to him now that perhaps some ring of race-track gamblers had conceived a new, horrible weapon and was using it, at present, to destroy personal enemies and to frame races. If that were true, it was no more than a routine job for the police; but suppose . . . suppose the criminals behind this strange new terror turned their thoughts to nation-wide conquest!

The *Spider* had seen many overwhelming reigns of terror begin thus trivially. He had learned the wisdom of striking quickly and terribly. So he had come tonight to determine what Latham knew of this strange, new, killing instrument.

The turmoil below was quieting. Soon the patrol of the grounds would begin again. The *Spider* had no fear that the man he had struck would regain consciousness and betray him. The jiu-jitsu blow would be effective for at least an hour and by that time, the *Spider's* presence would be known to them all!

A slow smile crossed the *Spider's* straight lips as he crept stealthily up the service stairway of the mansion toward the second floor sitting room, where, he knew, Latham kept his watch. There was a shotgun guard in the wide, upper hall. The *Spider* drew a length of silken line from a pocket of his cape, rope less than the diameter of a pencil which yet had a tensile strength of seven hundred pounds! The *Spider's* web, police had dubbed it. Well, he would use it now to catch a fly!

Carefully, he looped the cord, carefully tossed it. The unwary guard felt gossamer brush his throat; then he was yanked off his feet, his shotgun clattering to the floor. The *Spider* was beside him in an instant and once more he struck swiftly to render the man unconscious. He freed his line and, in two long bounds, was at the door behind which Latham lurked with his bodyguard.

That noise of clattering gun had been intentional. After its sound, all was utter, waiting silence. Then, abruptly, the door the *Spider* watched snapped open. A man with a gun held rigidly ready sprang out into the hall. He grated a curse as he saw the prostrate guard, moved toward him cautiously. The *Spider's* fist lashed out, caught him hard on the jaw. While the man still wavered on his feet, the *Spider* had yanked away his gun, was through the open door, had closed it, and the automatic was covering the room.

"Ah, Latham," said the *Spider,* his voice flat, mocking. "Let me compliment you on the efficacy of your guard!" He laughed softly, and that sound, too, was taunting, blood-chilling.

There were three men in the room and they sat—one of them half-stood—in attitudes of frozen fright. Only Latham's gun was in sight, upon a small, nearby taboret which also held whiskey and a soda siphon. He held a glass in his right hand and, the first to recover, he began presently to slosh the liquid about in it slowly. He was spare, but full-faced and distinguished with his smooth, brown hair which had whitened upon the temples.

"Damn glad you've come, *Spider,*" Latham said calmly. "Perhaps you know some way of stopping these damned bats."

"Just keep on drinking, Latham," the *Spider* said. "I wouldn't think of interrupting your pleasure."

The *Spider's* voice was gentle, but the grim, gaunt face with its lipless mouth and harsh beak of a nose was threat enough. Latham gazed at the sallow face, the hunch-backed figure in black cape that crouched behind the ready gun and his pale face became grayish. His glass moved jerkily away from the taboret and he touched tongue to his dry lips.

"Good God, *Spider,*" he said hoarsely, "I . . . I was just going to set my glass down."

"Certainly, Latham," the *Spider* agreed. "Tonight, Latham, you have no reason to fear me. I simply want to ask you some questions. . . . *Whose stable shelters the vampire bats?*"

Latham contrived a smile. "The guard I've got here tonight should prove to you that mine doesn't, *Spider,*" he said anxiously. "Hell, my men just drove away one attack . . . !"

The *Spider's* lipless mouth parted a little, but he did not explain the bats. Abruptly, tension whipped his body. He half-crouched and his gun jutted toward Latham's chest. Pounding footsteps were racing down the hall. In the darkness outside, a man screamed—a cry that choked off in mid-shout. With the suddenness of lightning, the lights clicked out and somewhere, wailing, quavering through the night, came a mourning note that was like the moan of a tortured soul in hell.

"Oh God!" screamed Latham. "It's the Bat Man!"

✪ ✪ ✪

For fifteen seconds after the first beat of footsteps, the *Spider* had suspected a trick. Perhaps someone knew the method of quickly reviving the man he had knocked out. There was a way. . . . But the sound of Latham's voice, the inarticulate fright in the cries of the others, convinced him that their terror was genuine.

The Bat Man . . . no need to inquire what they meant. He had suspected human agency behind the attacks of the vampire bats. These men knew and they called the master of the winged killers . . . *the Bat Man!*

The *Spider* waited tensely for this oddly-named man to show himself. His guns were ready. . . . Instantly, instinctively, the *Spider* had sprung from the spot he stood when the lights went out, but no one moved to attack him. There was a wild stampede of feet toward the door. Latham cried out.

"Keep that door shut, damn you!" His gun streaked flame out of the darkness. Near the door, a man groaned and thumped to the floor.

"Keep away from that door!" Latham shouted again, his panic barely under control. "I'll shoot the first man who touches it."

The *Spider* realized abruptly that the running in the hall had ceased. Either the man had seen the bodies there and fled in terror, or . . . *or the bats already had struck!* The *Spider* crouched to the floor, so that he caught the gray light of the window across the room—so that he could watch movement about him. No one budged. A man whimpered off to his right near the door and the one who had fallen at Latham's shot breathed with rattling breath. Latham had aimed well. He was cursing monotonously.

"You see, *Spider*," he whispered. "You see, he's after me. The Bat Man . . . !"

His voice was drowned in the bellowing blasts of shotguns just outside the window. There was a tearing, ripping sound of wire screen and the *Spider* saw against the gray square of the window the fluttering form of a bat!

"Cover your throat, Latham!" he shouted. "A bat just came in the window."

Even as he cried the warning, a half-dozen more of the black, loathsome things dodged in through the torn screening. A shuddering moan came from Latham.

"You can't tell when they bite," he whimpered. "You can't tell. Oh, God . . . !"

With his teeth set, the *Spider* whipped out his fountain pen flashlight, squeezed out its widely diffused ray. He saw a dodging, leathery-winged beast within inches of his face. The bat flicked away, but the *Spider's* bullet was swifter than its flight. The creature was torn to bits by forty-five caliber lead and the *Spider* pressed back against the wall, watching, watching. . . .

Abruptly, he became aware of two things. Within the house, all was silence. And there, but dimly heard, came a shrill, monstrous squeaking, as if a giant bat called to its kind!

It sounded again and black bat forms fluttered through the beam of the *Spider's* light, whirled toward the window and were gone.

One more of the creatures the *Spider* smashed with lead; then he was alone with the thumping of his heart, the reverberations of his shot. He lifted his gloved left hand and touched away the moisture that had oozed out through his facial make-up. He acknowledged to himself that in those few seconds, crouched against the wall, he had known the cold touch of fear. Bats with poisoned teeth . . . ! He fought down a shudder.

On swift, silent feet, the *Spider* crossed the room and peered out of the window. The entire mansion was dark and on the grounds nothing visible moved. The squeaking which clearly had recalled the bats had now ceased and far off, toward where the moon sank, a dog howled. Upward, there was nothing except the blackness of the sky. . . . Suddenly, the *Spider's* teeth shut upon a curse, his guns swirled upward. But he knew that shooting would be vain. His eyes were narrow as he stared. . . .

No bat ever had that wing spread, nor flew with that gliding, motionless ease. And yet, sliding effortlessly across the starry sky, the *Spider* beheld a creature *with bat wings fully ten feet across!*

Even as he watched, the thing steeped its angle of dive and sped out of sight over the close, clustering trees that reached upward toward the sky. For long moments after it was gone, the *Spider* crouched there at the window. He was aware of his quickened breath, of the aching in the forearm of the hand that held his gun.

"It was out of range," he whispered to himself. "Out of range!"

He jerked his head angrily, reached up a gloved hand to shut the window, then turned back to the room. Almost the *Spider* doubted his eyesight. No, no, he had *seen* the thing. His eyes had been too well trained in a thousand situations where life and liberty, a thousand lives, hinged on the accuracy of his vision. Breath hissed noisily out between his teeth. Latham had cried, "The Bat Man!" Was it possible that what he had seen was a . . . a man with wings!

The *Spider* spread the light of his torch over the floor. There was no doubt in his own mind of what he would find, but the horror written largely on Latham's twisted features tightened his own grim mouth. Latham had covered his throat, so the bat had fastened to his hand. He was dead.

Slowly, the *Spider* turned the beam upon the other two in the room. They were dead, too. He found the instrument which had smashed out the screening of the window—a spear with a special collar of light, steel blades which extended fully nine inches all around the haft. It must have been hurled with terrific force, for the screening was double, a heavier screen mesh outside the usual lighter wire.

The *Spider* made his way swiftly through the darkened house, avoiding the bodies of men that were everywhere scattered in distorted, tortured attitudes of death. There was no use in carrying the bats he had killed with him. He had recognized them as vampires of an ordinary variety, *Desmodus rufus*, a tiny creature whose body was no more than three inches long, with a wing spread of only seven inches. He could recognize it by its reddish-brown body and the black wings with edging of white. The heavy bullet had smashed the animal too badly for him to examine its teeth. However, that was scarcely necessary. The *Spider* was terribly sure now that human agency was behind the murders.

At the outer door, the *Spider* paused for a moment, his eyes dark and narrow. Twenty-seven men had died here tonight by the bite of non-poisonous vampire bats. He himself had seen the attack. A cold fury swept him as he realized what havoc these same tactics would wreak if they were used against the populace at large. So far, the Bat Man had confined his attacks to a few gamblers, also creatures of the half-world like the bats. The *Spider* could not mourn their loss to humanity—but suppose the man went power-mad? Suppose the agency behind these attacks turned loose his murderous creatures upon cities, upon entire countrysides . . . ?

The *Spider's* lean, taut-skinned face set in determined lines. It was his job to keep such things from coming to pass!

His gun was in his hand as he stepped outside the door. A blazing light slapped the *Spider* in the face. From the close-pressing shrubbery, a man called hoarsely:

"Hands up, it's the law!" The voice broke off in a gasp. "Good God, it's—the *Spider*! The *Spider* sent them bats!"

"That's the man," broke in a girl's voice, a deep, emotional voice.

Then another man, shrill, almost hysterical with his discovery. "It's the *Spider*! The *Spider*!"

# CHAPTER TWO
# "DEATH TO THE SPIDER!"

THE *SPIDER'S* GUN was ready at his side when the police behind the light challenged, but he did not fire. The *Spider* did not fight the law. He might go outside it in a thousand ways, kill, burglarize, kidnap. . . . But when he did, it was to smash criminals, to assist the law in its great work, because the police and other enforcement officers were hedged in by too many restrictions to operate effectively. He would die before he would fire upon one of the law's men.

Yet capture meant death for the *Spider*; it meant a revelation of his real identity and disgrace for his comrades and the one woman in the world who knew his secrets, Nita van Sloan. It meant even more than that. It meant that the law, for all its myriad successes against petty, customary criminals, would be without a means of combating this new terror that had arisen from the Underworld: the Bat Man, whose existence as yet they did not even suspect!

The thoughts flashed through the *Spider's* brain in the second he closed the door and felt the assault of the light. Useless to attempt a retreat. Before he could open the door and duck from sight, a dozen bullets would smash through his body. There were at least twenty men in the shrubbery out there. He could hear their rustling, their murmur as his identity was shouted hoarsely into the night. He might shoot out the light. It would give him an instant. But the night was scarcely dark enough to hope that he could flee unseen.

The *Spider* shrugged his shoulders, dropped the gun and raised his hands shoulder-high.

"I'm the *Spider,* all right," he admitted calmly, "but you'll have to hunt someone else to take the blame for the bats. I thought Latham was the man, but I was wrong."

Two men were coming out from behind the light now, walking wide lest they come between the guns and the *Spider.*

"What do you mean, wrong?" asked the hoarse voice that first had spoken.

The *Spider* allowed his straight lipless mouth to twist into a smile. "You'll find out when you take a look inside."

The two men were close now. Each had fastened a handcuff to one of his own wrists and held the other cuff open, ready for the *Spider's* hand. His eyes turned cold as he saw that. He could escape from handcuffs that were fastened between his own wrists, but if he were chained to two men . . . !

"We'll look into that," the leader growled. "But it'll take more than your say-so to clear you. This young lady seen you comin' in here with a cage. . . . Stand still. There's ten guns on you!"

The *Spider* had started uncontrollably at the information that he had been seen entering the grounds. Why, this was utterly damning! How could he convince these men that the bats he had let escape had been harmless?

"Who accuses me?" he demanded sharply. "Let me see the one who accuses me?"

The leader's voice dropped a note. "Never mind that now. You keep out of sight, young lady. He's up to some trick."

The *Spider* frowned, his heart thudding in his breast. He had had no definite plan in mind, but it was apparent these men were alert for any trick. They would be eager to kill. . . . The two men approaching him, both of them broad, tall farmers, were within a foot or two with their ready handcuffs. They were his only chance, the *Spider* knew. He must somehow use these two to escape, for once those handcuffs closed about his wrists. . . . The men behind the light were watching keenly, for they understood the situation as well as he.

❂ ❂ ❂

The *Spider* extended his left arm toward the man who approached from that direction, smiled at him with a thin parting of his lips.

"Come on, come on," he said impatiently. "What are you waiting for? You couldn't be afraid of the *Spider*?"

The man's young face flushed a little. He braced himself visibly and, holding the handcuff in both hands, stepped within reach of the outstretched hand, slapped the shackle about the wrist and fumbled to close the cuff. It was the very instant for which the *Spider* had waited. By offering his wrist so placidly for the bracelet, he had partially disarmed the man. But, even more important, he had obtained a hold on one of the men before the other had quite reached a place where he could act.

While the man still fumbled with the cuff, the *Spider's* fingers closed upon the chain between the shackles and, without a visible preliminary tensing of muscles—without a change in his face—he yanked savagely upon the bracelets. In his timidity, the man was leaning forward off-balance and the jerk pulled him directly in front of the *Spider,* between him and the guns that threatened.

The second man leaped forward and the *Spider* slammed his captive against him, slipped his wrist from the still-unfastened cuff and skipped backward through the door into the house. An excited man fired a shotgun and one of the struggling pair cried out in pain. The *Spider* heard all that as he slammed and bolted the door, then he raced to a window on the same side of the building.

The law men were already battering on the door. A window had been smashed in and gunshots were pouring death into the building. Guards were racing to surround the mansion. The *Spider* opened his window and waited. A guard started past the casement, paused and stared at it uncertainly, then inched forward. The silken rope snaked out of the darkness, yanked him to the window. A single blow knocked him out and the *Spider* was through the window and away. . . .

Once he was amid the shrubbery and trees, he was safe. Not even his namesake, the spider, could move more soundlessly than he. At the high, iron fence that surrounded the estate, he whistled softly in a weird, minor key. Seconds later, a shadow glided to the opposite side of the fence and a rope ladder, made of the same soft, silken cord, came swinging over. A moment later, he was speeding with that other shadow beside him, toward the hidden lane where he had parked the car.

"Wah! *Sahib!*" whispered the one beside him, "are we mice that we flee from battle?" He spoke in the Hindustani that was native to him.

The *Spider* chuckled. "They are men of the law, Ram Singh, more to be pitied for their stupidity than slain."

The turbaned Hindu, the *Spider's* servant to the death, grunted, but made no other reply. To Ram Singh, all men who opposed his master were game for his swift, keen knives. *Wah!* Mice!

The *Spider* flung into a black, low-slung Daimler sedan and the Hindu leaped to the driver's seat, sent the powerful car almost silently through the woods lane. In the tonneau, the *Spider* dropped his hand to a button beneath the left half of the cushions. The seat slid smoothly forward, turned half about and revealed in its back a closely hung wardrobe. The *Spider* folded upward a mirror about which neon lights instantly glowed. He pulled out a tray filled with the equipment of disguise. . . .

Five minutes later, as the car slid to the concrete highway which skirted the front of Latham's estate, the *Spider*—who was the *Spider* no longer—slid the cleverly contrived wardrobe into place, lounged back against the luxurious upholstery and drew a cigarette from a platinum case. When the police stopped him a hundred yards further on, he leaned forward politely to speak to the sergeant.

"Identify myself?" he said in the rich baritone that was his natural voice. "Oh, decidedly, sergeant!" He drew out a wallet, extracted a card and presented it between two perfectly manicured fingers.

The sergeant scowled at first, then his face cleared. He actually smiled. "A thousand pardons, Mr. Wentworth," he murmured obsequiously. "I've heard of you in New York, working with the cops to stop some of them crooks. Something here might interest you, sir. Them vampire bats killed about twenty men over there. . . ."

Richard Wentworth listened attentively. This was no masquerade, but his true identity. Scion of a wealthy family—its last surviving member—he had long ago pledged himself to the suppression of crime. He had created that other sinister character, the *Spider,* so that the Underworld might be additionally cleansed by a healthy fear.

Richard Wentworth, clubman, sportsman and amateur criminologist, was a friend of Governors and of Presidents, a man eagerly sought after by Commissioners of Police whenever the ugly head of super-crime was lifted. He sat there, his bronzed, strongly chiseled face keenly intelligent as he listened to the sergeant's account of the deaths at Latham's mansion. Finally he nodded gravely, a pleasant smile on his firm lips, his gray-blue eyes merry.

"Thank you, sergeant," he said, "if you will pass me through the gates I would be glad to look over the scene."

It was wasted time, Wentworth—the *Spider*—knew, but it would be suspicious to pass without inquiry. He hurried the inspection as much as possible, on fire with eagerness to pursue his quest. It was pretty well known in police circles that Latham had a tie-up with Red Cullihane, a Philadelphia brewer who in prohibition days had been one of the leading big-shots of the East. Wentworth no longer believed that Latham was connected with the Bat Man, but it was pretty obvious that Latham had been a target for especial animosity. It might well be that Cullihane would next be the target.

After leaving the grounds, he stopped once on the way northward through Maryland to send a night-letter. It began *Ma Cherie* and was addressed to Miss Nita van Sloan, Riverside Towers, New York City. Part of the message said *Dinner Thursday at the Early Quaker*. The rest of it seemed to be lovers' words but actually it bade the woman he loved—his ablest ally in the battle against crime—to hasten to Philadelphia with his speedy Northrup plane and bring with her his chauffeur, Jackson, who was much more than a chauffeur in the plans of the *Spider*.

Then the low, black car of the *Spider* sped northward again. To any one who gazed upon the man in its back seat, he would have seemed a bored member of the class of idle rich. To be sure there was a strength and intelligence about his face and a singular directness of gaze, a confidence of bearing that had nothing to do with a bank account, which might have surprised the onlooker. But, certainly, his face gave no evidence of the grim thoughts that were racing through his mind. . . .

Until now, Wentworth had had little opportunity to consider the events of the evening and now that he reviewed the attack of the bats, he felt a mounting sense of dread. There could be no doubt at all of human agency. Even without the wailing cry which had heralded the attack, the shrill squeaking as of a giant bat which had called the killers home, there was the spear which had smashed through the screening so that the bats would be able to enter and do their assassin's work. Yes, in that one venture, the *Spider* had confirmed his fear that a new menace had arisen for humanity.

Wentworth glanced at his watch, then leaned forward to turn on the radio. There was a news broadcast about now. . . . The announcer's voice came to him with unexpected harshness. There was excitement beneath the calm ordering of carefully enunciated syllables:

"Jack Harkins, ladies and gentlemen, bringing you the extraordinary news of the day. . . ."

Innocuous phrases, but the man's words were fraught with tension, with terror. Harkins had a stimulating voice. He talked in pounding short phrases that seemed to bring the action he described into the very room with his listeners.

"Does the world face another of those overwhelming madman's attacks which have struck terror to our hearts in recent years? May God in His mercy will that it is not so. But it looks as if it is. These winged horrors of the night, the vampire bats, have struck again! Twice tonight, in two widely separated parts of the country, they have struck. And, ladies and gentlemen, *one hundred and ninety-five people are dead!* Think of it, one hundred and ninety-five!"

Wentworth, listening to the hurried, staccato rhythm of the newsman, felt his hands clench in hard white knots. None could have detected the idler in his face now, for it was white and rigid with anger and his blue-gray eyes were almost black with fury. Then what he feared had already come to pass! The Bat Man had not been content with his attack upon Latham. . . .

"At first there seemed to be no danger except to those who were associated with horses in some way. It is a well-known fact that the vampire bat confines itself largely to horses, prefers their blood to most others. But tonight, that hopeful idea was dispelled once and for all, and terribly dispelled. In Centertown, Pennsylvania, the bats flittered down and kissed the throats of lovers in the parks, they tasted of the blood of brave policemen on their beats, brought their poison death to the gay crowd before the motion picture shows. A dozen people were killed in the panic, in the dash to escape, but many, many more were prey to the vicious poisoned teeth of these blood-thirsty little beasts. . . ."

There was more, much more of that sort of thing, all melodramatic, highly-colored and calculated to help the work of the Bat Man, whatever that was, by spreading the terror of the bats. Wentworth shook his head. There was no reason for the *Spider* to visit Centertown. Nothing to be gained by gazing on more bat-slain human beings. He must hasten to Philadelphia, hoping against hope that he had guessed right about the next target of the Bat Man. Abruptly his attention was pulled back to the radio. . . .

"And now, folks, to the most exciting part of the whole thing," the newsman went on. "And something you won't know whether to believe or not. The *Spider* was seen at Latham's place. Yes, sir, the *Spider!* And a girl whose brother was killed a week ago by the bats, says she saw the *Spider carrying a cage full of bats!* Now, what does that mean? Is it possible that the *Spider*. . . ."

With a grated curse, Wentworth shut off the radio and sat rigidly, staring straight ahead of him into the blackness of the night. No need to ask what lay ahead. Once more the nation would go mad and hunt the only man who could save it from the monster who had loosed his flying killers on the people. It would blame the *Spider* and throughout the country would ring the blood-thirsty cry of . . .

"Death to the *Spider!*"

A hard bitterness descended upon Wentworth. Damnable to have the very people for whom he had sacrificed so much—for whom he hourly risked death and disgrace—turn upon him in this way. He should have become accustomed to it by now, he who had served without stint in the face of persecution by law and criminal and civilian, but somehow the thought could still rankle. Not that the *Spider* ever wavered in his devotion to the pledge he had made so long ago. . . .

He caught up the speaking tube which communicated with Ram Singh. "I must be in Philadelphia within the hour," he ordered quietly.

He saw the tensing of the Hindu's broad shoulders, saw the turbaned head bend a little more over the steering wheel and heard the bass thunder of the engine deepen a full tone. The wind whispered past the car, but there was no other indication of its great speed except the occasional whine of tires on a curb. Within the hour. Yes, it was necessary to hurry. Wentworth had not anticipated that the Bat Man would strike again so quickly. Now that he had shown his versatility, there was no reason why he should not attack Red Cullihane, Latham's associate, at once.

Wentworth realized that it was merely his assumption that Cullihane would be attacked, a slim thread of hope. But there was no other clue to follow. It was desperately necessary that he find some more definite lead to this Bat Man immediately. If he could only be on the scene when next the vampires struck, he had a plan. . . .

When Ram Singh drew the powerful Daimler to a halt on a street that paralleled Philadelphia's waterfront, it was not Wentworth who alighted from the car, but a hunched and sinister figure whose very appearance was a threat . . . the *Spider*. The *Spider* knew—it was a part of his self-imposed duty to know—much about Red Cullihane. He knew of his home in the Heights and his gambling salon near the Early Quaker hotel where Wentworth had appointed a meeting with Nita the next evening. Actually it had been Latham who ran the place with Cullihane to provide protection.

Then there was a great, gaunt warehouse upon the hill overlooking the Quaker which was used as a depot for distribution of the Golden Stein beer which Cullihane now manufactured legally. It was this warehouse which Wentworth now approached for here was Cullihane's stronghold and, if he feared attack, it was the place where he would be most likely to barricade himself.

Swiftly, the *Spider* advanced on the building, invisible in the black shadows with which he merged himself, and, from an alley mouth across the street from Cullihane's warehouse, he stood watching. Three minutes passed and a black coupe cruised slowly past, turned a corner beside the warehouse and vanished. Four minutes later, it appeared again and followed the same course. The *Spider's* thinned lips parted a little, showing the white gleam of his teeth. He was right then. Cullihane was frightened. He had taken up his position here and the coupe was a patrol, a sentry on wheels, against attack.

When the coupe had crawled out of sight again, Wentworth darted across the street. . . .

"*Spider!*" It was a woman's voice, high, challenging.

Wentworth did not turn toward the call. It was too old a trick, that crying a name to attract attention, to cause a moment of motionless waiting while deadly lead was poured into a victim. He went flat down on the pavement of the street. The crack of a light automatic sounded strangely loud in the deserted street. The bullet splatted against the bricks of the warehouse. He had a moment to wonder at the attack, then he sprang to his feet. Jumping sideways, as the girl fired again, he charged straight toward her!

Dangerous work this, racing into the muzzle of an automatic, even though it was light in caliber and a woman handled it. But like everything the *Spider* did, it was a maneuver shrewdly planned in his lightning-swift mind. There was no cover for him there in the middle of the street. Within seconds, Cullihane's sentry would arrive at the scene. Only one chance and he took it, charging straight on the gun.

He had two hopes, one that his charge would confuse the girl. The other. . . . With his left arm, he billowed his cape wide to that side. In the darkness, his long cape, which almost swept the ground, would make him a confusing target as it spread out to one side—would make it hard for anyone to judge the position of his body.

The muffling folds of the cape served him in good stead. His charge did not frighten the girl, nor did the booming discharges of his automatic which he fired deliberately wide. But the cloak did the trick. The *Spider* felt two bullets tug at it. The failure of those bullets did what his charge could not. It terrified the girl. While the *Spider* was still twenty feet away, she turned and fled. . . .

Wentworth raced after her, his feet silent while hers beat a panicky tattoo upon the cement. The *Spider's* jaw was tight set. He sprinted at his best pace—and in his university days, Wentworth had broken an intercollegiate record! There was desperate need for haste. Any moment now, that prowling coupe with its two men, undoubtedly heavily armed, would be upon them. And that must not happen. It must not. . . .

The girl twisted her head about as she ran, saw his figure with the cape streaming from broad shoulders as he rapidly overtook her. She screamed, high, piercing sounds of terror. She fired blindly, uselessly behind her . . . and the *Spider* pounced upon her. He knocked the gun arm up, slapped an arm about her waist. He did not check his speed, but lifted her bodily from the ground and sprang toward a doorway a half dozen feet ahead.

Even while he hastened for the shadows that would mean life or death to them, the girl began to struggle. She could not strike with her fists, since her back was toward Wentworth, but she did use her feet. Her heels drummed against his shins. The *Spider* could hear the roar of the engine as the automobile he feared raced to the scene. He heard the squeal of skidding tires. . . . With a vaulting leap, he gained the doorway, thrust the girl into a corner and held her there.

"If you move, you die," he ordered sharply—and realized his mistake. The two men—the coupe which had rushed up the street—was not the patrol at the warehouse. It was a police radio-car with two uniformed men in it. But the *Spider's* action, his order, caught them unaware. They had both jumped from the car, both stood beside it. And though they held guns in hand, the *Spider's* weapons alone were ready to shoot. They could not know that he would not fire on them.

"This way," Wentworth ordered tightly. "Drop those guns and walk this way."

Their recognition was apparent in the whiteness of their faces. They hesitated, their guns tightly clenched. Wentworth saw the struggle in their faces. Should they submit, or lift guns and shoot it out with this arch-killer? If they were lucky enough to win in the gun battle, untold rewards would be theirs. Fifty thousand dollars had been posted on the *Spider's* head. There would be promotion. . . .

Wentworth's left hand automatic spat flame and the gun flew from one policeman's hand, rattled against the coupe. He gripped his numbed arm, cursing.

"Drop that gun!" Wentworth ordered again, quietly.

The second policeman obeyed and the two moved slowly toward the *Spider* at his order. Wentworth's eyes were probing the darkness beyond them. Where were Cullihane's two killers in the other coupe? Obvious that they had ducked out of the way when the police car had shown up, running silent under orders. But the men would not have gone far. They were even more vitally interested in the cause of the shooting than the police. . . .

Wentworth's hope lay in the throbbing police-car at the curb. If he could get the girl into that, escape would be certain. The girl, whose identity he did not yet know, might yield some secret. . . . The *Spider* became abruptly aware that the eyes of one of the police had flashed to the doorway behind him and that now the man was doing his best to pretend he had not looked there at all.

There was but one explanation. The girl was creeping out of the doorway, still bent on his destruction, as she had been when first her gun had spat at his back. Yet he could not turn to meet her with these two police before him. He could hear the girl's shoes making small rasping noises on the gritty pavement. Damn it, why couldn't she use sense? If she jumped him from behind. . . .

He shook his head. If she jumped him from behind, she would succeed in what she wished. She would achieve the *Spider's* death. She herself would suffer nothing. The footsteps crept closer. . . .

# CHAPTER THREE

# THE WINGED DEATH AGAIN

T HE TWO POLICEMEN now needed no prompting to move toward the *Spider*. Both had seen the girl creeping upon him from behind and they wanted to be near enough to attack when she distracted the *Spider's* attention. He let them come while he listened acutely to the girl's stealthy approach. There was a way out, but it would have to be perfectly timed. . . .

The footsteps of the girl were very close now. One more step and she would probably leap upon him. The final step was delayed and, with a quick tensing of muscles, the *Spider* lunged to the side while his guns swung with alert readiness on the two police. He was just in time. Even as he sprang, the girl catapulted herself upon the spot where he had stood. Thrown off balance, she reeled against one of the police and the two sprawled together to the pavement.

Wentworth turned the flurry to his own account. With a quick stride, he was beside them. His gun flicked out and the policeman collapsed, unconscious, upon the pavement. The second man sprang to the attack, but stopped a blow which felled him also.

The *Spider* took handcuffs and uniform caps from the policemen, jerked the girl to her feet and thrust her into the coupe. He secured her to the door post with the handcuffs, then sprang behind the wheel, hurled the car forward and traveled at maximum speed for a half dozen blocks before he cut the pace. He put one of the uniform caps upon the girl's fluffy, black hair, pulled the other down over his own head. The interior was dark and it was unlikely that anyone would see more than the silhouette of the occupants' heads. It would prevent detection for a short while. He glanced toward the girl. She sat rigidly, staring straight ahead. Her jaw was set and there was furious anger in her face. She was surprisingly pretty in that moment . . . abruptly the *Spider* recognized her. She was the girl who had accused him at Latham's place, whose brother, according to the radio, had been killed by bats. But how in the world had she come here so swiftly? How had she known so accurately where to lay her ambush? Wentworth's pulses quickened. Did not all this mean that she was an ally . . . of the Bat Man? He must find out. Even her brother's death did not preclude the possibility. He turned to the girl.

"Your name, as I recall it," Wentworth said quietly, "is June Calvert. What was your brother's name, Miss Calvert?"

The girl jerked her head about toward him. "Have you killed so many that you can't remember the names of your victims?" she demanded, her deep voice vibrant.

"I didn't kill your brother," Wentworth said. "If I had, I should not bother to deny it. There are enough kills on my conscience to make one more unimportant."

The girl's lips curled though her face was very white. "You have the courage to sit there and admit . . . admit . . . !"

"Those I kill always richly deserve death," said the *Spider*. "I did not kill your brother."

Something in his quiet tone seemed to pierce the girl's contempt and anger. The contempt left her face, leaving in its place a puzzled question.

"I saw you with a cage of bats," she said. "Bob Latham . . . I thought he might have a hand in Dick's death, I was going there to . . . to . . . I saw you with the bats."

Wentworth nodded slowly. "Yes, but if you saw, you also saw that none of my bats killed. It was fully half an hour after I went into the house that the vampire bats came. Mine were ordinary insect-eating bats that I captured to create a diversion there and open a path for my entrance."

His quiet manner seemed to be convincing the girl against her will. June Calvert's head sagged forward, her chin trembled.

"If you know anything about me at all, Miss Calvert," Wentworth continued quietly, "you must know that the *Spider* keeps his oath. I give you my word of honor that I did not kill your brother. I give you my word, also, to kill the man who *is* responsible!"

Slowly, the girl's head came up. She turned her dark, intent eyes upon him, her wrists, bound by the handcuffs to the doorpost, closed and opened nervously.

"But why," she whispered, "why are you trying so to convince me? If, as you say, you have already killed so many, how does one accusation more or less affect it?" The *Spider* had his eyes on the street in the flash of the headlights. He laughed shortly, bitterly.

"I do not mind just accusations," he said, "but when they are false . . ." He shrugged. "You will hear plenty against me from now on. You will hear that I am responsible for all the deaths that occur from these poisonous bats. Even when I kill the Bat Man himself, the idea of my guilt will not be entirely dispelled . . . Oh, forget it! Will you tell me how you happened to be waiting there for me?"

The girl lifted her shoulders in a slight shrug. "There is no magic in it," she said. "I knew that Cullihane and Latham were allies. Because Latham was attacked by the bats, I thought Cullihane would be also. I thought you'd be there to . . ."

The girl broke off as a shrill, rising whine came from the radio beneath the dashboard of the car. It ended and the announcer's dry voice intoned a call.

"Call two-thirty-five, car two-three-five, go to Seventy-first and Sullivan streets. Bat scare. That is . . ."

The announcer's voice broke off in the middle of the signature, then came in again, stronger, more alert.

"Calling all cars. Five men killed by bats at Seventy-first and Sullivan streets. Cars two-three-five, one-seven-four, Cruiser one-eight, go to Seventy-First and Sullivan. . . ."

A ragged curse forced itself out between Wentworth's locked teeth. Even as he feared, the Bat Man had struck again at once. The plans that he had laid for tracing the killers were nullified by a simple lack of time. A new thought struck him. The new point of attack where five citizens had been killed by the poison bats was nowhere near the warehouse of Cullihane, nor any other of his strongholds. Why then had the bats been loosed?

Wentworth started to whirl the car to race toward the spot where the bats were killing. That movement undoubtedly saved his life. From behind him came a stuttering drumroll of gunfire. Bullets tore the side of the car, pocked the windshield, then smashed it into glittering, slashing fragments. A shard stung his cheek . . . The *Spider* glimpsed his assailants in the rear-vision mirror, but already he was in action. He cramped the wheels of the car still further and drove head-on for a building on his right. The car behind him was Cullihane's prowl coupe. The men in it were still shooting. They must either have spotted him, or revived the police and learned from them that it was the *Spider* who kept watch.

As the coupe drove head-on for the building, Wentworth shouted to the girl to crouch to the floor and himself slid down behind the wheel, stomped his foot on the brakes. The force of the collision with the building wall half-stunned him, but the attacking car was already roaring away, convinced its work was done. Wentworth slapped open the door, leveled one automatic and fired three times carefully.

The gun car went out of control, skidded into a side street, and out of sight, hit something with a loud, splintering crash. Under the dash board of Wentworth's car, the radio was still squawking. . . .

"Calling all cars! Calling all cars!" the announcer's voice was harsh and excited. "Close all windows. Patrol cars put up curtains. Kill bats when possible. Warn all pedestrians to get behind closed doors at first opportunity. Twenty-two have been reported dead from the bats . . . !"

Wentworth's teeth locked. His eyes were hot flames. He freed June Calvert from the handcuffs. "Get under cover at once," he ordered.

He raced away from the wreck. He would have to cover a dozen blocks before he could reach his own car. Talking with June Calvert, he had traveled further than he had thought away from where he had left his own car. Small chance that he'd be able to get a taxicab. . . . He became abruptly aware that June Calvert was running after him.

The sound of her limping steps, one foot encased in a shoe, the other only stockinged, was close behind. Wentworth whirled.

"Get to cover," he ordered. "You must protect yourself or those bats . . ."

The girl stooped and snatched off her other shoe, came on toward him in her stocking feet. Her eyes were wide, determined.

"Wherever the bats are," she said, panting a little, "will be the killer of my brother. I'm going with you."

There was no time to argue with her. With a shrug, Wentworth turned and hurried on, hearing the quickened breath of the girl beside him. He kept an alert lookout for a cab, but none appeared. He ran lightly, conserving wind and strength. The girl presented a problem in more ways than one. If he reached his car, with her still beside him . . .

He sprang out into a cross street and halted, pivoting to the left. His Daimler was there, rolling softly swift, toward him with Ram Singh behind the wheel. But he could not permit the Hindu to greet him lest the girl who had proved herself shrewd enough to anticipate the *Spider's* next move, suspect his true identity.

Wentworth flipped an automatic into his palm, pointed it at Ram Singh and ordered him to halt. For a moment, surprise glared from the Hindu's eyes, then the girl burst out from behind the corner and he understood. His jaw trembled in simulated fear as he drew the car to a halt for Wentworth and the girl to enter. "Don't shoot, mister," he pleaded.

Wentworth hid a smile as he motioned June Calvert into the car, climbed in himself.

"I see there's a radio here," he said dryly. "Turn it on and let's see where the fight is the thickest."

Wentworth felt a keen disappointment while his heart was wrung with pity, with a bitter fury, at the knowledge of what must be happening here in this city at the moment with the winged death of the Bat Man fluttering from the sky. He had not anticipated any such wholesale attack as this, but he had expected Cullihane's place to be assailed by the Bat Man. He had hoped that when it happened he would be in a position to put a certain plan into effect, but this surprise assault had left him without recourse. Nita and his plane were far away. . . .

The radio came in with the clicking of the button. ". . . all cars. Calling all cars. *Spider* reported seen in neighborhood of Water Street and Sycamore. Suspected of connection with the vampire bats. . . ."

Wentworth's laughter was sharp and bitter. He was always fugitive from the law, but now once more the entire forces of a hundred cities, of the nation, would concentrate on his capture while the real persons behind the depredations of the bats went unhampered. Once more, it would depend on the *Spider* alone to find and destroy this new and overweening menace to the nation—handicapped by a thousand enemies bent upon his death. How the Bat Man must be laughing now!

The radio was squawking without ceasing. New reports of the bats sweeping death over the city. Now they were on Walnut Hill, now at Twelfth and Market streets. . . . As that last message came through, Wentworth leaned forward toward Ram Singh on whose back he kept the automatic centered.

"Get to Twelfth and Market Streets at once," he ordered flatly. "And make it fast or I'll give you a slug in the back to remember me by."

Ram Singh sent the Daimler hurtling through the streets. Wentworth leaned back against the cushions, apparently relaxed. He fingered a cigarette from a platinum case and lighted it with a snap of a lighter. Outwardly calm, he was aflame with anger. Twelfth and Market! It was in the heart of the downtown section. A few blocks away, the theaters would be loosing their gay crowds into the streets. There would be a mighty harvest for the bats this night, unless, unless . . .

He leaned forward. "That cigar store on the corner. Stop there!" he commanded sharply.

He handed an automatic to June Calvert. "Hold the car here," he said and sprang out without waiting for parley. He knew he risked death in the moments while he raced toward the store with his back toward the girl's gun. She was still not wholly convinced of his innocence. He had read that in her eyes, but she thought it wise to go with him in hope of learning more. This opportunity with a gun in her hand. . . . But the *Spider* had not acted without forethought. The very fact of his arming her and turning his back would militate against her suspicions. Wouldn't she hesitate to shoot a man who trusted her?

The drug clerk pulled up a startled head as a hunched figure in a black cape went past him toward the phone booths. He kept staring as Wentworth dropped a coin and dialed a number. The *Spider* watched him through the door which he opened just enough to extinguish the light within the booth. If he had been recognized, the police cars would soon have another errand than warning the people of the bats. . . .

Richard Wentworth, clubman and dilettante of the arts, was a personal friend of Commissioner Harrington of the Philadelphia police. The *Spider* called his home, got through to Harrington. He wasted no preliminaries.

"The *Spider* speaking," he announced, his voice flat, crisp. "You probably already know that the vampire bats are loose in the city. I think they are intended to attack the theater crowds. It would be wise to order all theaters to lock in their audiences until the bats are gone. You may save thousands of lives by that order. . . ."

So much Wentworth got out in a quick rush before Harrington interrupted. The *Spider* smashed through his words with sharp tones of command.

"Keep quiet, fool! Seconds are precious!" he snapped. "Send out loudspeaker cars to shout warning along the streets. Get a plane with a loudspeaker if you can. Don't forget that most of your people have not had a chance yet to learn about the bats."

Harrington was spluttering with his anger now. Wentworth's lips thinned to a smile. He could imagine the expression on Harrington's heavy face. It had been many a day, Wentworth thought, since anyone had dared to take that tone with the man. But it had served its purpose, had kept him silent while the message of the *Spider* was poured into his ears.

"For God's sake, act quickly," Wentworth urged, then he hung up softly and sped back out to the car. The cigar clerk stared at him, then staggered back a step against the wall. His eyes stretched wide and he pointed a trembling finger.

"The *Spider*!" he gabbled. "The *Spider*!"

He turned and ran toward a narrow door that opened in the back wall of the room, his voice going incoherent, turning into an hysterical scream. Before he had reached the doorway, the *Spider* was beside the car. He sprang into the rear, past June Calvert.

"Twelfth and Market!" he ordered again. "Split the road wide open."

He took the automatic from June's hand. Her dark eyes were frowning on him.

"What did you do?" she almost whispered.

Wentworth told her with clipped sentences while his eyes searched the way ahead.

He would do more when he reached the scene of activity, but what he wanted more than anything else was a chance to strike at the man behind these atrocities.

What was the reason behind this new threat against humanity? There could be no question that greed for money lay somewhere in the background. Money was responsible for all organized crime and, heaven knew, there was organization here—incredibly acute organization. . . .

The Daimler was gliding through the business section of the city now, all dark save where the sparkling of theater lights threw a multicolored glare against the heavens. A police radio-roadster, curtains tightly drawn, raced by with siren screaming and, at a word, Ram Singh followed. The radio still howled its incredibly mounting toll of deaths. Nearly a hundred human beings had been slain and the police undoubtedly could not discover more than half the victims so soon after the tragedy had begun. It was seemingly impossible that so purposeless a slaughter . . .

The Daimler swung a corner and a woman's screams rang out. Wentworth could see her, a dark, dodging form, as she ran frantically toward him along the street. She held a child in her arms and was bent far over it, protecting it with arms and head and bowed body. Wentworth could not see the cause of her terror, but he had no need. About her head, one of those poisonous vampires of the Bat Man must be flitting, seeking an inch of bare flesh in which to sink its deadly teeth.

Incredible that vampires should behave in this way—bats that were rarely seen, but came silently in the darkness of the night to flutter down on sleeping men and animals and take their toll of blood. But these bats were attacking as if they were hydrophobic—or as if they were starved! Yes, that must be it. Vampire bats starved until they would attack any living thing, against any odds, to obtain food!

The thought was a flash of light in Wentworth's brain. He had needed to shout no order to Ram Singh. The Daimler already was sprinting toward where the woman stumbled in a heavy, hopeless run, her screams despairing as she shielded her child against the attack of the flying beasts. Wentworth whipped open the door, felt the wind snatch it from his hand and slam it back against the body of the car.

"This way!" he shouted. "This way! I'll save you!" The woman cried out in joy and ran with increased speed toward the braking Daimler. Once let her get inside . . . Wentworth's automatics were in his hands. If he could only spot the bat that menaced her. Ah, a glimpse of a fluttering black form. The *Spider's* automatic blasted, hammered a bat into extinction. The woman was running toward him eagerly. She lifted her face, held the child out from her body in an effort to get it first into the protection of the car.

It happened in a heartbeat of time. Before the woman's face, a black shadow flitted. Leathery wings covered the baby's head. Wentworth could not shoot. He sprang forward and another of the loathsome black things flicked out of the darkness. The woman's scream rose high, higher, shrilling terribly. She stopped and stood rigidly, arms lifting the baby high. Its cries had ceased now and abruptly her own scream strangled into nothingness. She crumpled to the pavement while the *Spider* was still ten feet away.

As if it echoed her dying scream, another cry broke out. It was shrill, wailing and it ached downward from the heavens. It rose, wavering, to crescendo that made the cold flesh creep along Wentworth's spine, then died into a minor note that was like a death sob. The *Spider* shouted a curse. He knew that sound. It had heralded the death of those score of men in Latham's mansion. Hearing it, Latham had cried, "Oh, God, the Bat Man."

The Bat Man! Wentworth's eyes quested upward toward the muggy skies that threw back glare of street lights. Instinctively, he flinched. A bat dodged at his face and Wentworth's gun blasted upward deafeningly. The beast was hurled upward by the impact of lead, thudded softly to the pavement. The air was suddenly full of them, dodging, diving, sweeping on the *Spider*. His guns spoke deliberately, with a fearful accuracy. Through the night once more rang the wailing, blood-chilling cry of the Bat Man.

"Master!" Ram Singh shouted. "Master, quickly come to cover. A cloud of bats!"

Wentworth darted toward the Daimler, while his eyes still searched the heavens. Nothing moved there for the space of a half-dozen seconds, then far up there where the lights just touched him, the *Spider* saw again the incredible image of the huge bat-like thing he had spotted against the moon when Latham had died—Good God, was it only a few hours ago?—Wentworth's twin guns spat a deadly hail upward toward that gliding figure. But he knew it was futile, knew even as he continued to smash lead upward until his guns were empty.

"Master!" Ram Singh screamed the warning this time.

Wentworth sprang toward the car. He felt a gentle touch on his shoulder and brushed frantically with a gloved hand, knocked off a vampire bat. Then he was inside and the door thudded shut behind him. He was not a moment too soon. A cloud of bats blotted out for an instant the street outside, fluttering past the closed window.

A shudder swept over the *Spider's* body. He was no coward. No man in the world would ever call him that. But the sight of those hundred deadly little beasts with their soft flight and their teeth whose kiss meant death shook him as no gunman's lead had ever done. The black cloud lifted and he saw that the body of the woman and the child was a moving, black mass of leather-winged creatures. . . .

Beside him, June Calvert was sobbing, her face buried in her hands. Ram Singh was muttering harsh Hindustani curses under his breath. Up there where this dark side street intersected the brightness of Market, there was a sudden, dark rush of screaming people. Over their heads danced a myriad black, deadly forms. Wentworth's lips were motionless, thin against his teeth as he stuffed fresh clips of bullets into his automatics. He would do what he could, but in heaven's name, what could he accomplish with the slaughter of a few bats? Something like a groan of despair pushed its way out between his clenched teeth.

Up there in the heavens, that winged monster watched the work of his kindred fiends, the bats. And . . .

Once more came that wailing, mocking cry. Damn it, the Bat Man was laughing, *laughing.* . . . !

# CHAPTER FOUR

# BAT MAN VS. THE SPIDER

R AM SINGH thrust the Daimler toward where the crowd milled and slapped the air to drive off the deadly bats. Wentworth beat his knees with clenched fists. His guns were so futile against the hundreds of flying things. There *must* be some other method of fighting against them. . . . !

As the car rolled out into Market Street, men and women grabbed at the handles and sought to force their way inside. Wentworth had locked the doors. It was necessary if he were to accomplish anything at all. He might save a half-dozen persons inside the car, but that would keep him from work which might save hundreds. . . . He saw a fire-alarm box on a corner and shouted sharply to Ram Singh to halt.

He sprang from the car, fought his way through the crowds. The bats hovered just overhead. Now and again, one would dart downward and a man or woman would scream and die. Wentworth wore gloves, as always when he was in the *Spider's* disguise, and now he dragged his long, black cape up over his head, tearing a hole through which he might look. Twice, he felt the feathery touch of a bat lighting upon the cape and the hint of their poisonous death tightened his lips grimly. He reached the alarm box, jerked open the door and yanked the lever. If the firemen could smash through, there might be a chance. . . .

Across the street, a theater was gay with many-colored lights. Police stood behind the closed, glass doors, he saw. Despite his anger, Harrington had taken the *Spider's* advice. Perhaps a few hundred who might otherwise die terribly would be saved as a result of that.

Wentworth dared not uncover his head, lest the bats strike at him and without better vision, he could not shoot. Still, he did not dare return to the car lest he not be able to give the firemen the only suggestion that he thought might help. If they put on smoke helmets and covered their hands, they would be virtually immune to the attack. . . .

A crashing blast across the street pulled his startled gaze to the theater. He heard the crash again and saw one of the inner doors crash outward, saw an axe glitter coldly. Even as the police whirled with their nightsticks ready, other doors crashed outward and the entire audience of the theater came streaming out into the street.

"Bats!" a man screamed. "The theater is full of bats!"

Wentworth saw a woman attempting to cover her bare shoulders with a cape, saw a bat settle like a loathsome, black flower upon her bosom. The woman fell. He started across the street, but a new rush of terrified men and women drove him back. The hoarse sirens of the fire engines cut through the medley of terror and pain. The trucks were literally ploughing their way through the crowds. Wentworth saw that the men already had donned their smoke helmets. He nodded approval. If he could find the man who had ordered that, he wouldn't have any trouble putting over his idea. . . .

A battalion-chief's car jangled its way through solid ranks of screaming, dying people and the chief sprang out. He dodged as a bat flitted at him, ducked back inside the car and put on a smoke helmet. Wentworth rushed to his side, spat out his idea in swift words.

"Get hoses going," he shouted. "Knock people down and keep the streams going above them. Bats can't get through."

The battalion-chief was a gray-haired man. Wentworth saw his shrewd, smoke-narrowed eyes through the goggle eyes of the helmet. The driver of the car was rigid with fear, fear of the bats, fear of the man whose face he glimpsed when Wentworth lifted the hood of his cape. The chief nodded. He took off the smoke helmet long enough to shout orders. Wentworth dashed back to his car, ducked inside and began shooting.

"Get in front," he ordered June Calvert. "In front, but leave the glass slide open."

The girl hesitated, then clambered over the back of the seat. There were two panes of glass that slid in grooves between front and rear of the car. She left one open. Wentworth took off his hat, then flung open one door of the car. For long, dreadful seconds nothing happened, then a bat flicked into the interior, dropped toward Wentworth's face. He swept his hat swiftly up and knocked the bat to the seat. It would be helpless there. Bats have no way of taking off from a horizontal surface. They cannot take off from a porch which is less than several feet from the floor, for a bat takes off by dropping free, spreading its wings, then gliding. With its wings already spread, it might take off from a lower object, but the seat would not permit that. Wentworth waited, his hat poised, his split-second muscles set for the perilous task of capturing bats whose merest bite would be fatal.

One hose already was hissing out its stream of water into the crowd of Market Street. Men and women were bowled over and bats were washed out of the air to flutter helplessly on the pavement. Given time, they might work their way up the side of some building and fly again, but they would be given no opportunity for that.

Time after time, Wentworth's hat swept a bat from midflight to the seat and finally he slammed the door, crawled into the front section of the car and closed the glass slide. He sat looking over the water-flooded street. Many of the crowd had caught the idea of the hoses—a dozen were operating now—and were throwing themselves down beneath the protecting streams. The battalion-chief had evidently sent in a call for more trucks for the hoarse cry of their sirens filled the air.

Crowds were streaming now from every theater with cries that they were filled with bats. Wentworth's heart was heavy within him. It had been at his order that people had been kept prisoner in those theaters. Harrington would be glad to give the excuse that the *Spider* had advised the action. He could hear the man's grandiloquent voice now.

"Gentleman of the press, you all know what the *Spider* has done for us in the past. I thought him an honorable man, fighting for the law in his own peculiar way. Naturally when he advised a thing, I considered it seriously. Hold the people in the theaters—yes, it seemed a good idea. How could I know that the *Spider* had turned into a mad dog who should be exterminated on sight? I have given my men orders to that effect. To shoot the *Spider* on sight. . . ."

Yes, Harrington would talk like that. The *Spider* had tried to serve and he had led the people he sought to protect into a trap for the Bat Man. Regardless of whether he had convinced June Calvert, her earlier testimony that she had seen the *Spider* carrying a cage of bats would be revived. Wentworth laughed grimly. It only made his task more difficult. He closed his eyes, pressed them with heavy fingers. There was so much death, so much tragedy all about. What, in heaven's name, could be the purpose behind this wholesale slaughter of the innocents? If only he could have foreseen what was happening, have had Nita here earlier. . . .

Wentworth pulled up his head. There was work to do. Not yet had the Bat Man called home his charges with that thin, gigantic squeaking. . . . He turned to Ram Singh.

"I must thank you for standing by the *Spider* in time of trouble," he said crisply. "Many men would have fled from the scene of disaster the moment a gun was taken away from their back. You must tell me your master's name that I may commend you to him. Meantime, get us away from here at once. Miss Calvert, I am sure that soon it will be safe to go abroad. I am going to put you in the protection of some building. . . ."

Wentworth's words cut off as he met the black, blazing regard of her eyes. There was hatred there, more than suspicion, certainty. Good lord! Had she penetrated his subterfuge with Ram Singh? Had she detected the fact that they worked together, that the Hindu was in reality the servant of the *Spider*? If she had . . .

"You, you fiend!" she choked. "You almost tricked me. But it was *you* who kept those people in the theaters so that the bats could kill them. You are the Bat Man, and. . . ."

Wentworth shrugged, motioned to Ram Singh and the great car purred away from the spot where the dead lay in the streets beside the panicked living who crouched beneath the protection of the fire hoses. June Calvert ceased to talk and only glared at him angrily.

Luckily, she had no gun. . . . She was put out presently at the entrance of a subway that would shelter her from bats. Wentworth spun to Ram Singh.

"Find me a taxi immediately," he said sharply. When the Daimler surged forward, Wentworth rapidly instructed the Hindu in the course he must follow. Moments later, the Spider, stripped of cape and hat, part of the disguise removed from his face, sprang into a cab.

"Fifty dollars if you make the airport in twenty minutes," he ordered. "Ten more for every minute you shave off of that."

The taxi's forward lurch hurled him back against the cushions and he eased to a more comfortable position, drew out cigarettes and lighter. If only the Bat Man would delay for a while his signal to the bat horde. . . . He shook his head. There was small hope of that. Already the attack must have lasted for over half an hour, the hungry bats were becoming sated. Probably he would have no such luck.

The motor of the cab snarled with speed. They shot over the bridge toward Camden and the hiss of the wind increased. Wentworth had not doubted that Ram Singh would do his part. He had known just where to send the Hindu for the materials needed. . . . The Spider's mind was weary with futile contemplation of the tragedy he had seen, the hundreds laid in writhing death in the streets. He had certain lines of investigation he could start. That spear which had been hurled through the window of Latham's home. He had noticed certain of its characteristics and was pretty certain that it was of a type used by the headhunters of the extreme reaches of the Amazon, the Jivaro Indians. A ridiculous idea, that those fiercely independent Indians could have been brought to America, or could have come of their own accord. But then it was ridiculous, too, that vampire bats had invaded the temperate zones. Neither seemed possible . . . yet hundreds had died of their poisoned bite this night. Yes, literally hundreds. He glanced at his watch, then out at the dark buildings streaking past. The taxi was making good time.

Finally the lights of the airport came in view. The driver slammed up to the administration building, twisted about to blink behind horn-rimmed spectacles.

"I think you will find the exact time about seventeen minutes, sir," he said in polite, precise English.

Wentworth tossed him a hundred-dollar bill and raced toward

the main building. He glimpsed a low-winged monoplane on the tarmac of a nearby hangar, its motor ticking over and swerved in his race. Minutes were precious, terribly precious. It was barely possible that the Bat Man had not yet sounded the recall for the bats. Even if he had, swift action might yet win the day for the *Spider*. . . .

Wentworth reached the plane in a pounding sprint. A mechanic stood with a pilot at the door of the hangar and they turned in amazement at sight of the running figure. Something of his purpose they must have guessed, but not in time to accomplish anything. Even as they started forward, shouting, Wentworth toed the wing, sprang to the cockpit and instantly yanked the throttle wide. The plane's engine spluttered, then bellowed. The ship began to trundle down the tarmac. It was a Lockhead, a type with which Wentworth was entirely familiar. He jockeyed to gain speed rapidly. For seconds, there was danger that the pursuing pair could reach the tail and nail it to the ground. Then the ship gathered way. An air-liner was circling the field for a landing and the operations officer atop the administration building's conning tower flicked a red light at Wentworth frantically. The *Spider* glanced aloft, gauged his distances and sent his powerful monoplane off the ground downwind.

For seconds, the ship climbed sluggishly, then its speed picked up and he sent it racing at low altitude toward Philadelphia. He could not have wished for a better plane, but he longed for the machine guns of his scarlet Northrup. No way of knowing into what peril he flew tonight.

The lights of Philadelphia sprang at him. Within minutes, he was circling over its streets, peering down into the canyons and seeking the square to which he had directed Ram Singh. It was difficult at night, but after five minutes of circling, he located the place. His altitude was no more than four hundred feet. He drew an automatic and fired two shots. Staring down at the square, he saw the flashes of Ram Singh's answering gun.

Suspenseful moments passed then while Wentworth hung the Lockhead in the sky, watching, watching. . . . His panted breath of relief was almost a triumphant shout when, against the blackness of the square, he caught a dozen flitting bats which glowed as with phosphorescence. Ram Singh had succeeded then, had obtained the radiolite paint and sprayed the vampire bats with it, afterward providing them perches so that they could wing from the Daimler at the proper time. Now, if the *Spider* could keep them in sight and follow them to whatever place they had been kept, it was likely the Bat Man would not be far away!

At first, the glowing spots that were the bats flew about in seeming bewilderment, then they turned westward and, grouped loosely together, flew steadily in a straight course. Three times, the bats turned from their steady flight and each time a man in the streets died beneath their teeth. Wentworth, circling grim-lipped in the heavens, saw and could do nothing. But he swore a hard oath that the Bat Man and his followers should pay for each of these lives. They were martyrs to the cause of justice. . . .

Finally, the last of the houses of Philadelphia were gone from under Wentworth and still the bats winged on into the darkness. It was easier to follow them since the city lights no longer blinded him. It was necessary for him to swing in tight circles. The bats flew much more slowly than the plane, yet if he swung wide he might very well lose sight of their glowing bodies.

The flight moved on and on westward. Wentworth almost despaired of any definite goal for the bats. It seemed impossible that they should have been released so far from the city and yet sweep so directly there. Yet they flew fairly close together and bats generally traveled in pairs at most, generally alone. There must be some reason for this group migration. . . .

Suddenly, through the vibration of the plane's motor, Wentworth heard a shrill, wailing note that he recognized instantly. It was followed immediately by the squeaking rasp, as of a giant bat. The glowing flight below him faltered in its steady progression. He realized that they were no longer pushing forward, but were climbing straight toward him!

It was impossible. No one could so direct and guide bats, and yet—and yet here they came directly toward his swift plane! The answer came to him almost with the realization of their approach. The shrill squeak of the giant bat had come *from his direction*! The bats only flew toward the sound, then—then . . .

With a cold chill of apprehension racing up his spine, Wentworth tilted back his head to stare upward into the heavens. Then he kicked the rudder violently. The Lockhead rocked, spun to the left and Wentworth snapped a gun into his hand, staring with incredulous eyes at the black shadow that had seemed to float above him in the heavens.

Above him, almost within pistol range, was the huge creature that he had seen twice now upon the scene of vampire murder. Even as Wentworth spotted the thing, he saw flame streak from somewhere near its head and a rifle bullet cracked past his head!

An oath squeezed out between the *Spider's* locked teeth. No longer was there any doubt the thing was human. It might have wings, might skim the skies like a bat, but it was human. No bat could fire a rifle. With the thought, Wentworth yanked back the stick and drove straight at the thing, automatic ready in his hand. . . .

Once more the rifle cracked and the bullet dug into the fuselage beside Wentworth's shoulder. The *Spider* kicked the rudder, skidding the plane about. He was within range now and the *Spider's* lead never missed. . . . His automatic was ready, but its muzzle swept empty air! In the instant it had taken Wentworth's plane to wheel about, the Bat Man—it could be no other—had disappeared! Even as he made that discovery, lead whistled upward past his gun hand.

The *Spider's* lips twisted against his teeth. He shoved the stick against the instrument panel and the Lockhead dropped her nose like a plummet. In a heartbeat, he had lost two hundred feet. But he had not caught the Bat Man. He had a glimpse of him in the instant the ship's nose had gone down. The Bat Man had stood on his tail for that shot upward at the ship and as Wentworth swept by, he was in the midst of a whipstall. . . .

As the phrase *whipstall* snapped through Wentworth's brain, he gasped. Gasped even as he threw two swift shots at the Bat Man. There was time for no more. He was dangerously close to the ground and the Lockhead was heavy, its wing spread proportionally small. Down, down she went while he maneuvered rudder and ailerons. The Lockhead came out of it with twenty-five feet to spare. Wentworth zoomed, *viraged* to spot the Bat Man. . . . He was gone! As quickly as that, in the few seconds while the Lockhead dived for earth and zoomed out of it, the flying man had vanished.

Wentworth eagerly scanned the earth below, but there was nothing there, no movement, no sound—and no place where a plane might land even if the Bat Man were down there. Sudden wild hope sang through Wentworth's brain. Had those two swift shots, thrown in the midst of a power dive of terrific speed, knocked down the Bat Man? Slowly, the *Spider* shook his head. It was barely possible, but even his extraordinary aim would scarcely be equal to that task. Besides, he was certain that his zoom, his *virage* would have been quick enough to spot a Bat Man tumbling to earth. However, if he had dived. . . .

Wentworth's mind turned back to the idea that had flashed through his brain as he had darted past the Bat Man. *Whipstall!* That described the performance of the winged man. It was a phrase applied to planes that, rising too steeply, slapped straight down to the ground as if the tail were the handle of a whip and the nose the lash. A bird couldn't perform an operation such as that if it wished, nor could a bat.

To Wentworth that meant only one thing. That Bat Man was an ordinary human being. . . . *with wings attached to his body like a plane!* As the idea struck, a memory came to the *Spider*. Recently, at Miami, a "daredevil" had dropped from a plane with triangular canvas wings stretching from arms to his body and another fin between his legs. With their aid, he had looped and stunted in the air, finally using a parachute to land. Why wouldn't it be possible, by extending those wings to each side with struts and braces, to operate precisely as a motorless glider?

By the gods, the thing sounded possible! There was no time now, of course, to figure weight per square foot, gliding angles. . . . While he thought, Wentworth had been scouring the country below him, hoping against hope that he might catch some glimpse of the glowing bats. But it was in vain. The Bat Man had accomplished his purpose. He had almost killed Wentworth with his rifle, operated in what way God only knew, and he had distracted him until the murdering bats could escape.

*Spider* and Bat Man had met—and it was the Bat Man who had won!

# CHAPTER FIVE
# DINNER WITH DEATH

WEARILY, Wentworth turned the Lockhead back toward Camden airport. Undoubtedly all fields had been warned to watch out for a stolen ship. He smiled slightly, took the stick between his knees and stripped off the remnants of his disguise. Many things could be forgiven Richard Wentworth, especially if he paid well. . . .

He had no more trouble on landing than he had anticipated and found Ram Singh waiting for him with the Daimler. He settled gratefully into the cushions. A half hour later he was asleep at his rooms in the Early Quaker, an ancient and quiet hotel on the waterfront. He was astir early, found a note on his bedside table that Nita van Sloan already had arrived in response to his summons. A smile touched his lips. He lifted the note, in Nita's own handwriting, to his lips, and crossed to the telephone, got her rooms at once.

"Darling," he cried jubilantly, "could you find it in your heart to have breakfast with me, oh practically at once?"

"I thought the invitation was for dinner," she told him, "but it's just possible that I'm not engaged. . . ."

It was pleasant in the informal dining room of the Early Quaker. Its flooring was the ancient boards of a wharf and extended out over the river. Mooring rungs were still fastened there, and there was always the pleasant suck and murmur of the tide among the piles. The wharf had been glassed in and, open now, allowed the warm, morning sunlight to stream through.

Nita's smile, as Wentworth greeted her in the lobby, was warm and welcoming. Her violet eyes were deep and the bronze-lit curls that clustered about the perfect oval of her face were incredibly lovely. Wentworth told her so in a soft murmur as he took her arm and led her toward the sunlit dining room. Nita's lips were curved in a remembering smile. Their pleasurable moments together were all too brief. Greatly they loved, but the *Spider* could never marry. How could a man take on the responsibilities of wife and children when any moment might find the disgracing hand of the law upon his shoulder—when any night might bring his death at the hands of one of a hundred enemies?

No, Wentworth had sacrificed his hope of personal happiness for the sake of the thousands of others who would be denied peace, perhaps even life, if the arch-criminals that now and again arose, were not put down by the *Spider*. He had never regretted his choice, but their were times when bitterness touched his soul. . . .

At a table where they could gaze out on the blue of the Delaware River, Nita touched Wentworth's hand, her violet eyes gravely on his.

"I see that they blame the *Spider* again," she said.

Wentworth shrugged. "It is inevitable, I suppose. How do the newspapers explain the *Spider's* calling fire engines and directing the firemen to save the people with their hoses?"

Nita glanced toward the approaching waiter. "They don't explain it, Dick. They don't mention it at all."

Wentworth grimaced. The battalion-chief, then, had taken credit for the idea. Well, it did not matter. He began to tell Nita the events of the night before. He had no secrets from her. Often she helped him in his battles and more than once she had herself worn the *Spider's* mantle, and made the *Spider's* kills. . . .

The day passed without further event and Wentworth spent the time conferring with police officials, seeking some clue to the reason behind the wholesale slaughters of the Bat Man. He found no motive, but he learned one thing that made his lips thin with determination. The Crosswinds Jockey club was holding an annual banquet at the Early Quaker this evening.

It was a quasi-social affair and he decided at once to attend. Even though the Bat Man had been striking at random at humanity, it seemed likely he would still follow the aim of his first attacks— the race track. Even if there were no new assault, it was possible that Wentworth might pick up some lead to the killer. Certainly, the man must be some one familiar with racing and the coterie connected with it. He might very well still be associated with the turf himself. . . .

An invitation was easy to arrange and the dinner he had planned with Nita was shared with some hundred other persons, social celebrities and turf men. Commissioner of Police Harrington was there at the head table with Wentworth and Nita. His red-jowled face was far from pleasant. It was plain that the overwhelming tragedies of the last twenty-four hours weighed heavily upon him.

Wentworth had scarcely seated Nita when a blond, handsome man who towered even above Wentworth's six feet came eagerly to them.

"I say!" he cried. "Aren't you Nitita—I'm sorry—Nita van Sloan?"

Nita looked up questioningly then sprang to her feet and held out both hands.

"Piggy!" she cried. "Piggy Stoking. In heaven's name . . . !"

Wentworth stood politely by, smiling slightly, estimating the taper-shouldered strength of the man, taking in the youthful but determined face. Nita turned toward Wentworth, flushed a little.

"This is Frederick Stoking, who was my first beau," she told him, laughing. "He used to pull my pigtails when . . . when I wore pigtails. Richard Wentworth, Fred."

The two men bowed, shaking hands, taking each other's measure. Wentworth decided Stoking was intelligent, and steady, just as his wide-set, blue eyes were. There was a deep cleft in a firm chin. Without consciously willing it, he compared himself and this man who had been Nita's first beau. They were very much of an age, he and Stoking, but the trials he had undergone, the woes and the pains, had taken their toll of Wentworth's face. There were lines at his mouth corners, a sharpness to his nose. Stoking was gay.

"You must join us after the banquet," Wentworth said cordially. "I'd like very much to hear about Nita's pigtails."

Stoking's eyes were grave despite the laughter about his mouth. "They were just as lovely as her curls are now," he said. "I pulled them, but I assure you it was reverently."

Nita laughed at him. "None the less painfully!"

Stoking left and Wentworth and Nita both watched his superb figure as he moved back to his own party. Wentworth looked down at his plate, reflecting a score of yellow lights. His mouth was unconsciously grim. He was not thinking anything definitely, but there was a darkness, a depression, of his spirits.

Nita's hand touched his arm. "Why, Dick!" she whispered, "I do believe you're jealous!"

Wentworth straightened his shoulders, put a smile on his lips, but he spoke very quietly. "Darling, I am jealous for the normal happiness that might have been yours if you had never met me. Why should you be burdened down, as I am, with the cares of the world?"

Nita's hand tightened on his arm. "If you don't stop that, I shall kiss you right here in public," she said fiercely. "Perhaps I prefer to be burdened."

Wentworth laughed, patted her hand, and shrugged aside his depression. He leaned toward Nita, named all the celebrities present. "I am suspicious of all small men," he told her. "There's that jockey over there at the third table. An ex-jockey, rather, turned stables owner. He's very successful and bats haven't killed any of his horses. Sanderson is the name. He still doesn't weigh above ninety pounds."

"Why small men?" Nita asked.

"I've estimated the wing spread of the Bat Man, gliding angles, weight per square foot. He couldn't perform in the air as he does with that wing spread and weigh much over a hundred pounds. For instance, the man next to him, another ex-jockey named Earl Westfall, couldn't possibly manage himself on the wings. He's put on a lot of weight for his height, must weigh about a hundred and eighty to judge from his girth."

Nita's hand still clung to his arm. She tightened her fingers. "That red-headed man bending over Commissioner Harrington's shoulder . . . ?"

"Red Cullihane," Wentworth said briefly. "Partner of Latham, who was killed last night." He felt a tingling race over his body as he studied the stubby, powerful build of the man, a tingling of apprehension. Cullihane's presence here spelled danger for all of them. Suppose the Bat Man should strike at him tonight, at this banquet? If the man's intention was merely promiscuous slaughter, the gathering here offered an excellent opportunity, especially if people connected with the turf were still mainly his targets. Wentworth's eyes tightened, his hands beneath the table clenched into hard knots. He was suddenly sure that his premonition was correct, that there would be slaughter here tonight. . . .

He glanced swiftly about the banquet hall, built out over the Delaware river on piles, an ancient wharf actually. The glassed sides were open wide and through them now and then came the moan of a tug whistle, but there were tight-fitted screens. They could be smashed out by the same means that had been used at Latham's home, but Wentworth doubted that method. It would allow too slow ingress for the number of bats necessary to dispose of the entire gathering. . . . Nevertheless, he was certain that the attack would take place.

Wentworth's smile tightened, thinned his lips. Queer, these premonitions of his. They were rarely wrong and he had come to believe them to be based on the intuitive workings of his subconscious mind. He no longer strove to trace out the reasons, merely accepted the conclusion thus presented to him. There would be an attack here tonight.

Somehow, his mind refused to apply itself to the problem of defense. There was no reason for the lethargy. He was thoroughly rested after the strenuous activities of the previous twenty-four hours. Yet, instead of planning strategy, he found himself gazing time and again at the man who had been Nita's first beau. Fred Stoking's eyes kept straying toward Nita, too.

Nita's hand touched Wentworth's arm. "What's the matter, Dick boy?" she whispered.

There wasn't anything the matter, except that he felt a vast reluctance for the encounter that was approaching. Good God, would there never be an end of this ceaseless fighting?—Never an end of the warped madmen who sought nation-wide dominion through crime? He knew a strange rebellion that he, and he alone, should meet these terrors. . . .

"Nita," he spoke abruptly, "I want you to join Stoking's party and get them to leave here at once on some pretext."

Nita's fingers tightened on his arm. "What is it?"

"There's going to be a bat attack here," he told her, barely breathing the words. "I know it, but I couldn't persuade anyone to believe me. I don't even wish to prevent it. If I don't permit the attack, I won't be able to trail the Bat Man."

Nita started to protest, but a glimpse of Wentworth's bitter eyes stopped the words on her lips. She looked at him a bit curiously. His desire to remove her from the path of danger was understandable enough, but why Piggy Stoking?

Wentworth smiled at her slightly, reading the question in her eyes. "I rather like the lad," he said. "Besides I want to check up on your past and if he were killed, I couldn't do it."

He rose to his feet and Nita, perforce, stood also. She looked up into the lean, tanned face she loved, the smile fading from her lips. So often, so often they had parted like this on the eve of peril and death. . . .

"Be careful, Dick!"

"For you, sweetheart!"

Many eyes followed Nita and Wentworth as they crossed the floor to Stoking's table. They made a brave couple, those two, alike in proud carriage, with that touch of arrogance in the poise of the head, confidence like an accolade upon their shoulders.

"I'm called away unexpectedly," Wentworth told Stoking. "I'm sure I can trust you since there are no pigtails to pull."

"I make no promises," Stoking warned him. "Those curls tempt me, too."

Wentworth bowed his way from the table, his smile lingering mechanically on his lips. From the antechamber, he sent for Commissioner Harrington. The man came heavily toward him, shorter than Wentworth, a frown between his eyes.

"What's up?" he asked crisply.

Wentworth's face was as grave as his. "Bats," he said. "At least seventy-five per cent of the guests tonight are associated with the race track. They got Latham. Cullihane, with whom Latham was associated, is present."

Harrington tried to laugh it off. "You're of the belief then, that these attacks are sponsored by some crooks or another? You believe in this Bat Man?"

Quick anger throbbed over Wentworth. It was the unbelief of men like this, the slowness of authorities entrusted with the protection of humanity, that necessitated the activities of the *Spider*. Oh, for the keen strength of Governor Kirkpatrick in a time like this! Kirk, who had been police commissioner of New York City for years, had never hesitated. . . .

"Very well," Wentworth told Harrington coldly. "Doubt me and watch your friends die." He turned on his heel and strode away.

Commissioner Harrington came after him hurriedly. "No offense intended, Wentworth," he said. "Surely, you must realize it's hard to believe in a man with wings . . . ?"

Wentworth turned toward him. "It's no man with wings," he said shortly. "But a man who has rigged a bat-like glider. You've heard of motorless gliders, haven't you? I fought with him last night and he out-maneuvered me. Naturally, the shorter the wingspread, and axis, the more quickly the craft can pivot or dodge." He recounted briefly his battle with the Bat Man the night before. He stopped once to bow as Nita and the Stoking party passed them. His eyes saluted Nita for her achievement, then he turned back to Harrington and continued his story. When he had finished, the Commissioner frowned heavily, staring at the floor, standing with braced legs hands locked behind his back.

"I cannot doubt you," he said. "I know what you've done in New York, of course, against criminals. You must pardon my hesitation. The conception is a bit bizarre."

Wentworth acknowledged that with a short nod. "Quite, but I do not make statements unless I have ample reason for them. I tell you that the bats will attack here tonight. I do not know when, but. . . ."

His words broke off as a piercing wail, a sobbing moan swelled into the antechamber where the two men stood.

"The Bat Man!" Wentworth rasped.

As if his words had been a signal, the lights blinked out and a deathly stillness fell upon the gabble of the banquet hall, upon the entire hotel. Then a woman screamed.

"The bats!" she cried, and a panic roar followed her scream.

Wentworth's hand closed on Harrington's arm. He felt the man's start at his touch. "Perhaps next time," Wentworth shouted at him, "you *will* believe!"

# C H A P T E R   S I X
# WATERS OF DOOM

**W**ENTWORTH'S FACE was grimly set as he raced to the battle against the poisonous bats. If only he had begun earlier his attempt to persuade Harrington! But it was useless to reproach himself. He had acted immediately after the discovery of what impended. Only one thing to do now: attempt to save the lives of these trapped banqueters.

He fled headlong for the outer door and as he reached the curb, the long, low form of his Daimler rolled forward, jerked to a halt. He snapped open the back door, reached inside and snatched out a large drum-like object of glittering chromium. As he started back for the door of the hotel again, the driver sprang to the street and reached his side in long strides.

"Stay here, Ram Singh," Wentworth ordered. "Throw the switch as soon as I get inside."

The turbaned Hindu scowled at being barred from the battle, but there was no hesitation in his movements. He leaped back into the car. Wentworth shouldered open the doors of the hotel and instantly a wide beam of light blazed out from the drum-like object he carried. He hurried with it to the door of the banquet hall and its powerful ray illuminated the entire room.

The air was filled with the fluttering small messengers of death and streams of them poured upward through traps opened in the

170

floor. Wentworth cursed. He should have seen that method of attack. The wharf floor had been preserved in its original form. "Atmosphere" for the hotel. The Bat Man had merely opened the trap doors that once had been used by workmen and released his hordes of killers. Wentworth thanked the gods for his foresight in putting the powerful searchlight into the car. He had not expected this attack tonight, but had prepared for future frays. Now the blazing white beam was blinding the bats. Many of them were fluttering back into the pits from which they rose, while others swung blindly about the room in their heavy, laborious flight. Two score of men and women lay upon the floor, dead from the bites of the starved vampires—but the light had saved a hundred others!

Wentworth did not delay on the scene after placing the light. A single glance had pictured the hall indelibly upon his mind, then he turned and raced for the outer doors again. It would be impossible, he knew, to attack from here the men who had brought the bats. It would be certain death to attempt to descend through those bat-crowded trap-doors. But there was another way. . . .

As he sprang to the street he saw Ram Singh's knife glittering in the air. Four men were trying to slice the cable that fed current to the searchlight. Wentworth's twin automatics flew to his hands. He shot twice. Ram Singh's blade had disposed of the other two. His teeth flashed white in a smile as he faced his master.

"My knife is thirsty, master," he cried in Hindustani. "It has but sipped a drop or two . . . !"

Wentworth had not paused while he shot. Now he thrust his guns back into their holsters and, with a gesture to the Hindu, raced for a wharf from which he could reach the river. Ram Singh loped along beside him. He was chanting under his breath, a war song in which the exploits of his wonderful knife figured large.

A high board fence bordered the wharf. Wentworth sprang upward and seized its top. Instantly, Ram Singh caught his feet and helped him. Straddling the top, Wentworth reached down a hand to the Hindu. Below him the water was black with wavering white shadows of lights upon its surface. Under the piles which supported the dining room of the Early Quaker were only shadows. . . .

Wentworth stripped off coat and shoes. He thrust his automatics into Ram Singh's hands.

"Thy knife, warrior!" he ordered.

Ram Singh wiped the blade across his thigh and Wentworth gripped it between his teeth, dived into the black water. There was scarcely a splash to mark his smooth entrance. Ripples spread quietly and lapped against the piles, making zig-zags of the light's reflections. But Wentworth's head did not break the surface again. Under water, he stroked for the darkness beneath the Quaker wharf. Under there somewhere were the men of the Bat Master, loosing new killers upon the people above.

When he rose to the surface, it was with his fingers against the barnacle-studded base of a pile. His head lifted without a sound and he peered, narrow-eyed, through the darkness. Rays of light escaped from the banquet hall overhead. By that faint illumination, Wentworth made out the shadows of four boats. In each a man crouched beside a high cage from which the bats had been released. Even as he spotted them, the boats began to ease away from the trapdoors.

Noiselessly, Wentworth stroked toward the nearest. As he approached, the man in it slid over the side and vanished into the black water. Wentworth whipped the knife from between his teeth and dived. It was not the kind of weapon he liked, but this was no time for niceties. This man in the water was a knife at his back, a threat of death. What Wentworth sought was a live prisoner, but this swimming assassin. . . .

There could be no vision under this black surface, but Wentworth had marked the other's course and his knife fist groped before him. He touched living flesh, felt it flinch away and stroked mightily forward at the same time lunging with the knife as with a sword. Its keen point bit deep. He wrenched free and struck twice more, then swept backwards. There was a great, kicking commotion that made the water boil. The dying man's head breached and Wentworth heard a gasped cry in a language he did not recognize. Instantly the other three men took to water. . . . diving toward the *Spider*!

Wentworth stroked softly away from the spot where his victim had sunk. He must fight this out in the water for the air was filled with a soft fluttering of bats, and their hungry squeaking. He glimpsed one against the faint light from above and dodged beneath the surface as it fluttered toward him. His lips shut in a thin line, his eyes narrowed against the darkness. Death above from the fangs of a myriad bats; and in the water, death at the hands of three men whose companion he had killed. If only he had his automatics, dry and ready for action! But he had only Ram Singh's knife. A round head broke water within a yard of his face. . . .

On the instant, Wentworth flung himself toward it, his knife flashing in a cutting swing. The head flinched back out of range and instantly disappeared. But not before Wentworth had caught a glimpse of a knife between its teeth, a knife that now would be reaching for his groin!

Useless to try to flounder backward out of range. The knife-man would have the speed of a dive behind him. Wentworth did the only possible thing. He plunged forward and to one side at the same time. He had a glimpse of two other men moving toward him, then he pivoted to strike at his immediate assailant. The man's knife broke water first, thrusting toward the spot where a moment before Wentworth had been.

Wentworth did not wait for the whole man to show, but dived with the knife pointed for the body behind that arm. This time he felt his knife bite home. He did not attempt a second stroke, but swept on past the man, dragging his knife with him. Deadly blind work, this fighting in black water beneath a black, wooden roof. No telling where the knife had struck but no death flurry threshed the water above his head. . . .

Wentworth stroked cautiously beneath the water, knife hand feeling ahead for obstructions. He touched the shell-roughened surface of a pile, circled it and allowed himself to drift upward. His lungs were bursting, there was a heavy heart-pound in his ears. But when his head eased above the surface, he dared not let the air escape rapidly. Behind his post, he waited, listening as the humming in his ears subsided.

Not a sound broke the silence save the squeaking of the bats. Up there in the banquet hall was silence, too. But Wentworth did not push out into the open. Probably the two, or possibly three, men left were doing as he was, clinging to piles and waiting for the enemy to betray himself. Well, the *Spider* still had a stratagem in reserve.

Without a sound, he submerged and swam toward the spot where he had entered under the wharf.

It was laborious work. He dared not dive, lest the splashing betray him. He must waste precious time submerging, pushing off from the base of a pile and groping ahead lest he ram head-on into another. Twice he submerged before, in the dimness, he could detect open space ahead of him. Then he exhaled loudly, began to swim with small, secret splashings, deliberately making noise. Behind him all was silence.

He swam on, not too swiftly. He gasped out words in Hindustani that sounded like curses of despair to his pursuers. He ordered Ram Singh to shoot when the men appeared, yet spare one. When he had gone fifty yards from the edge of the wharf, he peered behind him. With the speed of fish, two men were swimming after him. He began to flounder, as if helpless with fatigue. The knives in the mouths of his pursuers were visible now, glints of steel. But only two. . . . Well, then, his knife thrust had gone home.

From the top of the fence, Ram Singh's automatic spat red flame. There was a thin, inarticulate cry and one of the heads vanished. They had been very close to Wentworth and with the shot and cry, he spun about and sped in a racing trudgeon toward the remaining man. The knife-man paused uncertainly, turned and began to swim back toward the wharf but at a pace that was markedly slow and burdened. Triumph shot through Wentworth. He changed to a powerful overhand so that he could watch his victim . . . and his sense of triumph lessened. Seconds before the man had been swimming swiftly, easily. Even fear could not so quickly destroy his speed. . . .

The thought had only half-formed in Wentworth's mind when he dived to one side, stroking with all his strength. He felt the faint concussion of Ram Singh's second shot and burst above the surface to find a second knife man beating up the water in a death-flurry. The original swimmer was making better time now for the wharf. It was obvious that, even as Wentworth's glancing thought had told him, the fellow's floundering was part of a trap. He had led Wentworth on until his companion could dive under water and knife Wentworth from behind. Only the *Spider's* keen powers of observation and split-second action had saved him. His face was set, hard. He raced on after the man whose antics had so nearly trapped him. . . .

The man's efforts were feeble again, a great deal of splashing and small progress. Wentworth overtook him speedily, but delayed just out of his reach. The man turned and hit out impotently with his knife. With a quick grab, Wentworth had his wrist. A wrench and the weapon was sinking to the bottom. But the battle was not so soon over. He did not wish to kill the man, nor to die himself. The other seemed too determined to drag him down, even at the cost of his own life.

As he lunged, Wentworth had a first clear glimpse of his features. He frowned in bewilderment even as the man reached out to seize him. The man was obviously an Indian, short of stature with a flattish face and black, heavy hair. But he had no time for speculation, for the Indian fastened upon him with arms and legs and they instantly sank below the surface.

Black water closed over them and they drifted lower and lower toward the bottom. Wentworth struggled desperately to free himself, to free even one arm, but the Indian clung with the strength of a madman, arms and legs wrapped about him, head buried under Wentworth's chin. Already, the *Spider's* lungs seemed squeezed with iron torture bands—already his blood was humming in his ears. Hope of capturing the man alive fled from him. It seemed possible now that he himself would not escape from this fight alive!

Colored lights danced in the blackness of the water and he knew that they signified approaching unconsciousness. But unconsciousness here meant death for the *Spider*—destruction for many thousands of others from the onslaughts of the Indians and their murdering bats! The Indian's arms seemed to lock more tightly about him. . . .

# CHAPTER SEVEN
# POISONED AMBUSH

WENTWORTH, suffocating beneath the waters in the grip of the Indian, had only one recourse. The knife between his teeth. He could not free his arm to wield it, but the Indian's head was beneath his chin. Slowly, with a sense of timelessness and enormous effort, Wentworth began to twist his head to one side, to turn the point of the knife between his teeth toward the Indian's neck.

The noise of his own laboring heart was thunderous in his ears. His lungs strained, strained. He blew out a little breath through his nostrils to relieve them, but instantly they were paining again. And he twisted his head, squirmed it sideways so that the long blade of the knife turned downward. All thought was done with now. Consciousness was almost gone, but still Wentworth's will drove his head to that slow twisting motion.

He was conscious of no movement, either in his own body, nor that of the Indian. They were resting on the slimy bottom of the river, but he did not know when they had touched there. With a final exhaustion of will, he achieved the position of head that he desired and jabbed downward with the knife. There was a pain in his neck, a stabbing brilliance of agony that made him think he had knifed himself instead of the Indian, then there was a vast, absorbing darkness. . . .

Even through that blackness, he had a sensation of lifting upward, though it seemed the Indian's arms were still about him. Impossible to know how long that oppressive darkness lasted, but finally he was looking up into the face of Ram Singh. The Hindu grinned widely.

"By Siva, sahib," he cried, "nothing can kill thee!"

Wentworth thrust himself up and found that he was inside of his car, the windows closed while black things hovered against it, the vampire killers of the Bat Man.

"Thy servant dived to help thee, master," Ram Singh went on, "but did not find thee until thou arosest thyself."

Wentworth took account of himself slowly. His brain came flashing back to full life ahead of his laggard body. He had succeeded then in puncturing the Indian's spine and relaxing his death grip. But even then, he would have drowned had it not been for the ever-vigilant Ram Singh.

"I'm afraid," he whispered, "that I lost thy knife, O warrior!"

Ram Singh held up the glistening blade. Wentworth was rapidly regaining his strength. His maneuver against the Bat Man had failed through the bravery of the monster's men. Indians. He recalled suddenly the Jivaro spear which had been driven through the window of Latham's mansion. He fumbled a flask of brandy out of a pocket of the car, took a long swig.

Ram Singh, squatting on the floor, was busy rewinding his turban.

"Wah! Those demons of Kali!" he exclaimed. "Thy servant was forced to hide his face in his turban to keep the bats from feasting on his blood while he sat upon the fence."

The potent liquor revived Wentworth's body, made his heart beat strongly. He leaned forward to his radio, tuned it carefully. From it issued a series of musical monotones . . . Ram Singh ceased the wrapping of his turban and listened. Wentworth began to smile.

"Quickly, Ram Singh," he cried. "That is Jackson in the plane. I set him to keep watch above on a chance that the Bat Man would strike. Jackson has followed. . . ." Wentworth stopped to catch the rhythmic beat of wireless signals: ". . . followed a plane from which the Bat Man dived. It was over New Jersey. Quickly, Ram Singh, by way of Trenton. . . ."

Ram Singh climbed over the front seat and dropped behind the wheel. Wentworth had seen at a glance that the lights blazed now in the Early Quaker hotel and he severed the cable that connected with the searchlight he had carried into the building. The Daimler was instantly in motion. . . .

For a while Wentworth rested. When Ram Singh had reached Roosevelt highway and was racing through the outskirts of Philadelphia toward Trenton, he opened the wardrobe behind the seat and substituted dry clothing for his ruined evening clothes. He donned dark tweeds. When the time came, he would add cape and broad-brimmed black hat, alter his face . . . and the *Spider* would step forth from the car in all his sinister fearful majesty. . . .

The wireless signals from Jackson continued to drum on his ears, repeating the message first sent and giving the new positions of the plane. Even if Jackson did not trail the ship to a hiding place of the Bat Man, they might capture the pilot and learn something from him. If they found a headquarters for the Indians . . . Well, there would be a new battle.

It was like the *Spider* that he should press on this way while his body still had not recuperated from a struggle that had nearly cost his life.

Because he was tired, he urged Ram Singh to greater speed in the pursuit. He warned the Hindu that, since they hunted Jivaros, they must be on the watch for poisoned blowgun darts.

"The Jivaros are headhunters," he explained. "They strip the skin from the skull, stuff it and smoke it down to about the size of a doll's head. If you don't want that turbaned skull of yours to be hung up at an Jivaro feast, be careful!"

Wentworth knew that Ram Singh was laughing. . . .

The Daimler rolled past a deserted, darkened air field and at Wentworth's quick order, Ram Singh whirled the mighty car about and sent it toward the hangar. It was necessary to use guns, even when Wentworth offered to buy a plane, before the single man on guard there could be persuaded to part with a fast ship. Wentworth left a check and sent the plane rocketing through the night. The ship was equipped with radio and Wentworth flashed a message to Jackson, received his joyous response. The Bat Man's ship was still boring steadily northward. . . .

Twenty minutes later, Jackson's wireless spluttered rapid signals: "Attacked by two ships with machine guns. Over Shrewesbury River near Red Bank. They're good and. . . ."

Then silence, blankness in the dark night above New Jersey. Wentworth caught at the throttle, but the plane already was doing its best, blazing through the black sky with its motor revving at dangerous speed. The *Spider's* mouth was a hard, uncompromising slit. Had Jackson, brave Jackson, paid the penalty of all who fought side by side with the *Spider*? A price of pain and blood and death? The empty sky gave him no answer. He pictured Jackson flaming down into the shallows of the Shrewesbury—Jackson who had fought with him in France, who had saved his life, and had his own saved in turn, a dozen times upon the battlefields of earth and sky! Jackson was battling for his life, had perhaps crashed in flames . . . !

Seconds dragged into minutes, each of which saw three miles of dark countryside slip past beneath hissing wings. Finally the dark shimmer of the river showed on the horizon and beside it spurted a bright gout of flame. Wentworth leaned forward in the pilot's seat, but he could make out no details of the scene below, no trace of hostile ships in the sky. At long last, he was circling over the spot of fire. It was the wreckage of a plane, but it was impossible to tell whether it was the Northrup. . . . Wentworth put the ship into a steep dive, circled and landed on the meadow by the light of the burning ship.

The *Spider* sat motionless in his plane, the motor just ticking over, and stared at the wreckage. It was a biplane as his Northrup was, but beyond that he could tell nothing. He climbed out of the cockpit and Ram Singh vaulted to the ground beside him. Slowly they made their way forward. . . .

"Master," said Ram Singh, "you warned me beware of blowgun darts."

At the words, Wentworth stopped short, a new thought striking him. Was this a trap? He had been so wrapped up in the idea of Jackson's battle, of his crash and death, that he had not paused to think of trickery. But now he threw swift, piercing glances into the shadows that ringed the plane's fire like waiting jackals at a kill.

"Thanks, Ram Singh," he said quietly.

He led the way even closer to the ship. Its structure greatly resembled a Northrup, but Wentworth could not be sure because of the smashing of structure by the crash. He became aware of automobile headlights speeding along a nearby road and turned heavily back to his own plane. They left the ring of dying red fire, stepped into the darkness, twice black now since their eyes were narrowed by the flame, and . . .

"Duck, major!"

Jackson's hearty deep voice rang out of the night somewhere. Even while a leap of joy convulsed his heart, Wentworth snatched Ram Singh's arm and pulled him to the ground with him.

"Roll," he shouted. "Roll toward the plane!"

Over his head, he saw tiny three-inch darts sail past. Off in the darkness, came the popping of blowguns, as if corks had been pulled from many bottles. As he and Ram Singh rolled desperately toward the ship, more of those butterfly harbingers of death buried their poison points in the earth beside them. Wentworth sprang to his feet and ran zig-zag toward the ship, snatched the throttle wide. Instantly a hurricane of wind whistled past him and Ram Singh stood beside him, hands locked on the wing. Wentworth had set the brakes, but with the propeller bellowing, the plane might get loose.

Leaning against the slip-stream, Wentworth pulled his automatics. He could no longer hear the popping of blowguns, but he could trace the course of the featherlight tiny arrows. He and Ram Singh were safe now, protected by the wind as by a sheet of steel, for the darts did not carry enough force, or weight, to penetrate that hurricane. Wentworth's guns began to speak rhythmically and screeches of pain came from the night. His heart beat joyous rhythm to his shots. He had thought Jackson dead and now he was restored. His lips moved grimly at each bullet he pumped into the darkness.

"Jackson," he called. "Come to the ship!"

"Coming!" Jackson's deep voice echoed, then he burst zig-zagging into the circle of light, crossed it and raced toward the ship. Wentworth's guns sought out the sources of the darts that flew for him and presently Jackson was beside him, his thick chest heaving from his run. He stood stiffly as the soldier he was, wide shoulders braced, broad face expressionless.

"Lost the Northrup, sir," he shouted above the roar of the propellers.

"Saved our lives!" Wentworth shouted back at him. "Into the plane, sergeant. Ram Singh, at the controls."

Ram Singh loosened his hold on the wing. The ship was quivering with the battle between propeller and brakes. Released, it bounded scarcely seventy-five feet before it lifted its nose toward the skies. Wentworth, crowded into the forward cockpit with Jackson, fitted on headphones and handed a pair to the sergeant.

"Report," Wentworth ordered briefly.

"Yes, sir," said Jackson, his voice at attention even though he himself was seated. "You know how I picked up a plane and followed. Got here, two other ships laid for me. Plane I followed kept right on. Tried to follow and two ganged up on me. Shot out my radio. Incendiary bullets got gasoline. Bailed out and parachuted into river. Got to wreck in time to see them sneaking devils trying to ambush you."

"Planes go away?" Wentworth inquired.

"Think they landed, sir," Jackson responded. "Not in sight when parachute opened."

Wentworth peered overside and found that Ram Singh was circling slowly, recalled he had not ordered any particular destination. Even as he looked, lights flared out over a field and three ships scuttled through it and bolted into the air. Wentworth laughed. Useless to attempt to fight three planes, when those ships had machine guns and he had only his automatics. But there was another way. He leaned forward and tapped Ram Singh's shoulder, shook his fist toward the lighted field.

Ram Singh twisted about and showed his gleaming teeth. While he still looked, the ship dipped nose down for the earth, diving straight toward the three rising planes!

# CHAPTER EIGHT

# TRIUMPH OF THE BAT!

T HE FANTASTIC COURAGE of that unarmed dive upon three machine-gun planes stupefied the pilots of the attacking ships for a space of seconds. They scattered from under the headlong plunge of the *Spider's* plane, breaking their formation, darting in all directions to escape what seemed a suicidal attack.

Wentworth's plane, under the steady hand of Ram Singh, flashed past them toward the field before they realized their mistake. When they whirled to the assault, it was almost too late. Ram Singh was floating in to a landing near the hangar at the upwind end of the field. The three planes, machine guns stuttering, swept in together on the slow-moving ship.

Watching them bullet-dive toward him, Wentworth saw certain death for his valiant men and himself. Their ship made a perfect target. He snatched out his automatics and sprayed lead at the lights that flooded the field with pale lavender illumination. His bullets smashed them into blackness and he sent his shout against the beat of the propeller, the lowered hum of the motor.

"Ground loop!"

He felt the ship tilt to the left as Ram Singh threw over the stick. There was a rending crash, the snarl of a bent propeller and Wentworth was hanging in his straps from an overturned plane. He was the first out and Jackson and Ram Singh were scarcely a second behind. They were jarred, but unhurt, and they followed Wentworth in a dash for the darkened hangar a hundred feet away.

Over their heads, motors roared and machine guns chattered. There was a beating of hard, leaden rain upon the earth near them, but none came too close and they reached the hangar in a hard run.

Inside the hangar, the liquid pop of a blowgun was incredibly loud. Wentworth cursed at this new attack. His gun answered almost of its own volition. There was a gasped cry and, after that, silence.

"Ram Singh!" Wentworth ordered sharply. "There must be a car outside. Get in it and speed away from here."

"Where to, *sahib*?"

"Philadelphia. Shake off pursuers there, not before. Report to *missie sahib*."

There was a movement of shadows, a muttered: "*Han, sahib!*" and Ram Singh had salaamed and vanished. Within a minute and a half, an automobile engine roared and dwindled rapidly into the distance. Wentworth and Jackson stood with their backs against the left wall of the hangar and waited.

"Any orders, major?" Jackson asked quietly.

"Just wait," Wentworth told him. "It's their first move. Must be more men here than the one Jivaro with the blowgun. Some will follow Ram Singh, thinking we've all escaped. When the others leave, we follow. The headquarters must be somewhere near here." Wentworth was hard put to hide the elation in his voice. He had played in luck tonight in spite of the destruction of his Northrup and his failure to capture a man alive in the battle under the wharf.

The machine guns had ceased to fire now and from the drum of the motors, it was apparent the planes were circling the field. Minutes dragged past, then a single flood light sprayed its ray over the ground. A second and a third followed and without waiting for complete illumination, the three ships swooped to a landing, rolled toward the hangar. From behind the lights, a dozen Indians in short scarlet kirtles ran toward the planes.

Goggled men sprang from the cockpits and the Indians prostrated themselves upon the ground. Wentworth watched, frowning, from the shadows of the hangar where, with Jackson, he crouched behind a gasoline drum. He was frowning, but what was going on out there was obvious enough. The Indians believed these flying men were gods. . . . One of the Jivaros leaped to his feet and raced off across the field. Moments later, all was dark again, but the planes were not trundled toward the hangar. There was absolute silence. . . .

"Something's up, sir," Jackson whispered.

Wentworth's eyes were tight and hard as he strove to accustom them to the darkness. No doubt that what Jackson said was correct. In some way, the Indians had detected his trick of sending only Ram Singh away as a decoy.

"Looks like we'll have to fight our way out," he said quietly. "Try to capture a white man. The Indians wouldn't know anything and wouldn't talk if they did. There must be a side door. . . ."

Leading the way, with Jackson just behind him, Wentworth crossed the dark hangar toward its opposite side. He found the door all right, turned the knob cautiously. That silence outside was prolonging itself suspiciously. . . .

A voice called hollowly from the main door and Wentworth wheeled that way, guns ready. No one was in sight.

"Surrender!" the voice called again, "or you will be killed instantly."

Wentworth pushed open the side door and slipped outside. Jackson was close behind him and they stood, waiting, peering into the darkness that crowded close upon them. A dozen yards away was a thick woods. Nothing moved. . . . With the abruptness of a gunshot, light bathed the entire side of the hangar, outlined the two men against it like black silhouette targets. Wentworth's gun blasted even as he flung himself to the earth. The light went out but behind him Jackson cursed raspingly.

"Got me, major. Blowgun dart. . . ." His voice faded and was punctured by a series of popping sounds there in the edge of the woods. Wentworth's guns blasted, his lips thinning back from his teeth. Jackson, good God, Jackson hit by a poisoned dart! . . . Two darts pricked his own skin, one on the throat, the other on his cheek. A dozen more thudded gently against the galvanized side of the hangar. With a shouted roar of anger, Wentworth leaped to his feet.

God! So the *Spider* had got it at last, dying not by the guns of the Underworld, but by poison on the end of a primitive arrow! His automatics blasted deafeningly. Screams beat upon his ears through the thunder of his weapons, but it was the end. No mistaking that this time. Here was no death trap, no plant he could wriggle out of, here was only death. . . .

Already a cold numbness was stealing over him. He wavered on his feet, squeezing the triggers of his automatics again. They kicked from his hands. For long seconds more he stood there, feeling again and again the prick of the darts, piercing his clothing, kissing his hands. By sheer will force, he fought down the numbness that washed up his limbs, that groped with cold fingers for his heart, his brain. . . .

A fierce, ringing cry welled up from his lips. The *Spider* fell. . . . A single glimmer of consciousness remained. He felt a great peace, a welling happiness of spirit. The battle was ended at last. Nita, *Nita*. . . .

He was dead, and yet he continued to realize dimly what was going on about him. In this fumbling way, he felt that he was lifted and carried. He remembered vaguely that *curare*, the poison with which the South American blowpipe users tipped their darts, paralyzed instantly, but did not kill for almost twenty minutes. He was passing through that intermediate stage of death now. . . .

Something pricked his throat. What the devil, were they injecting more poison into his veins? But there was no need for that. He was already. . . . But was he? The numbness was receding, the blackness withdrawing from his eyes. He could not understand all that was happening, but he could not doubt it. Had these Indians then found an antidote for the poison that had no antidote?

He heard a voice as harsh and grating as the squeak of a bat ranting impatiently. Then someone systematically began to slap his face. He opened his eyes and peered up into the impassive face of an Indian. The eyes glittered like points of obsidian knives. . . . Hands gripped his shoulders and hauled him to his feet. He was in an immense black room where the light was dim and red. The grating voice came from a great bat upon a throne of skulls. . . . what, a bat? But it wasn't possible . . . !

Wentworth shook his head violently to clear it, peered again at the throne. He saw now that it was a man seated there, a man with great leathery wings stretching from his shoulders. Now and then he waved them back and forth languidly. Wentworth saw these things without actually taking them in, but presently the last of the fogginess lifted from his brain, leaving it brilliantly clear. He peered into the face of the creature on the throne and, uncontrollably, a strong shudder plucked at his muscles. Was this the Bat Man then?

The face was incredibly hideous, the nose sliced off, the whole countenance drawn up toward that wound into a striking and hideous semblance of a bat's convulted face. He had even attached huge, pointed ears to his head, and those wings. . . . Wentworth pulled himself together with a bracing of his shoulders, a lift of his chin. There was that about the man and his face that made his blood run cold, but it was trickery. It must be. . . .

He looked about him with steady eyes, saw that Jackson stood nearby with four men clinging to his unbound arms even as Wentworth realized he also stood. About them stood ranks of impassive Indians, each kirtled in brilliant red with a belt about their waists of some curious whitish leather. . . . The monstrous squeaking of the Bat Man pulled his head toward the throne sharply.

"You are wondering why you are alive," he rasped. "It is not our habit to kill such prisoners as come our way—that is, not at once. You were shot with narcotic instead of poisoned darts. You see, our bats must have food."

He said the words simply, so matter-of-factly that for a moment the meaning did not penetrate. Food for the bats. . . . But these bats were vampires. They fed on blood! Wentworth's eyes tightened against a tendency to widen. He could feel the quivering of the muscles in his temples, but Wentworth forced his stiff lips to smile.

"I have considered many ends," he admitted casually, "but supplying oral transfusions to bats was not among them!"

He was conscious of Jackson's white face, his knotted, wide-muscled jaws, but he dared not look that way lest his sternly held composure desert him. The Bat Man made no direct reply to Wentworth's jibe, but the already contorted face was made revoltingly hideous by a frown. Jackson's breath was audible to Wentworth, a hissing, strangled sound. Somewhere behind the throne, a gong lifted its singing note and the Bat Man's frown faded. He smiled and lifted his right hand. . . .

Behind the throne, a door opened, revealing hangings of golden silk and through those portieres stepped a woman with glistening black hair that fluffed out from beneath scarlet fillets. She wore a scarlet robe, but one milk-white shoulder was bare, her breasts were outlined in bands that criss-crossed over her bosom in Roman style. Wentworth's teeth locked tightly.

"June Calvert!" he whispered.

The girl smiled down on him haughtily, her dark intelligent eyes half-veiled by their lids. "Who is this?" she asked imperiously.

The Bat Man's rasping voice seemed to soften a little. "Richard Wentworth, my dear, who is either a confederate of the *Spider*, or the *Spider* himself!"

Wentworth controlled the start that his muscles involuntarily made at those words. What, had he been discovered so early in the fight? His fists knotted and the Indians to each side, feeling his muscles harden, gripped more tightly, put their weight into their holds upon his arms.

"One of my men," the Bat Man was explaining, "saw the *Spider* knock bats into a car driven by a Hindu and later the Hindu released those bats coated with radioactive paint. This man attempted to trail them from the skies. The Hindu is this man's servant. . . ."

A remarkable change had come over June Calvert's face. It was still imperious, but it was twisted with hatred and rage. Her eyes, half-veiled, burned with living fires of anger and her hands became claws.

"The *Spider*!" she whispered. "The *Spider* who killed my brother!" Her hand slipped to her girdle and whipped out a curved dagger. She moved toward Wentworth on slow, crouching legs like a cat.

Wentworth smiled at her. "I am not the *Spider*," he said quietly, "but if I were, I could not have killed your brother. He died by the bite of the bats."

June Calvert laughed and the sound was more like a snarl. "Yes, bats killed him. His own bats. He was a partner of the Bat Man, but you turned the bats upon him. It was you, you, *you* . . . !"

"Calm yourself, my dear," Wentworth shrugged. "I'll admit that anger becomes you . . ."

June Calvert sprang toward him with her knife uplifted. The Bat Man squeaked. It was precisely that—not words, nor articulate sound—simply a squeak of peculiar timber. An Indian sprang between Wentworth and June, offered his breast to the knife. For a moment, it seemed she would strike him down to reach the man behind him, but the Bat Man was speaking now.

"My dear," he whispered raspingly, "I have another, juster, more delightful death in store for our friend here, be he *Spider* or not. As you know, the appetite for human blood of our cutely starved bats must be whetted. Sometimes when we have no prisoners, we are forced to call for volunteers from among our company, but now there is no need for that. Would you not consent, my dear, to feed him to the bats instead?"

June Calvert stood panting, just beyond the human barrier which shielded Wentworth. Gradually the hatred and rage in her face became more subtle, gave place to a cruel joy.

"Splendid!" she whispered. "Oh, splendid!" She turned toward the throne and bowed low. "Grant that I may watch the . . . bats feed."

The Bat Man's laughter was squeaky, too. It ascended the scale like the grating of a saw-file until it became inaudible in the ultra-human range.

"Yes, my dear," he whispered. "You may!"

He lifted his left hand in a peculiar gesture and Wentworth's captors wrenched him backward and pinned him to the floor. Other Indians tore his clothing from his body. To his right, he could hear Jackson cursing and fighting futilely against similar treatment. Then, birth-naked, they were thrust across the darkened room. Behind them, came a long file of Indians, marching, chanting a harsh paean. Their joy was obvious. On the throne at the other end of the long room, the Bat Man laughed and laughed his squeaky, unearthly mirth and June Calvert stood, proud in scarlet, with a cruel smile on her lips.

Wentworth and Jackson marched side by side now. Jackson twisted about his head. "Good God, what a woman!" he whispered. "She's mine, major. Mine! I never saw a woman who could stir me so. . . ."

Wentworth looked curiously as this staid soldier who had fought beside him through so many life and death struggles. A steady man, reliable and unimaginative. But now his chest heaved with something more than his exertions, and there was a set, determined jaw. He did not even seem to consider what lay in store for them.

"When we get out of this," Jackson said heavily. "I'm coming after her. I am."

Wentworth smiled thinly. Jackson said *when*, not *if*, we get out of this. But then, Jackson was depending on the *Spider* who had wrested him from many a fierce and loathesome doom. Wentworth felt the grimness of his own locked jaw, but he was fighting against an overwhelming despair. To be locked in a cage, naked, with starved vampire bats, could mean only inevitable death.

A steel grating was opened in a chamber whose walls were steel-mesh wire. Wentworth was hurled forward, Jackson behind him. They sprang to their feet as the door clanged shut, got their backs against a wall and strained their eyes into the twilight of their death-chamber. There on the floor were stretched two things that had been men. Their flesh was shrunken and folded in upon their bodies. Cheeks were sunken and shriveled lips bared locked teeth. But more than anything else, it was the *pallor* of the bodies that mocked Wentworth and Jackson in the cage of bats. Those bodies were . . . bloodless. . . .

Jackson still seemed in the daze which the beauty of the woman had afflicted upon him. Wentworth slapped him violently on the cheek.

"Later, Jackson, later," he said sharply. "Now, we must fight for our lives, unless you want to be as they are." His rigid pointing arm, indicating the bodies on the floor, snapped Jackson to attention. He paled. A shudder convulsed his shoulders.

"Good God, major!" he whispered. "What can we do?"

Wentworth shook his head slowly. There were Indian guards outside the cage with ready blowguns. There was no escape there. June Calvert had had a chair brought to the door and she sat there, languidly waiting for the torture to begin.

"What in God's name can we do?" Jackson whispered again.

Already above them in the dark upper reaches of the mesh prison, there were premonitory squeakings and fluttering. A bat winged through the air near them, circled, and swept toward Jackson. He struck savagely with his fist, then cursed and gripped his hand.

"The devil nipped me," he growled.

Wentworth laughed and there was a touch of wildness in the sound. The bats' teeth were not poisoned, it was apparent, since

Jackson had been bitten and still lived. But how long could they survive the blood-draining battle with the bats? There were thousands of them up above, to judge from the sound. But he knew the answer. It would be a matter of time only.

"We could make a barricade of those two bodies," Jackson said, without hope.

They did that, crouched behind the blood-drained corpses that warned them of what the future held. They settled themselves to fight for their lives. Abruptly the air was filled with a myriad black flutterings. Jackson and Wentworth flailed the air with their arms. Utter loathing gripped the *Spider*. The stench of the bats was nauseous and the thought of dying to feed such beasts. . . .

Jackson screamed with a hint of hysteria. "Take him off! Take him off!"

Wentworth smashed a bat that had fixed on the side of Jackson's face, then he felt leathery wings touch his throat and tore a vampire from his own flesh. Black wings were beating in his eyes. His breath came short and hot in his throat and it strangled him. He fought with locked teeth, without hope, but with desperation. Good God above, what an end for a man . . . !

# CHAPTER NINE
# THE WOOING OF NITA

N ITA WAS RELUCTANT to leave the Early Quaker with Fred Stoking and his party, knowing, as she did, the battle that impended. But there was nothing she could do to help Wentworth when the bats came, so she went at his bidding. The evening dragged at the night club to which they went and at midnight the group broke up. Newspaper boys were shouting extras when Fred Stoking helped Nita into a taxicab. The headlines screamed of the massacre at the Quaker.

Stoking looked at Nita, sitting erect though pale in the dim rear of the cab, then leaned toward the driver and ordered him to make all possible speed to the Quaker Hotel. Nita thanked him with a glance. There could be no news of Dick there, unless . . . unless, she forced the thought, he had fallen prey to his enemies. But she must know that much with all speed. She was scarcely conscious of the blond handsome man beside her, whose eyes were so attentively on her face. Her thoughts were all of Dick. . . .

The Quaker was a shambles and police sought to bar Nita and her escort, but Stoking was equal to that emergency. He and his family were influential; Commissioner Harrington was a personal friend. . . . They went in, but found no news of Wentworth. Nita brightened a little. He had found a trail then, and followed it.

Stoking led Nita into a small lounge off the main lobby and seat-ed her there.

"I'm sure you won't go to sleep for hours," he said.

Nita acknowledged that with a faint smile. Did she ever sleep when the *Spider* was abroad? Well Wentworth knew that and he would phone her when there was opportunity. . . . She sent word to the desk where she might be found. . . . Stoking found his way to the deserted bar and brought back drinks he had mixed himself.

"Now, Nitita," he said, "let's talk."

There was something in his tone that pulled Nita's head toward him, that penetrated her consciousness. She often worried about her Dick, but it seemed tonight that her fears were greater than usual. It was almost as if she sensed that at this very moment, far away in New Jersey, Wentworth was being thrust into the cage of famished vam-pires. But she could not know that of course. She forced herself to attend to Stoking's words. . . .

"Nitita," Stoking said again, using the name that he had given her long ago in pig-tail-pulling days. "Nitita, you are unhappy." He rushed on as she tried to protest. "It is not a secret, you know. When I came back from the Orient, you were the first person I asked for, and I heard such tales! Nitita, you have no right to be unhappy."

Nita laughed a little unsteadily. She looked up into the handsome face bending protectively toward her. Fred Stoking had always had nice eyes. They had acquired authority and depth with the added years, and they were tender on hers now.

Nita said, hesitantly, "Why, Fred, I believe you're making love to me!" She knew instantly that it was the wrong thing to have said. Stoking leaned closer.

"Nitita, you'll say I'm a romantic fool, but I always have loved you. Ever since . . ."

Nita lifted her hands in mock horror. "Not that line, Fred, please. The fiction writers have abused it so!"

Stoking refused to banter. He reached up and touched Nita's gleaming hair with a caressing finger. "I'm very serious about this, Nitita."

Nita was silenced. There was an intent directness about this man that could not be turned away with jests. She looked into the depths of his eyes and believed him. Her hand went impulsively to his.

"Don't, Fred," she said quietly. "I appreciate what you say, more than you can know. But I'm engaged to another man."

Stoking threw back his head and laughed. There was an edgy bitterness to the sound that was not pretty. "Engaged!" he said mockingly. "For how many years, Nita, have you been engaged to Dick Wentworth?"

Nita took her hand away and twisted her slim white fingers together in her lap. She looked at them, writhing there, and she smiled. "It's quite a while," she said quietly.

"He has no right!" Stoking declared fiercely. "I stayed away because I knew of this so-called engagement, but as it went on and on, I began to hope. Nita, I came home for you. I am going to take you back with me. No man has a right to inflict such unhappiness on any woman. . . ."

Nita lifted her head proudly. Her hands were quiet now. There might have been a time when domineering thrilled her, but she was a woman who had . . . good God, who had killed men! These slim white hands of hers could throw a bullet with accuracy that almost rivaled the *Spider's*. Her muscles were hardened by the physical instruction Wentworth had insisted she undertake when, defying his own opposition and the dictates of her own longings for normal, human life, she had pledged herself to the hard road of the *Spider*. Why, if she wished, she could tie even this powerful man beside her into knots with jiu jitsu! No, she could not be cave-manned.

Stoking saw his error at once. "Forgive me, dear, if I sound too excessively masculine," he said, with a touch of whimsicality, "but you can't guess how long I've eaten out my heart with longing."

"Stop, Fred," she said softly, "you make me very unhappy!"

Stoking laughed again, harshly. "Then I will stop. You have enough unhappiness. . . . Oh, my dear, I could give you so much. I know you do not love me, but you would, Nitita, you would! Don't tell me that you don't like the things I do, the far ends of the earth when you wish, and a fireside and children when you don't. Unhappiness!"

Nita's full lips straightened themselves with compression. "You are talking rather foolishly," she said, for all the stab of pain he had given her. Fred Stoking could read her all right. "Very foolishly. After all, I am, as the saying goes, free, reasonably white, and considerably over twenty-one. . . ."

"Twenty-six," Stoking said harshly. "Can you tell me anything about you I don't already know?"

"A great deal," Nita smiled into his eyes, so directly, so steadily that his own faltered a little. "A very great deal, Fred. But what I am saying is this: I am not unhappy in my present life. If there are . . . other things I would like, you must not think that I took my present course without great thought. It may be that Dick and I shall never marry. Dick warned me of that when we found we loved each other. He was unwilling for me to face that, but I insisted. We . . . love each other. I don't know what more to say." She reached for his hand, confidently now, steadily and he gripped it hard with both of his. "Fred, I've told you a great deal more than any one else has ever heard. I tell you so you won't foolishly nurture a vain hope. . . . If after all you're not merely . . . but that was unkind. I believe you and what you say."

Stoking held to her hand fiercely, his face drawn and lined with his struggle for control. His voice came out hoarsely. "All right. I accept what you say. But that doesn't mean I give up. Not if Wentworth said the things you indicate. And he would. I know it now. He would be the first to give me encouragement!"

Nita gasped, her hand flinching from his grasp. Before her rose the face of the man she loved, not the gay smiling Dick who first had won her love, but the white-faced battler whom peril created. She saw the hard bitterness that wrenched his lips, the cold, gray-blue strength of his eyes, and she could hear him saying just what Stoking declared.

"Darling, you know it is hopeless," he would say. "I love you. God knows I do. Love you enough to give you up. Seek happiness in normal living. The hell in which the *Spider* lives is not for a glorious woman like you. . . ."

Nita buried her face in her clenching hands. "No!" she cried, her voice muffled. "No, no, no!"

Stoking sat silent beside her, a little frightened at the emotion he had stirred, but his lips were grim-set. He was a fighter, too. Presently he touched Nita's arm.

"We'll forget it for the present," he said, "but don't think I've finished. I don't give up so easily."

There was a bleak coldness in his own blue eyes. He looked up abruptly as a movement caught his gaze. A bellboy stuck his head in at the door. "Phone call for Miss Nita van Sloan!"

Nita sprang to her feet. "Where?"

The boy turned and swaggered cockily across the lobby. Death nor tragedy, nor weeping women in the hotel lounge, could dim the brass that shone upon him—and not alone from his uniform buttons. Nita hurried to the telephone he indicated, aware that Stoking followed at a discreet distance. Now, Nita thought, now I'll hear Dick's voice. Dear Dick . . . !

"Hello," she faltered, then she straightened, her hands tight on the telephone. The happiness went out of her, but something else entered, the white, tight-lipped determination that was the other woman beneath her soft and lovely beauty. She spoke in Hindustani, her voice crisp, decisive.

"Is he in his own identity, Ram Singh, or . . . ? That helps some. Where are you? Wait there then. I'll come as quickly as possible. No, Ram Singh, there is nothing you can do now but wait."

She turned from the phone and Stoking strode toward her. He checked a half-dozen feet away, recognizing the change in her. It was present even in the way she walked. Still graceful she was, but there was business and determination in her pace.

"It's trouble," Stoking said flatly. "I've heard how you've gone to rescue Wentworth on occasion. You'll have to count me in on this."

Nita hesitated and her appraisal of him was as swift and competent as a marine captain's. "Very well," she said. "Get the fastest car and the fastest plane in the city. Have the car at the door in five minutes; the ship ready when we reach Camden field. Dick has been captured by the Bat Man!"

She moved swiftly to the elevators and, for a space of seconds, Stoking stood and watched her go, his eyes admiring, filled with longing, then he sprang to a telephone. . . .

It was just four minutes later that Nita stepped from the elevator, but Stoking was ready. He caught her elbow and was conscious of the bulge of a gun beneath the smart, tailored fit of her dark-blue suit.

Stoking felt distinctly out of place in his tail coat and faultless evening dress, but he made a joke of it.

"I carry armament, too," he told her gayly, "part of which you would probably disapprove. It is a knife strapped to my left forearm."

Nita said briefly, "Knives have their uses. Ram Singh has saved my life a dozen times over with his. Is the rest of your armament a revolver? If you have no firearms, I have an extra one in my purse for you."

They were in the car by now—Stoking's own, with a respectful chauffeur at the wheel—and the machine, which was a rakish Minerva, was muttering at close to top speed through the deserted streets. Stoking lounged on the cushions beside Nita and she noted with approval that he had the same manner of facing crises that so distinguished Wentworth, a calm, bitter readiness. Nita herself was tense.

"Don't you want to tell me about it?" he suggested quietly.

"You'll have to know if you're to help," Nita conceded, as if reluctantly. She told him of Wentworth's flight, the crash, and of Ram Singh's being sent away in a stolen car. "Ram Singh knew that he was supposed to be a decoy," she went on, "and when the Bat Man's crew didn't pursue, he stopped. He heard some fast, deliberate shooting and recognized Dick's guns. Then he heard Dick cry out. . . ." Nita paused, pressing her hands tightly down on the bulging black handbag in her lap. "Ram Singh does not scare easily, but he said that it . . . it sounded like a devil's death cry."

"Dick isn't dead," Stoking said quietly. "You would have known it, if he were."

Nita's voice was very low. "Yes, you do know me, Fred. You're right, I would have known. What Ram Singh said confirms it. He saw Dick and Jackson carried into two planes and flown away. Ram Singh tried to steal the third plane, but found the propeller had been bent in landing. He just escaped the Indians and came to phone me. He's in Flemington. We're flying there. Have to make a landing in a field with magnesium flares."

"I've got a two-seater Lockhead Vega," Stoking said casually. "I'm an indifferent pilot, but I understand you can handle ships."

"I have a thousand hours—transport license," Nita replied, tight-lipped. That was Dick's doing, too, teaching her to fly. Dick had been thorough. . . .

"I want to apologize again," Stoking kept his tone light, "for trying to caveman you. It was not the right tactic—not at all!"

Nita felt her tension easing a little beneath his banter. He was doing his part well, but even he knew that the ultimate effort must be hers. Well, she had never failed Dick yet.

The Vega was fast as Nita could have wished, but it seemed scarcely to move toward Flemington. She made a safe, though rough, landing on a meadow near the town and Ram Singh raced up in a car while they still clambered from the plane. The Hindu hesitated at sight of Stoking but, at a sign from Nita, accepted him and began to spill what supplementary news he had in a virtual downpour of words.

"What were the Bat Man's planes used for?" Nita asked abruptly.

Ram Singh lifted his shoulders in token of ignorance. "Perhaps, *missie sahib,* to distribute bats. There was a cage of them in the plane left behind."

Nita laughed exultingly. "To the field quickly, Ram Singh!" she cried as she sprang into the car Ram Singh had brought. "We must have that cage of bats!"

The car was fast enough, but scarcely comfortable. Stoking and Nita jounced miserably as the intrepid Hindu streaked over dark Jersey roads. He battled curves with squealing tires and motor roaring wide open, flew through unlighted anonymous towns that were no more than sounding boards for the car's engine.

"Why this wild enthusiasm for bats?" Stoking inquired mildly. "I must confess the poisonous little beasts don't interest me in the least."

"Later," Nita snapped. "Look for barbed-wire fences. If you see one, sing out. Ram Singh, stop at the first cry. *Stop, Ram Singh!*" Nita sprang from the car, groped in a pocket of the front door and got pliers, then strode to a barbed-wire fence on her side of the road. Within brief minutes, she was back with a coil of separate strands of wire. But still Stoking had no time for questions. Nita demanded his handkerchief, then the lining from his coat. Finally, she tore the upholstery of the car with the pliers and pulled out gobs of curled hair and padded cotton.

Ram Singh was traveling more slowly and silently. Everything in his manner suggested that they were near the field and that no chances must be taken of discovery.

"Bring me the cage of bats," Nita ordered.

Ram Singh sprang from the car and salaamed profoundly, lifting cupped hands to his forehead as he bowed in respect. *Wah!* This woman was a fit mate for his master—a tigress whose claws were as deadly as those of the old one himself. Bring back the bats? He would bring back heaven and hell, let her but command it!

As he strode off into the darkness, Nita sprang from the car and took the cap off the gasoline tank. She had fastened the torn bits of cloth to strands of the barbed-wire and now she dipped each one into the gasoline. When Ram Singh returned, she was ready. At her command, the Hindu maneuvered out one of the bats and held it so it could not bite. Nita fastened a string made of torn cloth through a small slit she made in the bat's inter-femoral membrane. The string was attached to wire, which in turn wrapped a bundle of gasoline-soaked cloth.

All climbed back into the car, then Nita touched a match to the gasoline rag and ordered the bat released. With the torch blazing behind him, the bat rose bewilderedly straight upward for a short distance. Then, with side excursions in which it tried to shake off the blazing tail that had been given, it made a laborious way southward. Nita watched until the ball of fire gave her the right direction, then she sent Ram Singh forward.

The Hindu was smiling broadly. *Wah!* Had he not said she was a veritable goddess? Wentworth *sahib* had sprayed bats with luminous paint and followed them. The *missie sahib* lacked the paint, but did that hinder her? By Siva, no! They would follow these bats to the hiding place of this unclean creature who flew through the air, then, by Kali, the destroyer, there would be an accounting! A hand stole to the hilt of the keen knife at his sash. . . .

They traveled five miles southward before Nita released the second bat. That left her three more. When they were gone. . . . But before that, they must have a clue to the Bat Man's whereabouts. They *must*! One by one those bats with their trail of fire fought upward into the sky and winged their way off into darkness, charting a course for the Bat Man's headquarters. The way was still southward. The next to the last bat had almost escaped them when the rays of an approaching car's headlights blinded them, but finally they detected the flying creature deviating from a straight, southern course, heading slightly eastward. They were near now, very near. That much was obvious, but how would they find the place with only one more bat? They might arrive within a hundred yards of the place and then. . . .

Resolutely, Nita prepared a larger bundle for the torch, burdened the final bat until it could scarcely lift itself toward the sky. It would be forced to fly slowly; the longer burning of the torch would help. Nita signaled a stop, alighted and stepped behind the car to dip the cloth in gasoline. As she struck a match to the torch, she breathed a little wordless prayer. If this hope failed them. . . . The bat struggled upward. Nita watched it go with aching eyes, then whirled as footsteps grated in the roadway. Flashlight glare assaulted her eyes and a gruff voice that carried the obvious burden of authority, rasped at them to: "Put them up!"

"We've got you, you damned murderers!" another man rejoined. "You was seen turning loose them bats along the road. Guy passed you and saw you. And now we catch you at it."

One man was on the running board with a gun against Ram Singh's side. Nita did not answer. She barely heeded them or realized their presence now, for she was watching the ball of fire that marked the bat's heavy flight as it moved directly eastward. . . .

"You're completely wrong about this," Stoking said sharply. "We have nothing to do with the poisoned bats. We. . . ."

A policeman's stocky figure came out from behind the light and his billie slapped Stoking unconscious to the ground. "Any guy that would turn loose them bats. . . ." he muttered, then turned to Nita.

Nita realized abruptly that, though she had at last approximately discovered the hiding place, at least of adherents of the Bat Man—the spot where possibly Dick was held prisoner—she was now helpless to render him any assistance. She caught the policeman by the arm, tried to explain what they had been doing. He only scowled and growled at her.

"Listen, baby," he said. "Only one thing int'rests me. You was turning loose them bats and you are going to jail. Come along!"

Nita gazed despairingly into his face. He couldn't mean what he said—but it was obvious that he did. She *must* get away. She had to save Dick—who must be very close now.

With a wrench, she freed herself from the policeman's hand and darted for the shrubbery at the side of the road. She reached it, but the bushes were thick and blocked her retreat. She snatched for the automatic beneath her arm, her breath sobbing in her throat. Dick never fired on police, not even to save his own life, but, but . . . this was for Dick!

She lifted the automatic. The policeman's stick slashed down on her wrist. Agony raced up her arm, then the policeman had her. Her arm was twisted behind her back until she moaned with the pain of it. She was tripped and thrown flat on her face, then handcuffs pinched home on her wrists. She lifted her head and saw Ram Singh unconscious on the ground beside Stoking. That hope was gone, too.

"Baby," growled the policeman, "when I say jail, I mean *jail*!"

Utter despair shook Nita. Sobs rose in her throat, but she choked them down. Surely, this time, destiny conspired against Dick! Was this, then, the end which the *Spider* and his mate had known must come some day . . . ?

# CHAPTER TEN
# IN THE VAMPIRE'S CAGE

IT SEEMED TO WENTWORTH, in the cage of the vampires, that he and Jackson had fought for hours against the bats. His arms became leaden with the ceaseless flailing against never-tiring wings. The upper half of his body was bleeding from half a hundred tiny wounds, but as yet, none of them was serious. Both men were panting through brassy throats.

"Can't . . . keep it up . . . much longer, major!" Jackson gasped beside him. The ceaseless whipping of his arms lagged for an instant and five of the brown furry beasts broke through his guard and darted at his face and throat. Jackson shouted, seized one in his fist and beat at the others with it. The captured bat squeaked and squealed and other vampires drew off, fluttering just out of reach of the defending arms of the men.

"Make it keep on squealing," Wentworth ordered sharply.

Jackson did, and while the bat shrilled its fright, the others held back.

"It won't last long," Wentworth panted.

"No, and there's no way out . . . unless Ram Singh comes."

Wentworth shook his head. "Sent him to Philadelphia. We'll have to get out of this ourselves." It was as if he knew that at this minute, within five miles of the house, Nita and Ram Singh and Stoking were helpless in the hands of the police. He knew a sickening despair. If he could only think. . . . Already the truce of fright was ending and the bats were fluttering to the attack again. Through their black cloud, Wentworth gazed toward where June Calvert still sat watching. She was leaning forward, her face cruelly smiling.

"Behold your love, Jackson!" he cried, "how she enjoys your torture!"

Jackson, flailing again with weary arms, peered toward her and, even in the midst of pain, Wentworth saw that she still drew him; that the strange attraction held. A glimmering of an idea began to shine in his brain.

"Jackson," he said quietly. "We're going to the door, back to back. You face the door. . . ."

Jackson turned a bewildered face toward him. "We'll be more exposed, sir."

"Quite," Wentworth conceded. "I'll stand first. Set your shoulders to mine and we'll walk across to the door."

Jackson was used to obedience. He knew that if Wentworth spoke, it was in furtherance of some definite plan. He did not question the strategy. After all, he had been a soldier. As Wentworth stood, Jackson sprang to his feet, and set his back against Wentworth's, walked slowly toward the door while they both struck out with their arms and kicked off the bats that flew low to attack their legs. They reached the grilled opening and Jackson pressed against it.

"Now, what, major?" he asked. His voice was strained and difficult.

Wentworth struck down a bat that bit at his face, caught another in his hand and held it, loudly squealing, before him. For a while the others held off. Wentworth laughed.

"Behold, Jackson," he cried, "the woman you love!"

Jackson did not answer, but Wentworth could hear his heavy, strained breathing. The bats continued to circle and with regular sweeps of his arms, he drove them back. He waited. It was a faint hope that he entertained. Jackson's instantaneous, passionate interest in the woman was a strange thing, but its reason was clear. The woman herself was intense, strongly emotional. The sight of her fancied enemy undergoing the torture of the bats made her breasts heave quickly. If she saw Jackson's overwhelming fascination, was it not barely possible that she might respond?

Jackson was a vigorous, handsome man, with a rugged, wide-jawed, wide-browed face. His chest was banded with muscle and the glistening perspiration caught every high-light, emphasized every ligament contour. There was something primitive about both of them: this savage fighter who had been an incorrigible in the army until he fell under Wentworth's firm hand, and this woman who could delight in torture and death. Elemental, both of them.

The *Spider* could not turn to watch the woman's face or actions. The bats would not permit, and even a glimpse of his own watching eyes might disrupt the spell he sought to weave. He could feel the quicker pumping of Jackson's sides, and finally, because he strained his ears through the ceaseless squeaking of the bats, he caught June Calvert's whispered words.

"Why . . . do you look at me . . . like that?"

Jackson made no answer. If he had guessed at Wentworth's plan, he gave no sign of it. Wentworth supposed that he was too much pre-occupied with emotion to think at all.

The woman spoke again, more strongly. "Why do you look at me like that?"

Jackson boomed out his deep laughter. "Because I hate you!" he cried.

Wentworth's eyes tightened and he nodded slowly. A bat broke through his guard and fastened on his throat. He tore it loose and felt his flesh rip, too. He laughed softly, battled on. The woman's voice was closer now.

"You don't hate me," she said. "You don't! I can see it in your eyes!"

Jackson said nothing and when the woman spoke again, Wentworth started, she was so near!

"Why do you look at me like that?" she whispered.

No sound from Jackson, no more from the woman. Wentworth could hear the breathing of both. He seized a bat and made it squeal in pain. The sound was piercing, hurt the eardrums, but it no longer drove back the vampires. They lanced in over Wentworth's arms.

One got past him and fastened on the side of Jackson's throat; but Jackson did not move to knock it off.

"The bat!" the woman whispered. "There's a bat on your throat. Take it off; please take it off!"

Jackson laughed again. "There will only be another. Let him stay and take his three ounces of blood."

"Please take it off," June Calvert cried. "Oh, there is blood on you, all over you."

Deliberately, Wentworth allowed another bat to slip past him and fasten on Jackson's upper arm.

Jackson spoke to the woman. "Come in here."

"No, *no!*" The woman was panting.

Jackson laughed, triumph in its sound. "You must."

After that, long silence, then Jackson's laughter again, the muscles tightening across his back. Presently, the woman sighed.

"You're hurting me," she whispered. "The bars. Wait, I will open the door."

Her footsteps hurried away. Jackson's weight sagged against Wentworth's back. "She's a devil," he whispered. "She takes my strength away. God, she's wonderful, wonderful . . ."

Wentworth said nothing, his mouth tightening as he continued the battle against the bats. Not much longer, thank God. A little more and they would be out of this cage of death. Even then, there would be fighting—but against humans, and a limited number of them—not against the winged vampires. . . . He made a mental note that Jackson, after this, would be useless to him against the Bat Man.

The woman's footsteps were running when she returned. "I had to kill the man," she sobbed. "I had to. He wouldn't give me the keys."

Metal rasped and Jackson sprang through the door. Wentworth whirled and went after him, slammed the cage shut. Jackson thought nothing of his escape. There was still one bat fastened to his arm, but it was the woman, leaning back in Jackson's embrace, who removed that. She pinched the vampire's throat and held it for a while, then dropped it to the floor. There was a smile on her red lips as she looked up into Jackson's face. She would have to go with them,

Wentworth thought, or the Bat Man would put her in their place in the vampire's cage. He cast swiftly about the black-walled room for a means of escape.

His clothing still lay upon the floor and he donned such pieces of it as were not impossibly torn. The bites of the bats were beginning to pain now. He was wrapped in their torture. He went back to Jackson and June Calvert.

"June, if you want him to live," he said sharply, "we'll have to get you both out of here quickly."

June Calvert looked at Wentworth without comprehension for fully thirty seconds, then she pulled herself out of Jackson's arms.

"Good God," she stammered, "what have I done? I have freed my brother's murderer!"

"I am not his murderer," Wentworth told her quietly. "I had nothing to do with his death, but you have freed us. If the Bat Man catches you, it will mean your death as well as ours."

June seemed still in a half-daze. She looked from Wentworth to Jackson and her gaze lingered longest there. Her face softened.

"You are right," she whispered. "We must escape. Come, I'll lead the way."

Wentworth motioned Jackson toward the remnants of his clothing upon the floor and, with a bound, he reached them and pulled them on. Wentworth had no weapon, nor did Jackson and June had only her curiously curved dagger.

"Are there any weapons we can get?" Wentworth asked.

June shook her head slowly. "The Bat Man allows none," she said. "None save his own and the blowguns of the Indians."

Wentworth thought grimly that the Bat Man did not trust his allies overmuch and nodded at the idea. That would be a help, perhaps.

"We would better leave at once," he said. "Soon the Bat Man will come back to see if we are dead, and then. . . ."

June Calvert nodded. She led the way with the stealth of a cat toward a curtained wall, pulled it aside and revealed a narrow passageway. "At the end of this are three doors," she whispered. "The one to the right leads outdoors. After that, there is no way to escape save by fighting through."

She walked ahead, carelessly, with assurance and behind her Jackson and Wentworth made no sound. Wentworth had no intention of leaving, but he must have a weapon before he could carry out his plan to kill the Bat Man. Jackson and the girl must go. . . .

There was no warning at all, but suddenly the hall ahead of them was crowded with the short, kirtled figures of Indians and a dozen blowguns were aimed at Wentworth and his companions. He whirled to retreat, but that way was blocked in the same way. There was no escape, not even by sacrificing his companions could the *Spider* win through to kill the Bat Man and rid humanity of this newest and most terrible scourge. For, to hold either girl or Jackson as a shield, would merely expose his back to the other force. . . . Wentworth shrugged.

"We surrender," he said shortly.

From somewhere nearby, but out of sight, the Bat Man squeaked an order. "To the bat cage with them. Strip the woman and throw her in with them. She is a traitor. That was for your benefit, my friends, now I shall repeat the order in their own language. . . ." The Bat Man broke into a gabbled tongue of the Indians. Instantly, they moved forward, half of them almost crawling to keep clear of the blowguns which the other half held ready.

Wentworth knotted his fists, his jaw set rigidly, but he knew it was useless. He would only bring on his own death, whereas if he submitted . . . But what hope lay that way? There would not again be an escape from the fangs of the vampires. He locked his teeth to hold back the curses of despair. Now, surely, there was an end of hope . . . !

If Wentworth surrendered philosophically, June Calvert did not. She swept, raging, toward the line of Indians and they parted before her, and seized her from behind, swept her helpless to the floor with a garrote about her throat.

A hoarse shout tore from Jackson. He hurled himself toward the struggling girl. Her dagger was out and she slashed about with it, hamstrung an Indian so that he dropped, screaming, to one knee. She took a second man in the groin with the blade. Jackson seized an Indian about the throat with his powerful hands, lifted him high and tossed him upon his fellows. Then a tiny dart blossomed on his shoulder, the hollow pop of a blowgun echoed down the hall. From his place of concealment, the Bat Man laughed squeakily.

Wentworth had shouted a warning when Jackson first charged in, but he had known in advance that it was hopeless. Yet he could not stand back while these other two fought. . . . The *Spider's* manner of fighting differed from theirs. Instead of rushing in against the blowguns, he threw back his head and laughed, an echo of the squeaky, bat-like mirth of the leader. While he laughed, he walked toward the place where Jackson and June still battled.

The girl was almost unconscious now, with the bite of the garrote on her throat. Jackson was staggering and Wentworth thought from his behavior that the dart which had pierced his shoulder carried the narcotic, not the deadly poison. . . . Wentworth continued his laughing advance. He could see that the Indians were puzzled, that they did not know whether or not to shoot. The Bat Man continued his mirth. Apparently, he could not see what went on in the narrow hallway. Wentworth stood now over Jackson, who had fallen, and the girl. Both were unconscious. Lord, it was so hopeless. What could he hope to accomplish, unarmed, against ten savages? Two lay dead on the floor, one still moaned over the gashed and useless leg. . . .

Wentworth helped the injured Indian to his feet and, still making squeaking noises, led the man down the hall. The blowgun men were puzzled, and as he continued, parted their ranks. Hope began to thrill through Wentworth, but it died in an instant. Apparently, he had shown himself to the Bat Man, for suddenly a high, shrill squeak rang out. Instantly, a flood of Indians hurled themselves upon him. Blowguns were forgotten. It was hand to hand, twist and wrench and punch. An Indian seized Wentworth's right wrist and attempted to twist it behind him. The man was powerful and his very grip was painful. Wentworth hurled himself bodily backward, tossing the Indian against the ceiling with the impetus of his fall.

The trick was a mistake. Though the man he had thrown fell unconscious, and probably dead, to the floor, four other Indians dived bodily upon Wentworth before he could rise to his feet again. He held one off with a kicking foot, got his elbow against the throat of a second, but the other two hit solidly on his chest. One got his fingers on Wentworth's throat and pressed crushingly on the larynx. Darkness began to whirl before Wentworth's eyes. He pulled up his hands, got hold of a finger with each and shredded the throttling hold off of his throat. He heard the fingers break and the Indian whimpered.

Another of the small, fierce men crawled into the battle. He had June's bloody knife and he moved its blade gloatingly toward Wentworth's throat. At the same time, five more Indians hurled themselves upon him, seizing arms and legs, kicking at his sides. Pain rippled over him. The knife caressed his neck . . . and a gun barked!

The sound of the pistol was deafening in the narrow confines of the hall. The Indian with the knife jerked to his feet and crashed down again in a crumpled heap, his forehead smashed by a heavy bullet. Three pistol shots smashed out together and three more of the small, savage men were slain. Wentworth hurled a body from his chest, bowled over another Indian and sprang to his feet.

"Catch, Dick!" It was a woman's voice, and an automatic arched through the air to his hand. A woman's voice . . . Who could it be but Nita? Wentworth threw back his head and laughed joyously. Nita . . . and a gun in his hand again.

"Brave work, Nita," he cried. He charged down the hall where the Indians were scrambling for their blowguns. He fired once as a man got his long tube to his lips, then he ducked from the hallway into an opening to his right. He no longer heard the squeaking laughter, or sharp orders of the Bat Man, but the creature could not be far away. Back in the hall, Nita's gun and those other two he had not identified were slamming death into the Indians. . . .

Wentworth was racing down a corridor between narrow walls, toward a twilight dimness that seemed to recede before him. He stopped abruptly, listening. The shooting and the shrieks of wounded and dying still came to his ears, but that was all. Nevertheless, he ran on, hoping against hope that he might find the Bat Man. Something clicked beneath his feet and he ducked backward, sensing an opening above his head. He went back three slow paces, eyeing that hole in the ceiling.

Suddenly he understood. A black form had dropped from the opening and leathery wings fluttered toward him. He cursed and fired a quick shot. No need to wonder whether the teeth of those bats were poisoned. Why else would a trap be set with them? He fired twice more in quick succession, then pulled his coat over his head, covered hands in pockets and raced past the spot where the bats whirled. He dared not use more of his bullets, lest there be none left when finally he came face to face with the Bat Man himself.

He burst suddenly into the open through a swinging door and stopped, peering about him. In the east, the sky was graying with dawn. In the woods that grew close to the house, sleepy birds were twittering with the promise of day. Wentworth looked down to the grass. It was wet with dew and here and there upon the blades, spiders had woven webs which were beaded with moisture. Straight ahead of him, a spider web had been torn.

With a cry that he scarcely suppressed, Wentworth sprang forward. The trail in the dewy grass was plain now. This way, the Bat Man must have fled. Abruptly, as he ran, Wentworth halted, made a circuit beneath a tree. There, for some reason, the tracks had left a gap as if the Bat Man had sprung into the air for a distance of ten feet. Even so, Wentworth barely escaped the trap he more than half suspected. His feet jarred the hidden trigger and from the tree overhead a sprung branch hurled a spear deep into the earth where, moments before, Wentworth had narrowly missed treading. If he had stepped there, the spear would have drilled him from neck to groin. Thereafter, he went more cautiously along the woodland path. He had gone perhaps seventy-five yards when, ahead of him, a plane roared into life. Wentworth sprinted for the clearing which he could see now vaguely through the trees, but as he burst into the open, the ship he had heard was just lifting from the earth, despite a cold motor, and climbing rapidly over the tree tops. . . .

The automatic jumped and slammed in Wentworth's hand. He was certain that he hit the plane twice before it slid out of range, but he could not have scored on the pilot for, though there was a slight faltering on the flight after the second shot, the plane kept steadily on. Wentworth cursed with disappointment. There could be no question that the Bat Man had escaped in that ship. He proceeded more cautiously along the trail back and found another trap which he had missed by sheer luck with his long, running stride. He discharged a small bow which hurled a poisoned dart.

Well, once more the *Spider* had met the Bat Man and this time, though he had failed to capture or kill the leader, he at least had not utterly failed. He was light-hearted as he loped back to the gaunt, low building where Nita had come to the rescue. The long, dim halls were as silent as before, more so, since cries and shots no longer echoed. For no apparent reason, an unrest seized him. His pace quickened until he fairly sprinted toward the place where they had battled.

Before he reached the spot, he saw bodies of red-clad Indians sprawled in the doorway. None of them even groaned. Surely, by now, he should hear the murmur of Nita's voice, the sound of her walking. But there was nothing. . . . He hurdled the stacked bodies, halted motionless in the middle of the hallway. Save for the dead—and the unmoving body of June Calvert—the place was empty.

"Nita!" Wentworth sent the cry echoing. "Nita! Nita!"

He waited and the echoes died and silence flowed back to his waiting ears. He sprang toward the spot where she had stood, shooting down the foes that crowded against his back. On the floor there, he found a scrap of lacy white that was her handkerchief, found two abandoned automatics. . . . He straightened with his face gone hard and white, his eyes glittering like deep glacial ice. There was no mistaking those signs, but, good God, Nita could not have been captured thus with those other two with her to help her fight! It wasn't possible . . . !

And then Wentworth saw another thing that filled his heart with leaden despair. The wall was pricked in half a dozen places by blow-gun darts. A groan came from the depths of his soul. He whirled and ran through other dim corridors, burst outside and circled the building, but nowhere was there any trace of Nita. Finally he came to a standstill again where her guns lay upon the floor. He lifted his clenched fists toward the ceiling and shook them twice. He had thought at least a partial victory was in his grasp, and in the moment of elation, he had lost everything . . . !

# CHAPTER ELEVEN
# AGAINST ALL HOPE

WENTWORTH TURNED once more to look about the hall and his eyes fell upon the supine body of June Calvert. Was she dead, then, with that garrote about her throat? With sudden hope, Wentworth approached her in long strides, looked down on her sullenly beautiful face. If it had turned blue with strangulation, then the stagnant blood already had been dissipated. . . . He flung down on a knee and felt for the pulse, held his polished platinum cigarette case before her lips. There was no indication of life either way, and yet. . . .

Swiftly, he turned June over on her face and began resuscitation, hands pressing down on her short ribs to expel air from her lungs, releasing sharply to suck in oxygen. Artificial respiration. He was desperately anxious that she survive. If she was seriously interested in Jackson, she might well reveal the Bat Man's secrets! It was heart-breaking work, this resuscitation of an apparently lifeless woman. If she should survive, he might speed the rescue of Nita, the smashing of all the Bat Man's demon plans. But if his work was useless, precious minutes were being wasted. For over half an hour, he continued the slow rhythm of breathing. There was a frown upon his forehead and curious, straight hardness to his lips. Almost he had despaired when there was a faint sigh from June's lips and, sluggishly, reluctantly, her lungs took up their work again.

She was alive! Wentworth almost cried the words aloud. He had no stimulant to administer, but he used what means of restoration he had, bathing her temples with cold water from a tap he found. Fear widened her eyes when first she beheld him, but presently she appeared to remember the situation. She tried to look about her, hand gripping her throat. . . .

"The Bat Man kidnapped them all," Wentworth told her harshly. "The woman I love, the man you love."

June Calvert thrust herself up on stiff arms and stared about the passageway, saw the heaped bodies of dead Indians and nothing more. Wentworth helped her to her feet and she began to stumble through the deserted halls and rooms. Finally, she sagged weakly against a wall and sobbed there, shoulders jerking spasmodically.

Wentworth watched her narrowly. He must judge her mood exactly if she was to be of help to him. Weeping was the wrong note. He jeered at her.

"I didn't expect you to spend time crying," he said. "Don't you realize that every second wasted brings the man you love that much nearer to the cage of vampires?"

June lifted her dark, disheveled head and stared into Wentworth's eyes. Her shoulders still jerked, but no sound came from her lips.

"Help me," Wentworth urged, "and we will save him."

Resolution hardened on the girl's face, a faint smile twisted her full lips. "You are not interested so much in saving him, as in capturing the Bat Man."

"Not capturing him," Wentworth corrected softly, "*killing him!*"

June Calvert's dark eyes widened a little, but she made no comment.

"But you are wrong about my not wanting to save Jackson," Wentworth continued. "He has been my comrade in arms for years. My Hindu servant is also a captive—and the woman I love. Come, June, the Bat Man ordered your death. You can no longer have any loyalty toward him. And there is Jackson. . . ."

"Jackson," she whispered. "A soldier? What's his first name?"

Wentworth fought for calmness. Seconds were so precious, but if he took a wrong move with this girl. . . . He smiled a little. "Jackson won't want you to call him by it," he said. "It's Ronald."

June was immediately indignant. "Why, I think it's a lovely name. Ronald," she tried it on her lips, softly. "Ronald Jackson."

Wentworth lost patience. "You'll never have a chance to call him by it if we don't hurry," he snapped. "Don't you realize that Jackson is going to be killed . . . by the Bat Man? Even while we stand here talking, he may be. . . ."

June shuddered. The tremor shook her shoulders, jerked over her entire body. "Yes, yes!" she whispered. "But I know so little. I don't know who the Bat Man is or where his other headquarters are, except that he boasted that only he could reach his hideout in the Rocky Mountains unless he went first and prepared the way . . ."

Wentworth was silent, letting her talk now that she was started, but bitter disappointment gripped him. Despair was a cold weight in his breast.

". . . I think," June was frowning, "that he was . . . quite fond . . . of me. He had a strange diffidence and made me rather timid offers to sit beside him when he ruled the world. Oh, it's not as unlikely as you think. He intends to practically destroy the United States. . . ."

A jagged curse forced itself from between Wentworth's lips. "But why? In God's name, why?"

"He intends to demand tribute of all the nations of the world," June said slowly, "in return for a promise not to loose the bats on their peoples."

"Preposterous!" Wentworth snapped. "They wouldn't pay." Then he frowned, remembering. There had been a time when nearly all the maritime nations of the world had paid tribute to the Barbary pirates of the Mediterranean, bribed them not to attack ships flying their flag. Only the United States had refused, and had sent great battleships to uphold that refusal. And that had been less than a hundred years ago. Only the United States had refused . . .

"He thought," June went on, "that the United States would refuse to pay, so he would make an example of her to the rest of the world. I think he plans to save New York for the last. His next attack. . . ."

"You know that? Good!" Wentworth began to know hope again. "Where will that be?"

"Michigan City," June replied briefly.

Wentworth uttered a sharp exclamation. Michigan City was an amusement resort at Chicago to which the city's population flocked in tens of thousands for swimming and other amusements. And in the entire place, there were not a half-dozen buildings into which the bats could not enter. In Chicago proper, it would be different. But in Michigan City, literally thousands would die. . . .

"Come," he said sharply, and hurried down the hall. He heard June's footsteps just behind him.

"Where are you going?" she demanded.

"Michigan City!"

"But you promised to save Ronald!" the girl cried.

Wentworth nodded, never slackening his pace as he pushed out into the morning that was reddening with sunrise. June Calvert caught his arm, tried to pull him about.

"You promised!" she cried.

Wentworth stopped and faced her. "Do you know where Jackson is?" he demanded.

"No."

"Do you know where the Bat Man is?"

"N-No."

"Then, June, we have to go to the only place you know of that the Bat Man will appear, don't we?"

June sobbed, pressed a clenched hand to her forehead. "Yes, yes," she whispered, "but before that, Ronald may be . . . may be . . ."

Wentworth's tanned face was drained of all color. June Calvert lifted her head slowly and looked at him. "Ah," she whispered, "I forgot. The woman you love is there, too!"

Wentworth said dully, "Yes." He turned and hurried off toward the airfield where, almost an hour ago, the Bat Man had winged into the dawn. June caught his arm.

"There are no more planes," she said. "There is nothing at all here to travel in, but there's a highway about three miles to the west."

They tramped in silence through the damp woodland, crashing over underbrush, jumping brooks, fighting thickets. Finally, they burst out in the highway and stopped, staring. There were two automobiles parked on the opposite side of the road. In one of them, two policeman sat.

Wentworth walked toward them and the man behind the wheel twisted about an angry face.

"Hey, buddy," he called. "Come here and get us loose, will you? We're all tied up."

Wentworth stopped beside the car. "How'd you get tied up?" he asked curiously.

"We was chasing them guys what's turning loose bats," the man, red-faced and angry, declared. "We has them all tied up, girl with them, too. Then one of them gets loose and pulls a knife on me and we can't do nothing."

Wentworth tackled the ropes, shooting eager questions at the policemen, but as the story unfolded, his eagerness died. It was apparent now that it was Nita the men had almost stopped. Nita and Ram Singh and Stoking. All of them were in the Bat Man's power now, food for bats. Wentworth's jaw tightened. . . . The police took him and June back to town, casting many curious glances at the girl's strange scarlet dress. When they had found the dead Indians there in the woods, they would remember this meeting, because of that similarity of dress. . . . Wentworth shook his head grimly. There was no time now to explain, even though trouble would follow later.

At Flemington, he found the plane Stoking had rented. He appropriated it and sent the ship racing into the West. At dusk, the attack would be made on Michigan City. There was ample time to reach Chicago by plane. Ample time, if there were no mishaps. . . . Persistently, Wentworth's thoughts reverted to Nita. She was in this situation, prisoner of the Bat Man, because she had striven to help him. God, this was no life for a woman! Better a thousand times, if they had never met. Better if she had married this Fred Stoking, who had been her childhood sweetheart. . . .

His bitterness came back overwhelmingly. What right did he have to wreck Nita's life this way, perhaps to bring about her death? If she had never met Dick Wentworth. . . .

Wentworth was snapped from his reverie by a spluttering motor. He glanced sharply at his instruments, but nothing was wrong there and the engine was drumming steadily again. He peered over the side. Beneath him lay the wild reaches of the Alleghanies. Good God, if he were forced down here, it would take him days to reach even a mountaineer's cabin! Days more before he could reach Chicago! The Bat Man would have struck and vanished. . . . The motor coughed and missed again!

❁ ❁ ❁

The *Spider's* face became hard and rigid. No use to conjecture now. The engine was failing. It was only a question of selecting a spot to crash. A bitter curse squeezed out. He leaned over the side, staring down at the jagged, forested sides of mountains below him. He realized grimly that it was not merely a question of landing in a spot from which it might be possible to reach civilization, it was even doubtful if they would survive the landing!

There was not a fifty-foot clearing anywhere in the tangle of mountains—not a roadway, nor a fire lane. The motor was missing badly now. Even though he pulled the throttle wide, the plane was losing altitude. Not rapidly, but losing none the less. He would have to make his decision quickly.

A mountain-top glided by beneath him, its trees no more than seventy-five feet under the fuselage, and the valley beyond opened. Wentworth knew a thrill of hope, for there was clearly a break in the forest down there. He swept a rapid glance over the country. No sign of smoke, or of human habitation. He laughed sharply. Would it not be better to smash against that rocky precipice that thrust out of the opposite mountain? When finally he escaped from these mountains, Nita would be dead—and Ram Singh and Jackson. . . . Every one dear to him would have died through his failure. Resolutely, he sought to close his mind to those facts. He was, he told himself, no longer a human being, but a cause. He was the *Spider*! He must live to defend humanity. . . .

Time after time, he had been compelled to abandon Nita to her fate while he battled new monsters of crime. For a single instant, however, his mind broke from his rigid control, and he pictured her thrown helpless into a cage of vampires, saw her white body fall under the fluttering black hordes. . . .

He screamed curses into the air, shook his fist at the skies that arched pitilessly above. By God, it should not be! It should not! The final splutter of the motor, the whir of the dying propeller snapped him out of his bitter tirade. He had been handling the plane sub-consciously, directing it toward that clearing in the valley which alone offered hope of safe landing.

Behind him, June Calvert's high voice beat on his sound-deafened ears.

"What's the matter?"

"Motor conked out," he called back to her, then leaned over the side to stare down at the clearing. It was a lake, full of black, jagged snags. The trees grew right to its shores. Once more Wentworth laughed, hardly, bitterly. It would be better if he did die—but he must strive to live. He sent the ship down in a sharp dive. . . .

# CHAPTER TWELVE
# RACE WITH TIME

A S THE PLANE SLOPED toward the lake, Wentworth's eyes swept the wooded shores hopefully. There was no beach anywhere. The retractable landing gear already had been lowered. Now Wentworth set to work to crank it back into the fuselage by hand. The hull of the plane would not resist water long, but he could use it as a pontoon in landing whereas the wheels would catch and tip the ship forward on her nose. His danger, without the wheels, would be in snagging a wing in the water since they would be so close to the surface. Fortunately, the craft was a Lockhead Vega, a high-winged monoplane, so even that danger was reduced. . . .

Swiftly the plane neared the mirror-like lake. The steep, wooded mountains were reflected and white clouds made their images below. It was strangely peaceful, but Wentworth knew no peace, only bitterness and mounting rage. . . . Another hundred feet and the Vega would breast the lake. Wentworth kept the stick waggling gently from side to side, leveling off the wings. He swept in over the tree-tops with scarcely a dozen feet clear, put the nose down and swooped toward the surface.

Down the center of the lake, there was a space fairly clear of snags and Wentworth had picked that as the only possible landing place. Now, as the ship settled in a stall, only inches above the surface, he spotted a submerged log fairly in his path. There was no help for it. He must drive straight for the log. The stick had already gone soft in his hand. . . . The ship squatted down on the water with a heavy impact, ran twenty feet and snagged the log . . .

"Let go and dive!" Wentworth shouted.

The nose went down, the tail whipped up and over, hurling Wentworth and June Calvert like catapult missiles through the air. Wentworth struck head first in a shallow dive, whipped to the surface and peered about for the girl. She broke water a few seconds afterward, smiled at him, white-faced.

"Don't worry about me," she gasped. "I can swim."

Side by side, they struck out for the shore. The plane, on its back, already was settling deep into the water, buoyed for a while by partially emptied gasoline tanks. But the pull of the motor was rapidly overcoming that. Even as Wentworth reached the shore and stood erect in the edge of the woods, the water lapped over the last inch of canvas and the plane disappeared.

Wentworth, his face set, leaned forward to assist June Calvert to her feet and she looked despairingly into his face.

"We're beaten," she said dully. "Beaten before we fairly start!"

Wentworth's lips moved in a slight still smile. "It's ten o'clock. We have almost ten hours to reach Chicago."

June Calvert gazed into his strong face, with its locked jaw and determined eyes and her own despair lessened. "But what can we do?" she whispered.

Wentworth turned and looked up the steep slope of the mountain, toward the bare outcropping of rock near its crest. He nodded toward it.

"From its top, we may be able to spot some help," he said. He turned toward the thick alder bushes that crowded close to the water's edge, the white-stemmed birches beyond. With a curt word, he started forward, wading first through swamp that rose to his knees. Among the birches, he stopped for a few minutes, whittling on two smaller trees with his pocket knife. Presently, they went on again, each with a staff.

The thickets continued and briars snagged at his clothing, tore his hands. He stopped and gave his coat to June Calvert. She thanked him with softening eyes, but his smile was thin.

"It's not chivalry, but wisdom," he said dryly. "You can travel faster with your shoulders protected."

She laughed at him and they went on again, Wentworth crashing through ahead to break a way. There was a hard desperation in his soul. He had to fight to keep from plunging forward at a mad run that would have exhausted him within minutes. A trotting horse travels farther, he reminded himself. God alone knew how much of this tramping there might be, but if he could get hold of a fast plane within the next six or eight hours. . . .

After they left the low shores of the lake, the underbrush was thinner, but the grade was steepening. It took a half hour to reach the crest of the hill, Wentworth discovered with a despairing glance at his watch. Then twelve such hills. . . . But there were the descents and the valleys to cross. Five, six such hills and his margin would be reduced to nothing.

"We'll have to run down this hill," he said shortly. "Jog, don't race."

He set the pace, the half-trot, half-lope that the woods-runners of the Indians had used over these same trails years ago. Half way down the hill, they struck a small path and June cried out in happiness.

"See, a path!" she panted. "Someone must be near!"

"Game trail," Wentworth threw over his shoulder.

But he swung along its course. As long as it went in the direction he wished, it would be swifter traveling. Unconsciously, his pace quickened. At the bottom of the hill, he realized that there were no footsteps behind him and halted. A hundred and fifty yards back, running doggedly at the pace he first had set, was June Calvert. Her red dress had been torn off at the knee and the coat looked strange with the silk robe, but she was plugging steadily along. She looked up, saw Wentworth.

"Go on, go on!" she cried. "I'm all right."

Wentworth waited until she was near, then ran on. The game trail stopped at a small brook in the valley, but another slanted up the hill, Wentworth pushed on, no longer running, but slowly regaining his breath as he pulled the hill. He had hoped from the ridge just passed, that he might detect some signs of human habitation. The hill ahead inspired him anew, but he said nothing. . . . The next valley was empty of hope, too. Wentworth stole a glance at his watch, an hour and a quarter gone. . . .

Doggedly, he held himself back as he loped down toward the valley. The game trail was gone now, wandering off down the valley and the way was constantly impeded by shrubbery. He kept his lips locked against the urge to pant. He could hear June Calvert gasp for breath. But, damn it, there could be no stop, no resting. Within a few hours, the Bat Man would strike. If the *Spider* did not then take his trail, it would be too late to save Nita and those two gallant men who had thrown in their lot with him. It might even be too late to strike at the Bat Man, for if this chance failed, future contacts would depend on luck alone.

These thoughts worked maddeningly in Wentworth's brain as he loped downhill, and labored up the next grade, the third. If this one also proved an empty hope . . . But it would only mean pushing on to the next and a further reduction of the possibility of success. He scarcely dared look at his watch.

It was hot in the woods where the trees choked off all breeze. Black flies and midges danced about his perspiring face and his shirt clung damply to his body. Nor were his shoes fitted to this type of walking. The soles speedily grew slippery on leaves and the fallen needles of pines so that walking became an exhausting labor. At the top of the third hill, June was three hundred yards behind him and he himself was panting through stubbornly resisting lips. Almost he dreaded to peer into the valley beyond and search the opposite slope, but hope urged him on. He looked—it was empty . . . !

June Calvert toiled up to him, glanced and passed on, pushing herself into a labored run. She was panting, too, but there was a stubborn set to her chin. Wentworth loped after her, drew abreast.

"What time?" she gasped.

Wentworth looked reluctantly at his watch. "Half past twelve."

June said nothing and they ran on. At the bottom of the hill, a spring bubbled water into a small brook. Wentworth halted and they drank sparingly and pushed on. The three hours that followed were nightmares of exhausting action. There was no more running down hills and at the crest of each they stopped for long minutes. The heat had increased, and they dared not drink heavily lest cold water bloat them. When they struck a game trail, they followed it, but mostly there was dense underbrush that must be circled or crashed through and in the bottoms, alder bushes made almost impenetrable thickets.

Each hill had burgeoned hope of what might lie beyond, but each crest brought disappointment, so that Wentworth scarcely dared to gaze on the scenes below. The seventh hill seemed interminable, its crest was a bare ridge where rocks jostled the clouds. Twice, on the climb, Wentworth halted and June Calvert toiled to where he stood and went past him. The third time, he was just on the edge of the barren ridge that crowned the rise.

He stood there, gathering strength for the last pull, for the disappointment that must meet him from its top and once more June moved up beside him. Not even glancing in his direction, she traveled on heavily. Her stockings long ago had ripped from her legs and the flesh was torn and lacerated by thorns. Her head sagged so that her black hair half-hid her face and she moved with the steadiness, the stiffness of an automaton.

Wentworth watched her mount toward the crest; then he tramped on himself, head hanging, the white birch staff helping him up the grade. He did not look again at June, but abruptly he stopped, his down-gazing eyes seeing June upon her knees, head sagging, hands clasped together before her. He lifted his eyes and saw slow, blue smoke rising from the opposite slope of the hill. Was it already too late? He said nothing, but looked wearily at his watch. It was half-past four. If he could get a plane by six . . . It would take a half hour or more to reach that smoke.

He bent down and raised June to her feet and together, his arm supporting her, they went down the hill. The bottom was incredibly overgrown, but nothing could have stopped Wentworth now. He crashed through like a bull. On the far side, he stopped, peering upward. Laurel grew thickly ahead of him, screening the ground from view, but he could still see the smoke above the trees. What it portended, he did not know since there had been no house visible from the opposite ridge. But surely there were men here. They would be able to speed him on his way.

He turned, waited for June; then he pushed on again toward the laurel. He was looking at the ground when a rasping voice called out.

"You can stop right there, furriner!"

Wentworth glanced up sharply. A rifle muzzle yawned at him through a thick clump of laurel. . . .

Wentworth looked very calmly into the muzzle of the rifle. He had looked into similar eyes of death many times, but it was not that which calmed him now. It was his determination that nothing should stop him.

"Our plane crashed in a lake seven hills back," he said shortly. "I want a horse or some other means of getting to the nearest town. I'll pay for it . . . by check." He mentioned the method of payment as an afterthought. It would be very easy for the hidden man to shoot if he thought there was any chance for loot.

"We ain't got no hawses," he said flatly. "I reckon you better mosey back over them mar seven hills."

June Calvert was at Wentworth's shoulder. "Stop being a damned fool, Lemuel," she said. "We're not going back and you're going to help us to get out."

"Yuh know Lem?" another hidden man asked cautiously.

June Calvert said, "Oh, go to hell!" She walked to the right of the bushes where the rifle was poised. Wentworth was as puzzled as the rifleman obviously was, but he followed June. Two mountaineers came cautiously out of the laurel, tall, lanky, with squinting blue eyes.

"Where'd yuh ever meet up with Lem?" he demanded.

"I reckon I'll let Lem tell you that," June said steadily. "You tell him June Calvert said you were a damn'-sight faster with your rifle than you are with your brains. We want a flivver and we want it quick."

The older mountaineer blinked at June Calvert's words, moved his feet uncomfortably and spat tobacco juice at the bole of a tree.

"Wa'al," he mumbled, "if yuh know Lem, I reckon you be all right. We got a flivver over the hill a piece. You wantin' me to drive it?"

June shook her head, started up the hill. Wentworth followed her lead and the lanky mountaineer stood, with his arms folded over the muzzle of his rifle watching them go.

"Just leave the flivver at Pop Hawkins' store!" he yelled after them. "Tell him I'll be after it directly."

Wentworth felt the weariness drop from his legs. He went up the hill as freshly as he had started hours before. He ranged up beside

June, glanced at her curiously. Her lips were curved in a wide smile and she seemed hard put to choke back a laugh.

"You tricked him," Wentworth whispered wonderingly. "How in the world did you do it?"

They topped the hill before June spoke, then she laughed. "I used to teach school in the mountains," she said. "There isn't a family of them that hasn't got a Lemuel in it. If there wasn't one in this family, the chances were that they knew somebody pretty well who had the name. It wasn't half as wide a shot as you might think. They've got a whiskey still on the hill. That's the reason for the rifle."

At the crest, Wentworth swept the valley beyond with a quick glance. It was fully five miles across and far down toward the north was the smoke of a small town. But, best of all, there was a narrow, rutted road only a few hundred feet down. They went toward it rapidly.

"It was a very clever trick, June," Wentworth said. "I owe you one for that."

"You owe me nothing," June said sharply. "I was as much in danger as you were. What time is it?"

It was five minutes after five and Wentworth's lips drew tight and hard against his teeth as he hurried toward the ancient Ford that was parked in the middle of the road below. Wentworth had to crank it, but once started, the motor ran smoothly. He backed up a sharp embankment, wrenched the wheels about and sent it bounding down the steep hill.

The road twisted and wound between trees and rocks and bulging roots of trees. There were two ruts and between them grass grew. A more modern car would have scraped off its crank case in the first mile, but the high-wheeled Ford bounded as lightly as a goat from bump to bump and they made incredibly good time. Once a creek, which they forded, splashed water as high as the carburetor and almost stalled the engine, but it caught again and hurled them joyously down the valley.

Five miles of that and the road swung into a wider, dirt highway in which two cars could pass by running one wheel into the ditch. Three miles more and they came to a town of a dozen shacks with a general store labeled: "P. J. Hawkins, Merchandise, Groceries, Dry

Goods, Seeds, Plows, etc." Wentworth jerked to a halt before it and went inside.

The town was Hawkinsville, Penn., and the railroad was twenty miles straight down the valley. Pop Hawkins wasn't sure whether there was an airport there, but there might be one at Pittsburgh. He said *Pittsburgh* as some people whisper *Heaven!* Yep, one of the boys did hire his car out sometimes. He went to the porch.

"Lem!" he shouted. "Lem Conley!"

June, from the auto, winked at Wentworth. It was ten minutes before this Lemuel backed a wheezy Dodge from the stable and sent them rolling down the valley at a mad thirty-five miles an hour. Ordinarily, Wentworth would have enjoyed this out of the way corner of the world, but there was no time for dalliance. It was close to six o'clock. . . .

It was seven, and the sun was slanting toward the hills, when the Dodge wheezed up to the railway station of Dry Town. There would be no more trains that night. Airplanes? Well, now, over the hill there in Goochland County, they was having a fair and a fellow did some dad-fool stunts up in the air. . . . No, 'twasn't fur, no more'n ten miles.

Wentworth almost despaired. He was dubious of the plane, too. Ships used for stunting would not be the racing type he would need if he were to reach Chicago before the Bat Man loosed his hordes upon Michigan City. But there was still a chance.

The Dodge labored up roads that seemed perpendicular, finally crested the mountain and swooped down into Goochland with bolts rattling like castanets. The aviator at the fair wheeled out an old Waco that would make ninety miles an hour in a pinch. . . .

The red ball of the sun was balanced on the horizon and they took off into its eye. A half hour later, they set down at Pittsburgh and Wentworth chartered a fast Boeing, the only speedy job available on the field. Two hours from Chicago. . . . and it was already deep twilight. How long before the Bat Man would release his murdering hordes?

Wentworth blindly watched the dark landscape sliding beneath the plane, the yellow lights of homes prick out. Those windows would be dark with death soon if the Bat Man were not overpowered. Michigan City was the only hope of contact with him, and yet—did

Wentworth have the right to risk the lives, nay to sacrifice lives, at the amusement park tonight so that he could meet once more with the Bat Man if he was not already too late. It was true that many hundreds would die if he did not find and kill the man, but was he justified? Was he not thinking more of the urgency of rescuing Nita and Jackson and Ram Singh, than of those thousands at the park tonight?

Wentworth's lips twitched, became ironically twisted. He got heavily to his feet and walked through the cabin to the cockpit. There was only one pilot on this chartered trip and Wentworth dropped into the copilot's seat.

"Radio or wireless?" he questioned.

"Only wireless is working," the pilot yelled above the engine roar, "but I can send for you if you wish, sir."

Wentworth shook his head and leaned forward to the key, began tapping out the call signals for Chicago police. He had been wrong, he acknowledged to himself, in delaying so long with the warning, but he had hoped against hope that he could reach the city before the fatal hour.

HXW, he called, HXW, until, closing the circuit, he heard the answering call, WT, HXW, WT, HXW. Then he began to pound out his warning, identifying himself first of all, for he was known to Chicago police also.

"Bat Man raiding Michigan City tonight with poison bats," he rapped out while the pilot glanced at him, admiring his sending fist. It was rapid, but clear and rhythmic. "Have information from escaped prisoner of Bat Man. Suggest that park be cleared instantly and information put on radio to keep windows shut, throughout city."

"Commissioner MacHugh sends thanks," the wireless buzzed back at him. "Will follow suggestions."

Wentworth signed off and switched off the set, leaned back in the seat with his eyes gazing off into the black sky. Well, it was done. He had thrown away the only chance he had of saving Nita from the death of the vampires. He argued with himself that he could not have behaved otherwise, but his heart felt cold when he lurched to his feet and stumbled back into the cabin.

June Calvert frowned at his white, drawn face. "What's the matter?" she demanded sharply.

Wentworth shook his head. No use in destroying her hopes of Jackson's rescue. Actually, he was despairing before there was need of it. It still was possible that the plane would reach Michigan City before the bats flew their lethal way through the night. He walked restlessly back and forth along the aisle of the ship, hands locked behind him. June caught his arm as he passed and stopped him.

"Something has gone wrong!" she said. "I know it."

Wentworth shrugged. "We'll be too late, you know that. The Bat Man will have attacked and gone before we get there."

"No," June protested, her dark face flushed despite the drain of fatigue. "He couldn't do that."

"Why not?"

"He just couldn't, not after the struggle we've put up. Why, things don't work out that way!" June was desperate.

Wentworth smiled at her wanly. "I hope you're right, June." He resumed his pacing. Abruptly, the door of the pilot compartment flung open. "Chicago police calling you," he shouted.

Wentworth ducked into the cockpit and fitted the headset to his ears again, waited until police had ceased signaling, then sent his answer winging through space, followed by a question.

Chicago's reply came with staccato speed. "Please repeat warning. Commissioner MacHugh, seven others in headquarters killed by bats."

Wentworth leaned forward tensely as he hammered out his message again. Chicago answered that Michigan City was in hand, advised him to fly to Elgin, Illinois, and land at a field that would show a light. The Bat Man had been seen there, the police continued. Wentworth thanked them and signed off, but sat for a considerable while without ordering a change of course. An hour had rolled by and Columbus lay behind the plane. He turned to the pilot.

"Did that last sending seem the same tone, the same strength as the other?" he asked.

The pilot turned toward him, dropping the companion headset that he wore about his neck. "Funny you should mention it," he said. "I had the same feeling about it—that it wasn't the same."

Wentworth's lips parted in a grim smile. "A decoy message, if I'm not mistaken," he said flatly. "Hold for Michigan City."

The pilot nodded cheerfully. "Yes, sir. Will there be a fight?"

"Pretty apt to be," Wentworth nodded. He got to his feet and started toward the cabin. He heard something hit with a rapid hammering thud just behind him, heard the pilot gasp and whipped about. The pilot was sagging forward over the controls, his head and body a mess of blood and across the twin windshields of the cockpit ran a stitching of bullet holes where machine gun lead had struck . . . !

# WHEN THE BATS FLY!

An instant after the discovery, Wentworth was hurled toward the front of the ship as it answered the pilot's push on the controls. Wentworth's lips moved with his furious curses as he fought to reach the co-pilot's seat. A glance at the altimeter showed him that he must move swiftly, for already the ship had plunged a thousand feet. The gauge showed nine hundred feet!

No need to wonder about the shooting. That decoy message actually had been used to trace his plane so that a killer from the Bat Man could locate him with a radio direction-finder and shoot him down. And it would have succeeded had he moved a moment later or a few minutes sooner. Had he left the cockpit, he could not have reached the controls in time and had he been later, the bullets would have sewn him to the seat as they had the pilot.

The altimeter read five hundred feet when Wentworth got his hand on the stick and began to ease it back. The ship continued to drop at terrific speed and the wings shook with the strain of his attempt to lever out of the dive. For long seconds, it seemed the mighty ship would plunge its engines into the earth, but finally the nose began to lift. Something scraped along the fuselage, tossed the ship wildly. Wentworth tripped off the lights, peered downward through the bullet-pocked windshield and saw the treetops just beneath. The plane's momentum pulled it through.

In a trice, it was zooming and Wentworth caught a glimpse of fiery exhaust blossoms high up in the heavens where the murder ship was circling to watch the finish of its work. Wentworth was grimly thankful that his own exhausts were muffled, so that his flight would not be detected. He made the big Boeing hop hedges for a dozen miles before he dared to let it surge upward toward the skies again. He had no means of defense but he thought it probable that he could outrace his attacker in a straight-away pursuit. He did not sight the plane again as he drove on his course toward Michigan City.

He could turn now to the pilot in the seat beside him, but there was nothing he could do there. The man had made no sound or movement since the bullets had drilled him. His breath had not even rattled in his throat. There could be no doubt he was dead. Wentworth's face was impassive, but there were cold fires of rage in his blue-gray eyes. Another man who served the *Spider,* even though briefly, had died. Was he forever to bring only death to those who helped him?

Grimly, he tugged the throttle of the ship wide until the motors were raving out there in the darkness and the propeller whine rose viciously. He must reach Michigan City before the Bat Man could strike and flee.

It occurred to Wentworth suddenly that June Calvert had made no sound since the shooting and he peered back into the cabin, saw her stretched on the floor with a bloody wound across her temple. It did not seem to be deep, but Wentworth could not leave the controls to investigate. He bent more tensely over the wheel.

Ahead of him was the glow of Michigan City, its thousand lights reaching up challengingly toward the sky. Still the radio did not speak of an attack there. Perhaps he was in time after all! He realized the ship was vibrating dangerously, as he continued to push it at peak speed, but he could not slacken off now. Within fifteen minutes, he would be circling over the myriad lights. . . .

The radio squealed into action. "Calling all Michigan City cars. Calling Michigan City cars. Two men reported killed by bats in front of carousel. Car twenty-four investigate. Proceed with caution. All others stand by."

It had started then, this new mad murder-jag of the Bat Man. His warning had come too late. . . .

He berated himself bitterly for his neglect, his selfishness in keeping the secret so long. Now Death would stride with seven-league boots across the park, taking great swaths of lives with each sweep of his keen scythe. . . . Wentworth was directly over Michigan City now, swinging in great circles about its borders, searching for some trace of the Bat Man. He could see the bats, even from his height, clouds of fluttering killers. A touch on his shoulder startled him. He looked up into June Calvert's face. It was very pale and he knew that she had seen the pilot's body. The air made a keen hissing through the bullet holes that effectively prevented speech.

Twice more, Wentworth swung about the resort, then, suddenly, he spotted his enemy, the Bat Man. With great wings spread, he was gliding over the fleeing thousands who left many dead behind. With a great shout, Wentworth gunned the ship, put the nose down and dived directly on the Bat Man. If he struck him, the propellers would be ruined, motors would fly apart, death would hurl the ship downward. Wentworth knew those things, but it did not matter.

This black, gliding thing was the creature who had destroyed so many hundreds of lives, who had killed this brave man beside him, who had snatched Nita from his side. There was a snarling smile on the *Spider's* lips as, resolutely, he hammered downward at the Bat Man. Only two hundred feet from him, now only a hundred and fifty and the motors bellowed like hungry lions.

When Wentworth was only a hundred feet away, the Bat Man glided smoothly to the right. Wentworth wrenched the plane about in an effort to follow, but his momentum was too great. He shot on past the slowly moving man and plunged toward the milling crowds below. With a frantic effort, he pulled the great ship's nose upward, whirled it in a *virage* and darted to the attack again. He was handling the powerful Boeing as if it were a light pursuit ship and the wings quivered and vibrated, the engines labored.

The Boeing dodged under the Bat's flight, whirled upward toward him with clawing propellers, the touch of which would slice the man in two. Wentworth had a glimpse of the drawn, frightened face of the Bat Man, saw a rifle spurt flame from near his head. He caught no bullet wind, but the man's effort pushed him just out of reach of the propellers. Savagely, Wentworth whirled the ship about and spotted the Bat Man fluttering downward like a wounded bird, sliding from side to side, whirling. Had he sliced the devil, then?

Wentworth took no chances. He sent the ship plunging toward the Bat Man, though they were now only two hundred feet above the earth. Even as he dived, he saw the Bat Man straighten out of his fall and speed earthward in a straight, controlled glide.

Grimly, Wentworth recognized that pursuit was now hopeless, for he saw the Bat Man glide downward between the high-reaching ferris wheel and a switchback structure. No chance for the Boeing there, but he was quite sure the Bat Man could not wing his way upward again. Those wings would not provide him with enough lift for soaring. He whipped about toward June Calvert.

"I'm going to land on the beach," he rapped out. "Got to follow him. Go to the tail and strap yourself down."

June Calvert smiled slightly. "A parachute would be faster," she said. "I can handle the ship!"

Wentworth's smile was a cheer. He slipped out from behind the wheel and June Calvert took it with practiced hands. Within a minute, he was strapped into the parachute.

"Land it on the beach," he shouted at her, then went to the cabin door. He fought it open against the slip stream, crouched and dived below the tail group, snatched out the ring at once. June had shoved the ship upward, but the altitude was barely adequate. Wentworth landed heavily behind the switchback, sliced through the parachute shrouds with a keen pocket knife and raced for the open. He wore a flying helmet with goggles from the ship and his coat collar was turned high. Only the lower half of his face was exposed to the attacks of the bats, for his hands were gauntleted. Even so, he kept alert for the flying death.

It had been impossible to watch the landing of the Bat Man, but Wentworth had traced out his course and now he ran swiftly toward the spot his calculations indicated. He had gone a hundred feet when a revolver spat from the darkness ahead. Wentworth fired at the flash and zig-zagged on. The revolver lanced flame at him again.

Wentworth wasted no more shots. It was evident that the man who fired was behind some bullet-proof shield. For the Spider's lead always flew true to the target. . . .

Twice more the revolver was fired and only once did the lead hum near. The man was a wretched shot, Wentworth thought. He raced on, heard his opponent flee crashingly through formal shrubbery that was planted nearby.

As he ran swiftly in pursuit, Wentworth saw that the man's shield had been a concrete bench. There was a strange odor of bat musk on the air and Wentworth's eyes were narrow. Certainly, the Bat Man did a thorough job of impersonation! He went lithely through the shrubbery, hurdled a hedge, raced along a gravel path. . . .

Out of the darkness came the screams of men and women fleeing in panic before the bats. Wentworth owed his escape thus far from the poison vampires to the fact that all of the killers were hovering where the crowd was thickest. He realized this and saw, too, that the chase was leading directly toward the concourse of the amusement streets. Did the Bat Man then have some means of protection against his small assassins?

Changing his course, Wentworth ran parallel to the flight of his enemy. If he could outline him against the light from the thousand electric bulbs which still beckoned their invitation to the crowd, there would be an immediate end to this slaughter. As if the fugitive guessed his purpose, he doubled back on his trail and fled again toward the formal garden and the switchback.

As they turned, Wentworth saw the huge Boeing slant to a landing on the sands. It bounced violently, but did not loop. Wentworth guessed that June Calvert had never before handled so large a ship, certainly not at night. She had courage! He had a new proof of that fact almost at once. The ship, once landed, did not remain stationary, but turned toward the park and trundled forward, its propellers lashing the air. June intended to shelter as many fugitives as possible in the cabin. . . .

Now, at last, Wentworth caught a glimpse of the man he pursued. Good lord, the Bat Man still wore his wings! Wentworth flung lead after him, saw him trip and fall. A great shout welled out of the *Spider's* throat. He dashed forward, then abruptly flung himself flat to the earth also. From the shadows ahead came the liquid pop of blowguns. The Bat Man had led him into an ambush!

Wentworth lifted his head and grimly leveled his automatic. He realized that the Indians were moving rapidly to surround him. They would close in slowly until sure that the *Spider* was dead. He had eleven cartridges and there were easily thirty Indians . . . !

# CHAPTER FOURTEEN
# IN THE BAT'S TRAP

T HE FEELING OF DESPAIR that had never been far from Wentworth's heart since the first battle against the Bat Man surged over him again, but it received a sudden check. Unbidden, without preliminary, the thought rose in Wentworth's mind: *Nita is not dead!* And there was a reason for the thought. The Bat Man had not had time to go to more than one bat depot—and the bats of that group must be kept hungry for the night's attack! No, Nita had not yet been fed to the vampires.

With the thought, Wentworth felt a flood of new vigor come into him. If Nita lived, he would save her, despite this ambush of poison darts. There was one way . . . They would not begin to close in until they had completed the circle about him and there was yet an opening of twenty feet in the rear. Wentworth made no move toward it. Instead, he rapidly began to wriggle out of the parachute harness from which he had sliced the shrouds, rather than discard it in his need for speed. He gouged out a deep hollow in the ground, set the butt of his gun in it and packed the earth down tightly about it. He fastened an end of the parachute harness, whose straps he had cut to stretch it to the greatest possible length, to the trigger of the automatic and the other end he held in his hand as he crawled straight toward where the Bat Man had fallen!

When he had gone a few feet, he pulled gently on the harness until the automatic fired. He smiled grimly. He was giving the poison darts a target, but it was a false one.

The rain of darts increased behind him as he crawled to the attack. There were four shots in the automatic. They lasted him twelve feet, half the distance to the Bat Man. He tried then to drag the empty pistol to him but the strap slipped loose and he was compelled to abandon it. To return there through the fire of the Indians would be fatal. Besides, the circle was complete and the blowgun men were beginning to close in. Unarmed, he pushed rapidly on.

The innocuous seeming pop of the deadly guns sounded strange against the background of panic screams out there where the bats were thick. Through the middle of sound, he caught, too, a distant rumble as of a train. Were police coming by rail? But that was foolish . . . He realized abruptly that the sound came from the switchback where cars were running wild, empty, about the tracks, abandoned by the operators who had fled, or been killed by the bats. The scent of bat musk was heavy all about him.

Already, Wentworth could make out the black hump that marked where the Bat Man lay. The sight tightened his mouth, narrowed his eyes to a steely hardness. He was only six feet away— now only three! He hunched himself up on tense thighs, hurled himself bodily upon the middle of the wings! He fell on fabric. A metal brace prodded him in the side, but that was all. *The Bat Man was gone!*

The sound of Wentworth's leap had not passed unnoticed. While he lay, half-dazed by his fall, an Indian called in a nasal shout that was a challenge. Wentworth could not answer. He did not know the language. A bat-like squeak in the wrong tone might be equally betraying. But there was a way out. He thrust himself to one side of the brace which evidently supported the wings, got to the edge of the queer contraption and crawled underneath it. His lips were smiling. Even the light fabric of the wings would be enough to protect him from the darts—if the Indians dared to fire at the spot where their master had been!

Wentworth began to wriggle along flat on his stomach, carrying the wings with him. His acute ears heard the advance of the blowguns as their popping grew louder. When they were almost upon him, he halted. When they passed, he began again the slow crawling. Fifteen feet outside of their circle, he slid out from under the wings and, bent double, raced away on silent feet.

Where had the Bat Man gone? Wentworth found himself sprinting toward the high, spidery structure of the switchback. There, he could escape the Indians.

Under its shadows he crept, and crouching there, he became aware again of that strange, over-powering scent of bat musk which he had detected earlier in the night. He twisted his head about, sniffing like a dog. Unless he was fooled by the wind, the scent was stronger toward his left. Without hesitation, Wentworth crept in that direction. The Bat Man was armed and the *Spider* was empty-handed, but it would have taken more than that to turn him back tonight!

The scent was stronger now. Wentworth crouched low, seeking to outline his enemy against the sky but there were only the slits of the switchback. He pushed on. The scent grew fainter. He pivoted back again, frowning in perplexity, angry in frustration. Then there was an infinitesimal squeak, as of leather on wood, almost directly above him. He tilted back his head and saw, outlined like a spider in a squared web of wood against the sky, a man climbing among the braces of the switchback.

Strangling down the cry of triumph that rose in his throat, Wentworth sprang to a horizontal brace just above his head, and swung up, clambered to his feet. The structure was built with high verticals and horizontals like the floors of a house. Then in each oblong made by the crossing of uprights and crosspieces, there were X-braces, stretched diagonally from corner to corner. It was a simple matter to walk up one of these diagonals, using the crosspieces as a handrail. Wentworth clambered swiftly in the wake of the little man who was making panicky speed for the top.

Wentworth recognized the Bat Man's plan. At the top of the first incline toward which the man climbed, the cars moved at a snail's pace. It would be an easy matter for him to climb in and sail over the runways to safety before Wentworth could overtake him. There was one defect in his plan. He could get out only at the spot where he had entered, on the long initial incline up which the cars were drawn by a chain—unless one of his henchmen could operate the brakes which ordinarily stopped the cars, but which were independent of the cars themselves.

The Bat Man was half-way to the top now, climbing like a monkey among the cross-braces. Wentworth was fully thirty feet below him. He abandoned walking the X-braces and started scrambling up them like a ladder, X-brace to crosspiece, to X-brace again. It was dizzying work and every second increased the distance above the ground and the peril. Out there in the darkness, the flying cars squealed on curves or rumbled down inclines that were almost perpendicular. At the bottom of the incline, a car was beginning its clanking rise to the peak which the fugitive sought.

Wentworth realized with a despairing cry that the Bat Man would reach the top in time to board the car, and that he himself could not. He threw a sharp, estimating glance about as he fought upward at top speed. The rails of the first dip were only about half the distance of the top from him, and to walk the crosspieces to it would take only seconds. The string of cars, four hitched together, would be gaining the momentum for its entire run there, but the point opposite Wentworth was less than half way down the swoop. It would be accelerating—not yet at its peak speed. . . .

Grimly, swiftly as always, the *Spider* made his choice. Already, he was footing it along the cross-piece. He reached the track before the car arrived at the top of the incline where the Bat Man was even now scrambling. While there was yet time, Wentworth scrambled ten feet higher along the track. Then he crouched and waited for the car. There was a railing here and he poised on its top, which would be barely on a level with the side of the car seats. It would be a perilous undertaking!

Wentworth's jaw locked rigidly, the muscles in his thighs tautened. . . . The cars had reached the crest. The Bat Man scrambled in and, with a rising roar, the train plunged down the rise toward where Wentworth waited.

The Bat Man saw him, raised up in the front seat with his revolver in his hand and a despairing cry in his throat. There would be a split-second when he was directly opposite Wentworth—when he could shoot at him at point-blank range. He would, at that time, be moving at about thirty miles an hour. Wentworth estimated his chances, crouching there on the rail, and his lips drew back from his teeth. The cars roared toward him . . . !

Wentworth was not standing broadside to the cars, but was facing the same direction in which they were traveling. He had no way of estimating the velocity of his leap, but it could not reasonably be more than fifteen miles an hour. That difference was enough to make it damnably dangerous. Added to that was the fact that his footing, both in jumping and landing, was extremely uncertain. He did not need that threatening revolver to make it a life-and-death attempt. He must spring into the air at exactly the right heart-beat of time. There must be no hesitation, no slip-up.

And yet, as the car hurtled toward him, Wentworth flung his laughter into the air—reckless, taunting laughter. The Bat Man leaned forward, stretching the revolver out before him. He was almost upon Wentworth.

"Look out, fool!" Wentworth shouted.

His cry was at just the right moment. It caught the Bat Man squeezing the trigger—the front of the car almost level with Wentworth. At the same instant, Wentworth jumped. If he could, he meant to hammer the Bat Man to the floor with the bludgeon of his body. But he miscalculated—either his own speed or that of the train—for his feet caught on the back of the cushion of the third car. The blow smacked his feet out from under him and hurled him, headfirst, into the seat of the fourth car.

The car whirled sickeningly around a curve, jamming Wentworth over against one side of the seat; then it straightened out for another dive. The rush of wind helped to clear Wentworth's brain and he thrust stiff arms into the cushions, shoved himself erect. He was almost thrown out as the car plunged again. He peered ahead, saw the glint of a revolver and pulled his head down as the bullet whined.

The *Spider* still did not have complete control over his body, but there was no time to be lost. The moments when he could crawl forward to the attack were terribly limited, for the track led under the cross-braces of other tracks and to stand up would mean a broken neck. Likewise, the sidesway of the U-turns would hurl him off by centrifugal force.

Nevertheless, Wentworth set himself grimly to climb forward. He jerked the cushion from the seat and, when next there was an instant of clear overhead, he hurled it forward against the blast of the wind and threw himself head first into the third car of the train.

The cushion did not reach the first car, but it had made the Bat Man duck and before he could shoot, Wentworth was under cover—one car nearer the front! He thought that the next cushion he hurled would reach its goal.

Already, the train was starting the last and lowest circuit of the structure. Wentworth realized that he would have no further chance to advance on his enemy until a new circuit was started. Meantime, the Bat Man would have the long, slow climb up the incline in which to escape. His hands clenched with determination as he crouched behind the protection of the car's front. If the Bat Man attempted to get off this car, he would have the *Spider* on his back!

"If you jump out," Wentworth called to him, "I'm going to push you off. I won't have to touch you. A cushion. . . ."

Wentworth did not again lift his head above the seats, but he leaned far over to the side and peered toward the front car. He saw a foot thrust out cautiously. He started to shout a warning to the man to get back, but shut his mouth grimly and held his cushion ready. The Bat Man's foot reached out farther. They were almost to the top and he must hurry if he was to get away before that. Wentworth saw the foot lift a little and hurled the cushion.

The heavy combination of wood and leather struck the walkway beside the track just as the Bat Man stepped down, hit the same place. The Bat Man screamed, lost his footing and fell flat. He rolled against the side of the car, bounced toward the low guard railing. Wentworth sprang to his feet to hurl himself upon the man, but at that moment the car gave a lurch and surged over the top of the incline!

Wentworth cursed, peered back and saw the Bat Man roll onto the tracks which the car had just quitted, then the train carrying Wentworth whipped down into that first, terrific dip. The *Spider* sat and cursed under his breath the entire way around the switchback. The circuit that last time had been so swift—stretched out interminably—but at last the train swept toward the chained incline. Wentworth sprang out, peered eagerly upward and—*The Bat Man was gone!*

Both the Bat Man and the Indians had vanished. Heavily, he

turned toward the plane, and while he went, by back-ways where the bats were not, he heard the piercing, gigantic squeaking which he knew was the recall signal for the vampires. There was no tracing the sound. It seemed to come from everywhere. . . .

Wentworth broke into a run. The battle was not yet lost. If all roads were blocked and all small men detained for examination. . . . At the plane, he found a group of uniformed police and, inside their circle, Commissioner MacHugh, of Chicago, was shooting questions at June Calvert.

June was taking it languidly, leaning against the side of the Boeing with a glint of humor in her dark eyes. She had taken advantage of the interim to fluff her black hair about the piquant oval of her face. But her beauty was only a mask for grim determination. That much, Wentworth knew.

He thrust through the circle after MacHugh had identified him. MacHugh was small, but he had a big, hearty manner. His energy was tiring to watch. He sprang forward to grasp Wentworth's hand. "By all that's holy, Wentworth!" he shouted. "I was about to string the girl up by her thumbs because she wouldn't talk. How do you pick 'em, my boy? How do you pick 'em?"

Wentworth grinned into the Commissioner's face. The man was infectious. "Commissioner, the Bat Man was here just a few minutes ago. I fought with him, but he got away. I suggest that we stop all roads and search for small men, not above a hundred pounds. . . ."

MacHugh made a move. His complexion was dark and his frown made his face ugly. "I escape by one pound! Is the Bat Man small?"

"He is," Wentworth said grimly. "After all the small men are together, I want to look them over. There's a bare chance I might identify him."

"I say, there, Commissioner MacHugh!" a man's voice piped. Wentworth spun about to stare beyond the circle of police. He caught his breath. Sanderson, the weazened ex-jockey turned stable owner, was just outside the cordon, waving at MacHugh.

"Let him in," the Commissioner called. He turned to Wentworth. "Sanderson came out with me. We were at a show and just got here a few seconds ago. Sanderson wanted to look about."

Wentworth stared suspiciously at Sanderson as the little man sauntered up, swaggering a bit. His mind was racing. Both of these men were small—both had just arrived on the scene. Was it possible that . . . one of these men was the Bat?

Wentworth moved to June's side, turning his back on the others.

"When the big squeak was made," he whispered, "was MacHugh here?"

June shook her head, glanced over his shoulder at the Commissioner. "Do you think . . . ?"

Wentworth shrugged. "I don't know," he said, suddenly weary. Once more, the Bat Man had won. . . . There was no longer any need to starve the bats. Nita, dear Nita. . . .

# CHAPTER FIFTEEN
# A CLUE AT LAST

A DRAGGING WEARINESS rode with Wentworth back to Chicago in Commissioner MacHugh's sedan. He sat on a kick seat beside Sanderson, who kept up a half-apologetic conversation on the horrors he had seen at Michigan City. The dead were estimated at three thousand five hundred.

"Some of them must have suffered horribly," Sanderson went on in his subdued voice. "One boy had strangled a bat in each hand, but he had at least a dozen bites on his face and neck. I picked up a bat, and ever since then, I fancy I smell like the damned things."

Wentworth said nothing, but his thoughts were swift. Now that Sanderson had called attention to it, he did catch a faint whiff of the bat-musk which had been so powerful in the vicinity of the Bat Man. Suspicion leaped full-grown into his brain. It wasn't possible that bat scent should cling so to a person who had only handled a dead one. He decided that Sanderson's movements should be watched, his whereabouts at other appearances of the Bat Man checked.

Where did the scent that the Bat Man used come from? Surely, not from merely handling bats, nor from the glands of the bat itself. To generate such a powerful taint of it, hundreds of bats would have to be slaughtered and certainly, the Bat Man could not have a great enough supply of bats to warrant such butchery. Only one explanation was possible then. The scent was artificial, and. . . .

Wentworth sat abruptly straight, spun toward MacHugh. "Commissioner, will you have your men gather every dead bat possible at the park and rush them to me at the Blackstone hotel? This is important! It may mean the solution of the case!"

Sanderson shuddered. "I should hope so. Vampires! Brrrr!"

Fatigue and mental fog lifted from Wentworth's body. At last he had a trail which might lead to the Bat Man. And it was one that could be followed swiftly. . . . He engaged a suite of rooms at the Blackstone and, one hour after the dead bats had been delivered to him there, he left with June Calvert for the airport. The Boeing had been refueled and new windows substituted for those the machine gun had wrecked. At Wentworth's orders, these were bullet proof. The pilot was a United States Marine officer whose mouth was straight and pugnacious below a pointed nose. His eyes were direct.

"What the hell's up? And who are you?" he demanded when Wentworth entered.

Wentworth smiled slightly. He mentioned his title and regiment of the reserves, his name. The Marine came sharply to his feet, saluted with a crisp efficiency.

"Begging the major's pardon," he said flatly, "but they got me up out of the first night's sleep I've had in a week. Lieutenant Carlisle, sir."

"At ease," Wentworth told him briefly. "I asked for a pilot without nerves, who was reasonably good with an automatic and better than good as to courage. I'm satisfied. Take off at once. All possible speed for the Rocky Mountains, about fifty miles south of Hooligan Pass."

The lieutenant saluted, fairly jumped to the controls. The plane swept down the field, lofted gently and swung about in a bank that almost scraped off the wingtip.

Wentworth's face was drawn with harsh lines of fatigue. There were dark smudges beneath his eyes, a deeper crease at his mouth corners.

"We're going to the Bat Man's main headquarters," he said shortly. "The purpose is to kill him and save certain persons who are his prisoners."

"But how do you know where to go?" June demanded.

Wentworth smiled faintly. "I've got a good nose. I'm going to sleep."

It was not the least of Wentworth's miracles that he could sleep when all his soul and body stirred with anxiety. But there was nothing he could do now, and how many hours had it been since he had last slept . . . ? Two hours after the takeoff, Wentworth sprang up from the cushions. Many of the lines had been erased from his face and, after a swift toilet, he was fresh, and vigorous. He went into the cockpit, dropped into the co-pilot's seat.

"Mr. Carlisle," he said. "We're going to kill the Bat Man."

The lieutenant turned his head briefly. "Yes, sir."

"Do you know the Rockies, Mr. Carlisle?"

"Yes, sir."

Wentworth smiled faintly.

"Interrupt me if I'm wrong, Mr. Carlisle," he said. "About fifty miles south of Hooligan Pass, there is a section in which hot springs abound. Also, due to the action of this hot water upon limestone, there are large, far-reaching caverns. In the recesses of those caves, it is likely that the heat—due to the water—would approximate that of the tropical river regions of South America where vampire bats live. In those caves, vampire bats could breed just as they do in the tropics and thus produce the overwhelming numbers which have been loosed on America. Do you agree with me that far, Mr. Carlisle?"

"Yes, sir!" There was a rising enthusiasm in the lieutenant's voice.

"How long, Mr. Carlisle, before we'll reach that section?"

"Twenty-two minutes, sir!"

Wentworth nodded and got to his feet. "I am looking for a canyon in that district into which it would be impossible to descend, Mr. Carlisle. Signal me when you reach Hoot-Owl Center."

Wentworth returned to the cabin and found June Calvert sitting up sleepily. He crossed to a long paper-wrapped package that he had picked up in Chicago, which had been brought from New York by plane. He unwrapped it quickly and revealed a pair of wings, folded flat together. June sprang to her feet.

"The Bat Man's wings!" she cried.

Wentworth shook his head. "No, mine," he said, "but modeled after the Bat Man's. Because of my greater weight, I had to increase their size. Will you help me, please?"

✪ ✪ ✪

He lifted the wings and adjusted the straps over his shoulders. The wings folded flat together and pointed out rigidly some nine feet along the cabin. There were straps also about waist and ankles to support his body. When he jumped from the plane, a jerk would snap the wings out to each side and lock them there. A kick would move the rudder into position just behind his feet. There were tip ailerons which he could operate by twisting his wrists and his feet rested on the rudder rod. There was no elevator. The ailerons and the shifting of his body would take care of dives. There would be little climbing.

June Calvert looked at him with wide eyes. "But why, why?" she whispered.

Wentworth laughed. "Didn't the Bat Man say no one but himself could reach his hide-out unless he willed it? Well, I am now the Bat Man so far as aerial navigation is concerned!"

From up forward came a queer hooting sound and for a moment, Wentworth did not identify it. Then he realized its meaning. Lieutenant Carlisle had signaled that the ship was over Hoot-Owl Center. Wentworth smiled slightly as he released himself from the straps, leaned the wings against the wall and walked forward. The little mountain town lay beneath them and ahead lifted the barrier of the Rockies. A small, crooked road wove its way upward into the fastness and on it Wentworth made out three auto trains of seven or eight cars apiece. His eyes narrowed at the sight and he caught up a pair of field glasses and focused them on the road.

The cars were trucks and each carried big boxes that would be far too heavy a load for the vehicles if they contained weighty cargo. Furthermore, the men who manned the trucks were Indians, not the lithe, red men of the North American wilderness, but the stubby, fierce savages from the Amazon, each with his blowgun.

Wentworth's hand dropped on the pilot's shoulder. "These are the men of the Bat." he said. "Climb as high as possible while still keeping an eye on them. See where they go, and then—I have some twelve-pound bombs."

Lieutenant Carlisle said, "Yes, sir!"

Wentworth strode sharply back into the cabin with elation singing in his veins.

June Calvert stood up and moved toward him. "What is it?" she demanded, whispering. She had to repeat the words before Wentworth looked at her.

"We're close now," he said. "Very close." He moved toward the wings that were shaped like a bat's.

Carlisle's voice rang out from the cockpit, "Major!"

Wentworth hurried to him.

"They've stopped, sir," Carlisle said. "They're getting out."

Wentworth took the glasses and peered down. The plane had climbed three thousand feet, but was still easily visible to the men below. Their flattish faces were turned upward. Wentworth's lips thinned. He lowered the glasses.

"They've guessed we're following! Bomb them. Drop down to fifteen hundred. I'll throw the bombs out of the door."

Carlisle spun the ship about and Wentworth dragged out two wooden cases from opposite walls of the cabin, opened them and took out two bombs shaped like tear drops, but with fins on the tails to keep them nose down. He forced open the door and waited while the Boeing circled downward. Wentworth could see the upturned faces without glasses now. He held the bombs ready.

June Calvert came and stood beside the box. "I'll hand them to you," she said.

The three motorcades had merged and were strung out along the road for over a half-mile. Wentworth waited until the ship was in position, then darted the first bomb toward the head of the line. It struck ten feet to the side of the road and splintered a huge pine. The second bomb made a direct hit on the second truck. The body went to pieces. The big cages of bats were tossed a hundred feet and the steel frame soared and crushed the front of the fifth truck in line.

The Boeing zoomed, viraged and swept back over the road again. Indians were scattering in all directions from the trucks, blocked permanently by the first bomb Wentworth had thrown. The last truck was trying frantically to turn about and retreat. Wentworth's third bomb hit close by, dug a pit under its wheels and flopped the car over on its side. Systematically then, Wentworth pelted the rest of the trucks until not one remained undamaged.

"One of the trucks got away," June told him tensely. "The first one in line. You missed it and it went up into the mountains."

Lieutenant Carlisle evidently had noticed it, too. The ship was sent hurtling after the truck, but Wentworth put his last two bombs back into the case, went forward to the cockpit.

"Keep the truck in sight," he ordered.

There was a drumming thud upon the roof of the cabin. The hammering moved forward and in its wake appeared a seam of bullet holes. A machine gun! Wentworth cursed. He pulled June Calvert far back into the tail of the ship, saw the windows of the cockpit sliver under the hail of lead, but resist the attack. The tail of the ship whipped over, wind roared in through the open door as Carlisle put the giant Boeing into a side-slip to dodge the attacking plane.

The bomb case lurched toward the opening and, even as Wentworth darted forward to seize it, plunged outward into space. The roar of wind through the door abruptly checked and Wentworth knew the Boeing was sliding in the opposite direction. He saw a jot of earth leap upward where the bomb case struck. The road was blocked! That accidental discharge of high explosive had struck squarely in the middle of the mountain trail and dug a twenty foot pit across it. And the truck they were following was on the far side of that pit!

Now there would be no trail to lead them to the headquarters of the Bat Man. They would have to guess at its location. . . . Wentworth shouted forward. "Turn your port side to the plane!"

The Boeing zoomed, whirled in a vertical bank and, peering upward now through the open door, Wentworth had a glimpse of a speedy little monoplane diving toward him. There was a flicker of flame behind the propeller that showed his machine guns. . . .

"Up!" Wentworth shouted.

He felt the plane lift even as the machine gun fire dipped. The bullets missed. . . . The ship was close enough now. No need to aim. Wentworth held both automatics on the nose of the ship, held on the face of the man just visible behind the windshield of the attacking plane. He pumped the full charge of both automatics.

The monoplane zoomed, fell off on the left wing and screamed downward in a whipping, screaming tail-spin. Wentworth, stepping back from the doorway to reload his automatics, could see the pilot lolling helplessly back against the crash pad. The *Spider's* eyes narrowed as his lips parted in a smile. The man was dead. That much was obvious, but was it the Bat Man? Grimly, he hoped that it was, but he doubted such luck. The Bat Man usually made his attacks on his own wings. . . .

Wentworth slipped the loaded weapons back into his holsters and pushed forward. There was nothing to do now but follow the road and hope that they would be able to spot a canyon that might fit the description Wentworth had given. He dropped in the co-pilot's seat and waited while the Boeing made slow wide circles over wild, mountain country.

A squealing sound, not unlike the squeak of a giant bat, came from the wireless headphones and Wentworth, frowning, lifted them to his ears. The squealing continued, but now it was broken into short and long sounds. Wentworth cursed, pressed the phones closer. . . . It was Morse code! Swiftly, Wentworth deciphered the message:

"Unless you at once return the way you came," ran the dots and dashes, "you will forfeit the lives of three friends and the woman you love. Furthermore, I shall shoot you down, as I am in a position to do at this moment. Consider, *Spider,* the lives of four people against a strategic retreat. Which do you choose?"

The squealing stopped for a moment, then began again, the same message. Coolly, Wentworth moved the coil of the radio direction-finder. "Two points east of north," he said to Carlisle, "and very near. He is threatening to shoot us down. Keep a sharp eye out for attacking planes."

Wentworth moved hurriedly back into the cabin then and donned the wings, tightening all the straps. Just short of the tip ailerons, there were two holsters and into these, Wentworth thrust his automatics. He stood by the door, peering down at the mountains sliding past below him.

Carlisle shouted, "Plane is attacking ahead, major. Something funny . . . Good God, *it's the Bat Man!*"

Wentworth turned about and smiled at June Calvert. "Tell Carlisle to dodge the plane and circle aloft. He'll have the ceiling of that monoplane. Tell him to look for a signal from that canyon we're passing over."

June Calvert nodded, staring at him with wide eyes. Wentworth shouted forward, "When I shout, kick the tail to starboard!"

"Yes, sir!"

Wentworth paused in the doorway, gazing downward, his hands moved over the buckles of the wings that jutted oddly from his shoulders. There was a grim, drawn tension about his mouth. He poised in the doorway like a diver, shouted at Carlisle, then sprang head foremost into space, with only those queer wings and his skill to save him from inevitable death on the rocks five thousand feet below . . . !

# C H A P T E R   S I X T E E N
# THE JAWS OF DEATH

W ENTWORTH plunged downward at terrific speed, falling
free, the wings of no more value than a tangled parachute.
He spread his legs so that the fin between them straightened, the rudder whipped back into position. He was falling headfirst
now and it was easy to pull the wings about into flying station.

He twisted the ailerons, kicked the rudder and immediately felt
the lift of the wings. He shot forward on a level with the momentum
of his plunge, peered about and a shout of anger and hate rang out.
The Bat Man was diving headfirst toward the Boeing and, even as
Wentworth shouted, the giant plane faltered, slid off on one wing
and nosed down. It took only a glance to realize that the Bat Man's
rifle had penetrated the bullet-proof glass and that the Marine pilot
and June Calvert were plunging to their deaths!

Instinctively, as Wentworth saw what had happened, he tilted
back his ailerons and zoomed up toward the Bat Man. It was not
until then that the man saw Wentworth, flying on wings so like his
own. When he did, he staggered uncertainly for a moment, his flying
speed falling off. Instantly, he overcame his surprise and dived to
gather momentum.

It was only then that Wentworth realized the difficulty of the
thing he had undertaken. He had intended the wings to enable him

to penetrate the Bat's hiding place, now suddenly, he found himself forced to fight in a field in which his opponent was easily the master. He was plunged instantly into a life and death struggle!

Wentworth realized these things when he prolonged his zoom too long in an effort to gain altitude on the Bat Man. He lost flying speed, whip-stalled and found himself plunging for the earth at a furious pace. Ailerons and rudder kicked him out of it, but he found the Bat Man sweeping toward him nose-on. The rifle which Wentworth now saw was strapped to the top of the wing and was aligned with the man's body. It spat flame and a bullet whipped past within inches of his head.

Wentworth's face was grimly set. If the Bat Man expected any armament at all, he would naturally conceive it to be of the same type as his own. Actually, Wentworth's automatics were pointed straight out to each side, slung in holsters through whose tip they could fire as readily as if held freely in the hands. As Wentworth wheeled out of the line of fire, he pointed a wingtip toward the Bat Man and squeezed the trigger. The recoil kicked the wing upward slightly and Wentworth had to twist ailerons to straighten out his curious craft. The bullet went wide.

Wentworth completed a circle but found the Bat Man had the speed on him, from his dive. His enemy shot about in an almost vertical bank which Wentworth would have believed impossible and the rifle was leveled once more. A bullet from the Bat Man's rifle struck the wing and tugged at Wentworth's sleeve. A second shot, close on its heels, struck the duralumin brace and whined off into space.

Wentworth dived. It was the only thing he could do. The Bat Man followed and the *Spider* saw that he had one advantage—speed of descent. In a vertical plunge, of course, both would drop at the same pace, but at a glide, Wentworth's greater weight, his higher ratio of weight to wing spread gave him the advantage. But he could not outfly bullets. . . .

Lead cracked over his head viciously. Wentworth kicked the rudder and dodged. He repeated that while bullets sang and whined about him. The wing was struck again. Wentworth twisted his head about and saw the Bat Man was gaining on him slightly because of his dodging. As he looked, the squealing, rasping signal that was a call to the bats rang out. Good lord, was the man summoning the vampires to his assistance?

Wentworth whipped about and tried once more to down the man with automatic shots, but his lack of lateral control handicapped him badly. He dared not empty his guns with such poor assurance of success and he was forced once more to turn and run. The *Spider* run from an enemy! It was incredible, but it was so. The man had greater skill.

They were dangerously close to earth now. No more than a thousand feet. Wentworth continued to dodge while he searched the earth with eager eyes. Over to his right was the deep slit of a canyon. Beneath him, all was dense woods. There was no spot to mark where the Boeing had crashed. Desperately, Wentworth searched the earth for some spot in which to land. There was none.

Abruptly, Wentworth remembered the reason for his wings. They had been for the purpose of entering the secret hiding place of the Bat Man, of invading the canyon cave in which, Wentworth deduced, he had made his headquarters. There was a canyon, and the attack upon him had been begun near it. He would have to chance a dive into its tricky and turbulent wind currents.

With his mind made up, Wentworth slanted directly for the darkened mouth of the canyon. Behind him, the Bat Man screamed again and it seemed to Wentworth that it was more than a signal. The sound held a touch of fright, perhaps of anger. The Bat pressed him more closely, dived steeply to intercept his approach to the cliffs. Wentworth smiled thinly. He had guessed right then. The hiding place was there! He would enter that canyon or die in the attempt.

The Bat pressed closer, closer, his rifle barking again and again. Wentworth watched him come with worried, angry eyes. There was death for one of them here on the lip of the cliffs, or in that narrow bit of air that led downward into the throat of the canyon itself. In that confined space, there could be little dodging, little hope of escape. Bullets would fly. . . .

On the point of darting downward into the canyon, Wentworth whipped upward into a zoom almost head on toward the Bat Man. He twisted the ailerons and side-slipped toward the valley below. As he slipped, holding his wings steadily vertical so that he plunged at terrific force toward the stony death below, he began to shoot. For the first time, now, in that perilous position, he had the stability he needed for accuracy. His first shot caught the right wing of the Bat Man. His second plucked at the man's clothing. But in his steady dive, Wentworth exposed himself to the fire of his enemy's rifle and the bullets whipped closer, closer. . . .

A knife of fire slit down Wentworth's right arm and his hand went utterly numb and useless. He knew that one of the bullets had touched him at last. It was a superficial wound, but it might well mean death! The crippling of that arm loosened one of the ailerons to flap as it would. It halved his armament . . . !

A wild challenging shout rang from the *Spider's* lips. Its echo battered at him from both walls of the canyon, but it seemed to him that there was another shriller voice shouting, too. He fought grimly to hold on with his numb hand to the handle of the aileron. He did not seek to use it, merely to hold it stationary while with his other hand and the rudder he maneuvered his other wing uppermost. As the rudder turned him, first, head-down, then over again, he caught a glimpse of a black cave's mouth far below and, on the edge before it, several figures stood with arms uplifted. By the gods, if that Bat Man did not kill the *Spider* in the air, then the man's Indians would slaughter him when he landed!

Bitterly, Wentworth completed his whirl, thrust his gun-hand upward. If he died, he at least would not die alone!

His hands moved, his feet kicked the rudder. Before his eyes whirled the black opening of the cave he had seen and the gesturing figures. They were going to kill him, were they? He tried to kick a wing about so that he could shoot, but he forgot to bank or his hands failed on the ailerons when he did it. He skated sideways, twisting his head about to see the death that presently would strike into him.

In God's name, who was this who held out waiting arms to him? That face! Nita! *Good God, Nita!* He felt that he was still skidding sideways toward that lovely face that floated before his eyes. He saw men leap toward him, then . . . nothing!

Impossible to tell whether he was unconscious for an hour or a second, but the crooning of Nita's voice drifted away and returned to him in waves of sound. He pushed his eyes open, looked up into Nita's face. He struggled up. . . .

"The Bat Man! The Bat Man!" he cried. "Where is he?"

"Dead, darling," Nita told him. "You shot him down out in the canyon there, before you sideslipped into a landing here on the ledge."

Wentworth moved his arms stiffly and found a biting pain in the right one, found the left unencumbered by the wing. He looked about him. June Calvert was standing near, with Jackson's arm about her. Fred Stoking and Ram Singh smiled at him. The Marine lieutenant. . . .

"Mr. Carlisle," Wentworth said weakly, "how in the hell do you happen to be still alive?"

The Marine grinned. "I faked out-of-control and landed in the canyon valley. There's a rope ladder up here. Had quite a tussle with some of those vampire bats up there. They came out when that guy screamed up here in the air, but they couldn't see in the daylight very well and we got the best of them."

Wentworth sank back on the hard rock of the ledge gratefully. "Well, Earl Westfall will never be electrocuted then."

Nita smiled at him. "How did you know the Bat Man was Westfall? We found out when we came here that he wasn't the fat man he seemed at all. He had a rubber suit that he blew up. It made him look huge. And that Bat Man face of his—it was a mask."

Wentworth looked about, found June Calvert's eyes. "You ought to know how I found out, how I learned where the headquarters was."

June Calvert shook her head. "I haven't the faintest idea," she said happily, "but I don't see that it matters much as long as you did." She looked up into Jackson's wide, grinning face.

"Really," Wentworth complained, "won't somebody inquire how the great Wentworth learned the secret?"

Nita laughed and brushed his forehead with her lips. "Tell me, darling," she whispered. "I'll always want to know."

"The bat musk secret," Wentworth said. "None of the Indians was ever attacked by the bats and there had to be a reason. It was because they smelled like bats."

They were interested now, all of them. Fred Stoking looked at Nita with wistful, but hopeless, eyes.

"It wasn't possible for the Bat Man—or Westfall—" Wentworth went on, "to get enough bat glands to make the odor, so he had to make it artificially. The bat musk was strangely like some perfume I had run across. Basically, of course. I identified the perfume— Chatou's Oriental—and found out where large shipments of it had been made. It came to Hoot-Owl Center, and would you believe it? Westfall actually had it addressed to his stable manager! But I had been suspicious of Westfall for some time. I found out from some of my newspaper clippings that he had recently been to a sanitarium for drug addicts and I looked up his weight there. It's exactly ninety pounds."

Wentworth pushed himself to his feet. His side ached from a flesh wound and his right arm hung useless at his side, but there was a smile on his face. He put his good arm about Nita's shoulders.

"Darling," he said, "I think that—when I get out of the hospital— I shall go on a real bat."

Nita shuddered, laughed up at him. "I'm willing, but for heaven's sakes, let's call it something . . . something else than . . . a bat!"

# THE
# OCTOPUS

# CHAPTER ONE
# WHEN THE BEAST HUNGERS

THE YOUNG NURSE NODDED downward at the mummy-like thing on the cot in Ward Seven. "She's been trying to move, Doctor," she said. "Are you sure you need the stimulants?" Dr. Skull nodded absently. His keen brown eyes, the liveliest thing in his gentle old face, were appraising the swathed figure of Mrs. Purvins, and there was an ancient satisfaction in them, ancient as medicine itself. He remembered the day, almost a month ago, when a frightened woman stripped herself in his office, and whispered, "Is it cancer, Doctor. Will I die soon?"

She had been ghastly, that woman, with the hard black growth ridging her body like the tentacles of a deep sea monster. Ghastly even to the case-hardened eye of the surgeon.

There had been something about the growth that suggested more than medical abnormality, something uniform and patterned, as though a deliberate perverted will had planned it so.

"Only the skin," Skull had told her. "It's operable. There's a good chance. You're young—you have a young woman's heart, a young woman's capacity for recovery. . . ."

She had been brave, that frightened little Mrs. Purvins. And so she had taken the chance, a greater chance than her surgeon cared to tell her, and for weeks she had lain in a ward cot at the Mid-City

Hospital, too sick to speak, swathed like a mummy, but blessedly, beautifully alive! Alive, and with the malignant growth ripped out root and branch. Yet her greatest battle was just beginning.

With justifiable triumph Dr. Skull began to snip at the white bandages and behind curtains veiling the procedure from other occupants of Ward Seven, his surgeon's handiwork came to light. To no one but a doctor or a nurse, used to the ravages of suffering, would Mrs. Purvins have seemed anything but a horribly scarred and suppurating grotesque imposed upon a human form. But to the two who watched her, she was neither unbeautiful nor disheartening.

"It's a marvelous job, Doctor," the nurse said fervently. "Such a clean incision. . . . I don't think there's another surgeon in the world who could have accomplished anything with her. And a man with your skill, giving all his time to charity cases. . . . Sometimes I just don't understand it."

It was more than either skill or charity that the case of Mrs. Purvins had called for, but the nurse didn't know that. And even now, Dr. Skull, his brown eyes fixed almost unbelievingly on Mrs. Purvins, wondered if he had succeeded. For she had been more than a charity patient with cancer.

Her poor scarred body had been the battleground between Dr. Skull and whatever it was that had been foisted on her—those marks that were like nothing so much as the puckered souvenirs of some cruelly hungry orifice, sucking at her skin!

A battleground for salvation against a fate medically uncharted— Dr. Skull stared into his patient's eyes, and her own eyes stared back unblinkingly. Suddenly he realized that those large grey eyes, which had gazed on Ward Seven through slits in the bandages for days, had not blinked before, either. . . . No, he could not remember seeing her eyelids move! His brows drew together thoughtfully. No, not since the operation!

The raw sutures would heal in time, he knew. The body would be smooth again, and skin-grafting could take care of the scars that might be left on her face. But—those markings! And those eyes!

He made a hurried examination, and a ghastly suspicion crossed his mind. "Nurse," he said brusquely, "please leave me alone with the patient for a few moments."

Alone with Mrs. Purvins, Dr. Skull repeated his examination, more carefully—but his hands still shook as though with ague, and his lined old face was drawn and pale.

The sick woman seemed barely aware of the hands which felt for her pulse, strove to locate her heartbeat—she did not even try to talk, and her fixed, staring grey eyes had somehow an eerie, glistening witlessness.

Dr. Skull took a blood sample, called the nurse back in, and went to the laboratories on the third floor.

It was incredible, this thing that had apparently happened to Mrs. Purvins; yes, utterly, fantastically unbelievable. . . . But still it made his palms wet and his heart race!

Under the white light of the laboratory lamp he tested the blood sample. The thin fluid did not clot, didn't even smell like blood. . . .

And then he steeled himself to the ultimate chemical analysis. He felt his pulse pound in his veins as once more he repeated the test, to make sure. There could be no mistake! The blood was of the temperature and approximate consistency of sea-water!

A telephone sounded in the laboratory anteroom. Someone murmured, "For you, Dr. Skull."

It was the nurse from Ward Seven. "Dr. Skull," she said tensely, "your patient, Doctor—I started to take her pulse, and—and she hasn't any. . . ."

Softly, Dr. Skull put the phone back on its receiver. No pulse . . . ? He had found worse than that. Mrs. Purvins hadn't a heartbeat, either. And yet, when he had taken the bandages off, she had given every outward indication that the operation had been a success.

Sea-water! He opened a drawer marked with his own name, rummaged in it for the newspaper clipping which had first interested him in Mrs. Purvins: "Delirious Woman Picked Up Near East River," the headline read. . . .

They had found her, battered and half-crazed, the victim of an inexplicable assault that left her almost drained of blood. And she had moaned, repeatedly something about an octopus. . . .

Dr. Skull frowned. There are no octopi in the East River—nor anywhere in that part of the Atlantic coastal waters, for that matter. And from his later conversations with Mrs. Purvins, after the first scars of that attack had healed, leaving in their wake a still more inexplicable cancerous growth, he was sure that her attacker had been no monster of the deep, but rather some equally monstrous human being.

Yet the sea was the cradle of all life, for before living organisms had made their slow progress onto land, aeons ago, unicellular creatures had taken their nourishment and vitality from the water of primordial oceans. And all life still—even man himself—must carry the chemical composition of ocean water within itself. All living protoplasm cells on land are bathed in blood, which has the same elements as sea-water. The lower forms of life are still bound to ocean.

But blood and sea-water, as media of life, are separated by a million million years of evolution—and it was those millions of years that had slipped from the heritage of Mrs. Purvins!

Either the phenomenon was inherent in those strange puckered markings which had been unlike ordinary cancer—or else, he—Dr. Skull—had created an atavism!

Dr. Skull rushed back to Ward Seven. Surgery couldn't—but it *must* have been his own surgery, his clean simple excision of an cancerous growth. Yet what strange, eerie quirk of the laws of chance had upset in this woman a balance older than the oldest mountain ranges . . . ?

He brushed past the curtains which still veiled Mrs. Purvins from the rest of Ward Seven. And then he paused, some deep-seated instinct muffled the cry in his throat. . . .

Mrs. Purvins' mouth was fastened like a suction pump on the nurse's bosom, and in the staring grey eyes there was stark, maddened hunger!

Dr. Skull seized his patient's shoulders, his muscular fingers pulled against that sucking, intractable force even as he gasped at the hideous strength of those hungry lips. . . . Then, with a soft *whoosh,* he pulled her clear.

The nurse dropped like a dead weight, with a three-inch circle of raw muscle bleeding over her heart, and even more terrifying in its implications, he saw the shredded, torn remnants of part of her uniform on the floor!

The Thing that had been his patient turned its shining unhuman eyes on the doctor. Suddenly it reared—not on its legs, but with a swift upward surge that seemed to involve every molecule of matter in its body. He felt the white surgeon's jacket torn from him as though it were cheesecloth, and suddenly he understood why the nurse had been unable to give alarm when she had been attacked.

The Thing's clammy hand slapped against his mouth, jammed into his throat, nearly suffocating him, while, with the swiftness of a striking snake, that terrible mouth fastened on his shoulder, its suction rending his skin, tearing with intolerable pain at the muscular flesh beneath.

He lunged desperately with arms and legs—felt himself free, and gasped for air. He cried out then, trying to call for help as his staring eyes saw his erstwhile patient rear up at the window, and with a peculiarly undulating movement slip outside. He staggered after it, his fingers clutching the sill as the Thing descended the fire-escape with unbelievable rapidity. . . . And then he saw something else that momentarily caused him to forget his pain, and his horror.

As the Thing passed the third floor, a snakily prehensile arm whirled a net from the window, trapped the creature that had been Mrs. Purvins, and pulled her back inside the hospital.

And that, he knew, was one of the windows opening from the maternity ward!

He heard himself shouting orders to the internes who were streaming into the curtained enclosure. The room was swaying crazily about him, but someone had to look after the young nurse who was lying unconscious on the floor. And someone had to capture the monster that a short while ago had been his patient, Mrs. Purvins; someone had to capture and kill the monstrous thing that had trapped her.

One of the internes was applying a hasty dressing to his shoulder wound when Dr. Borden, head of the hospital, was suddenly and excitedly among them.

Borden cried, "What's this about?"

Dr. Skull didn't answer, but he felt Borden's restraining hand on his arm as he lunged forward.

"Come along, Doctor!" he gasped, "We've got to get—to the—maternity ward!"

He leaned dizzily against Borden in the corridor, struggling to retain consciousness in the descending elevator. The car came to a stop at the third floor.

Skull started out, but a human form slammed into him with stunning impact. He felt his knees folding, felt darkness sweeping over him, and Dr. Borden's grip relaxing on his arm.

Desperately he twisted his body, even as he began to fall—through the humming, drumming darkness that was closing over him he saw Borden struggling—not in the grip of a monster, but of some human adversary. A knife glinted in the hand of Borden's attacker.

His own hand stabbed downward, almost reflexively, and his fingers grasped the small automatic which he carried with him on night-calls about the slum districts of the city. He hardly knew he had pressed the trigger, but there was a deafening explosion in the clean white corridor, and the man who had been grappling with Borden slumped to the floor.

Incredulously, Skull stared at the man he had shot, as Borden shouted: "Do you know this man, Doctor?" Nor did Skull miss the vitriolic accusation in the hospital chief's voice.

At last, Skull nodded. "The—the husband of my patient—Henry Purvins. He tried to kill you, didn't he?"

"Does it occur to you that he might have had a grievance?" Borden asked coldly. "After what you did to his wife—Look!"

Skull's eyes followed Borden's pointing finger, and he saw internes wheeling a stretcher out of the maternity ward—a stretcher on which something formless and gelid struggled frantically against sheets that tied it down—sheets covered with the pale pink compound that had passed for blood in the veins of Mrs. Purvins.

Borden, with almost venomous deliberation, went on, "*You* did that to her. . . . And now, you try to silence a husband's reasonable indignation by murder! Doctor, is it your duty to create malformations, and to kill?"

# CHAPTER TWO
# THE SKULL KILLER

SKULL'S EYES TRAVELED from Borden's face to those of the three internes who held him; to the nurses who stood about, almost hysterically tense, and the white-jacketed orderlies who bent over that body on the floor.

In the eyes of his accusers he read a completely unreasoning hatred—and something more! Behind the irises of everyone of them, with the exception of Borden, he saw flickering specks of color. . . . And he recognized in that color the mark of insanity! He had seen it before in human eyes. . . .

Again he looked at the face of the man he had shot. Even in death, the gaping unseeing eyes had that unearthly purplish glint. . . . Dr. Skull remembered that even Mrs. Purvins had warned him of her husband's "oddness." Oddness? Most damnable oddness! Murderousness, rather. . . . How close Skull had been to suspecting that Henry Purvins might have been his wife's attacker when she had been found wandering by the East River!

Then Borden stooped sanctimoniously over the corpse, and suddenly the beginning of an incredible conviction snapped into Dr. Skull's mind. The hospital chief's watch fob dangled from his waist. It was of gold, heavy and carefully wrought, and repulsive as artistry could make it. A golden octopus, with one jewelled purple eye gleaming in its head. . . . In her terrified delirium, Mrs. Purvins had babbled about an octopus—and now Mrs. Purvins was hideously, unhumanly dead!

The internes holding Skull were not prepared for the strength and fury of his attack. He bent over swiftly, and the man directly behind him doubled up with his breath knocked out. With an ease that belied his years, Skull ripped his arms free and sent another colleague spinning with a hook to the jaw. As Borden was leaping for him, Dr. Skull side-stepped and swung. Then he jumped for the elevator.

The man at the controls tried to rush him, and Skull grasped his arm, and with a jiu-jitsu hold, threw him into the melee in the hall. He slammed the doors, and his fingers were cold on the control lever as he started the car downward.

His shoulder ached agonizingly, and after that brief desperate spurt of energy, he was again dizzy and weak . . . twice the car bounced jerkily against its basement springs before Skull remembered to release the controls. Blindly, he levered the doors open, and staggered into the cellar's cool dusk.

Into the darkness behind the huge heating unit he delved, leaning heavily against a dusty, jutting plank. There was a brief whir of chains, and a section of the wall gave way. Skull lurched into the opening, and sank to his knees, completely exhausted. Behind him, he dimly heard again the soft whir of the chains, and then he was alone in the cool darkness of an unsuspected hollow in the wall.

Silent seconds passed, bringing with them some return of strength to the old doctor's nerves and muscles. And with the strength, a fiery determination-glinted again in his eyes.

Sparing the torn shoulder as best he could, he slowly removed his white surgeon's jacket, and began briskly to rub his face with it. Then it seemed as if a miracle occurred, for the sunken wrinkles disappeared completely from his jaws, cheeks and forehead. . . . He tore off the strips which secured the grey wig, revealing a head of lustrous dark hair beneath. The removal of two padded wire hooks from his lower jaw altered the shape of his face considerably. It was a far younger Dr. Skull who finally turned on his back, and lay motionless, staring upward into the darkness with alertly thoughtful brown eyes.

A half-naked young man, his were an athletes' trained and rippling muscles. . . . Weary as he was, with the bloody shoulder bandage, there was an aura of health, strength and competence about him. Hospital authorities would have recognized him as Jeffrey Fairchild, son of the late Dr. Henry Fairchild, who had achieved medical fame and a sizable fortune before his death.

Jeffrey, as administrator of his father's estate, had been instrumental in the erection of the Mid-City Hospital, and from that estate, large sums were still available to the hospital on request. That much he had done for humanity in his father's name and his own. There were people who said he might have done more, for Jeffrey, a brilliant student, had graduated at the head of his class from the best medical school in the country, and was not known ever to have started practice.

But people did not know about Dr. Skull. . . .

It was as Dr. Skull, the kindly philanthropic little East Side surgeon, that Jeffrey Fairchild had been able to fight more battles for humanity than confining his skill solely to the struggle against disease. He had been born with a love of adventure and a genius for compassion, and inevitably he had allied himself against those who have no compassion, and who prey upon the defenseless and helpless. In the slums, breeding-place of crime, Dr. Skull had been the unyielding adversary of all criminals.

No Park Avenue surgeon could have done what Dr. Skull had done, known what Dr. Skull knew. They came to him in the slums, the victims of poverty and ignorance and fear, and they trusted him to heal more than their bodies. For behind Dr. Skull himself, unknown even to his patients, there was the almost phantom figure of the Skull Killer, known only by the corpses he left behind him.

It was typical of Dr. Skull that he should have tried to find a reason for that unholy glint of purple madness in the eyes of Henry Purvins when he first began to treat the man's wife. Another doctor would have either disregarded it entirely, or considered it a phenomenon he had not been called upon to delve.

He'd labored through months and years of untiring research, research that was also adventure—and then, in the half-factual, half-superstitious chronicles of forgotten medieval savants, Dr. Skull had found the reference he sought.

He had been excited, moved—and at the same time wondered if he were allowing his credulity to be conditioned by the inevitable superstitions of the patients with whom he worked. He remembered the article he had actually written, intending it for the *American Medical Journal,* and which he had then decided not to send, as too fantastic for men of science to accept:

> During every great social catastrophe in ancient history, purple eyes have made their appearance as eternal harbingers of destruction. They have been either the cause or effect of terror among a people already ravaged by war or pestilence, inducing an unaccountable mass hysteria, often leading to wholesale atrocities.
>
> This mass hysteria reduced the population in some cases as high as seventy percent in certain districts of Central Europe, after barbaric invasions, and ruined entire sections of civilized society. By dint of incredible and impoverishing taxes, terror-ized peoples have sometimes bought off self-claimed leaders of the purple eyes, whom many insist to have been the same person, living through centuries.

Superstition? Certainly. And yet, there was the undeniable fact of those purple eyes in modern, up-to-date New York. But whereas the medieval leaders of the purple-eyed ones had been able to operate openly in a superstitious civilization separated by the thinnest of veneers from chaos, their modern counterpart would be driven to operate through the weak-minded and credulous. He would be forced to use some startling and fear-invoking disguise. . . .

The Octopus! Mrs. Purvins, who had been marked for a sentence worse than death, had babbled its name. . . . Again, Jeffrey Fairchild remembered Borden's watch-fob of the purple-eyed octopus. Did Borden know its implications, or was he an unwitting tool in a more sinister hand, as Henry Purvins undoubtedly had been?

Jeffrey trembled slightly, as he rested in the coolness of his base-ment chamber, which was the terminus of an abandoned water main reaching far under the city's streets. He came to his feet, steadied himself, and moved deeper into the subterranean passage. From a wall niche, he took a concealed gun, to replace the weapon he had lost in the scuffle upstairs, and thus armed, re-entered the basement of the Mid-City Hospital.

Through the shadows he skulked, a pale moving figure in the darkness, toward a little white-washed door. For a moment, he listened behind it, and then Jeffrey Fairchild slipped into the cool, sterile-smelling interior of the hospital morgue.

One by one, he drew the sheets from cold white faces, with some innate reverence in him asking forgiveness of the helpless dead for this intrusion. One by one, among those silent speechless people who had passed beyond earthly help or harm, he sought the man he wanted—the man he himself had killed.

Jeffrey stared with growing concentration into the wide eyes of Henry Purvins' corpse, and his mouth went grim. Was his imagination running riot, or did he actually see even in the darkness, those inhuman jewel-like eyes glowing purple . . . ? No; someone had been behind that series of concerted and unrelated incidents which he had just experienced, a series too concerted not to be directed by some purposeful malevolent agency. In life, Henry Purvins had been the tool of the most malignant personality ever spewed out of hell, and in death, the devil would claim his own!

There was just a chance—more than a chance—that the evidence he needed was here, in the form of Purvins' body, with those ghastly, purplish luminescent eyes. . . . Did it point to a hospital whose staff would not bear investigation, to someone unknown who must, for some evil purpose, soon commune with this body?

He uncovered the corpse, placed it on another stretcher. Then he took its place, and pulled the sheet over him. Quiet as the dead he lay, and the only sound in that half-way station to the tomb was his own whispered breath.

Old Angus Burke, the morgue-keeper of the hospital, didn't like the tone they'd used when they brought down the latest corpse.

"Shot?" grunted Angus. "Now that's the damndest yet! You've brought me some funny stiffs lately, lads, but for a man to die of hot lead in a hospital . . . !"

"You're not being paid for your opinions," the young interne had answered tartly, and old Angus didn't like that. He'd been handling stiffs before that whipper-snapper was born, and he knew how people died in a hospital, and how they didn't.

They didn't die, for instance, of diabetes and lockjaw at the same time. Not in a proper hospital, that is. Maybe in some beleaguered army ward where the enemy had cut off surgical supplies—but even in war, old Angus remembered, you didn't get much blood-poisoning.

He thought uneasily of the sort of cases they'd been bringing down there recently. Tetanus, elephantiasis, and other things he couldn't even name, and didn't like to think about—sure, they'd been bringing him mighty strange stiffs lately!

And now this one, with a bullet between the eyes. . . . The doctors must be crazy, he thought; like as if they didn't know their business, and the poor folks who trust 'em might better have saved their money and die peaceful.

Well, he was glad to know about it, old Angus thought, as he played double solitaire against himself in his cubby-hole of an office. He'd been thinking of asking one of the doctors for something for his rheumatism. He wouldn't now, no-sirree! Except he'd been sure of that nice old Dr. Skull. A real gentleman, he was, who didn't treat a man any different because he kept dead stiffs instead of dying ones.

But it was Dr. Skull, so they said, who'd made the latest stiff, the oddest one of all. Shot him dead, they said. Old Angus shook his head. A mighty peculiar business, and he didn't like any of it. Shouldn't be surprised if they all lost their jobs of it, either. . . .

"Can't you hear anything?"

Old Angus stood up, looking at his visitors, two of them, dressed in civilian clothes. "I ain't so deaf that you have to yell loud enough to wake these poor peaceful dead folks down here," he said with asperity. And he added, "I'm the keeper here. I suppose you're look-ing for that Purvins fellow?"

One of the men nodded. "I'm his brother. Where is he?"

A pretty strange sort of a brother, old Angus thought. Usually folks came down here with their eyes red and sniffling, not caring what you said to them. . . . It's the world these days, he considered, as he led the unfeeling brother and his companion into the morgue itself.

Old Angus hobbled up to the latest stiff, and lifted the sheet from its face. . . .

And then the corpse yelled at him, "Duck, they'll kill you!" And a bullet sang above the old man's head! . . .

He hadn't really ducked, it had been more like his knees gave way. And then, in the darkness, the corpse and his brother started firing at one another. . . .

Angus tried to whine for help, but nothing audible was coming out of his windpipe.

Like nothing dead, the stiff was letting them have it with the revolver. . . . Old Angus shut his eyes, and his brain busied itself with a prayer.

When the shots stopped, he peered dazedly about. The two visitors were dead, and the corpse was doing something to their faces.

"*A-aah!*" managed old Angus.

The corpse glanced at him briefly, and then it darted out of the room.

Minutes later, the old man looked at his visitors. Red and plain on their foreheads, the corpse had branded the mark of a human skull!

Later, when he told the newspapermen about it, old Angus realized that he had been a hero.

"So that was the Skull Killer?" he mused aloud. "Him as always leaves his mark, and never gets caught?"

"That's right, Mr. Burke," said the reporter. "You're the only man alive who's ever seen him make a kill. It's a wonder you're here to tell the tale. If you're not afraid—and I don't think you're the type of man who scares easy, Mr. Burke—suppose you try to tell us what you noticed about him. It would be a great help to the police, and a big story for us."

Old Angus peered importantly at the reporter. No, he wasn't afraid. He leaned over close. "They brought him down here dead," whispered old Angus solemnly. "One o' my regular stiffs, with a bullet between the eyes. And mister, they don't come deader than that!"

Newspapers didn't print it quite as old Angus gave it to them. They didn't swallow that bullet between the eyes, although they did ask if the Skull Killer were vulnerable at all.

For six years, that phantom image had preyed on the population of New York's underworld, sporadically and without detection. No one had ever seen him, but everyone had seen pictures, on the front pages, of the corpses he left in various parts of the city, with that red brand burned into their foreheads as if by acid.

His motive? The newspapers guessed him to be some lone fanatic, crusading against crime. Or, as one newspaper guessed, he might be a higher-up in the Police Department, for he knew so much about criminals and where to find them. He must be a gangster, said another, for it's the gangsters who kill their own kind. A prominent psychologist, when interviewed, explained technically and at great length, that a killer who left his mark was an incurable exhibitionist. He had probably had a thwarted childhood, said the prominent psychologist, quoting effectively from Freud and Jung.

In the end, people knew as much about the Skull Killer as they had known before, which was nothing. There was a momentary connection between the fact that a certain Dr. Skull had left the third floor of the Mid-City Hospital under hurried circumstances, only twenty minutes before the Skull Killer appeared in its basement.

But old Angus Burke, whose opinion had to be respected, since there was no one to contradict him, swore that the Skull Killer was a young man, a good thirty years younger than Dr. Skull, whom old Angus would have known if he'd met him in hell. This seemed to tally with the facts, for it was ridiculous to suspect an old man who has spent his life in study and medical practice, of murdering the toughest gangsters in the city single-handed, over a period of six years.

# CHAPTER THREE
# A SURPRISE FOR DR. SKULL

C AROL ENDICOTT, standing beside an old-fashioned roll-top desk in the clean and shabby doctor's office, stared wide-eyed at a slip of paper in her hand. For the second time she read the neatly typed words:

My Dear Dr. Skull:

I have followed with the greatest interest your efforts in behalf of the unfortunate Mrs. Purvins, whose remarkable story regarding my existence received so little credence on the part of the authorities.

Fisherman's luck! I find I am to be congratulated on the size of my catch! When I set poor Mrs. Purvins out as bait for an old East Side medico, I had no idea that I should shortly be playing a most extraordinary young man on the end of my line.

By the time you receive this note, you will have met—and found out how you may co-operate with

*The Octopus.*

Carol's slim fingers sought out and rested on the bulky thing in the pocket of her neatly starched nurse's uniform, and she frowned almost imperceptibly. The note had arrived in an unsealed and unstamped envelope in the doctor's morning mail, and she had neither been able to reach the doctor—who had an important appointment at the Mid-City Hospital in connection with the Mrs. Purvins whom the note mentioned—nor had she been able to figure out the meaning of the missive. So she had spent the past half-hour oiling and cleaning the old revolver which her father had used twenty years ago in France.

Consequently, at this moment, there was about Carol Endicott little of the immaculate nurse whom Dr. Skull's patients were accustomed to seeing. Her white uniform had grease smudges on it, and a large smudge bridged her freckled, pert little nose, while there was a rather unprofessional competence about her movements. She was again the independent and rather harassed New York slum girl whom Jeffrey Fairchild had persuaded to trust the old East Side doctor in order that she might have a home, decency and security.

Decency had always been one of Carol's attributes, though often, in the old days, she had had to fight for it. Young, tall, with a clear ivory skin and lustrous dark hair that carried in it a reddish glint, she had attracted considerable attention in the tenement district where she lived. Personal danger wasn't exactly a new thing to her. This particular type of danger, however, was.

She shivered a little, remembering Mrs. Purvins as she had looked when the doctor had first interested himself in her case, shortly after they'd found her unconscious near the East River, mumbling incoherently about "the octopus." She shivered, and took a slightly firmer grip on the butt of the old revolver. She didn't know whether she could actually fire it, or what would happen if she tried, but its comfort was good.

The ringing of the telephone almost made her jump. Then, wiping her hands on her skirt, thereby adding a few more spots to it, she picked up the phone.

"Dr. Skull's office," she said.

"Board of Health calling. This is a routine call. Is the doctor in?"

"I'm his nurse. I'll take a message."

"Very well. We're warning all doctors not to hospitalize their patients unless it's absolutely necessary, until further notice. We're checking all hospitals, doing the best we can. Thank you."

"What!" she exclaimed. "Say, what's been—" Then she realized that she was talking into a dead phone, and hung up.

This was serious, Carol thought. She couldn't tie things together, but this was the second extraordinary telephone call she had received that morning, after discovering the crank letter.

Dr. Steele had called, asking if Skull couldn't join him at once in a consultation . . . and Steele had been most unprofessionally vague about details. Then a little Italian boy, one of the doctor's former patients, had run in a short while ago, to say his father was looking for the doctor, and the doctor had better watch out.

She'd tried calling the Mid-City Hospital then, but the hospital authorities had been most uncooperative about disturbing the doctor, and she hadn't even been able to put her message through.

And now this warning about hospitals. Dr. Skull had another patient at the Mid-City, besides Mrs. Purvins—one Robert Fairchild. Robert Fairchild, the crippled eighteen-year-old, who idolized the old doctor so that he had become a resident patient.

Robert had been taken to the Mid-City a few weeks ago for another of a series of operations through which the doctor eventually hoped to cure the boy, and lift him from the wheelchair, to which he now seemed condemned for life.

Carol decided to try the Mid-City again, and see if she could talk to Robert. . . . Not that anything bad would happen to Robert—about whom too many people worried already. There was Dr. Skull, for one, who treated him like a son. And there was Jeffrey Fairchild, Robert's brother, with whom, oddly enough, Robert couldn't get along at all. . . .

Carol smiled a little grimly when she thought of the relationship between the two brothers.

It was Jeffrey, whom she privately considered worth a half-a-dozen Roberts, who made all the overtures, and it was Robert who rejected them—the spoiled, ungrateful brat!

She dialed Mid-City Hospital again, and got the switchboard girl.

"Private Pavilion," she said, and tried to light a cigarette during the ensuing pause. She had to laugh at herself, she was so nervous. Three matches, and none of them took!

"Mr. Robert Fairchild," she demanded, when they gave her the floor phone.

"Who's calling, please?"

"I'm his nurse. This is Dr. Skull's office."

"Oh—is the doctor there?" the voice inquired.

"No," said Carol. "He should be at the hospital. If you could find him for me, it's impor—"

But a definite click at the other end of the wire told her that the connection had been killed. And the operator informed her, "Your party hung up, miss."

Carol's cheeks flushed, and then went white again. She was as angry as she had ever been in her life—almost angry enough to forget what she had tried so very hard to remember lately, namely, that she was a lady.

It was Jeffrey Fairchild who had first impressed that idea upon her, when he had gotten Dr. Skull to give her her present job, and it was for the sake of Jeffrey that she nearly forgot it now. If anything were to happen to Robert Fairchild, it would break Jeffrey's heart . . . and Jeffrey, at one point in her life, had been her very real saviour.

The tough look that came over Carol's piquantly lovely features had nothing lady-like about it. Rather, it reflected a portion of her life she had nearly forgotten—her upbringing in a rough-and-ready slum neighborhood, and the battle she had waged continually not only for respectability among the worst elements of humanity, but for her very survival.

She lifted the phone receiver again, and dialed Jeffrey Fairchild's Park Avenue apartment. While she waited, her fingers again sought the reassuring bulge of the ancient revolver in her pocket.

There was no answer.

Slowly Carol Endicott replaced the receiver. A stony determination spread over her face as she turned toward the closet for her coat. If the hospital authorities chose to be snooty about giving her information about Robert Fairchild, she'd find a means of getting it out of them!

It was at this point that the door opened, and a perfectly strange voice told her to stand right where she was.

Her unexpected visitor's command to Carol carried farther than Dr. Skull's office. In a small chamber hidden behind a basement wall in the same building, a tall young man was in the act of changing from a blood-stained surgeon's uniform into a custom-made tweed suit. He put his ear to a wall amplifier as the stranger's command snapped out to Carol Endicott. Jeffrey Fairchild, after his battle in the morgue of the Mid-City Hospital, had again taken his secret exit from the hospital basement. From there, he had proceeded through a maze of abandoned gas and water mains which peppered the earth under New York's streets. Relics of another era, these passages had been forgotten by citizens and authorities alike. Jeffrey had come upon them accidentally as a young boy, and later they had suggested to him the feasibility of his double life.

The terminals of that underground maze had been Jeffrey's chief reason for the location of Dr. Skull's office, of his own apartment, and even of the site he had chosen for the Mid-City Hospital.

The chamber where he was now dressing had been furnished with a cot, a chair, and a bureau. Its wall amplifier enabled him to keep posted on events in the office above, and its location made it a convenient dressing-room for exchanges of personality between Dr. Skull and Jeffrey Fairchild.

"What do you want?" he heard Carol demand.

There was a sinister purring note in the reply. "We're waiting for the doctor—got a little present for him. O.K., boys, bring in the crate."

Shuffling sounds, the scrape of wood across the floor—and then staccato little footsteps.

"You stay right here, sister!" snapped the intruder's voice. "You're not going anywhere till the doctor comes—this is a surprise party!"

As Jeffrey finished dressing, into the silence above broke the screech of metal, the scream of the girl. Carol, the innocent gambit in a desperate battle whose stakes Jeffrey could only guess, was alone up there with the spawn of hell. . . .

Swiftly Jeffrey moved through the coal-bin door, took the cellar staircase three steps at a time, and emerged through the rear door to Dr. Skull's office, his gun drawn.

A startled oath broke from a man's lips, and the girl cried out defiantly. Jeffrey saw the flare of explosive brilliance before he heard the shot . . . and then Carol, entrenched behind the roll-top desk, swayed dizzily. Her bloody hand unclenched and dropped, and the shattered remnants of the revolver she had been holding fell to the floor.

Somehow that gun had exploded in her grasp at her first attempt to use it!

Jeffrey's bullet snarled just as one man reached the unconscious girl. The startled intruder spun to his knees, and as Jeffrey leaped into the room, he realized that he had drawn fire from two hostile guns.

He lunged forward as lead whined past his cheek, and let them have it again. Two men were sprawled on the floor, and the third was retreating. Agonizingly, Jeffrey shifted his bandaged shoulder to avoid a shot and fired half-blindly in the same gesture.

The third man had fled.

And then *they* crawled out of the open wooden crate which Jeffrey had barely noticed on Dr. Skull's floor. With a sick sense of fatality, Jeffrey realized that he could not fire upon those obscenely crawling, even if they killed him. His physician's instinct, outraged and muted by the ghastly sight, still was strong enough to make him lower the smoking weapon in his hand.

Once they had been a man and a woman. Jeffrey recognized their grayish flannel bathrobes as the regulation equipment in the city's largest charity ward. But the bodies under those bathrobes, spindly as matches in the bony structure, hideously swollen and protruding at every joint, were like no patients Jeffrey had seen in that hospital or any other.

The man's shoulder-joints were bulbous as huge gourds on the frail vine-like torso, and the woman's pelvic girdle was flattened, wide till she seemed to be sitting on a portable chair even as she moved painfully toward him.

And their faces! The wide eyes stared, hideous with hatred and pain, from their shrunken mummy sockets. The lower jaws were huge, contrasting inhumanly with the shrunken craniums, like platters supporting a pointed pudding.

So this was the surprise party!

Slowly, deliberately, the creatures were advancing on him. . . . These ghastly abortions, obviously abducted from hospital wards, would have been further damning evidence against Dr. Skull—if there had been anything left of Dr. Skull when his enemies were through with him.

"What do you want of me?" Jeffrey asked softly. His nerves were stinging with pain and shock, but he stood erect and untrembling. "Can I help you?"

The man-thing's monstrous lower jaw moved gigantically, and a hoarse, unearthly laugh with no joy in it ripped from the match-stick chest.

"There—is no—help," he stated in harsh, deliberate gutturals, as though speech had become difficult. "If you're—a doctor, I want to—kill you."

The woman-thing started to laugh in high, tinny laughter. Maybe the damned laugh that way in hell, Jeffrey thought feverishly. But this wasn't hell! This was New York, civilization. . . .

"I am a doctor, of sorts," he admitted to the monstrous creatures. "And I don't want to hurt you. As you see, I have a gun. I can defend myself, but hope that won't be necessary. I want you to trust me!"

He didn't finish, for at that moment, the two foul distortions of human shape leaped upon him. Their huge hams of hands covered his throat, his face, pinned his arms to his sides . . . unutterable revulsion rose in him, as he smelled the faint but undeniable tinge of putrescence in that sick flesh. . . .

He twisted his body at the waist, used his upper torso as a club, and then he was free. A guttural howl thudded against his ear-drums, and then a powerful lower jaw sank into his arm. With both hands, Jeffrey seized the man-thing's throat, squeezed till the eyes popped and the jaw loosened.

The woman-thing fell to her knees beside the sprawled figure of her mate, and from her round bulbous eyes a few tears squeezed out.

"He's not dead," Jeffrey gasped. "He—won't die. You two . . . I've got to—help you."

The man's body was clumsy, but no heavier than any other body. As Jeffrey dragged it haltingly down into his cellar, the woman followed. He noticed that she stopped for something which had been in the crate, wondered if it were some kind of weapon.

It was only when he had stretched the man-thing on his cot in the underground chamber behind the coal-bin that the woman stretched out her hand. In that vast swollen palm, there was an ordinary glazed electric bulb.

"Light," said the woman. "Give us light, or—we die."

Jeffrey frowned at the pleading, half-beaten quality in that harsh painful voice. He removed his own bulb from the wall socket, and inserted the bulb she gave him.

Instantly, the subterranean room was flooded with a pale but glaring indigo radiance that hurt Jeffrey's eyes. Ultraviolet! Why, what . . . ?

"Go!" commanded the monstrous woman. "It will hurt you; we need it. We need it because doctors have . . . done this to us. . . ."

The glare was dizzying. It hurt his skin, tickled a vibrant heat into his bones. On the cot, the man-thing began to stir.

"There's a box of package groceries on the shelf," Jeffrey said, "and water in the tap there. Here—" he made some adjustments in his wall amplifier, transforming it into what it had been originally, a radio loud speaker, "if you turn on that switch, you'll have a radio. I'll be back later, with books, cooked food—"

The woman nodded again. Her gnarled flattened body might have been twenty years old or a hundred, but it seemed now as ancient as human tragedy itself. "Go," she said again.

The ultra-violet light was beginning to break his skin. Jeffrey left them there and cautiously locked the door from the outside.

What had they been, what ghoulish distortion of the scientific mind had made them monsters?

The question seared Jeffrey's brain, blazed a new scar of hatred across it like the hot blade of a branding knife. There was a passion in him for health and normalcy, and he had discerned the ghost of those things in that ungodly pair.

Their vengeful attack was understandable.

Beyond that murderous rage, their minds seemed unimpaired. He thought again of the woman-thing's tears when she thought her mate was dead, and of the way she had followed him. . . .

Would he really be able to help them, as he passionately hoped to do? He had not helped Mrs. Purvins—so far.

Suddenly the sick certainty dawned on Jeffrey that there would be more cases, and more still, until the very name of doctors and healing medicine were anathemas to an outraged humanity!

# CHAPTER FOUR
# HELL'S HOSPITAL

SHORTLY, he guessed, there would be more intruders in the office of Dr. Skull. They would be men with badges from the police and health departments, who had been informed that two medical monsters, additional damning proof of malpractice, were to be found in Dr. Skull's office.

He uttered a fervent inward prayer of thanks for that hidden chamber where the two monstrosities might be safe until he found out what had deformed them. In that discovery lay his only chance of helping them.

He stopped upstairs, dragged the unconscious Carol to a couch, and bathed her blasted hand with antiseptic. That right hand would be useless for weeks, but no other harm had been done.

"Good little soldier!" he whispered.

The homeless girl Jeffrey had befriended when she had no one else to turn to did not hear him. But her strong slender body seemed to relax, as though she knew a friend was near. . . . And Jeff guessed that this wouldn't be the last time he got Carol out of a tight spot, just as it wasn't the first.

He stared briefly at the two dead faces on Dr. Skull's office floor, faces in which the sightless eyes glowed like purple grave-lights! That was the characteristic of those who had given their souls to a devil's keeping, but for what reward, Jeffrey did not know.

He bent down, and with a rubber stamp whose handle was a vial containing acid, he burned the Mark of the Skull on the two cold brows. Contrary to erudite psychological opinion, that brand was no mere braggart gesture. In Jeffrey's ceaseless war on evil, he had found that the brand gave him a definite authority over his enemy. Sometimes indeed, it acted as a deterrent, for those marked corpses were proof to the living that the Skull Killer was alive and active. . . .

His hands moved swiftly after that, exploring the clothing of the two, in an effort to find some mark of identification. In the breast pocket of one he found a sealed envelope—and its contents, as he eagerly scanned them, caused him to forget everything but his immediate mission.

Now, with the ghastly knowledge which a brief glimpse at the dead man's papers had given him, he wondered if he would be in time. One thing was sure—he had to leave Carol, and surmised that the next intruders in his office wouldn't harm her. As a police siren sounded outside, he raced into the street and hailed a taxi.

It was night, a cold starry November night, with Orion making a clear pale pattern above Manhattan, as it had done for the past five thousand Novembers. Dark stone buildings squatted or soared in contemplative peace above the small streets. But the Mid-City Hospital—that modern medical colossus—seemed no part of the pattern, seemed to be breaking out of the background in an ominous haze of color.

Dim but unmistakable in the darkness, the hospital walls glowed like a new earthbound star. Nor were they the color of stars—they were purple!

He had seen that color in human eyes. . . . He had seen it half an hour ago in the incredible ultra-violet life-ray of two who were heirs to hell. It was the color of damnation—and ironically now the color of the building dedicated to the relief of human suffering!

Robert was in that building—Robert, who was the point and meaning of his brother Jeff's existence. . . .

As the cab slowed to a snail's pace then stopped amid a blare of horns and calls of doormen in the Monday night theatre traffic, Jeffrey handed his driver a dollar bill, and proceeded on foot.

If he could make it in time! But in time for what?

He didn't know, couldn't know yet, in just what fashion hell would break loose in the Mid-City Hospital—whether it would take seconds or hours before horror burst like shrapnel upon the thousand helpless inmates. Whether, in some vile secret part of that magnificent edifice, it had not already happened. . . .

A nurse nodded to him pleasantly at the desk, and he brushed past hurriedly into an elevator, and was soon in the eighth floor pavilion where Robert had a private suite.

The boy was sitting in his wheel-chair, reading a book of sonnets. One lamp cast its glow on the chiseled beauty of the boy's dark head . . . there was something almost unearthly in the boy's sculptured profile, Jeffrey thought with a sharp pang of solicitude.

He himself was rough-hewn, fit for the hard eventualities of life, but Robert wasn't. A fierce tenderness welled in the big man for the crippled boy, a tenderness that played through his first half-humorous phrase.

"It's moving-day, Robert. I've come to take you home."

"Are you crazy?" the boy asked petulantly. It was his whole greeting. "If you think I'm just *playing* sick, I might tell you that Dr. Skull said—"

"I don't give a damn!" Jeffrey told him, and then he lifted the boy bodily from his wheel chair. Robert gasped, shut his eyes, and then relaxed in his brother's arms. The book fell from his grasp, and Jeffrey noted its title hastily, planning in some corner of his mind to replace it later.

He ran into the corridor, and with that living burden clutched against his chest, began a rapid round of the rooms.

"If you can walk or crawl or move in any way at all," he shouted to one startled patient after another, "get out of this place! It's no spot for the sick or the well!"

Screams echoed behind him, as patients and nurses alike recognized in this enraged young man the chief patron of the hospital. The corridors were becoming a chaos with those who tried to flee, and others who tried to hold them back. And a few times, Jeffrey intervened to help some frantic refugee get clear passage to freedom. . . .

"Jeffrey Fairchild, are you insane?" There was excitement and anger on the dignified professional face before him, as the man in white who had appeared in the corridor excitedly waving his arms. "I've always liked you, but you've gone too far this time. . . ."

Jeffrey swept Dr. Borden, staff director of the hospital, aside with one gesture of his left arm, and continued down the corridor, yelling commands for exodus.

"Stop that maniac!" he heard Borden shriek behind him, and then three husky orderlies were trying to wrest Robert from him. . . .

It was then that the queer crackling began to echo ominously through every part of the building's structure. For a second Jeffrey's heart went acrobatic. . . . And then the *smell* came!

It made him gasp. It was a little like acid, but stronger, a little like smoke, but more throttling, and as yet invisible. The crackling sound grew like the laugh of a giant devil.

An orderly shrieked,, as he ran headlong from the man he was supposed to detain. "The X-ray films! My God, the X-ray room's on fire. That means poison gas!"

Jeffrey didn't remember the details later, but he would hold all through his life the hectic impressions of that roaring chaos. . . . How he carried Robert to willing helpers in the air outside, and then plunged back into the building.

How heavy the old woman was, when she fainted on her bed, and he had to drag her to safety because everyone else had forgotten her. How the young man went berserk, using the plaster cast on his arm for a club, and had to be knocked out before Jeff could save him. And always the dreadful, suffocating smell grew heavier, and the enormous crackling laugh of the burning walls more taunting and hateful. Through it all, his brain screamed in pain and desperation for vengeance on the conscious agent who had caused all this. . . .

Everywhere, now, firemen were dragging, wheeling and carrying the shrieking patients to safety. The lower floors had to be vacated first, for that was where the deadly fumes were heaviest.

Jeffrey had nowhere seen Mrs. Purvins, who was reported under observation at the hospital. He choked his way up a staircase at last, passing white figures of the thickening, swirling, deadly mist. Had she already been taken from the hospital? Suddenly he found himself in a corridor where the trend was downward, downward, with a frantic stream of refugees making their tortured way toward the exit and into the blessed air of night.

He lurched against the door of the psychopathic ward where he guessed the rescuers would arrive last. Here, most likely, they had sent Mrs. Purvins.

And then he broke into inferno. . . .

All who were left were strapped to their cots, or confined in strait-jackets. The others must have fled. A howling like the howling of purgatory clangored with the wall-crackling. Crazed, twisted shapes wormed across the hot floor, humping in torture toward escape, bound as they were. . . .

There was fury in Jeff's heart as he freed them, working over those bonds with a superhuman reserve of strength, allowing the mad-dened human things to scamper for their lives.

He found one cold and shapeless form on a far cot, knew it for Mrs. Purvins. Was she dead, then? He didn't know, couldn't tell, for there was no heart-beat to guide him. He slung the sloshing mass of flesh over his shoulder, and fought through the smoke to freedom.

Fury rose hotly in his heart, and death seemed to clot his lungs. . . . He was blind, drowning in a sea of white acrid smoke, but he clung tenaciously to that burden in his arms.

Then life was coming back to his tortured body, and somewhere above him the stars were glowing serenely. He felt the burden lifted from his arms, heard men's voices. Someone was holding cool water to his mouth.

He saw—when he could be sure of what he was seeing—that he was on the veranda outside the hospital, and that the men about him wore black and red helmets of the fire department. Suddenly, from the bowels of the doomed building, Jeffrey heard a woman scream in mortal terror.

Maybe the others heard it—maybe they could persuade them-selves of the futility of rescue. Jeffrey didn't stop to argue. But before any one could stop him, he burst back into the hot white hell of fire and radium fumes that had been the Mid-City Hospital. . . .

When Carol opened her eyes, the office was dark. She touched a hand to her forehead and felt the cloth.

Her hand—someone had bandaged her hand! She remembered now, how her father's gun had exploded in her palm. Poor old Pop! He'd come back from over there with an army gun and a lot of faith in nothing at all. Other men gave their lives, and Pop had given his soul. . . . She might have known he'd never leave her anything useful!

Those men who had been waiting for Dr. Skull—had they gone? She stumbled toward the wall switch, still puzzled by that big salt-smelling bandage, thinking that possibly Dr. Skull had come after all. . . .

Carol cried aloud, a little cry of fear that died in her throat. Two men—she recognized them as the intruders—were sprawled on the floor. Gingerly, she looked at them more closely, afraid to wake them to further activity. But there was no cause for such fear. They were completely dead.

And on the foreheads of each, was the Mark of the Skull. The Skull Killer! That half-legendary figure whom Carol, and many other New Yorkers, had half-believed a fabrication of the newspapers. . . . He had been here, he had killed her attackers. And it must have been he who had bandaged her hand!

She leaned against the wall, trying to puzzle out what had just happened to her. There were things in herself that were new to her. There was this desperate, uneasy foreboding, that was somehow worse than actual fear. . . . And then she remembered Robert!

That was where she should have gone, hours ago. She had been on her way to the hospital when those men. . . .

Carol struggled into her coat, ran out into the street. A policeman looked at her idly, and she had the fleeting thought that this was no moment to report a double killing. She hadn't the time. Later, perhaps. . . .

The streets were crowded with people, coming home from work, going to the movies, laughing and talking and getting last-minute purchases for dinner, but Carol's nerves were raw and angry with that queer unease. She wanted to warn all the people, tell them it was no good going to the movies or taking life calmly, while the forces of some cryptic hurricane gathered over them, ready to bring its tragic destruction to blight their lives.

What would she find in the hospital, what would it mean to her and to all the cheerfully noisy people about her? She couldn't, no matter how hard she tried, assure herself that it would be all right, that the hospital would tower as it had always done over central Manhattan, with every polite interne ready to explain that visiting hours were almost over, but if she really wanted to drop in. . . . No, it wasn't going to be like that!

She knew it three blocks away, knew it from the sudden change in tempo of the crowd about her, from the loud wail of hook-and-ladder sirens. . . .

The hospital was on fire!

Uniformed men were beginning to throw a cordon about the flaming pile of stone as she fought her way through the thick crowd. She heard shouts, screams. . . . And through it all ran the half-meaningless phrase, "It's the X-ray films! They haven't a chance!"

Fires don't *smell* like this she thought, with that queer, cold tension in her tightening to a certainty. Something unearthly, something devastating as an earthquake, had happened to Robert, and to all the other people in there!

It came to her, then, like a bolt from hell. Suppose that Jeffrey were in there with Robert! The thought sent her whirling lithely through the press of people right to the half-formed cordon of fire-fighters. Her coat was ripped off and lost in the crowd as she pressed closer. The hot flames made a blazing summer out of that November night, poisoning the pure air with soaring smoke.

Behind that screen of smoke, she managed to slip into the doomed building.

Heat and gas rolled like ocean waves through her body . . . She could hardly bear it, she would die here, and no one would know what had happened to her!

Figures brushed past her in the mist, and she could not identify them. She merely guessed that they were refugee and human. . . . She would never find Jeffrey or Robert!

Out. . . . She must get out, into the clean air. . . .

Carol stumbled forward through the roaring smoke, arms outstretched before her. She was nearly there, she could see the vague outline of an exit ahead of her.

Someone caught her waist and she murmured faintly, "Take me—out of here. . . ." Then she relaxed limply into strong masculine arms, her swaying body grateful for that support.

The smoke was getting worse, she thought dully; it must be all over the city by now. And then she realized with sharp fright that she was being carried away from the exit—back into the burning heart of the building!

"It's the wrong way!" she screamed at the man who held her. "We'll die if you don't—"

A strangely hollow laugh cut short her protest. She looked at the man who carried her, and even in that heat, she felt a quick, hideous chill. For it wasn't a human face at all! It was a—a—gargoyle . . . And now there were other gargoyles, scampering toward them, returning to sport in the hell they had created.

She had not thought herself capable of the mighty effort which pulled her loose from the thing that held her . . . but she was on her own legs again, running like a hunted thing for freedom. . . .

They circled off her escape, all of them, devil-faced creatures of poisoned smoke, and then they were carrying her back with them, into unimaginable torment.

They were not gargoyles, Carol realized; they were men in gas masks. She saw that as soon as they passed the door marked, "X-Ray Room. Keep Out."

Here the smoke had cleared, but the heat was unbearable, and that ghastly smell was stronger than it had been outside.

"Everything here's burned itself out," one of the masked men remarked tersely, "That was quick."

Carol looked about wildly at the blackened interior. Strips of charred wood clung to the twisted steel frame-work. She could only guess at the immense heat which had twisted that steel. Her strength, she felt was growing less. And meanwhile, the men's voices echoed in her ears, like voices heard in a dream.

"The girl's going to die soon," she heard one of her captors say. "This air must be terrific. Are we leaving her?" As he spoke, Carol felt the hold on her relaxed. She sagged to the floor, shrieked as her skin blistered at the contact.

One of the figures picked her up, held her at arm's length—and then hot air seared her lungs as she gasped it in and began to scream—but regularly, repeatedly. An evil staring mask wavered before her eyes, seemed to grow larger and more hideous, just as the body beneath it seemed to swell. A million tearing pains shot through her tortured flesh, seeming to rend it asunder, and she knew that not one but four arms encircled her, arms that held her not by a grip, but by powerful suction.

The Octopus! It seemed to her as though a sudden silence had fallen in the room, a silence through which a meaning clearer than words floated into her consciousness.

"The Skull's nurse," it seemed to say. "She'll be a good object lesson by the time he finds her!"

Into the dim haze of her consciousness came the memory of the morning, and of the arrival of the threatening missive. This monster was human, then; and the thought revived some of her ebbing courage. She tried feebly to struggle.

But there was no strength in Carol anywhere, save in her voice, and even her shrieks were growing fainter. . . .

She had not quite lost consciousness—she insisted later—but she could not remember how she came to be upright and on her feet again, with the blood streaming dizzily through her veins, and the various suction cups on her skin releasing their hold. She was leaning against the wall, also against someone, and the fiery little room was loud with shouts.

Fearfully, she turned her head. Jeffrey Fairchild had found her. How, or when—that didn't matter. She realized that all the laughing gargoyles had lost their masks—excepting one who had last held her. There was a smoking gun in Jeff's hand. He was raising the gun and taking point-blank aim at the remaining devil—the Octopus.

Simultaneously with Jeff's pulling the trigger, she saw one of those long green arms snake out and fasten around his wrist, and she thought she could hear the audible click as the gun-hammer hit on a spent cartridge. Jeff seemed suddenly torn from her side, but then she realized that he had hit the monster with a flying tackle that carried them both across the room.

They squirmed and rolled in a tangle of flying limbs, with those long green arms encircling Jeff. Jeff had switched his gun into his left hand which was still free, and with it he kept beating the monster back, hitting it in the face, while he had managed to get his right hand near his side in spite of the gripping scaly tentacle.

She saw his fingers flick briefly into the side pocket of his jacket, and come out holding something that glistened in the dim light of the smoke-filled room. He swung his fist, holding the shining object toward the side of the monster's head, but the other eluded him by throwing himself backward and releasing Jeff altogether.

The monster rolled over into a corner, one of the long arms reached far back and threw something, and suddenly the room was dark, filled with acrid, lung-searing gas.

She coughed, struggled for breath with which to scream, and then she felt Jeff's arms around her again, lifting her up, carrying her outside.

She tried to ask him about it, when at last they were outside; what was it that had made the monster suddenly release him and act as if he were afraid? But Jeff wasn't listening. He wrapped his own torn coat around her, and then she was in a taxi with Jeff and Robert. She was growing ill, for that smell seemed to linger on every square inch of her body. . . .

Jeff seemed to know about the poison that seemed to be eating into her skin. In his own apartment, he sponged her aching body with warm water and some kind of liniment.

"Sorry to make you play nursemaid," she smiled faintly.

He didn't answer, merely pulled the cool sheet over her, and reached for her wounded hand. Carefully, he began to wind a new bandage about it.

"Where's Dr. Skull?" she asked. "There were some men, and a letter—from that thing. . . ."

She told him about the letter that had come in the doctor's mail, and Jeff listened, quietly.

"I think Dr. Skull will take care of himself," Jeffrey said then. "You try to sleep. And—better leave guns alone!"

She writhed into some kind of comfort in the cool darkness. How had Jeffrey known that her hand had been hurt by the explosion of an old revolver? Did it look that bad?

She fell asleep in the middle of plans for securing an up-to-date, non-burstable, conveniently concealable police revolver. It was all very well to be a lady in normal times—but when armed intruders entered your place of business, and when you were likely to meet an—octopus—in a place several degrees hotter than hades . . . well, even a lady might be pardoned for packing her own protection!

# CHAPTER FIVE
# WHILE THE CITY SLEEPS

T HAT MONDAY AT MIDNIGHT, a new beacon flared in the Manhattan skyline. It seemed to waver at first, like a star trying to be born, and then one brilliant plume of violet light shot upward and southward. A sparkling spray edged electrically bright from either side . . . and then the ray thickened, rose and seemed to comb the constellations. Feeling its way among the scattered clouds like a thing alive—huge, probing tentacle!

Then, after the momentary display which attracted a thousand eyes, it settled into a steady purple glow.

Having erected a new and notable skyscraper on Columbus Circle, the owner of the just-completed Victory Building had crowned his work with a signal so starkly beautiful that the other steel peaks of Manhattan paled by comparison. There was something eerie about the purple light, something that suggested the island's future as it towered closer and closer, dynamically victorious, towards unattainable heights of sky.

So the men in the streets thought, as they clustered in little groups to gape at the star-searcher. So the lone pilot thought, as the wing-tip of his empty transport plane seemed to catch momentary violet fire, two thousand feet above the crest of the Victory Building. But almost instinctively, for reasons he could never explain, he sent the ship into a steep bank, to avoid that purple glow.

Jeffrey Fairchild, watching from his northwest window, read another significance in the blazing beacon. It was the same light, multiplied by millions of watts, as the one that those pitiful lost souls in the basement chamber required for life. It was the same light, concentrated and directed, as he had seen glowing on the walls of the Mid-City Hospital an hour before its collapse!

The color of Satan victorious. . . . In that beacon, Jeffrey thought, he saw the risen flag of evil conquest over an already doomed city. Had the Octopus laid his plans so well, was his position already so firm, that he could hoist his eerie standard boldly in plain sight of the City's millions?

Desperately, Jeffrey assured himself that there might not be a connection. The purple beacon was—must be—only a purple beacon. But after all that had happened that day, he could hardly believe in such coincidence.

It was the end of Dr. Skull—at least for a while. Already the city itself was ready to prosecute that mild-mannered professional man for murder and worse. If the enemy had raised his standard, *his* next attack on the quarters of Dr. Skull would be neither insidious nor subtle. Rather, it would be the high-handed devastation of the conquering invader—there was no room in the same city for two buildings representing such opposing philosophies as the humble quarters of Dr. Skull, and the arrogant new temple of the twentieth century Satan!

Some day, Dr. Skull might continue his offices and functions, and heart-brokenly, Jeffrey hoped that he could. In the meantime, it was for Jeffrey Fairchild to discover the true nature of that ominous and brightly sinister banner.

Carol woke with cold sweat draining from every pore. She had dreamed of that time in Dr. Skull's office when two fiercely garnet-colored eyes had attempted to stare her into hideous obedience. . . . But now she was safe in Jeffrey Fairchild's house and it was only the Broadway dawn coming through the blinds that had caused her troubled dream of that time when she had been kidnapped.

The Broadway dawn—New York's nocturnal neon life—but

what a strange color! She rose on her knees in bed, and drew the curtains.

A mile tall in the sky, sharp and radiant as a sword, pierced the shaft of purple light. Carol gasped, and rubbed her cold arms. Was this the end for them all; had the nightmare been realer than she thought? Her body ached with weariness. It had been a hard day, a dreadful day and she could still feel the chafing in her ankles where those men. . . .

Outraged, her mind shrank from the memory. Another woman might have been hysterical for days. Not Carol—but she didn't want to think. . . .

Someone else had to think for her, someone stronger than she. She could act, she could fight, she could endure. But to anticipate and face the terrors she knew to be waiting—no, she couldn't do that, till her nerves and muscles forgot that too-recent torture!

No one but Jeffrey was strong enough to help her. With Jeffrey beside her, she could kneel and be calm in the valley of sinister shadow. . . .

She pulled the curtains against that stark image in the sky, and lurched forward on her pillow.

In the morning, she thought drowsily, when true dawn cleaned the sky with serene sunlight, she would be sure that she had never wakened; she would only think that her nightmare had taken some odd and realistic twist. . . .

Jeffrey passed softly into the dark room where Robert slept. Before he went out into the night, he wanted to look once more at his brother's face. That one look might perforce last him through eternity.

A wind rustled the half-drawn shade, and the boy sighed quietly. Was he awake? Jeffrey half hoped so. If he could hear Robert's voice now, the night ahead would be easier. . . . But Robert did not stir.

The very darkness had a purplish cast, and that glowing arm of radiance was clearly visible from the window. As his eyes grew more accustomed to the dimness, Jeffrey saw that Robert was propped up in bed, his face turned toward the window. There was an open book in the boy's lap. He must have been reading it when the glow came, and he had turned the light off the better to watch that curious beacon.

Jeff sat beside the bed and waited for Robert to speak.

"Funny looking thing, isn't it, Jeff?"

"Very. What were you reading?"

For seconds, Robert did not answer. Then he said, "Jeff, did you notice, just before the hospital caught fire, that the walls were just that color? Sort of—purple and alive?"

"Why, yes," said Jeffrey.

"It's funny," said Robert, "that you always show up when I need you. Guess I wouldn't be here if it weren't for you . . . It's too bad, Jeff, that we can't see eye to eye on things. I sometimes wish that I could get along with you. If you'd only drop your sloppy way of living. . . . If you'd only look at things the long way, care about the things that matter, the way Dr. Skull does. . . ."

"Skull?" Jeffrey breathed. "Well, where's your Dr. Skull now?" In spite of the fact that he himself lived in the two personalities, so clear and separate an entity had Dr. Skull become to Jeffrey, that he was almost jealous of his brother's affection for the old doctor. Especially so since that affection was denied to him.

Robert's voice grew lower. "I think he's hiding somewhere, Jeff. They're after him—oh, for all sorts of things he hasn't done! Murder—human vivisection, or worse! You know, Jeff, I almost understand why people believe that. Once I—" the boy broke off, then spoke again. "It's hard to believe at first that anyone can really be as kind and unselfish as Dr. Skull is. At one time, I even thought he was the Skull Killer—and of course, that's crazy. But he's not that way! He's good, clean through, and I wish I could find him and tell him so!"

"I might find him for you," Jeffrey murmured.

"You? You wouldn't even know him. You've always been too busy, or too lazy, or just too snobbish, to meet him when I asked you to. . . ."

To change the subject, Jeffrey said, "You still haven't told me about that book you were reading."

"This book? It really belongs to Dr. Skull. He gave it to me a long time ago, when he wanted me to do research for him on something called the Purple Eye. He was writing a paper for the Medical Association. There's something here I didn't tell him. Look here, Jeff—if you should happen to run into him any time, if you should recognize him, you tell him what it is, the way I'm going to tell you. Tell him about the Mid-City Hospital fire, too.

"But this book. . . . It's a book of legends—most of them just can't be swallowed in any shape. And I didn't tell him what I found, because it didn't have anything to do with eyes. There's a story here about Rome—the night before it burned. They saw a purple light around the Coliseum, and then the flames came. Only one man told about it—Dorican Agrippa—but he isn't generally considered a reliable source."

"I'll tell Dr. Skull if I see him," Jeffrey said, his eyes narrowed and thoughtful. Purple lights in the walls of doomed buildings! And now the very sky was threaded by that forewarning of destruction. "Think I'll let you get some sleep, Robert."

"Good idea," said the boy quietly. He sighed, and fell back against his pillow.

Jeffrey turned for another look from the doorway, but Robert no longer seemed aware of him. His face turned to the window, the boy motionlessly watched that arrogant purple signal in the sky.

Half an hour or so later, Jeffrey heard a faint scratching sound as he tunneled toward the underground chamber below Dr. Skull's office. It grew louder; and as he opened the door, he saw his monstrous pair of half-human things scraping the wooden floor under his cot with the nails of their thick spatulate fingers. The violet light there hurt his eyes, and he blinked, standing there on the threshold.

Before he could open his eyes again, a shrill cry of surprise echoed through the little chamber, and a rancid-smelling hand reached for his throat. Helplessly, he flailed at the flesh that hemmed him in.

"It's—the other one!" he heard the woman say, and then he was free. "Wait," she continued, her form seeming to waver and seethe crazily in that dazzling light. "We can change the lights for a few minutes, so you can stay—and talk to us."

In the charged darkness, Jeffrey scarcely knew whether or not another attack would be forthcoming, and then the room seemed half-normal again with the steady blaze of his own old hundred-watt bulb.

"We can last an hour without the other light," grunted the

man-thing. His great shrunken eyes traveled unblinkingly the length of Jeffrey's person. "Are you—Dr. Skull?"

Jeffrey nodded.

"They hate you," the woman said. "They came for you." She paused. The pair took turns in speaking, as though it were difficult for one alone to sustain a conversation.

"I switched your radio," said the man. "Switched it both ways. Upstairs—we heard men upstairs. They talked—they were detectives. They wanted you—and us. They went away soon."

"Then the others," said the woman. "The doctors—the bad doctors—and the one they call the Octopus. . . . They came to find if Dr. Skull—had been arrested. You're not one of them. They said so. They want to kill you. You—may be all right."

"Help us," the man grunted in that thick, half-dead monotone.

Jeffrey backed against the wall. If he only could! Those pitiful outstretched reeds of arms, flattened into hideous fronds at the joints! He had come here to help them, but they would have to help him, too. They would have to tell him what was the matter with them, as best they could; who had done this to them; where he could find the man or men responsible for these atrocities.

"Who was your doctor?" he asked. "When this happened to you, I mean?"

"His name was Borden," the man answered. "But he—there's another, who tells him what to do. Another man—maybe another devil—the one whom I told you about."

"Who is he?" Jeffrey almost shouted.

Tragically, the woman shrilled, "We don't know. We don't know who he is, or how he did it. But he has his people all over. They call him the Octopus, but they all have crazy eyes, except Borden, who's their front. They took us here from the hospital. . . . For a long time they kept us apart. They were bad, bad. . . . But we can't—prove anything. . . ."

Who was the man behind the whole hellish scheme? Jeffrey tried agonizingly to think of a clue to his identity. "Why did they do it?" he asked. "What reason could anyone possibly have for doing this to you?"

For answer, the man squatted, and pulled something out from under the cot. "Maybe—this is the reason," he said.

Jeffrey couldn't answer; didn't know how to answer. Cold little waves of revulsion traveled up and down his spine, and he choked back the spontaneous animal cry that welled in his throat.

The thing under the cot had been a man once, before those tooth-marks had flapped the skin of its throat to loose ribbons.

There was no trace of blood at the severed jugular, no trace of blood in the entire, shrunken, half-naked frame. It was a grey, dried body, suggestively withered, with the flat layers of muscle and fat sagging against a limp bony structure . . . even the whites of the eyes were as bloodless as the belly of a dead fish. But the irises were a livid, staring purple!

"You took his blood!" Jeffrey whispered, when he could speak at all.

The bulbous misshapen head of the man-thing slowly rose and fell. "We must—have living blood. Otherwise—we die. That may be why—they did this to us. They are men who hate many people. They wanted us—to drink the blood of their enemies."

Jeffrey remembered Mrs. Purvins . . . and he tensed expectantly, waiting for some further attack on himself. It was impossible to tell from those hoarse gutturals whether the monsters feared, respected, or *hungered* for him. Their tones were utterly flat and emotionless, save for that heavy undercurrent of dread tragedy. "He came here," the woman said. "He—looked for us. He came in—but he never told the others he had found us. He will never tell now—about anything. We had to silence him. . . . And then we were thirsty."

So the enemy had committed one boomerang atrocity! It was the first time, to Jeffrey's knowledge, that such a thing had happened.

The man repeated, with a tense desperation somehow threading the harsh, lifeless guttural quality of his speech, "Help us. Please help us—Dr. Skull. . . ."

Jeffrey said, "I'll need a blood sample."

The man's lips moved in what might have been a smile. He rolled his bathrobe sleeve, baring a yellowish gash in his arm. "*He* did that," said the man. "That's—all I have for blood."

Jeffrey didn't have to analyze it. He tried to find the pair's pulses, and couldn't. The yellowish stuff . . . was like that cold, primitive compound which had been in the veins of Mrs. Purvins. Sea-water, in human bodies! That's why they needed the constant renewing warmth of living blood. But these people, unlike Mrs. Purvins, gave evidence of logical reasoning.

Jeffrey asked them who they had been, their ages, and how they had come under the care of Dr. Borden.

Her husband caught pneumonia, the woman said, and then she caught it from him. Because there was no one to take care of them, they had both gone to the hospital. And that was where, in the secrecy of a private room, its horror guarded from public knowledge by the almost military discipline of a hospital, the transformation had taken place.

The man was thirty, the woman twenty-six. Their name was Halliday, Stephen and Eleanor Halliday.

From the wall amplifier, came a thudding interruption. Someone was *leaving* the office of Dr. Skull . . . leaving in a hurry!

# CHAPTER SIX
# THE PURPLE WARNING!

THE MAN-THING threw himself on Jeffrey, keeping him from running up to investigate. "You can't go!" the monster gutturaled. "We know what they're doing—we heard them planning it!"

A deafening detonation roared through the chamber, rocked the walls. For a breathless second, the fore-wall cracked and swayed, and then the quake was over, with all walls in a jagged ungeometric pattern, but they were still standing.

The man-thing kept his broad fingers clutched on Jeffrey's coat. "I saved your life," he rasped. "Remember that. And unless you help us, we will claim that life, as we claimed his—" his malformed thumb, gestured awkwardly toward the drained corpse on the floor. "We will find you, wherever you are. *They* will help us find you, if we go back to them. We don't care—we're not afraid of anything—not even of them. That's why we were made like this—nothing worse can happen, and there's nothing left for us to fear. That's why they expected us to be good tools for them. But they made a mistake—when they brought us here."

These monsters, even with their desperate threats, gave Jeffrey more hope than anything else he had encountered. They seemed to know more about the Octopus than anyone else was willing to admit. . . .

"Do you know anything about the new purple search-light?" he asked. "There's one over Manhattan tonight, and I think it's theirs."

The monsters looked at one another, and shook their great heads. "No. And you'd—better go soon," said the woman, "We—must have our own light on again."

Jeffrey turned toward the door.

"You can work for us in peace, Dr. Skull," said the man. "They think you're dead, now. When one of their men disappeared—the one who found us—they were sure you were somewhere—in the building. We heard them say so. That's why they blew up the building. They think now that you died in the explosion. . . . Remember us. . . . And we shall not forget you!"

The woman busied herself with the light-bulb. "I'll remember," Jeffrey promised.

He could not lock the door again, for that first intruder had smashed the lock. But he was sure the man and woman would await him peaceably enough, secluded both from their enemies and cruel public scrutiny if he came back within a reasonable time.

He wanted to stop at the office, to see if there was anything he could salvage, but debris blocked the way. He couldn't even get past the coal-bin into the basement. Then growing louder above him, he heard the hungry crackle and roar of flames!

Through that voracious sound of destruction came the approaching clang and whine of the fire-trucks. . . . But Jeffrey knew that before those raging flames could be tamed, the whole building and everything in it would be lost beyond redemption.

For an instant a pang of heart-ache assailed him as he thought of the associations which that humble edifice had for him during the past six years. . . . For Dr. Skull had made it a haven for the poor and the ailing of this downtrodden neighborhood.

Then, after a few minutes, he emerged out on the street, the flaming structure blocks away. He entered a drug store, stepped swiftly into a phone booth, and dialed the number of his garage.

Excepting for the powerful Diesel motor which he had designed and installed himself, there was nothing to mark Jeffrey's car as different from a thousand other sedans on the streets. He nodded to the garage mechanic as the car was brought up to the drug store, then, alone behind the wheel, he headed southward, toward the Holland tunnel to New Jersey, while the purple beacon sprayed its light into the heavens above Manhattan . . .

A hundred miles out at sea that night, sleepless navigators stared with marvelling eyes at a harbor-light no sailor had seen before. On Long Island, and in the Westchester and Connecticut suburbs to the north of the city, residents wondered at the new splendor of New York's nightlife reflected in the skies.

And in Manhattan itself, people stared—as Manhattanites will at each new marvel their city produces—and some wondered if the glaring ray would not blind aviators rather than guide them. . . . And if there shouldn't be a law, or an ordinance. . . .

Jeffrey headed under the Hudson, and on the Jersey shore he hit for the Newark airport. Occasionally, he had found use for a trim little two-seater kept there. It had a lofty wing-spread, which gave it some of the qualities of a glider, and powerful little motor. At the airport he was known as a wealthy and idle young man, with a penchant for playing with air currents and the scientific side of flying.

The little ship took to the heavens like a bird, and in ten minutes he was circling above the heart of Manhattan, with the jewelled crest of the Victory building glowing below him. He dared not fly through the beacon itself; if its nature were what he feared, such an attempt might mean suicide.

He cut his motor, doused his riding lights, and silently circled in the upward air currents caused by the canyon streets. As he neared the column of purple glare, he felt an almost unbearable heat in his open cockpit.

Holding the stick between his knees, he reached into his pocket for a piece of cloth, which he smeared thickly with a heavy, tar-like substance from a long, narrow flask. After waiting for the cloth to dry, he wrapped it around his hand.

Despite the upward air current, the weight of his little plane carried him lower and lower. The heat intensified momentarily as he dipped into the purple glare, and he felt his hands and face almost blistering—all but that part of his right hand which had been covered with the saturated cloth.

A grim look of satisfaction on his face, he pulled back on the stick, and soared skyward. The beam of light trembled beneath him, then swung slightly, seeking him out. He threw the plane into a steep bank, barely avoiding that purple radiance, and momentarily the little craft, not built for such quick maneuvering, fluttered like a leaf. He steadied her in a long glide, and again nosed up. . . .

Then he knew! The ray on the Victory Building was the purple arm of death—an ultra-violet ray!

Now he was sure that the new building in midtown Manhattan was his enemy's citadel. From the air, it was impregnable. No craft could hope to remain aloft above that death-dealing flare.

By land. . . . Jeffrey frowned, guessing that the light could be deflected downward as well as up. No army in the world could march through a street swept by the purple beam.

Excitedly, Jeffrey tried to imagine the purpose of the citadel, and its connection with the monsters that the Octopus had created. It was important now for him to warn all aircraft in the vicinity about the light.

His plane was equipped with a two-way transmitter. As he switched it on, he heard a loud spluttering that ran through all wave lengths, as though an important political speech were being broadcast over every station.

As he tried to clear it, he ran into the broadcast itself. It was the most bizarre and unholy announcement, Jeffrey realized, that had ever gone through ether:

> Station WVI, on top of the Victory Building, New York City. We bring you our half-hourly announcement again. All other stations please sign off. The life of every man, woman and child in New York City is at stake.

A short, spluttering pause. And then a deep, indefinably sinister voice that sent the nerve-ends in Jeffrey's spine into a dizzy jig.

> Citizens of New York! You are in the grip of an epidemic with which your ordinary health facilities cannot and will not deal. Even more than your lives are at stake.
> Tonight there will walk among you the patients of your hospitals. They have been hospitalized for the ordinary

diseases, but now they come from the hospitals *unrecognizable as human beings.* They are monsters.

Another pause. Jeffrey's plane stirred southward for seconds, poised above Radio City, and circled there during the broadcast.

Not one of you is immune to this spreading plague. Do not trust your doctors! Do not trust your hospitals! They are the chief agents of this unnamable disease! In their hands, you too may become unfit to bear the name of man.

There is one way, and one way only, to keep the plague from torturing your' selves and your families. We have gathered here, in the offices of the Victory Building, all those doctors who are still worthy of the name—men of national and international reputation, who will co-operate with you to stamp out this plague. They have come together under the name of The Citizens' Emergency Medical Committee.

Tomorrow, all citizens employed in gainful occupation, whether by private or government enterprise, are requested to send one day's pay to the Citizens' Emergency Medical Committee, address, the Victory Building, New York City, as the only safe form of health insurance for yourselves and your families. Thus insured, you will receive medical treatment by New York's only safe doctors in the event that disease strikes.

To outlying territories, we broadcast this warning: Do not permit trains, busses, pleasure cars, boats or aircraft to cross your borders from metropolitan New York, lest you bring the epidemic on yourselves. Warning especially the State of New Jersey, Westchester County, and the City of Yonkers in particular. Since all of Long Island has been stricken also, we warn the State of Connecticut to prohibit ferry traffic across Long Island Sound to and from the counties of Nassau and Suffolk.

Do not hesitate to comply. This is for your own good. Do not attempt to enter the Victory Building until you require the services of a physician. Send all insurance money by mail, and you will receive your receipt-cards the following day. To those cranks and fanatics who are always ready to attack a new development, we broadcast a warning: By attacking the Victory Building, you cut New York completely off from medical salvation. You doom three millions of innocent human beings! We welcome an investigation by proper authorities, peaceably conducted.

We will bring you another broadcast within the half hour.

Jeffrey stared at the silent transmitter as the broadcast ended, almost wishing it were alive, so that he might throttle the thing that had uttered those words. Extortion—with the stakes not mere loss of reputation, nor even life itself, but a warping in body and mind of great sections of the population!

He was almost directly above Radio City, then he switched on his own shortwave transmitter, and spoke into it. "This is the Skull Killer, calling Radio City. Please rebroadcast over your regular wave length. Reply when ready."

There was no answer. . . .

"Skull Killer, still calling Radio City. This is in relation to the broadcast by the Citizen's Emergency Medical Committee, which you have just heard. Please reply."

For silent seconds, Jeffrey despaired of receiving any response. They must have taken the first broadcast as a practical joke, as they might be taking his own plea. And then, faintly and uncertainly, a voice said, "Ready. Go ahead, Skull Killer. . . ."

And so that night, the voice of the Skull Killer, whose face no man could describe, was heard through the length and breadth of a thousand square miles through the City of New York.

"Citizens of New York!" he began fervently. "This is the Skull Killer. . . . I wish to advise you about this so-called Citizens' Emergency Medical Committee. It is not a joke. Neither is it to be taken at face value.

"I have only this to go by: The purple light seen over the Victory Building tonight is an ultra-violet ray of hitherto unknown strength.

All aircraft are warned not to venture near or through the light. The motives of the new medical committee seem bent more toward destruction than conservation of human life.

"They have invited the investigation of authorities; see to it that your authorities really do investigate. And in the meanwhile, on my own part, I tell you that there will be a thorough private investigation. That is all."

As Jeffrey flew southward from Radio City, there was a fresh broadcast from the Victory Building:

> Tonight we are submitting to the authorities undeniable proof of the Skull Killer's identity, and of the fact that he himself, in the guise of a doctor, is responsible for several of the monstrosities which you see on the streets tonight.

What would New York's streets be like, during the remainder of the night, Jeffrey wondered as he headed again toward Newark. As he had expected, no emergency measures had as yet been adopted; no cordon of official planes were quaranteeing Manhattan. Most people who had heard that early morning broadcast from the Victory Building would have taken it as a practical joke—gruesome, perhaps, but a joke still.

And that broadcast of the Skull Killer? Didn't the very fact that the Skull Killer had been granted a use of popular airwaves bespeak the fact that the Citizens' Emergency Medical Committee's speech had made some impression. He wondered how many people he had reached, and what they thought—or had they really given him a wavelength at all?

They must have, for the Medical Committee's last words had been an oblique answer to his message! Jeffrey Fairchild felt a thrill of elation. He was starting his greatest battle; already he had made some progress and must make more if he hoped to save the nation's greatest metropolis from ghastly destruction!

He was allowed to land at the airport without interference, and to drive back to the City through the tunnel.

He wondered at the ability of his enemy to make broadcasts at regular half-hour intervals without interference from the authorities. WVI must be a newly-licensed station—and the threat in those announcements of the Citizens' Medical Committee had been so cunningly veiled, that outside their definite disquieting influence, even those who took them seriously might never recognize them for the sinister demands they were. Unless the true nature of that purple beacon was known, listeners would not even look upon those announcements as threats.

That much he had accomplished, but even now some sort of account must be had from the City authorities regarding the Committee. . . . And that account he knew, it was his responsibility to get at once.

# CHAPTER SEVEN
# CREATURES THAT ONCE WERE MEN

D R. ANTHONY STEELE took the position which had been assigned to him, at the entrance to the Victory Building. It was an hour after midnight, and up the steel canyons, came a sharp Hudson wind. Dr. Steele shivered—the War must have been like this, he thought, the War in which his uncle had been an army doctor, from which he had not come back.

Thus it was to serve your country, or even your city, against a still-unconquered enemy, an enemy even more formidable in its hidden, sinister mystery. Dr. Steele had been shivering a little bit all day.

When they'd told him that old Dr. Skull was responsible for a new and ghastly form of disease, he'd been upset about that, and had tried to get in touch with the man. But Dr. Skull could not be reached. . . .

Then, the call from Borden, at Tony Steele's customary comfortable bed-time, impressing him into this Emergency Medical Committee. . . .

Wild talk, frightening talk—that had been his impression of the first Committee meeting in the new Victory Building. If it hadn't been for Borden, he wouldn't have been there; he wouldn't have trusted any of the others. And if ever he had seen the fires of insanity reflected in human eyes, he had seen them in the eyes of several of the supposed leaders of the Committee, and they all seemed to belong to a secret order of sorts; all wearing watch fobs in the shape of a purple-eyed octopus.

But how could you tell? Those might have been fever-lights, signs of this growing pestilence! The men might have been stricken with the first stages of the malady, and were working on nevertheless, sacrificing themselves for their fellows, for nobody could tell yet how this thing really started.

There was nothing really to go by, except the talk, and a few apparently unrelated facts. The Mid-City Hospital had burned down, and some Committee members had openly accused the monstrous patients, who apparently hated doctors and hospitals. Borden and a few of his medical friends had accused Jeffrey Fairchild, of all people! Said his wealth had made him a thrill-criminal. Borden even claimed to have seen Jeff at the fire, purposely, he said, contributing to the confusion. Jeffrey Fairchild, that amiable and intelligent young man about town who had been so helpful when Steel first started practice, four years ago!

And now the monsters were coming, for aid, for treatment, and it was Steele's job to admit them. It hadn't been hard getting them out of hospitals, he surmised, or away from the care of their private physicians—it seemed part of the disease to mistrust any known sort of medical help. Tony Steele looked at them, not realizing how he trembled. . . .

Hundreds of headlamps, from ambulances and private cars, played a false dawn on the pavement about the Victory Building. Escorted by police, by internes and nurses, by private citizens who seemed normal in all but their distraught perplexity, *they* were coming. Hundreds of them, scrambling for the lighted doors of the Victory Building. As though the lame and halt of the world had converged at the purple point. . . . As though the lame and the halt of history had risen half-rotting from their graves for some weird rite of resuscitation.

And the overpowering odor! Not even the effluvium of stale sweat, this thing; It was more like the humors that might arise in an overheated morgue. . . .

And he was supposed to help, to cure, he who had specialized in those diseases which are a luxury.

A policeman joined him, and then the crowd became something between a mob and an Act of God. For what seemed hours, Dr. Steel stood there, assorting those who sought to surge inward, allowing only the damnably sick to pass, and in spite of the dark morning's chill, he began to sweat. His voice grew hoarse with shouting directions. All about him, he sensed the press of grotesque and tragic humanity, hobbling toward possible salvation from God knew what hell of self-loathing. . . .

He didn't know! He hardly knew what great work he was engaged in, what was the beginning and the end of this process which began when the monsters left their ward beds, to end their grim trek upstairs on the forty-fourth floor of the Victory Building. He somehow felt himself a sentient tool, taking orders, standing at the doorway between mystery and mystery. . . .

How had they sickened? How would they be cured? What was he about here, and how had this vast and grisly chaos come so unpredictably, so violently, into his pleasant life? He wondered if Charon had felt as he did, bound forever to the Styx, witlessly rowing souls between remembered life and anticipated death. . . .

Another man tapped Tony Steele's shoulder, and said, "I'll relieve you, doctor. You're needed upstairs."

Steele sighed, the breath coming hard through his nostrils. Upstairs, at least, was more where a doctor belonged. Tony Steele was no tough-minded man. He liked people, liked to see them well and happy. It was for that reason, as much as for anything, that he had concentrated on rich patients. The rich, when they were ill, could be cheered so easily, could be sent to handsome hospital suites, could be ordered to take Napoleon brandy as a tonic, or luxury cruises on palatial liners. . . .

But the poor. . . . No, there was less you could do for the poor. You had to see them hungry-eyed and listless, in those airless sunless flats, worrying about money, worrying about bills, worrying about the cost of medicine. . . . You had to see a fifth child born into a three-room hovel, knowing that from its birth that the child would have to fight for its right to food, its right to a corner of the world, its very right to live. . . .

But now, Tony Steele was looking on human suffering in a stark and inexplicable shape. What good was a bedside manner for these shapes that might have been conceived in hell?

It was more than a clinical manner they needed, something of the all-wise, little father attitude. . . . Tony Steele went up to the forty-fourth floor, where the emergency clinic had been equipped to diagnose these patients.

Shuddering at some internal chill, Steele took his place in the busy clinic, and waited for the monsters to file in. He had not long to wait, for a nurse escorted a hobbling *thing* to him, a thing that looked at him with strange malevolence out of its huge unblinking eyes. . . .

"Name?" he asked, trying hard to remember the clinical manner.

The thing grunted its response. Steele asked the other questions, insanely irrelevant questions, about age, address, and occupation. Those are the things you ask a *man*, he thought. But this thing isn't a man—not any more! It's a shell around a private hades. . . .

"You cannot help me," the thing said, after it had answered all the questions. There was the ghost of manhood in those harsh tones. "I prefer—to die."

"Now, now, Mr. White. . . ." Steele protested, half-heartedly. Hell, why shouldn't the thing prefer to die! Who was he to interrupt that choice? "If you'll just trust us, we'll do so much for you. . . . We'll make you well again!"

The man said, "Fool." That was all, and the nurse led him away.

Steele stared after him, trembling. He was unaware of another patient in front of him, a patient whose mind had gone, who struggled wordlessly, and had to be held by two strong young men.

"Fool." What had that meant? It had been so concise, so unemotional. . . . Steele saw another doctor at his elbow. There were a lot of them standing around.

"Here," he shouted at his fellow-practitioner. "You take the cases. I've got to see somebody."

It wasn't quite suspicion—it was more like a passionate disquietude. So much suffering, so much madness. . . . Fool, the monster had called him, after saying also, I prefer to die.

That living, suffering organism who had once known a man named White—he'd sounded so like an educated man. A little like

Steele's usual well-mannered patients. There might be something, maybe neuro-vascular tests that could relieve him. Perhaps it had been done already, but Steele knew a million men could take the same experiment and only one of them read anything like a correct diagnosis out of it.

He'd have to check with Borden on that! Borden would have to give him that much of a free hand. It might be simple; there might be a simple magic solution that would make the world right again, that would send Tony Steele back to his fine offices on West End Avenue, where he could believe again in the innate cheeriness of things.

Monster and nurse were vanishing down the corridor. He knew they were going to the treatment rooms on the floor above. Borden was in charge of all that—Borden was there, too.

Steele went down the corridor after them, but he took a different elevator. Somehow, he didn't want to face White again. . . .

Borden was sitting in that important-looking office, giving directions to tired and respectful-looking doctors. Steele considered that he hadn't been paid a cent, and so owed no respect to anyone.

"Give me a laboratory," he demanded of Borden without prelude.

Borden's eyes assumed a surprised expression. No one else spoke. "Why should I?" Borden inquired.

Steele, a nerve specialist, attacked the problem from that angle almost out of habit. "It's their whole systems," he explained. "I'm sure of it. There isn't a breakdown in any one place—it's the whole system getting wrong stimuli, as nerves transmitting wrong stimuli to the body cells. Almost as though they were reacting to a different environment—as different, say, as though they'd all been transplanted to the moon."

"Pardon me if I seem skeptical," Borden remarked wearily, "but I've been approaching the problem from so practical an angle myself, that I haven't much patience with theories. Medicine is medicine— it's complicated, detailed, difficult. . . . And you don't get cures by saying your patients have been transplanted to the moon."

"I didn't say that," Steele answered hotly.

Borden shrugged. "Very well. You're needed downstairs, but if it's going to make you any happier, you can have your laboratory. I'd suggest, however, that you first take a good look into the ward, unless it's against your theories to clutter your mind with factual details about the people you're supposed to cure."

The two older doctors in Borden's office snickered, and the three younger ones looked sympathetically crushed. Steele felt the hot flush under his cheeks, checked an impulse to tell Borden to go to hell. The old coot was getting so darned officious lately. . . .

"I'll take a look," he said, mustering some kind of calm into his tone. Borden pointed to the large door on his left.

"Right down that corridor," Borden directed. "If you have the heart to waste time on theories after you see those people, you're a harder man than I think."

But he wasn't hard! Tony Steele only wished he were. He was sorry now, that he made the gesture of going into the ward. As he walked down the short corridor between Borden's office and the ward, he had an overwhelming sense of repugnance. He knew they were sick, not ghastly, only sick. . . . But he could smell them even before he entered the ward. . . .

As he stepped across the threshold, an eerie howl, like the baying of a dog, sent the short hair bristling up his spine. Then the howl turned into a chorus, and Steele turned, would have fled, but a shapeless and gelid *force* grasped him, pulled him back into the room.

The monsters—what did they want with him?

As they circled about, pawing and clutching at him, he screamed that he was a doctor, that he had come on a routine examination.

The last thing he heard, before the blood roaring in his ears drowned out all external sound, was the wild unearthly laughter that greeted his protest. He realized that he was being held as a rabbit is held by a pack of dogs . . . that naked teeth were ripping the covering of his flesh . . . searching for veins and arteries. . . .

Weakly, he could see his own blood dribbling richly over their enormous chins, the stuff of his life. He could feel the seeping of cold air into his emptying arteries. . . .

And then he saw the monster called White standing a little way apart, arms folded over his chest.

It seemed in a dream of drumming revulsion that White's lips moved, repeating the word, "Fool." And now Steele knew what he had meant when he said, "I prefer to die."

Borden—Borden had sent him here. Borden must have known, and wanted him out of the way, after he proposed a cure!

If he could only make them understand, these people! Understand that he was worth more to them alive. . . .

The last thing he saw was White walking toward him, but he never knew whether White reached him or not. . . .

# C H A P T E R  E I G H T
# WHEN HELL LOCKED ITS GATES

A S JEFFREY FAIRCHILD drove up out of the tunnel under the river, he looked again at the sky. Suddenly, he stiffened at the wheel. The purple beacon atop the Victory Building went out even as he looked at it. It was out for a full minute, while Jeffrey's roadster wormed its way through the nearly empty Manhattan streets—and then it flashed on again.

But now it was a different light. That illusion of topless height had gone; the beacon's tip lost itself visibly into darkness. The glow was steadier, without that eerie sparkle which had given it a queer light of its own.

Jeffrey could have sworn that now the beacon was dead and cold as it had not been before . . . Perhaps, he hazarded, there was an investigation going on as a result of his warning broadcast. He stamped on the gas pedal, and raced northward.

An ambulance siren's scream warned him of his recklessness. As he slowed down, he heard others—ambulances, police cars, private automobiles whose drivers seemed to jam one hand to their horns, as they bore down, all toward the same point—the Victory Building in Columbus Circle.

Jeffrey traveled with them, and it was soon unmistakable what grim cavalcade he had joined.

318

The monsters were answering a summons that had been tacit in the strange broadcast from Station WVI. In terrifying quantities, they had come from their secret places, with their twisted and hideous bodies, with unimaginable things reflected in their wide unblinking eyes. . . .

And then Jeffrey saw the windows, knew why they came. For even behind drawn curtains, a splash of purple threaded out from various lofty angles of the Victory Building's interior—that was the life-light for creatures of sentient death, the ultra-violet salvation of the dreadful and pitiful malformed things that breathed and moved. He parked his car, and pressed into the crowd.

Near the doorway, the pack thickened oppressively. From the harried policemen who were keeping the thing from becoming a stampede, he knew the authorities were in on this, at least to the extent of cooperating. How much more did they really know. . . . How far did they really trust that surprise broadcast from the new station?

Soon Jeffrey would know . . . a heavy hand fell on his shoulder, and someone said, "Jeffrey Fairchild!" in a voice almost too weary for surprise.

Jeff looked up into the haggard face of Captain Manning, a grey-haired and soldierly police officer, in uniform. "Hello, Captain," Jeffrey said quietly. "You're just the man I want to see."

Captain Manning said, "Is it important, Mr. Fairchild? If it's not, I've got my hands full enough. . . ."

"Damned important," said Jeffrey grimly. "I want to search the Victory Building, and I want you to come with me."

"It's been done," said Manning tersely. He added, in a lower voice, "You shouldn't be here, Mr. Fairchild. The Commissioner's in there now, talking to the head of this medical committee, whatever its name is. I think they're talking about you. You'll probably never hear of it—it's so cockeyed, but if you want to wait at the entrance and talk to the Commissioner when he comes out. . . ."

Jeffrey was known throughout the force as one of the Commissioner's oldest friends, and though he would never have used that influence to deter the humblest rookie cop from his duties, his word carried weight with the entire department. "Suppose you tell me what it's all about," he suggested. "Why are they talking about me, and who's the head of the Committee, as it calls itself?"

Manning swore, then answered, "Some of these docs are damfools when they get away from medicine. Fellow named Borden—a big doctor, they say—is boss in there. He's been talking high, wide and handsome, about what the department ought to do to you for the Mid-City Hospital fire."

Jeffrey gasped, and Manning continued, "Of course, there's nothing for you to worry about. We'll settle that headache before it gets to you."

Jeffrey's lowered eyelids almost concealed the hard thoughtfulness of his gaze. Borden! Borden, whom the monsters in his own basement had accused of almost unbelievable malpractice . . . Borden, whom he himself had elevated to a position of trust and importance in that ruined hospital . . . Borden, head of this mysterious Committee . . . the streets were violet with filtered light, but the lights in Jeffrey's brain were red.

He thanked Manning, and pushed back toward the entrance. If he could make Tom Wiley, the Commissioner, understand what was going on . . . the Mid-City Hospital had been Jeffrey's, and at the core of Borden's guilty soul, there must be a desperate, snakelike urge to accuse before he was accused himself.

Borden couldn't be dismissed as a medical man gone haywire out of his own sphere.

There was a man behind Borden—maybe a devil, the monsters had told Jeff. And that could only be the Octopus himself! Everything Borden said or did would be calculated to dupe organized medicine and organized justice until it was too late to retrench, until New York was delivered over to the enemy. . . .

But it wasn't yet too late. It couldn't be. There'd been no report to the public of an official investigation, and Jeff could reach Tom Wiley before one was made. . . .

But what if Tom Wiley never came out of that building? No—the man he had to reach was Borden! And the report that must be made was the revelation promised by the Skull Killer!

Jeffrey found himself in the great entrance hall of the Victory Building. He had seen other skyscrapers when they were new, he had seen the Queen Mary when that giant floating palace had first docked in New York; he was accustomed to the city's newest and finest hotels. But he had never—not in all his life—seen an interior like that great hall.

It was lofty, nearly five stories high, with starkly subdued indirect lighting that gave the impression of unfathomable violet depths and heights. Each wall panel held its mural—and so cleverly had the murals been designed, that the figures represented there also gave that topless, boundless impression. Jeffrey realized that the representations were simple, most of them merely huge, realistic, portraits or impressions, of contemporary scenes from the city. Yet somehow, they seemed to be the work of an artist with torture in his eyes. . . .

Then it came to him. They were exactly like the thing the city was fast turning into! An eerie and uncertain place, with limitless possibilities of stark tragedy, of malformed beings with crippled, tortured souls!

Jeffrey shuddered, and made for an elevator. The crowd that had been so dense in the street outside had ample room in the hall. . . . Here, even those incredibly warped figures seemed dwarfed to inconspicuousness by the chamber's shadowed proportions.

"I want to see Dr. Borden," Jeffrey told the uniformed elevator man, whose hard eyes measured him.

A denial seemed to hover on the other's lips.

Jeffrey said, "I'm Mr. Fairchild—Jeffrey Fairchild."

If Manning's warning hadn't been unfounded, and if the things he himself suspected of Borden were true, that name should have an effect on a henchman of Borden's—and it did. The hard look in the elevator man's eyes was replaced by a queer purposefulness. "Forty-fifth floor, sir," he muttered.

Jeffrey entered the car. He noticed that he was the only occupant of the elevator, which made no stops between the first floor and the forty-fifth.

In the gleamingly sterile corridor of the forty-fifth floor, a woman in white sat at a desk. The place looked exactly like a hospital, Jeffrey thought. This must be the headquarters of the Citizens' Emergency Medical Committee. But a queer sort of hospital, for no sound echoed through the long corridors, there were no red-cheeked young girls in blue-and-white uniforms wheeling trays and smiling at internes. About it all was that ominous sterility which seemed to extend farther than germ life.

"I'd like to see Dr. Borden," Jeffrey told the woman at the desk.

Mechanically, she inquired, "Who's calling, please?"

"Jeffrey Fairchild."

The woman's eyes stared up at him. "Straight down that corridor, then turn to your left."

Uneasily, Jeffrey strode down the long hallway. No lamps were visible, but the windowless hall was bright as the sky at early dusk. . . .

After narrow yards of walking, he came to a cross-hall, and took a left turn. He had met no one, heard no one. It was almost too easy, this entrance of his, and he sensed some abrupt reception that must have been waiting in these silent offices for him.

The left hall ended after twenty yards it a sort of booth where a young man in white sat cleaning surgical instruments. Jeffrey asked him, "Can you tell me where to find Dr. Borden?"

A small dagger-like scalpel slipped from the young man's hands, but he did not look up. In a strangely monotone voice, he countered, "Who did you say you were?"

Jeffrey again gave his name—and the young man looked at him through eyes as opaquely sharp and radiant as the steel of his surgical blades. "Straight ahead," he directed, pointing down a turn in the corridor. "Fifth door on your right. Just walk in."

The young man did not look up again as Jeffrey passed. . . .

He opened the fifth door on his right, looked about before he entered. The room seemed empty, but there was a curtain stretched across its width, and he guessed Borden might be behind that curtain.

Jeff left the door ajar and stepped softly inside. . . .

Then behind him the heavy door clicked quietly.

He wheeled about, pulled at the inside handle. The door was locked. Jeffrey cursed aloud, and darted behind the curtains.

There was nothing. Not a chair, not a stick or a straw to indicate that the windowless square chamber had ever been entered before. The walls were white, and gave somehow the impression of porousness, like the sound-proofed walls of a broadcasting studio. Jeffrey had been locked inside a white square box, with ten cubic feet of air and a curtain.

He tried shouting, and the sound of his own voice hit back at his eardrums with hammer-force in that sealed chamber. From a distance of a few feet he fired his revolver at the invisible door-lock, and the detonation nearly deafened him, while his bullet caromed harmlessly from a steel plate beneath that porous white substance.

He felt at those walls with his hands, searching a weak spot, and suddenly felt the walls warm under his touch. That warmth was increasing. . . .

Jeffrey stepped back, and then, from under the white porous wall-covering there shone a violet radiance, a strange pulsing light that seared his eye-balls and radiated heat that seemed to penetrate with rhythmic sequence beneath his skin, into the very marrow of his bones!

Now the walls seemed alive with that shimmering fluid glow, the light and the heat were somehow rendered indirect by that asbestos-like substance that coated the walls, so that his skin did not break, but he felt the veins in his body swelling with excruciating pain, as though his blood were reaching a boiling point. Then, as he fought for breath to find release through his vocal chords, that seething irradiance died, and the walls once more became dull and white.

The insufferable heat was seeping out of his veins, his heart, which had momentarily seemed to cease beating except in harmony with that pulsing glow, slowly came back to normal. Jeffrey found himself crouching unnaturally in the middle of the room, as though his flesh had shrunk, causing contraction in all his muscles, dried and seared by the heat.

Slowly, with infinite effort, he was able to knead his limbs to normal semblance, then he stood silently—and waited.

For he knew now that the "treatment" would be repeated. It would be repeated over and over, until he—Jeffrey Fairchild—had become a monster, a dried and rotting corpse, requiring for its abnormal functions the indigo glare of the ultraviolet light—needing for sustenance the warm blood of his fellows.

The cause and the cure were the same—ultra-violet radiance differently directed first caused these malformations, and later enabled the monsters to survive. Penetrating into the very marrow of the bony structure where blood corpuscles were manufactured, its heat brought about an aberration of functions, broke down the stages of evolution, reduced blood to its simplest elementals, and at the same time effected the necessary changes in the living cells to enable them to survive, provided they were subjected to that very radiance which had first caused their distortion.

Far back, in the very first stages of evolution, when the simplest forms of life had crawled out of the primordial swamps, the ultra-violet contained in sunlight must have caused parallel changes in the structure of living things—distorted them, changed them into what their fellows must have felt were monsters, until sunlight had become a necessity, without which their life could not continue.

It was a matter, in some respects, of resistance, which culminated in the building of a new type of life. The process would not be too rapid, Jeffrey knew, as he experienced his breathing spell. These things having become clear to him, certain elements of the fiendish activities of his enemy were more understandable, also.

The Mid-City Hospital fire, and the purple glow which had seemed to bathe the walls of certain parts of the building, had emanated from walls built as the walls of his chamber were built, from rooms in which transformations such as he was about to undergo had been effected on other unfortunate humans. . . .

Borden was behind it, and Borden had been ready to resume operations elsewhere! The Mid-City Hospital had been destroyed so as to obliterate all evidence of those indigo walls. . . .

Borden, then, Jeff figured, had found another backer for his nefarious activities than the philanthropic patron of the Mid-City Hospital, and that backer was the builder and owner of the Victory Building. He must be the Octopus himself!

But the other hospitals—the other sick-wards whence also human malformations had emanated—what about them? Would they too be destroyed tonight so that there would be no evidence, so that the enemy would remain triumphantly unsuspected, entrenched in the very heart of Manhattan in the guise of a philanthropic organization which stamped out its own corruption and bled society in the process?

The walls were cool again, and Jeffrey moved painfully about the room. Like a trapped animal he sought desperately for an opening in his trap, a means of escape from this locked, white-walled hell. . . .

# CHAPTER NINE
# JEFF PLAYS A LONE HAND

IT SEEMED A LONG WHILE before he could actually bring his mind to bear on any practical plan of escape. The torture he had undergone seemed almost to have induced amnesia in his brain. Then he went berserk, and, brutishly, desperately, insanely clawed at the walls of his prison, while something he had meant to remember teased agonizingly at the back of his mind.

Too many other things intruded. There was the futility of his own plight, the ominous threat to all decency, all peace in this greatest of all cities—all these things seemed to batter like a million fists at his consciousness and prevented his concentration. He knew he was wasting precious seconds, and was unable to do anything about it.

There was something he had anticipated, and desperately he tried to think of what it had been. It hadn't been capture—at least, not this kind of capture—but something else. Almost mechanically his hands explored his person. There should be something, he felt, some precaution he had taken. . . . And then he found it.

It was a long flat tube of make-up grease. There, in his hands—Jeffrey's mouth quirked a little crazily at the thought—he held nearly all of the identity of Dr. Skull. And Dr. Skull was completely unrecognizable, compressed, as it were, in this little tube!

Feverishly, Jeffrey's hands tore into his clothing, ripping open the inner seams. Concealed in the shoulder padding of his coat, in the upper seams of his trousers, were other tubes of make-up, but these were the things he always carried . . . yet there was something else, something important. . . .

As he threw his coat aside, with a puzzled gesture, the thing he sought rolled out of the inside breast pocket—a long, narrow flask. . . .

His brain suddenly clear, Jeffrey looked hastily at his watch. It had stopped, the glass had smashed at some point in his struggles. He tried to compute, from his knowledge of ultra-violet rays, how long it would be before they would judge he could stand another dose, but all concept of time had fled him and he set to work.

He undressed completely, and tore his inner garments to shreds. Then he wound them puttee-like over as much of his anatomy as they would cover. Bits of handkerchief he trussed into his mouth, inside the cheeks. Then he attacked the curtain which had been hung in the middle of the room, presumably to lure him in, and with thread-thin strips of this managed to cover the rest of his torso.

Then he went to work, covering himself with the substance of the various make-up tubes. The stuff sufficed barely to give him a coating of tenuous grease, like a transparent, oily outer skin, through which his bandages showed. Over his face spread the pale-yellow color of age—and then Jeffrey Fairchild paused.

His fingers held the long black flask while his ears sought desperately to detect some sound beyond the room. But there was only silence.

He took a deep breath, and uncorked the flask. From it he shook some of that thick, tarry substance with which he had experimented in the plane—a zinc composition. Carefully, he began to smear himself with that, then put on his coat and trousers.

The stuff congealed into a flexible, airtight covering over his body. He wouldn't last long with that, even with the loose padding of porous strips of cloth next to his skin, for it would close his sweat pores. Somberly he hoped it would do what he meant that it should—protect him, at least to some extent, from those penetrating rays. . . .

He had barely time to slip on trousers and jacket, when it came again. The room began to grow warm. Jeffrey threw himself flat on the floor, and cradled his unprotected face in the shelter of his arms. He could feel the heat sweeping over him, feel his body struggling futilely to exude moisture, and almost a wave of insanity crossed his brain at this violence to his body processes.

It was worse than the first time, and as the heat abated Jeffrey lay limp, unable to move. But there wasn't that dry contraction in his muscles that the first treatment had given him. . . . And then the door opened.

Jeffrey Fairchild could hear it, though he didn't dare to look. Somebody was coming for him, as he had expected they would. If they didn't intend to kill him, they had to come in, as soon as they thought him powerless, to prepare him for future treatments.

As the footsteps neared him, Jeffrey felt the enervating limpness disappear from his muscles at the approach of danger. When the newcomer came to a stop beside him, he rolled, groaning, on his back. Then, almost in the same movement, his hands shot out to grasp the ankles which came to his view, and he heaved with all his strength.

There was a startled exclamation from the other man, as Jeffrey swarmed over him, but the yell was cut short by Jeffrey's hands closing the other's windpipe. The man sputtered, tried to smash something he held in his hand into Jeffrey's face, but Jeffrey dodged the blow, and his own fist sent the object spinning from the other's fingers.

Then the cold rage in him settled him grimly to his task. His adversary's eyes grew wide and popping, then assumed that familiar purple glow. Convulsively the other rose half-way in a last desperate gesture, as though the evil spirit symbolized by that unearthly gleam in his eyes were giving him strength to the last, and then the man fell back limply.

Jeffrey rose to his knees. Caution against disclosing his identity precluded his marking the corpse with the mark of the skull— besides, the Skull Killer was stalking bigger game! But where was his deadly quarry?

Jeffrey, as he staggered to his feet and out of the room, into the lofty, medically clean corridors of the Victory Building, did not know.

❁ ❁ ❁

He wondered a little at the emptiness of this part of the building. Peering cautiously up and down the gleaming hall, he could see no living soul, but slightly to the left and across the hall he saw a door marked WASHROOM.

Lurching towards it, he made it, still unseen, and once inside, again stripped himself. Carefully, he peeled off as much of the zinc coating as he could, and then dressed once more, again emerged into the empty corridors.

From the death-like silence of this part of the building, he drew one important conclusion. It must be near that section of the Victory building which was purposely kept secluded. He wondered if even the police, in conducting their baffled and openly invited investigation, had penetrated here. . . .

A glance at the washroom mirror had told him that the disguise his practiced hands had applied in that torture chamber a short while ago would pass muster. The facial creams he had used to give the aged color to the skin of his face, when he had wanted to masquerade as Dr. Skull, now gave his smooth cheeks the pale, sweaty look of illness, and the strips of rolled handkerchief in his mouth gave a swelling to his lower jaws, which was at least a good imitation of the facial shape of the monsters.

His speech through these impediments to the movements of his tongue, would carry the resemblance further, and the bandages crisscrossing his body produced the effect of deformity, which he could accentuate with a dragging limp.

He passed slowly down the long corridor, and came to a door. There were sounds beyond the door, and for a moment he listened, then slipped through. Another long hall stretched before him, a hall through which moved slowly a line of deformed monsters, not unlike himself in appearance.

He joined the procession, which was flanked occasionally by orderlies and nurses, and which led past a desk where a white-coated doctor sat, taking down the case histories of the patients.

As he neared the desk, Jeffrey recognized the doctor. It was Anthony Steele—a man whose acquaintance Jeffrey had cultivated after the other had become a professional admirer and friend of Dr. Skull.

Was Steele involved in this, also? Jeffrey could hardly believe it. His turn came, and Dr. Steele's eyes, tired, and with something aghast struggling in their depths, were lifted to his.

"Name?" muttered Steele.

"White," said Jeffrey, "Robert White."

He knew suddenly that as far as Tony Steele was concerned, the deception was unnecessary. Tony Steele looked as if he'd been through hell, and might drop any minute—but because of that very fatigue, he might not be able to keep a secret.

No, Jeffrey had to play a lone hand. Nor was it hard for him to become immersed in the part he elected to play. . . .

# CHAPTER TEN
# FRESH BLOOD FOR THE OCTOPUS

T HE SUN POURED into Carol Endicott's bedroom, and she woke to an evil memory. "It was only a dream," she thought, as reassuring daylight made a bright thing of her room. "Only a bad dream . . . ." She turned, and tried to sleep again.

But the thing which had awakened her would not be silent. Persistently, in another room, a telephone was ringing, and she knew by its tone that it was the private wire between Jeffrey Fairchild's apartment and the offices of Dr. Skull. Jeff had it installed in order to keep in constant touch with Robert, who, when he was not at the hospital, lived with the doctor.

Who, she thought through her troubled drowsiness, would be at the doctor's office now? For she and Robert were here—and the doctor was missing.

She lifted the receiver, and announced primly enough, "Mr. Fairchild's residence."

No response. Only a soft click. . . . Alarmed, Carol tried to ring the other end. It didn't work. The line was dead.

"Jeff!" She knocked at the door of his room, for it was a puzzle that justified her awakening him. But Jeffrey did not answer either. . . .

She heard the back door-bell ringing, and recalled that it was time

330

for the cook to come to work. It would be a relief, she thought, as she went to the service entrance, to have someone else in the house to talk to—Her hand turned the knob, and a smile of welcome was on her lips when suddenly she stopped.

A scream eddied to her lips, a scream that was choked back by the huge hand that closed clammily over her mouth.

They were vast, distorted, grotesque, the man and woman on the threshold; half-human, half-nameless beasts. Carol struggled with all the power of utter revulsion against that gagging grasp, but the man was stronger than she.

"Don't be afraid," the man was saying in a harsh guttural whisper. "I don't mean to hurt you. . . . I only want to find Dr. Skull. Don't scream when I let you go; I *must* talk to you—"

The grip on her mouth relaxed, and Carol took a deep breath. Something in the creature's tone banished her fear and oddly now—she felt only pity.

"I'm Dr. Skull's nurse," she said. "But I don't know, myself, where he is. What made you come here? Was it you who called a moment ago?"

The man nodded. "He had us—in his house, in the cellar. We found a tunnel and it came to this building, but there were so many apartments. Then we used the phone. You told us which apartment you were in, and we found this place by the directory in the basement. No one has seen us. No one—ought to."

"I'll call Mr. Fairchild," Carol said helplessly. "He may help you more than I can. Just wait inside; I'll be right back."

She went back to Jeffrey's room, knocked again, and then opened the door. Incredulously, unhappily, she stared at four walls and a ceiling, at the bed which had not been slept in. For Jeffrey was gone.

A queer sort of grimace, half-leer, half-tragic, came over his ghastly features. "There must be lots of—people—disappearing," the man-creature said in his toneless, grunting voice.

"But, Jeffrey. . . . You don't understand," Carol mourned.

For the first time, painfully, the woman of the pair spoke. "The purple light," she said slowly. "Last night—he said—there was a purple light. Maybe—that's where they all are. Do you know anything about that?"

Carol remembered her dream—or was it a dream? "No," she said slowly, "I don't know—but it's on that new building. . ."

"You've got to take us there," he said.

Carol took a last shocked glance at her visitors, and went for her coat. No sense waking Robert—it wouldn't matter to him that Jeff was gone. And he might be a nuisance about being left alone. So, to insure privacy, she went down the back stairs with the grotesque pair, and hailed a taxi.

She had expected, at the very least, that the cabbie would be surprised, but he only looked at her with a queer I'm-glad-I'm-not-in-your-shoes kind of sympathy and said, "Victory Building, miss?"

"I guess so," Carol answered bewilderedly. Things seemed to have proceeded vastly during the night, so that the city was altogether changed. She felt like a pawn in a game whose rules she did not know, and she could not imagine at what point in the future she would be again allowed to take her fate into her own hands.

Then she saw the traffic converging as though by design, upon a single point. A whole corps of uniformed policemen were directing traffic either to or from one central point—and ahead loomed the Victory Building, its peak barely discernible in the low-lying late autumn clouds.

As the cars packed closer to one another, she realized that hers was not the only ghastly cargo of deformed humanity. There were others—hundreds of others of the gruesome half-human Things.

A sob caught in her throat, and the woman-thing beside her said, "Not nice, is it?"

Not nice . . . no, decidedly not nice. It was vast and terrifying and inexplicable, like watching a stray star rush toward the earth, knowing that collision would mean the end of history and of men. It was cruel and mad, and there was almost nothing to do about it but press through the crowd and wait. . . .

The taxi drew up in front of the entrance, and a man in white helped her get her passengers out. All three walked in the slow file across the sidewalk, and at the great portals, a man with a badge asked officially, "Your name, miss?"

"Carol Endicott," she said. "I'm a nurse, and these people are my doctor's patients. We want to find him . . . it's Dr. Skull."

Even before the man-monster behind her gasped, "Don't tell *him!*" she knew it had been a mistake.

The man with the badge stiffened; one hand fell heavily on her shoulder, and the other brought a whistle to his lips.

"It's the Skull's nurse!" he shouted. "Don't let her get away . . . !"

The pack behind her thickened. Only ahead, into the building, was there any sort of passage to escape. Carol writhed in the official's grasp, and her eyes widened as she saw the man-thing slam into her captor with terrific force. She felt the clasp of a cold hand on her wrist, and one of her patients whispered, "Run!"

They ran—up stairways, into elevators, down bewildering corridors, always with the hue and cry behind them, "The Skull's nurse! Don't let her get away!"

This is how a mouse feels, Carol thought hectically, with a cat after it . . . for she was not choosing her own route. Always, the pursuers seemed to circle at all but one point, as though they were deliberately leaving clear passage for her, but she dared not defy the route they seemed to have chosen for her. After all, that might just be an accident. . . .

Suddenly, in a short hall between two doors, the sound of pursuit ceased. Carol had no idea where she was—and when she looked questioningly at her patients, she realized that they were looking at her in the same manner.

Echoes of the chase sounded beyond the door to the right—that settled it. Carol opened the left-hand door, and walked in.

It was very dark, but there were people moving about. Something rose up in front of her, something that was sick in an ungodly way, and it said, "What are you doing here? Do you want to be killed?"

Carol blinked, and then she saw the shape of the other occupants of the room. They were dozens of monsters, in all stages of physical and mental deterioration. Carol's monster-guide stepped in front of her as though for protection, and she heard him ask hoarsely of the creature which had just accosted her, "We were chased here. Are there many of you? Will they hurt this girl?"

The creature—he was a man once, Carol realized—shrugged his flattened shoulders. "Someone else got chased here," he said. "I'll show you what they did to him. . . ."

He elbowed his way through the sniffling pack who stared at Carol with avid, hungry eyes, led them to a narrow cot on which lay a man. He seemed well enough, save for the long angry gashes on his face, throat, and bared chest.

Carol looked at him, and uttered a little gasp. "Dr. Steele! What have they done to you? Does anyone know?"

Dr. Anthony Steel lifted his head ever so little, and tried to grin. He didn't succeed, and Carol hadn't the heart to grin back at him. "You're that cute little nurse—of Dr. Skull's," said Steele. "I remember you—God, I'm glad to see—someone I know. . . ."

Carol knelt beside the cot, unmindful of the stench of the sick flesh all about her. Somehow, she was glad, too, that someone he knew would be on hand when merry young Dr. Steele. . . . No, she couldn't even think the word. But he was very low; very low and helpless. . . .

"You tell—your doc—it's Borden," Tony Steele whispered. "He—thought I was trying to—find out too much. These people—half of 'em O.K. in the noggin; the others . . . plain nuts. They—did this to me. Carol, listen: Save the sane ones. Electric heart-beat—start the heart working right again. Step it up. Seventy-two a minute, like it should be. Just a hunch—but I'm sure."

Carol stared miserably at Steele's white face. And at a light tap on her shoulder, she turned.

The thing she faced was more bloated and twisted than the others, and his skin was a vile yellowish color. . . . But his brown eyes had bright memories.

"You know what he means?" the monster whispered. "He means that electric stimulation will cure this condition. When you get out of here, tell that to the police!"

Something about the man's voice struck a familiar chord. . . . She must have met him somewhere, Carol thought, before this happened to him. "The police are looking for me," she said bitterly. "I'm Dr. Skull's nurse. That seems to be a crime."

The man said, "You are also someone's friend." He stepped backward, and Tony Steele was trying to talk to her again. . . .

"That's White," he said. "A good guy, White, and lousy trick they played him. . . . Carol!" He sat up suddenly, and his eyes were wide with fright. Carol reached her hand into the groping clasp, felt it squeezed hard. "Carol—it can't be over for me! I—didn't want to die! Didn't even want—to be a damn hero! Don't let me go—for the love of God, don't let me go!"

Carol put an arm behind the young man's shoulders, supporting him in a sitting position. "Steady," she murmured. "It's all right . . . all right. . . ."

"Sure," said Tony Steele, somehow more calm. "That's better. . . . Sure, it's all right, now. . . ."

This time, he succeeded to grin. It was a transient, brave gesture, then suddenly Tony Steele's body went heavy and inert against Carol's arm. As Carol laid him back slowly against the cot, she saw the blood spurt with scarlet finality from the long cruel line on the left side of Steele's chest. . . . It was his heart's-blood they had taken.

Borden, he had said, was responsible. The eminent Dr. Borden was a murderer.

And then Carol heard someone else say it, heard the monster named White crying at the others, "You all know who's at the bottom of this—you all know now, all of you whose minds haven't been wrecked, who your real enemies are. I'm going after Borden and his gang, and if you won't come with me, I'm going alone!"

A babel of shouts broke out, and Carol realized that most of the monsters were following White as he hurled himself against the door. She knelt beside Tony Steele's body, and wondered if the same thing had happened to Jeffrey. . . .

Someone grasped her wrist roughly; White had come back for her. "Some of these people are staying," he said. "They're killers. . . . You're coming with us. You'll be safer."

There was something in the hideous man's brown eyes. . . .

Carol rose, and walked by his side through the open door, down seemingly endless corridors and rooms, and then one more door. White kicked it open, and they were facing a green-colored figure wearing a pointed mask, sitting across a desk on the other side of a glass partition.

Carol gasped, "That's the man! The one who calls himself the Oc—" but she could not finish. .

For suddenly, underneath the mask, a purple light began to glow, grow stronger and larger, until it covered the whole of the face of the mask. Two gigantic eyes seemed to focus upon her, blinding her, stopping her speech.

A tremendous wave of heat seemed to shrivel her skin, as it had done on that previous occasion at the burning hospital. She heard guttural shouts all about her, miraculously heard someone calling her name, and then she was falling, falling, into purple depths of oblivion. And from a great distance she seemed to sense, rather than hear, the cruel thin laughter of the Octopus!

## CHAPTER ELEVEN

# BLOOD-BANK OF THE DAMNED

THE EFFECT of someone speaking seemed to filter into Carol's understanding as she opened her eyes. Through the dull ache of her semi-consciousness she felt she had been aware of that sound moving through her dream like the murmur of evil doom.

She saw that she was in the same room where the flash of purple light had rendered her momentarily unconscious—and about her were the same monsters. White's arm circled her slim body with an impersonal protectiveness—and somehow, though he was hideously sick as the rest, that contact did not repulse her.

The monotone effect of their speech lingered with her, seemed to pound with peculiarly sympathetic cadence against her tortured eardrums. Perhaps it was because the very elements of her understanding had so recently been outraged; perhaps, she thought, she was still only half-conscious. Then suddenly it seemed to her that it was no human speech she was hearing.

She couldn't distinguish words in that monotone murmur, that felt as though it exuded from some sort of mechanism, yet the sound had carried conviction, as though by cadence rather than by words, and it seemed to penetrate somehow into the bases of her comprehension. . . . And it carried a message.

337

She looked about her again, and saw all the monsters, including White, listening attentively. The message related to them. Carol became somehow aware that these monsters had rights—they had a right to live, they had a right to kill and perform atrocities, to preserve the living spark that animated them . . . just as much right to all these things as she had, as any normal person had!

Yet certainly these convictions of hers did not grow out of her own reason! Her eyes transcended her immediate surroundings, and she became aware of a cloudy glass-like partition in the middle of the room, behind which were two figures. One was Borden, the other that shapeless, bulbous mass with the long tentacles and the oddly gleaming eyes, whose light was no longer directed at her. . . . Its motionless lack of feature suggested something ageless and evil that might have come down through centuries of untold suffering and darkness. . . .

The message she was hearing must be emanating from that gelid mass. . . . The purple orbs were moving, shifting. Perhaps this Thing was speaking words, but before they came through the glass screen which divided the room, they must have passed through some sort of mechanism that removed from them the elements of speech, reduced them to an eerily comprehensible murmur that carried with it a persuasive undertone of menace.

"You'll believe, or you die. . . ." Somehow that thought intruded into Carol's mind, and every instinct in her body shrieked its willingness to believe, crying for safety and self-preservation.

White's arm tightened perceptibly about her, and her bewildered awareness was now absorbing another part of the message: The Victory Building, she found herself realizing, was the only place where the monsters could live. It was the only place where they could be fed the food they required—the blood of living things. . . .

The man who was speaking was their saviour; it was he who had set up Borden in this most modern of all hospitals, specifically built to withstand the ravages of this new disease that was turning men into monsters with no blood in their veins. . . . It was an altar dedicated to the salvation of those unfortunates, who were what they were through no fault of their own. . . .

Abruptly she heard White exclaim beside her: "How will you provide us with what we require—how can we be sure that you won't fail us. . . . That the authorities won't stop you, for you know what we need. Let us take our chances on the outside. . . ."

The monotone murmur seemed to snap an order. The room grew dark behind the glass partition, and somewhere a door opened.

Carol screamed at the sight that met her eyes.

They were chained in a slave-file by the wrists and ankles, and their faces were the faces of the damned. Carol sobbed aloud when she saw them led in, for the prisoners of that evil orator were neither sick nor mad. Except for the despairing horror on their faces, and the marks of struggle on their persons and clothing, they were as normal as Carol herself.

There was an elderly woman who might have been sweet-faced two days ago, and there was a boy of thirteen who had forgotten the meaning of courage. Young and old, of mixed sexes and conditions . . . nearly forty of them, Carol reckoned, were led in chained by the purple-eyed guards who applied whips and clubs when the file threatened to become unruly.

The evil voice continued, and Carol knew that the people in chains were intended food for the monsters that had been human. Knew also, with a strangely hopeless assurance, that these victims had been carefully chosen for their ambiguous background, they were people without relatives and without friends who might send authorities investigating their disappearance!

That was the Satanic orator's answer to White's objection! "If you were on your own, on the outside," that toneless murmur asked, "could you do better. Indeed, could you do as well?"

She heard White cry out then, and as the pane lifted, angry-eyed guards rushed toward him.

They were rushing toward him because he still retained enough of his humanity to be unwilling to sacrifice those helpless ones for his own survival. . . . And they were also intent upon wresting her from his protective arm.

How long, she wondered, had he been protecting her from his hungry fellow monsters, who were now making hungry gestures in her direction?

Startled, she heard them ask White whether he wanted her . . . and why he wanted her, and she could read their thoughts in their shriveled eyes. Sudden fright brought her close to collapse as she tried desperately to divine White's intentions, and the other's brown eyes remained unreadable.

She realized, through the stampede of bodies that jolted the struggle between White and the guards, that the monsters were rushing upon their victims. Shrieks pierced her ear-drums, which would reecho to those ghastly sounds as long as she lived—if indeed she could live for more than a few minutes in this charnel-house of misery.

God in heaven, she thought, *nothing* that had been born of woman should value its own life so highly! Life wasn't worth the rending of your fellow-man, the bloody mouthing of raw and unkilled human flesh. . . .

Carol heard her own shrieks joining with the rest, and she knew she was not quite sane at that point. But sanity had ceased to exist, sanity was a hopeless memory that had gone into limbo with all other good things. . . .

White was playing for space, dodging through the stampede, with the guards gingerly following him, as if they feared that these Frankenstein creations might slip from control, and turn red-toothed upon those who fed them. . . .

If it had not been for White, Carol realized, she would have gone shrieking with the rest, to tear into the monsters as they tore into their helpless victims, to be trampled underfoot or torn to shreds for her blood. . . . But White never relinquished his hold on her, he always kept a shifting arm's-length between her and the blood-crazed pack.

Through the hungry cries and the shrieks of the dying rose the evil voice, again and again as, with monotone deviltry, he was urging his guards to capture White.

And then one of the guards reached them. Carol felt hasty hands laid irreverently on herself, and even before she cried out, White's fist came crashing against the guard's face. There was something sharply shining in her champion's hand, and she heard the startled man screech with pain as that shining thing landed between his eyes.

For a moment, they had a breathing-space, as the guard plunged headlong before them. His face was turned, but not turned so much that Carol could not see, between his staring purple eyes, the Mark of the Skull.

White, her rescuer, was the Skull Killer!

In an awed voice she whispered "You've killed him!" though she did not know how it happened.

White grasped her wrist, and pulled her rapidly through the crowd. Voices jelled into a chorus—and the burden of the chorus was that the Skull Killer had come among them.

Now the guards were even more loath to press toward the deformed figure of that famous avenger, and even the blood-starved sick gave him clearance of a sort in that awed moment of recognition.

It was only a moment, but by the time the madness had broken again, this time on an even more terrifying note of rage and murderousness, White had led Carol through the milling monsters.

She heard the rising babel of pursuit as he bolted the door behind him. If they were caught now, she knew, the tortures of those pitiful chained souls would be as nothing compared to her own. At the concept of pain and horror such as that, her knees wavered under her, and her breath came in sharp cold stabs through her lungs.

White looked at her, and something in those clear brown eyes gave her a reckless courage. "Don't be afraid," he said. "I won't let them get you."

Into a hidden corner of her soul she shelved her fears until such time as the cause for them should be over. In the meantime, unthinking as a child and glad of it, she trusted herself unreservedly to this monstrous champion. Outside, the clangor of attack resounded ominously against the door which was their barricade, and it could not hold forever!

They made a silent exit through another door, into the sterile white corridor, only to hear the approaching echo of many feet. They were being headed off. She must not doubt, Carol told herself, that this man could save her, for she would go mad if she doubted.

From both directions, that sound was growing in volume as White bolted up the corridor, and hurled his weight against a jammed door.

Twice he rammed into it, and their pursuers were coming nearer. Desperately, the third time, Carol also pitted her weight against the door—and hurtled inward as it suddenly gave.

They were in another ward, she realized, with a sudden fresh access of fright, and among other unspeakably alive things. Curiously, the lumbering creatures stared at them.

White gasped breathlessly, "They've found a cure for us. If we can only get out of here!"

A humming, monotone message interrupted him. It was the same sort of message, half-words, half-sensation, that Carol had sensed in the divided room where they had left other monsters to their dreadful feeding.

"The Skull Killer is loose," it seemed to say. "There's a girl with him, a girl with fresh red blood and they have disobeyed the rules of the institution. Be careful—he's dangerous. . . ."

Still, the lumbering monsters only stared, and the monotone message droned on. It was clear to the girl that doors were no barrier against that incarnation of evil, and Carol's hand tightened spasmodically about the Skull Killer's.

The monsters stared and began to close in on them, in an ominous circle. White's brown eyes met theirs, and there was a tension that would break, if it broke at all, in murder—or worse. . . .

But when it happened, the episode was too swift for Carol to realize details for seconds later. She was aware of one of the malformities springing directly at her in a wave-like, hungry surge. But even before her nerves had time to carry a message of fear to her brain, White's arm traveled in a semi-arc; there was an ear-splitting yell of pain, and the monster seemed to crumble at her feet.

On the sloping, fish-belly brow, the Mark of the Skull made a smoking outline—but a fraction of that flashing action made her gasp her horror. For she noticed that as the Skull Killer pulled back his arm, the small object in his hand parted from his victim's forehead with a distinct wrench, and she caught a glimpse of a sharp point in the middle of the tool that made that fearsome print—a point that in the practiced hand of White must have smashed right through the skull-bone.

"That was self-defense," she heard White murmur—and then she was screaming a warning, as the door opened behind them.

❂ ❂ ❂

Later, she was conscious of remembering a sickening struggle of nightmarish proportions. Through that open door had emerged two more of the malformations, but these looked somehow familiar, and afterwards she decided they must have been the monsters who originally brought her into the Victory Building.

They delved past her and White, into the mass of those others, fighting on her side. . . . With peculiar dexterity she felt herself extricated from the melee and drawn back through that door, and then she and White were once more running through the endless, gleaming corridors.

Something in the words White gasped to her while they were running should have given her some kind of a message, she felt, though at the moment she was unable to grasp it. "They won't kill their own kind," he said. "At least—I hope they won't. I've got to get you away. . . ."

What was there in the simple statement that she felt she should have understood—and didn't?

In the world outside, it would be late morning, a grey November morning, with no harshness in it. But here in the Victory Building there was neither night nor day, there were only miles of sterile, luminous corridor. . . .

"What are we looking for?" Carol asked. Partly, the Skull Killer was leading her, partly he was dragging her. Her legs had long ago ceased to feel as though they had life of their own. . . .

"There's some way of getting to the part of the building behind that glass-paned room," he whispered. "We'll get back the keys of the city if we reach that far—and I'm pretty sure we're on the right track, because the building's full of authorities and investigators, and none of them seem to have gotten here." A queer grim smile came over his yellowed, face. "And if we persuade a few of these poor creatures, on our way, that the Skull Killer is a better gamble than the Octopus, it won't hurt our cause, either!"

And Carol shivered at the sight of his smile.

As their continued escape brought her never long-downed feeling of confidence nearer its healthy norm, it occurred to her that she was being something of a burden to this man—and her brain busied itself with plans and schemes for getting into the stronghold of the enemy.

The toneless voice was sending its message out again—"The Skull Killer is loose among us. Be careful—he is dangerous. . . . you are urged to kill him on sight . . ." And then followed directions for the chase, giving what Carol surmised was their approximate location in the building.

Carol said, "That must be a sort of broadcast—it follows us all over, right through this part of the building. That means there's a wiring system, maybe with photo-electric cells. He knows where we are because we shut the connections. . . . If we could find the wires, and trace them, we'll have him. I'm going to look for them right now."

The brown eyes turned searchingly on Carol then, warmly appreciative. "Bright girl," White said. "Though I doubt it's so simple."

Still, he made Carol feel good—so good that she immediately began the search for hidden wiring, pressing her palms up and down the wall, against the floor. Then a small electric shock made her hop back to an erect position, and with rapidly beating heart, she announced, "I've found it!"

The wiring appeared only as a thinnish white ridge along the gleaming floor. It was almost imperceptible to the casual glance, but once recognized, it was easy to follow. Momentarily Carol wondered that it hadn't been hidden more thoroughly, and the same idea seemed to have occurred to White.

"He probably didn't want this wiring out of reach of handy repair, if it ever went wrong," White murmured. "That's why it's not in the wall—thank God! Look, that's the direction we've got to go, because there's a junction."

Suddenly the constant messages changed in tenor, became addressed directly to Carol and her companion.

"Don't be fools, you two! I know you're coming—and what you seek to do is hopeless. The city is full of the dead and deformed who have only incidentally displeased me—how much more terrible do you think my vengeance will be on you who deliberately seek to ruin me? You still have a chance to save yourselves. Go back, before it is too late!"

Carol shuddered, then she heard White whisper exultantly, "He's scared! We must be almost there. He's afraid his men won't get to us in time, and he's starting to bluff!"

Carol tried hard to be sure of that, and kept her eyes downward on the guiding white ridge. Suddenly she cried out with dismay, for the ridge ended in a blank wall.

And from somewhere on the other side of the wall came a muffled series of shrieked pleas, as of a human being in prolonged death agony.

Carol looked about the jointure of wall and floorboard, almost as though she might find a loose seam there—and suddenly she was less concerned with further progress than with defense. For people were coming toward them, and already she was conscious of the peculiar overpowering smell heralding the approach of that evil and parasitic life.

White knew it, too. He stepped rapidly in front of her, and his brown eyes, the only recognizably human feature in his face, grew suddenly cold with alarm.

There were two people, a man and a woman. Carol recognized them as the pair with whom she had come to the Victory Building. They hadn't seemed evil then, only sick. . . . But now she didn't know. For, as the two came nearer, those grotesque faces were utterly without expression.

The omnipresent murmuring voice broke into command to the two approaching monsters. "Capture these people, and bring them to me! They are enemies of your own kind."

Carol braced herself for swift attack, but there was only the guttural voice of the man-thing, saying, "Give us light. Without the light, we are too weak."

Instantly, a dull steady indigo glare flooded the corridor. It was not strong enough to send Carol again into semi-consciousness, but her eyes smarted to the point of dizziness and her whole body trembled.

She heard White's startled exclamation, and when her eyes could penetrate the glare she realized that the dead-end wall had become transparent in the glow. And beyond that wall was the thing whose voice had followed them through the building.

A young girl's nearly nude body was hanging taut, and suspended by the wrists from a rope in the ceiling, her feet barely grazing the floor. Her body was pitted with little black holes—and it was only too obvious what had caused those holes.

The gruesome Thing with its weaving tentacles stood beside the girl; she could see the dark blood on the rim of the knife-like circular suction cups of its tentacles. On the girl's other side stood a deformed monster, drawing still more of the life-fluid from that white body, by means of a sharpened metal pipe which he had inserted in the victim's side. Carol stared, weak with horror, while the shapeless living mass was finishing its ghoulish feast with passionate greed!

Carol looked behind her, almost ready now to run recklessly back the way she had come, shrieking for human aid, but the passageway was closed.

Over a score of the misshapen, ravenous monster-things choked the corridor!

# CHAPTER TWELVE
# VOICE OF THE SKULL KILLER

WHITE'S HAND CLOSED about hers firmly, as though he knew what berserk madness was hatching in her brain. "They won't kill their own kind," White had said—but she, Carol, wasn't their kind! The girl—the girl whose blood was being drained. . . . They'll do that to me, Carol thought, with only death as the end of agony. . . .

But the monsters, though they circled impassably about, made no move to attack. Their bodies seemed to wax in the purple glow, and an eerie sheen played on the sick flesh. . . .

The green Octopus seemed to laugh softly as a tentacle reached out with a sinuously caressing movement that meant death. The nude girl's body writhed a very little bit. . . .

The voice came again: "When I raise this wall, my people will attend to the young lady. You, White—you're going to see that girl with you drained as this girl is being drained. I know what you are, and it's not what you pretend to be. The Skull Killer, monster though he appears, is *not* one of our patients."

Carol could almost hear the rigidity of the diseased bodies about her as they stiffened. "They won't kill their own kind!" but, as she had half suspected, the Skull Killer wasn't their kind at all.

347

He was disguised, and now the Octopus had shattered the Skull's safety.

Then she realized that it was another thought which had caused the monsters to become so tensely rigid. She could not read it in their immobile expressions, but that very immobility was eloquent. It was not the Skull Killer their leashed fury waited to attack, for the Octopus, by stating that the Skull Killer was not one of his patients, had undermined the very reason for the monsters' allegiance! The disease was supposed to be epidemic, and in an epidemic, no man can say who will, and who will not be stricken. Looking upon the hideously malformed White, how could he say then, that the Skull Killer was positively not afflicted? To all practical purposes, the monstrosity had admitted to his victims that there was a deliberate plan behind their deformity—and that the plan was his!

Carol's heart pounded almost triumphantly. She looked again at the man named White, and her terror-numbed brain struggled with the thought that she should have known him. Those brown eyes. . . . No, the identity eluded her. Leering like a carrion thing about to strike, the Octopus rose erect, his snake-like tentacles slowly waving, and the wall began to raise!

Carol and White were fairly swept into the chamber by the onrush of waiting monsters. Now the murmuring voice was loud with hatred. Carol, strangely fascinated by the weird, sea-green thing before her, the cupped, weaving tentacles, the hideously malformed legs, and the small mask through which glowed the purple, luminous eyes, heard orders concerning herself that chilled her to the marrow, but only for a tense moment.

After that moment, their throats raucous with a battle cry of the vengeful damned, the monsters rushed to the attack. But the object of their attack was—the Octopus himself!

Now a new voice arose in command, clear and calm. It was the voice of the Skull Killer beside her and he seemed not at all surprised at the turn of events. As Carol flattened herself against the wall to avoid the trampling, seething mob of monsters, she realized that White and the two man- and woman-things with whom she had come to the Victory Building were working together as though by some carefully pre-arranged plan.

Again her mind flashed back to the time when those two monsters had aided her and the Skull Killer's escape from their fellows. Though she had been too dazed to realize it then, that room where the monsters had been kept must have been a pre-arranged meeting place between White and his malformed helpers. They must have made their plans at some point either when she had been unconscious or had her attention diverted.

It had been the duty of those friendly monsters to convince their fellows that, in White's words, "The Skull Killer was a better bet than the Octopus." They had succeeded, and then followed White and herself through the long corridors, biding their time, waiting for the opportunity to avenge their wrongs.

The sight of that vengeance now sickened Carol. Man after sniveling man, Borden, and the white-jacketed orderlies, were being torn to shreds by the fury of that attack. She felt the Octopus screaming, saw the room grow darker, as those indigo eyes were extinguished. Then merciful darkness closed over her . . .

Slowly she became conscious of the Skull Killer's voice again. He was speaking into a microphone contained in a little glass cage set apart in one corner of the room, like the control-room of a radio station.

"This is station WVI, on top of the Victory Building, New York City. Skull Killer speaking. In reference to my previous broadcast, which promised an investigation of the Citizens' Emergency Medical Committee, that investigation has taken place. The Committee has been purged of various vicious and deadly elements which had control of it.

"The disease against which you have been warned in previous broadcasts from this same station, is no natural disease at all—but was the work of fiendish human beings. I speak of them in the past tense, because they have ceased now to exist."

There was a pause, then White went on, "You will be glad to learn that there is no further danger of contamination to you, nor need you send any but voluntary contributions to aid your stricken fellow-citizens. A cure has been suggested for them by Dr. Anthony Steele, late member of the Emergency Committee, who died heroically, doing his duty as a doctor.

"Authorities are requested to come to the west wing of the

forty-fifth floor of this building, where they will find corroboration of what I have just said, in a hitherto inaccessible part of the Victory Building. . . . That is all!"

White suddenly rushed out of the glass-enclosed booth. He paused before her, his hideously swollen, yellow face inches removed from her own.

He whispered, "I must go now. When the authorities come, tell them what Steele said. That'll clear you—then tell them everything else. These—people," his arm gestured briefly towards the monsters, who had fallen silent and stood regarding him, "will corroborate your testimony, and help clear any friends of yours from charges. . . . Do your best!"

He reached for a switch, and the room became dark. Carol was conscious of an almost overwhelming physical relief as the purple glare of the ultra-violet light was extinguished. She had hardly noticed its torturous presence in the recent excitement, but now she was weak and faint.

Strong arms encircled her, supported her. She thought they were White's, but when presently the room was flooded again with the light, she saw that he had disappeared. A frightened cry escaped her lips. She was completely alone and surrounded by the hideous, half-human malformations, and it was a woman who held her up.

"Don't worry," the woman said gutturally, "you'll be—all right."

And then the police, with their red and healthy human faces, were entering that place of deadly violet dusk. . . .

Jeffrey Fairchild picked her up at Police Headquarters. She had told her story, and had only been half-believed. Still, Jeffrey's influence had been sufficient to secure her release, and the pending investigation, the quizzing of the monsters, was all in her favor, and thus, automatically, in favor of her employer, Dr. Skull.

She wondered a little where Skull could be, and remembered the brown eyes of the monster, Robert White, the Skull Killer. She realized, shuddering, that with a little altering of the lines about them, those eyes might have been Dr. Skull's.

Had the elderly physician given himself those same treatments, that turned men into monsters, simply so that he would be able to fight that dread disease? Then she remembered the youth and strength of White . . . it was impossible that old Dr. Skull could have been as strong as that.

Seriously, however, she offered her surmises to Jeffrey, who laughed at them.

"Silly kid," he said indulgently. "You've just risked your life with the net effect of clearing Dr. Skull, and now it seems you've convinced everyone but yourself! Personally, I always thought those rumors about the doctor and the Skull Killer were so much dream-stuff. I just saw Dr. Skull, half an hour ago, and he was no more diseased than I am."

Carol shook her head perplexedly. "I wish he'd have let me know that earlier," she said. "I suppose my job's still open?"

Jeffrey nodded. "Dr. Skull's going to do some special work at the Victory Building. You'll probably be working right there with him."

Already Jeff had opened negotiations for purchase of the skyscraper whose owners could not be found. For he realized that, with its magnificent medical equipment, the Victory Building would be a logical substitute for the ruined Mid-City Hospital in service to the community.

But the Octopus—that incredibly evil personality who had been the skyscraper's first master—would his presence really be gone forever from the place he had lorded? Jeffrey recalled those old legends of the Deathless One, and he couldn't swear that the man was dead. It had been impossible to identify all the mangled bodies after that dreadful revenge.

He forced himself to think sensibly of the whole matter. It was true that he could not account for the Octopus, nor for his purple-eyed followers, neither in their origin or nature.

Albinism, attended by a mental aberration—he thought of that as an explanation. But why should there have risen a leader for these suddenly-appearing purple-eyed albinos?

Jeffrey sighed. He had done his part in the freeing of his city; he could only continue to do his part in the interests of its welfare. If sometime in the unpredictable future that essence of evil threatened once more to tests its malignant, deadly powers, the new owner of the Victory Building would have to do his part again. . . .

# CHAPTER ONE
# DARK PORTENT

I T WAS one of those neighborhoods found only in New York City. On one side of the street were exclusive apartments, their subdued lights glowing warmly against the blanket of cold fog. On the other side, there was rank squalor.

Here the buildings were unclean and condemned, tenement slums and cheap shops from which figures slunk with the cringing furtiveness of wild beasts.

The imported limousine seemed out of place in such a street, under the glow of the street lamp. Dark and sleek it stood there, its motor silent. Drops of fog condensed on its windows slid quietly down. There was no sign of movement from within.

Like the street, it waited.

The night waited. There were no sounds save the hoarse moan of fog whistles as tugs prowled through the murk of the East River and the far off rumble of elevated trains. Overhead, a row of dim lights crawled through mid-air, where other lights hung like drops of blood . . . . Queensborough Bridge.

There was a faint thin note in the air that seemed to come from above. It resolved itself into a whistled tune, but such a tune as this street had never heard before! It was weird, throbbing, with something of the eerie wailing of a Chinese flute . . . a sound that might have come straight from the heart of the mysterious Orient!

Suddenly the waiting ended!

In the limousine there was a hint of movement. A pale face showed against a window. It was a lovely face, shadowed somehow with tragedy and apprehension. From behind the car, a tall figure slid forward, a man with broad towering shoulders, arms folded across his chest. He made no sound. There was a turban bound about his proud head.

The whistle died . . . and abruptly there was movement where the shadows clustered most closely against the tenements. A figure melted out of the blackness into the half-light.

It was a man muffled to the eyes in a long flowing black cape. Beneath the broad brim of his black hat his eyes glittered coldly.

The turbaned man swept a low salaam before this sinister figure . . . and just around the corner, a police whistle shrilled in the night!

The man in the cape laughed softly, and a few crackling words in Punjabi issued from his lips as he sprang toward the car. The turbaned man salaamed again, sprang to the rear of the limousine. The door of the tonneau swung open. For an instant, the woman's face showed. Fear and apprehension were gone now. Instead, there was a welcoming smile on her lips.

The man swept off the hat as he leaped through the door. His face was covered by a ruthless looking steel mask. Then the door clapped shut.

A police radio car whooped into the street. Blue-uniformed police raced on foot around the corner, their feet loud in the moisture-laden air. The corner light glinted on their guns. They converged on the black limousine.

"Hey, you!" one snarled at the turbaned man. "What you doing here?"

The man straightened imperturbably. His bearded face showed nothing, but fierceness flashed in his eyes.

"Are you a fool to ask such a question?" he said scornfully, "Use your eyes!"

A tire on the limousine was flat.

THE door of the limousine opened and a light flashed on in the ceiling. In the rear sat a woman, beautifully gowned, and a man in evening attire. His silk hat sat jauntily on his head, and his face was pleasant, kindly, despite the strength of the jaw, the firm line of nose and brows.

The man opened the door, "Is anything wrong, officer?" he asked quietly.

"I beg your pardon, sir," the officer said, more mildly. "Did you see anyone pass here in a hurry? You see, there's been a murder."

The woman gasped, "Horrible!"

The man frowned. "Any number of people have passed, I suppose," he said. "But I noticed none of them in particular. No one running. My man took a short cut to avoid traffic, and we had that beastly puncture. It's a wonder the street department wouldn't sweep here once in a while. . . . If I can be of any help to you, let me know." He fingered a card from a platinum case and held it out to the officer.

The cop frowned at it, "Mr. Richard Wentworth!" he said. "Gee, I didn't know it was you, Mr. Wentworth! You'd better let me leave a man on guard here until your tire is mended. This murder—it was The Spider done it!"

The girl in the car shuddered again. "The Spider! How horrible!" she gasped.

The cop rubbed his jaw, "Yeah, well. . . . It's murder, like I said, but the guy what got it—"

"Who was it, officer?"

The cop started to spit, glanced at the woman and didn't. "He was a lawyer. Mortimer Hurd."

Wentworth nodded gravely. "I remember. He just beat some disbarment action against him. Supposed to have worked with a dope ring."

"Supposed!" snapped the cop. "Supposed! He was the whole works, if you ask me. Only he was too slick. The law couldn't touch him. . . . Well, I got to get going. I'll leave a man here until you're fixed up."

Wentworth said, "Thank you, officer." He closed the door, and the hand of the woman beside him slid into his. "Nita, my dear," Wentworth said, "your hand is quite cold! When will you get over being nervous over the operations of . . . The Spider? This wasn't even close."

Nita van Sloan shuddered a little, drew her fur-edged wrap more closely about her shoulders. "I . . . worry, Dick," she whispered.

Wentworth laughed gently. "You heard what the policeman said, Nita . . . 'He was too slick. The law couldn't touch him.' Still, I don't think The Spider intended to kill him. Not if he'd turn over all his money to the poor and leave the country. He preferred to be slick—and try for his gun. When the law can't act . . . The Spider will!"

Nita's hand twined within his. "Oh, Dick," she whispered, "you talk as if you . . . and The Spider . . . were two entirely different people!"

Wentworth stared straight before him. His blue-grey eyes were not narrow, but wide and thoughtful. The smile on his generous mouth held regret, but no weakness. "Sometimes," he said softly, "it would be . . . nice if it were so. There's so much to do, so many criminals to be punished. . . ."

The turbaned man swung behind the steering wheel, set the limousine in swift motion. Wentworth saluted the policeman on guard, picked up a microphone.

"Nice work, Ram Singh," he said softly and saw the turbaned driver nod.

"Switch on transmission. . . ." He pressed a button on the microphone, and knew that his voice, when next he spoke, would be broadcast over the car's two-way radio. He did not speak. Instead, he whistled softly a few bars of an old English folksong. Then he replaced the microphone, and he was frowning a little.

"I didn't need any of the precautions I took," he said.

# NEXT!
# BAEN BOOKS
# PRESENTS

IN

# *CITY OF DOOM*

## THREE EPIC ACTION THRILLERS

*THE CITY DESTROYER*
*THE FACELESS ONE*
*THE COUNCIL OF EVIL*

BY NORVELL W. PAGE